THIS WOMAN . . .

Well, she certainly wasn't his usual pick; they often looked much more delighted the morning after. Still, a woman was a woman, and with her hair loose about her shoulders and her lips relaxed and soft, he knew she'd be beautiful.

A smile tugged at his mouth but he could manage to lift only one corner. "Morning, darlin'."

He didn't think it possible but her lips pressed even more tightly, hiding them altogether. Who in God's name was she? Perhaps she was the new maid he'd ordered last week, although he'd been expecting a native. Was she a captain's wife down on her luck?

"Excuse me," she demanded, her English accent so sharp it could have cracked the plaster.

He winked, trying to lighten the mood. "Sure, why?"

She sighed again and looked heavenward as if praying for patience. "You're lying on my book. I'd like it back."

He lowered his gaze. From under his tan breeches, he could just see the top of a novel.

The Lifecycle of the Butterfly.

"Sounds delightful." The reason for the sharp pain. His confusion mounted, as did his interest. What sort of maid read about butterflies? "I wondered what that was." He rolled onto his side, his back to her, and looked over his shoulder. "Go on."

Her lips parted on a gasp of outrage. "You . . . you don't expect me . . ."

"What?" He glanced down.

She, apparently, didn't wish to go near him . . . backside or any other part. He frowned. Definitely not some chit he'd brought home last night.

BOOK YOUR PLACE ON OUR WEBSITE AND MAKE THE READING CONNECTION!

We've created a customized website just for our very special readers, where you can get the inside scoop on everything that's going on with Zebra, Pinnacle and Kensington books.

When you come online, you'll have the exciting opportunity to:

- View covers of upcoming books

- Read sample chapters

- Learn about our future publishing schedule (listed by publication month *and author*)

- Find out when your favorite authors will be visiting a city near you

- Search for and order backlist books from our online catalog

- Check out author bios and background information

- Send e-mail to your favorite authors

- Meet the Kensington staff online

- Join us in weekly chats with authors, readers and other guests

- Get writing guidelines

- AND MUCH MORE!

Visit our website at
http://www.kensingtonbooks.com

Wild Desire

LORI BRIGHTON

ZEBRA BOOKS
KENSINGTON PUBLISHING CORP.
http://www.kensingtonbooks.com

ZEBRA BOOKS are published by

Kensington Publishing Corp.
119 West 40th Street
New York, NY 10018

All Kensington titles, imprints and distributed lines are available at special quantity discounts for bulk purchases for sales promotion, premiums, fund-raising, educational or institutional use.

Special book excerpts or customized printings can also be created to fit specific needs. For details, write or phone the office of the Kensington Special Sales Manager: Attn. Special Sales Department. Kensington Publishing Corp., 119 West 40th Street, New York, NY 10018. Phone: 1-800-221-2647.

Zebra and the Z logo Reg. U.S. Pat. & TM Off.

ISBN-13: 978-1-4201-0866-8
ISBN-10: 1-4201-0866-2

First Printing: March 2011
10 9 8 7 6 5 4 3 2 1

Printed in the United States of America

Chapter 1

India, 1857

She was naked. Naked as the day she was born. Naked as the winter was long in Scotland. Naked as the days were hot in India. Naked.

But the drunken sod who'd burst into her room didn't seem to notice. He didn't bother to glance Bea's way as he cursed in slurred words and wavered about the moonlit bed-chamber as if he owned the small abode and had the right to be there, which he *most* assuredly did not.

Completely and utterly shocked, Bea stood frozen in the dark corner. Not bolting. Not screaming. Not fainting into a naked heap at his feet. Even when the wet cloth that was pressed to her chest dripped warm water between the valley of her breasts, over her stomach, and tickled lower regions a refined woman best not mention, she didn't dare move.

He turned. The moonlight filtering through the open windows hit his face. In one breathless moment, Bea took in his features. High cheekbones, square jaw, and an aquiline nose were highlighted under a silver glow. Mythical, really. Or perhaps the light was playing tricks, for he looked almost handsome. One would think he was a spirit, or some beast come to seduce her soul. Yes, at first glance one would think he was magical, and that person would most definitely be wrong.

Bea didn't need a lantern to know this person was nothing otherworldly. And he was no gentleman. A gentleman would not burst into a lady's bedchamber. A gentleman would not curse. And a gentleman would most assuredly not smell of alcohol, smoke, and the same spice that seemed to permeate the entire blasted country.

"Damn it," he growled in what sounded decidedly like an American accent.

Surprised, the grip on her washing cloth eased. What was an American doing in Delhi?

Better yet, what was an American doing in this tiny room?

He stumbled closer to her cot, closer to her. Bea swallowed her squeak of protest and stepped back until the sensitive skin on her shoulders rubbed against the rough stone of the walls. Her breasts rose and fell with each sharp intake of breath, but he didn't seem to hear. In fact, he seemed completely unaware of her presence.

She thought for sure he'd collapsed upon her tiny cot, but somehow the inebriated man managed to keep to his feet, wavering closer to her. Sweat beaded on Bea's brow, her toes curling into the reed mats that covered the floor. Oh, how dreadful! How wretchedly dreadful! Why had she ever agreed to leave the sanity of Britain? Because Leo and Ella had practically begged.

"Come along," Ella had urged. *"My dear cousin Colin is in Delhi and we'll reside with him. When would you have another chance to visit such an interesting country? Think of all the butterflies you'll be able to study."*

Bea almost snorted. Interesting, indeed. If one found extremely hot weather, the constant feel of sand in your corset, and horrible men bursting into your bedchamber *interesting*. Oh yes, she'd pay dearly because of her urge for adventure, just as Grandmother had always warned. Stuck in a moldy, drafty castle in Scotland for the past ten years didn't seem so terrible now.

Not only was Colin's home ridiculously primitive and small, but the man was nowhere to be found, leaving dear Ella to worry and pace all night before she'd finally given up hope that he'd return home. Ella and Leo had retired to their room next door only two hours earlier. Were they fast asleep, or were they alert and awake enough to hear her scream?

"Damn boots," the intruder snapped, spinning around and stumbling farther away.

Bea released the air she hadn't realized she held. The bloody humidity pressed down on her lungs. The urge to cough settled on her chest like an anvil. A blasted cough she'd picked up only days after arriving in India. Dear Lord, she couldn't cough now. She closed her eyes for the briefest of moments. *Concentrate, Beatrice Edmund.* She prayed until the spasm passed.

But as the urge to cough faded, she was once again left with the realization that she was naked. Completely and utterly naked. And even in the dark, the man would surely notice. Frantically, she searched the room until she spotted her white robe lying like a sleeping spirit on the end of her cot.

Could she reach it before he spied her?

If he noticed, he may very well attack . . . or worse. She'd heard stories of men going mad at the mere sight of a woman's ankle. What would one do if he saw a woman completely naked? The thought sent a shiver of disgust over her skin. Perhaps before she bolted across the room she should arm herself. As Grandmother said, always be prepared.

Taking her lower lip between her teeth, she eased her hands from her chest. The air instantly hardened her nipples, an embarrassing reminder of her lack of clothing. Ignoring her body's reaction, her fingertips grazed the table holding a pitcher of water and her dagger.

Her hand inched along the smooth teak toward the metal blade. A dagger Cousin Leo had given to her when they'd first arrived in India. A gift she thought completely barbaric at the time yet she'd accepted to be kind to a relative she hadn't seen in years.

The intruder turned. Bea froze, the handle just out of reach.

Had he heard her? Could he see her? Dash it! She couldn't tell.

He sighed and rested his hands atop his head. "For God's sake. I know I left the damn thing here somewhere."

The man shuffled toward a trunk not five feet from her. Thank the heavens he didn't seem to see or sense her standing so close that if she exhaled too strong, the curl that touched his ear might take momentary flight. Surprise was an element still on her side. She started to reach for her dagger once more when the meaning of his words seeped through her muddled mind.

The thing. Somewhere.

He'd left something here? Bea frowned. She'd been given the room to occupy, and assumed, because of the trunks, it was used for storage. Perhaps he wasn't an intruder after all. Fear eased into curiosity. Maybe he was a servant in Colin's small household?

But no, he didn't have the typical Indian accent and she'd never heard of an American working as a servant in India.

A friend of Ella's cousin Colin? Her frown deepened. Certainly Colin wouldn't befriend a drunken imbecile who barged into rooms without the mere courtesy of a knock. Then again, she'd never met Colin and perhaps he felt the need to hobnob with cads.

She gave her head a slight shake, her long locks brushing across her lower back. He most decidedly must be a friend. There was no other explanation. If so, this certainly complicated her plans, which, at the moment, consisted of screaming and slashing at the stranger with her dagger.

She uncurled her fingers, forcing herself to relax. If

friend, then it was only proper she introduce herself. Her gaze traveled to the far corner where her luggage rested, her clothing still packed. Reaching her valise for her calling card wasn't possible and he'd hardly be able to read it in the dark.

Could she reach her robe before he noticed? Really, it was rather difficult to decide on a plan of action when she was naked and wasn't sure what exactly he was, gentleman or cad? Bea resisted the urge to sigh in frustration.

Steeling her resolve, she inched closer toward the cot. Dare she ring the bell for Ella to introduce her? But if Ella didn't know the man, she'd have to ring for Leo and . . . well, that could take a rather long time with an endless line of people waiting for introductions and she doubted he'd wait patiently by. He most certainly did not seem the patient sort.

As if to justify her conclusion, the man threw open a chest that had been left in the room by some unknown occupant. The lid banged against the wall with a thud that rattled the room and would surely attract someone's attention. That would not do at all. If anyone found her with the strange man, her reputation would be shattered. And even halfway across the world she knew, somehow, Grandmother would hear about it by morn.

She shuffled another step toward her robe. Best to be a brave girl and confront him herself. Of course, it would be horrifyingly shameful, but even Americans had some sense of decency. Didn't they? Yes, he'd realize his mistake, apologize, and leave. There'd be embarrassment on her part, but she could live with the repercussions as long as he kept his mouth shut.

There was a clank of metal as he tossed an object aside and it rolled across the reed mats covering the floor. Bea shook her head. Really, he'd wake the house like this. Was he completely lacking in manners?

Slowly, she dropped her washing cloth on the cot. A mosquito buzzed around her ear, humming a melody of seduction. She waved aside the pest and stepped closer to her robe. If only she could reach the garment before he noticed her, she wouldn't have to be quite so humiliated. The floorboard underfoot squeaked.

Bea froze. The man spun around. Metal flashed in the moonlight.

A sword. He had a sword in hand.

Bea screamed.

"Son of a bitch!" the man roared, dropping the sword with a clank.

Frantic, Bea stumbled back, focused on nothing but escape. Her foot caught on the netting that hung from the ceiling and gathered around her cot, tripping her steps. Off balance, she grasped on to the material. A rip screeched through the room like a dying cat. Suddenly, there was nothing but air beneath her. Steel arms banded around her waist. Was he trying to save her, or murder her?

Her backside hit the floor with a thud. His body followed, crushing her into the reed mats. The netting floated down around their prone bodies. For one long moment, neither of them moved, their harsh breathing the only sound. Finally, Bea squirmed underneath him, but the movement only made his clothing rub against her sensitive skin in a most embarrassing way. Her breasts grew heavy. His breathing was harsh across her neck, harsh, but warm. She should push him off, kick him, scream again. Yet she couldn't seem to think, let alone move.

Frozen in surprise, or was it fear, she merely lay there, feeling every inch of his body, every long, hard muscle. Underneath the scent of alcohol and smoke, she smelled him—warm and musky, male. An oddly . . . pleasant aroma. Slowly, his hands moved up the sides of her naked form. Bea stiffened, but her traitorous body reacted, sending shivers over her skin.

Hesitating, his large hands settled at the curve of her hips, touching places no man had ever touched. "A gift?" His deep voice had turned pleasantly husky.

"Wh . . . what?" she gasped.

"My dear, Delilah, you do surprise me." With those words he crushed his mouth to hers.

Bea's cry of outrage was lost in the back of her throat. Stunned, she merely allowed the beastly man to explore her mouth. He tasted of alcohol, but more . . . something heady, something spicy, something rather delicious.

When his tongue slipped between her lips and rubbed against her own, an odd and not entirely unwelcome heat spread through her body, tingling her nerve endings. Shocked, Bea merely lay there, reveling in the moment. She'd been kissed before . . . sweet, simple kisses. But this was no sweet kiss. This man took control, his mouth demanding, hard.

His hands slipped around her hips, farther, until suddenly his palms were cupping her bottom, lifting her higher into his body . . . into something hard, pulsing . . . The realization of just what that hard, pulsing thing was jerked her back into reality. Bea's lips burst wide open in a scream.

Outraged, she shoved the heels of her palms into his muscled shoulders. The man pulled back just enough so she could reach up and slap him soundly across his face. The sound lingered in the room like thunder after a storm.

"What the hell?" He pressed his hand to his cheek. "Delilah?"

Bea curled her fingers, ignoring the sting of her palm. "Of course not, you bloody brute!"

Before she could scream again, a thump sounded from somewhere in the small abode.

He stilled, hovering over her. With his gaze pinned to the door, he reached toward the cot and snatched up her dressing gown.

"Dress," he demanded, sounding surprisingly sober.

Bea wasted no time, and shoved her arms through the light, silky gown she'd purchased in Lyon.

Leo? Please let the noise be Leo. Was her cousin finally

coming to her rescue? The man was only next door; surely he'd heard her scream.

Before either could react, the door exploded. Wood splinters skittered across the floor like dancing marionettes.

Leo's tall, dark shadow filled the empty space. "Bea?"

Her cousin didn't wait for a response. Fortunately, knowing danger when he came upon it, he burst across the room and slammed into the man hovering over her. The stranger was torn from her body, and together Leo and the man landed with a thud that rattled the windows.

Bea was finally able to breathe. She squirmed, but the netting around her bed twisted between her ankles, holding her captive. Leo wasted no time and slammed his fist into the man's stomach. There was a loud grunt and the men became a jumble of dark shadows, tossing about the floor so she couldn't decipher one from the other. Frantically, she tried to untangle herself from the netting, but the blasted thing seemed to only catch all the more. She felt like a fly in a web, doomed to be a spider's next meal.

"Bea!" Ella called out as she raced into the room. Bea immediately ceased struggling. She'd never been so happy to see her cousin's wife. The woman's nimble fingers worked the netting until Bea was free from her confines.

"Are you all right?" Ella's hands clutched Bea's shoulders. "Bea, my dear, what happened?"

"I was . . . bathing," she managed to get out.

Ella helped her to her feet. "Dear, why were you bathing in the dark?"

The heat in her cheeks intensified. She leaned closer to Ella, keeping her voice low. "I couldn't sleep because it was so wretchedly hot and I had the windows open. I didn't want anyone to see me and then he barged in. I can only assume he didn't have a lantern because he didn't want to be seen. He's a thief . . . or . . . or something equally as terrible!"

"Don't be ridiculous," the man mumbled, "Christ, Leo! Get the hell off me."

Bea stiffened and at the same time she heard Ella suck in a breath. He knew Leo? But how?

Leo stilled, his fist raised in the air. "Colin?"

"Yes, you ass," the man growled and shoved Leo aside.

Colin? Colin! Ella's cousin? *This* was Colin? The very man they'd come to India to visit? Bea's gaze jumped to Ella, looking for confirmation, but she could read nothing in the darkness.

"You said he was English!" Bea confronted.

Ella shook her head. "No, I didn't."

Bea parted her lips to argue, but realized the woman was right. She'd only assumed Colin was English because Ella was.

"Colin's mother was American," Ella explained. "He lived there."

Colin rubbed his jaw. "What the hell are you doing here? I wasn't expecting you until next week."

"We're early, obviously," Leo said.

Colin. Ella's cousin Colin. Heat shot to Bea's cheeks. Thank God no one could see her in the dark. He'd touched her naked flesh. Ella's cousin had touched her naked flesh. She didn't think she could be any more embarrassed. The sudden urge to throw herself from the window held certain appeal. With her luck, she'd merely break a leg and lie sprawled half-naked across the street for all of Delhi to see. Bea wasn't sure if she wanted to laugh or cry.

Leo stumbled to his feet, but Colin remained on the floor like an enormous ragdoll, most likely too drunk to stand. How could the cad possibly be related to Ella? Bea couldn't deny she'd been expecting someone rather bookish, thin, perhaps with glasses and a shy smile, for Ella had claimed Colin had come here to study Indian culture. But this man . . . this brute of a man . . . well, he didn't fit her thoughts in the least. Oh, how she hated surprises, and Colin Finch was most definitely a surprise.

"Colin!" Ella finally cried out as if the words had just sunk in. She abandoned Bea and raced to the man's side.

"I'm fine." He waved her away.

Bea gave the man a doleful glance and sank onto the edge of her cot, still too confused to do much of anything else. *This* was the infamous Colin Finch? Surely there had to be a mistake. Ella, sweet, caring Ella could not be related to this . . . this atrocity. Yet Ella slipped her arm around his waist and helped him to his feet, an act much too intimate for a man not related. Bea pressed her fingers to her lips. What would Ella say when she realized Colin had kissed her? Even worse, what would Leo say?

"*Merda*, Colin," Leo snapped, settling his hands on his hips. "What the hell was that about? Bea, are you all right?"

Suddenly, three sets of eyes were pinned to her, all glowing eerily in the moonlight. Bea nodded. Of course she wasn't all right. She'd been scared nearly to death, had a cough that wouldn't seem to go away, and was bloody exhausted from traveling across a country she was growing to despise. Sudden tears stung her eyes but she refused to let them fall. She'd survived a decade as an Englishwoman in Scotland—an outcaste. She could survive this.

"Yes," she managed to get out over the lump in her throat.

Colin started laughing, a deep chuckle that set her teeth on edge. How could he find this amusing? She'd been torn from the intimacy of bathing only to find a strange man in her room. She'd even thought her very life was in danger and he was *amused*?

She stood on trembling legs, intent on telling him exactly what she thought. Before she could get a word out, he straightened to his full height and Bea fell silent. Intoxicated or not, he was tall, taller than she'd deduced in her haze of fear. She had the sudden desire to step back.

"I didn't realize someone was in my damn room." His teeth flashed white in the darkness.

He was grinning, finding sport in the situation. Once more,

anger replaced her fear. Bea clenched her jaw and narrowed her eyes, the glare completely pointless in the dark.

"Yes, well, Leo and I took the other chamber and gave Bea the cot in here. We left you a note. Did you not see it?"

"No, darlin' cousin, I did not. A bit preoccupied."

Ella gasped and waved her hand in front of her face. "You're foxed!"

He flashed another brilliant white grin. "If by foxed, you mean drunk, then yes. I believe I am." He slipped his arm around Ella's shoulders. "So lovely to see you, my little daffodil."

"Oh, Colin." Ella shook her head like a mum annoyed with a misbehaving child.

Colin stumbled back, holding his hands up, palms out as if to ward them off. "Now, now, don't get your hide up. I had to . . . to . . ."

Leo lit a flint. Light flared to life in the dark room, the flame too strong at first, and there was a moment's silence as they all blinked, attempting to focus their gazes.

"Colin!" Ella gasped, cupping his cheeks. "What happened to your face?"

Before Bea could truly study his features, the man spun around and stumbled toward the cot. Without thought to the company awaiting answers, he threw himself down as if he belonged there. The bamboo frame groaned under his weight. With an angelic smile, he turned his head and looked at them.

For the first time, Bea truly saw the man. Dark, purple bruises stood out on his tanned skin, marring the area underneath both eyes . . . blue eyes . . . so blue they looked like the deepest part of the ocean. Beautiful eyes. Romantic eyes that seemed to pull her under . . .

"Really, Colin," Ella admonished, sharing an exasperated glance with Leo.

But Bea found herself stepping reluctantly closer, transfixed by a face that she hadn't expected. Her gaze moved to his hair, golden locks that curled softly against his forehead and ears. Her fingers itched to touch the strands, to see if they were as soft as they looked. Even with the bruises marring the harsh planes of his face, Bea had the good sense to realize he was quite handsome. Her heart did a strange, quick beat. She couldn't quite seem to breathe.

She frowned, annoyed with herself. She didn't want to think of him as handsome. He was Ella's cousin, for God's sake. And he was obviously an imbecile. She was merely surprised he was so attractive, what with his horrible manners. That combined with the excitement of the evening and any sensible being would find it difficult to think . . . to breathe . . . to swallow.

Bea stepped back, hoping distance would soften the wild beat of her heart. Yet distance did not diminish the taste of Colin, a taste that still hovered on her tongue and lips.

"Marco likes to drink," Colin said, scratching the scruff that covered his cheeks. "What could I do?"

He laughed after he said this, although Bea wasn't sure what he found so amusing. She tightened the belt around her waist to preserve at least a bit of modesty, not that he was looking at her. Was he even aware he'd nearly crushed her? Was he even aware how close his hand had been to her . . . Bea fanned herself, unable to finish the thought. The least he could do was acknowledge her presence and apologize. But of course he didn't. Just like an American. Just like a man.

"Who the hell is Marco?" Leo crossed his arms over his bare chest as if he was annoyed. She didn't blame him.

Colin pushed himself up on his elbows, his eyes half-closed with drowsiness. "Hmm?"

Leo released a sigh that reeked of exasperation. Stomping closer, he raked his hands through his indecently long hair. "Who the hell is Marco?"

Colin frowned. "How do you know Marco?"

Bea bit back her sharp response and tapped her bare foot on the reed mat. The man was exasperating, to say the least.

"Colin." Ella rushed forward, perhaps sensing her husband's increasingly foul mood. But then Ella always seemed to sense Leo's mood like no other.

"You just told us you were meeting with this Marco. Who is he?"

"Ah, right, Marco." He chuckled, then fell back against the cot and closed his eyes.

"Colin!" Ella demanded, non-to-gently nudging his shoulder with her fingertips.

He lifted his lids. "Hmm?"

"Who is Marco?"

The confused haze in his eyes cleared. He blinked up innocently at them. "Why, the man who's coming to kill me, of course."

Chapter 2

No one said a word.

Finally, after what seemed a ridiculously long amount of time in which they continued to stand there staring at Colin while he slept, Ella turned toward them. "Did he just say . . ." Her voice trailed off as her wide gaze flickered from Leo to Bea.

Since no one else seemed inclined to answer, Bea nodded.

Leo stomped across the room toward the small table that held her dagger. For a moment, she thought Leo was going to arm himself. Instead of her knife, he picked up the pitcher of water. She knew immediately what he planned to do. Bea bit her lower lip to keep from allowing the bubble of manic laughter from escaping. A completely inappropriate response given the circumstances. Gads, the heat and exhaustion must be making her mad.

"Leo," Ella warned, apparently aware of his intentions.

He merely looked at her, quirked a dark brow, and without hesitation, poured the contents over Colin's face. Water splattered his handsome features, before splashing to the cot and floor. The tepid liquid wasn't shockingly cold, but it did the job.

Colin jumped from the bed, sputtering and cursing words that no decent woman should hear. As offended as she should be, Bea found she had to press her hands to her lips to keep from laughing out loud. The night was becoming rather like a Comedy of Errors.

"What the hell?" he demanded, swiping the water from his face and shaking the drops from his long fingertips . . . fingers that had only moments ago been roaming her body.

Ella glared at her husband as she moved closer to Colin, the hem of her soft blue nightgown swooshing over the reed mats. "Well, in his defense, you did say someone named Marco was coming to kill you."

Colin raked back his wet locks, confusion flickering across his gaze. "Marco?"

"Yes, Marco," Bea blurted out before she thought better of it. Everyone's attention snapped to her. Well, really. The entire situation was so utterly ridiculous, someone needed to be the voice of reason.

Colin's gaze slid down, then back up her body, leaving behind a trail of heat. She crossed her arms over her chest, feeling oddly as if he'd just touched her all over again.

The left corner of his lips lifted, revealing a deep dimple that sent her heart fluttering. "Hello, darlin'. I don't believe we've met."

"For God's sake," Leo muttered.

"Of course, how rude of us." Ella glanced at Bea and smiled politely as if they were making introductions in the parlor of a London townhome. "Colin, this is Miss Beatrice Edmund. Leo's cousin."

The heated look in his gaze fled. Those brilliant blue eyes turned steely. "Henry's sister?"

Confused, Bea looked to Ella and Leo for an explanation but they were decidedly avoiding her gaze. How did Colin know Henry? She'd barely seen her cousin Henry in years. Most recently, she'd heard he'd vanished to the Colonies, although she had her doubts. Most likely the man had gotten into gambling trouble and was hiding from his debtors.

"No. Not Henry's sister." Leo replaced the pitcher on the table. "Another cousin with a different father than Henry's."

"Oh, just wonderful. A damn family reunion." Colin threw his arms in the air. The movement was apparently still too much and caused him to stumble. Ella was first to his side, slipping her arms around his waist and taking the brunt of his weight.

"And is she evil, too?"

Bea stiffened at the comment, heat shooting to her cheeks. She'd known Henry was a bad seed when they were children. The few times they'd visited, he'd called her names, pushed her down until she cried, had even poured honey in her hair. But really, for Colin to stand there and defile her family name was too much.

She glanced at Leo, waiting for the man to come to their family's defense. Leo merely stood there with his arms crossed over his broad chest, not looking the least bit put out. Then again, Leo had been raised in the jungles of India for half his childhood—perhaps he didn't understand that one was supposed to defend one's family honor.

"Of course not. Bea is nothing like Henry," Ella said, her words not exactly putting Bea at ease.

"Bea," Colin repeated, and he was back to grinning. The man couldn't decide on a mood. "Like . . . like a bee. Buzz." He found this immensely amusing and started laughing, a deep rich chuckle that seemed to vibrate the very air around them.

Ella slapped his arm and Leo sighed long and loud.

"Perhaps," Bea said, feeling someone should take control, "we should cease discussing our family lineage and discuss this Marco who is coming to murder you?"

Colin stopped laughing, his face growing serious. "Yes. True. Very true."

She didn't believe in this Marco for a moment, but decided it'd be best for her own temperament and sanity if they changed the subject. Surely no one was coming to kill anyone. After all, Colin was much too relaxed to be caught in the middle of such a dire situation. In his inebriated state, he'd imagined this supposed man.

Still . . . by the bruises on his face, it was obvious *something* had happened.

"So, there's someone coming to kill you?" Leo asked, his face as passive as Colin's and confirming Bea's suspicion that this was all a misunderstanding.

Colin shrugged his right shoulder. "There is a very good possibility."

"Cazzarola." Leo snapped the curse word in Italian, his mood changing like an ocean breeze and surprising Bea. If this Marco wasn't real, why was Leo so upset?

Leo scooped up the discarded sword and gripped the hilt, the muscles in his arm flexing and bulging under his golden skin.

More importantly, if Marco wasn't real, why was Leo gathering weapons?

Bea drew in a deep, trembling breath. "What will you do?"

Leo slid her a glance that spoke of amusement and exasperation. The same look he'd just given Colin. Her cousin had never been one much for conversation, but he managed to answer. "What do you *think* I'm going to do?"

Bea frowned at his surly tone. As if sensing her hurt and confusion, Ella moved to Bea's side and slipped her arm through hers. "I believe we have no choice but to fight. If someone's coming." Always the voice of reason. But there was no rhyme or reason to this absurd situation.

Bea released a shaky laugh. "But surely, no one's—"

A loud thud shook the house, rattling the glass in the windows. She didn't need to finish her sentence. Suddenly the absurd situation had taken a turn toward reality.

The blood drained from her head, leaving her dizzy. Bea slumped back against the rough stone wall of Colin's abode. Heavens, someone really was here.

"Bea, dear, are you all right?" Ella's face wavered before her, the concern evident in her puckered brows.

All right? Of course she wasn't all right! Bea's heart hammered against her chest, threatening to explode. She pressed her hand to her breast. Adventure. She'd wanted adventure. It was why she'd agreed to this ridiculous trip halfway across the world. Why hadn't she stayed home and married a respectable man? Why hadn't she listened to Grandmother? *Proper ladies do not sail around the world.*

But part of her didn't want to be a proper young lady any longer. She was tired of being stuck in a dreary castle for years with only an old, bitter woman for company. And this was what she received for disregarding everything Grandmother had taught her.

Colin held his arms wide and grinned, his smile as annoying as it was perfect. Those dimples deepened, mocking her. "Apparently, my friends have arrived."

"Shall I ring for tea, or just kill them straightaway?" Leo asked drolly.

Bea's mouth dropped open. Ridiculous. Utterly ridiculous. Why was everyone acting as if being attacked were an everyday occurrence? But there was Ella, sweet, happy Ella going to the trunk and pulling out a sword long enough to take off a man's head and making Bea wonder if, indeed, being attacked was common for her newly acquired family.

For all she was aware, perhaps her cousin and his wife enjoyed fighting as a sport. She'd known Ella and Leo for only a year. They'd appeared at the castle in Scotland claiming to be her relations. Thinking Leo had died over ten years ago, her poor grandmother had fainted on the spot.

Bea sucked in a deep breath, attempting to gain control of her rapidly beating heart.

Although Bea had been thrilled with Leo and Ella's sudden appearance, her grandmother had been more than leery to have her supposedly dead grandson suddenly appear from the grave. They'd seemed rather respectable and

genuinely kind. Certainly they'd seemed respectable enough
to take her to India. Now, she wasn't so sure. Why hadn't she
heeded her grandmother?

"You're frightening Bea," Ella admonished, handing her
husband the sword, while her concerned gaze remained
pinned to Bea.

Yes, yes he was. Shouldn't he be? Yet no one else looked
overly fearful. Colin looked amused. Leo looked annoyed.
Ella merely looked resigned.

"How many?" Leo shifted the weapons in his hands, as if
testing the feel of the leather-wrapped hilts.

Colin shrugged, completely indifferent and completely
unhelpful.

No, this was not happening. Bea raked her dark locks
from her face, trying to calm her rapid breathing and make
sense of the situation. "I . . . I don't understand."

A loud shattering crash resounded from below. Someone
was most definitely in the house. Her heart jumped into her
throat, but everyone else seemed unconcerned. What in
bloody hell was happening? Her arms fell to her sides, her
palms flattening against the cool rock wall behind her.

Leo narrowed his eyes. "Sounds like . . . two . . . or three."

"He has a dog," Ella piped in.

Bea turned her disbelieving gaze toward her cousin's
wife. How Ella knew there was a dog was beyond Bea. But
then nothing was making sense. Leo moved to the door,
swords in hand, apparently one sword for each intruder. Bea
felt the ridiculous need to laugh. Surely if she just glanced
toward the cot, she'd see herself sleeping. But when she
looked over her shoulder, the cot lay empty and her amusement faded as quickly as it had come.

Leo pulled open the door and glanced back at Colin.
There was a telling amusement in her cousin's eyes, amber
eyes that matched her own. Yet she knew hers were not
sparkling with laughter. "You'll stay here with the women."

Bea practically huffed at that comment. As if Colin were

capable of protecting them in his sorry state. But reality set in and the breath died before it passed her lips. Heavens, they'd all die. She'd die here, in this foreign country, and probably be eaten by jackals.

"Don't be insane," Colin muttered.

Leo stabbed his finger toward Colin. "You'll stay. We need you here in case . . ." Leo slid Bea a glance and didn't finish his sentence. She wasn't sure if she should be offended.

"Leo," Ella whispered.

His gaze shifted to his wife and there was a noticeable softening of his entire body.

Ella raced across the room and threw her arms around his neck. "Do be careful."

Leo pressed his lips to the top of her head, the affection for his wife evident in the way he held her tight. "I will. I love you."

Ella smiled. "I know."

Bea looked away, giving them a moment's privacy. Usually their constant show of affection made her heart warm . . . gave her hope that, indeed, love could exist. But now, of all times, she was more than annoyed. They were going to be killed, for God's sake! There was no time to kiss and cuddle.

"I'll take care of the dog," she thought she heard Ella whisper.

Bea jerked her head toward them, pondering the comment, but Leo had already moved into the hall, merging into the shadows like a thief in the night. Ella closed the door and locked it with a click. Her movements were quick, efficient, as if she'd done this before. Had they done this before? Bea pushed aside that discerning thought and focused on the situation at hand. Perhaps she should arm herself? What *did* one do when one was being attacked?

"Ella," she asked, deciding to ask the only other sane person in the household. "What shall we do? How serious is the situation?"

Ella took Bea's hands, her blue eyes wide and solemn. "I wouldn't have brought you if I'd known this would happen. I thought we'd merely uncover information."

"Information? Information about what?" she demanded, her voice coming out shrill. "A trip, you told me we were going on a trip to see the sites and visit your cousin! Now you tell me there was another purpose?"

She didn't know what was more annoying, that Ella had lied or that they'd put her in a dangerous situation for no valid reason.

Ella looked away, but not before Bea saw the guilt lingering in her blue eyes. "I'm so sorry. Really, it was for your own protection—"

Bea jerked her hands away, hurt and offended. They'd lied. Ella had lied. "Ella, why are we in India, if not to see the sites and visit with your cousin?"

"Shhh," Colin whispered, shaking his head and moving to the door. "Quiet, woman."

The way he commanded set Bea on edge. Her eyes narrowed, her temper flaring, heating her blood. "Quiet?" she snapped. "You led them here and you tell *me* to be quiet?"

He ignored her and pressed his ear to the door.

"What do you hear?" Ella abandoned Bea and rushed to Colin's side. Most likely to avoid Bea's many questions.

"Nothing."

"That's helpful," Bea muttered, gaining a glare from the man. Well, really, what did he expect? Gratitude? He should be downstairs assisting Leo, not cowering up here.

Muffled shouting interrupted the silence, people arguing in a language Bea didn't understand. Curiosity got the better of her. She edged closer to the door, tilting her head to better hear.

"Leo," Ella whispered, all color draining from her face.

Colin latched on to Ella's shoulders, forcing her to look at him. "Is he afraid?"

Bea sucked in a sharp breath. If something happened to Leo, they'd have no one to protect them.

"Leo's never afraid." Ella let her lashes drift down, her body frozen in concentration.

Colin rolled his eyes. "Is he in trouble, or holding his own?"

With her eyes closed, she started to nod, then paused, her brows drawing together. "No, he's worried."

Bea didn't understand. Didn't understand anything. How could Ella possibly know what Leo was feeling? She latched on to Ella's arm. As if breaking from a trance, the woman blinked up at her in surprise.

"How do you know that Leo—"

"Shhh!" Colin held up his hand, rudely interrupting Bea. "I have to go downstairs." He stumbled to the trunk, his body still more drunk than sober, and pulled out a pistol.

Ella jerked away from Bea and raced across the room. "No, absolutely not." Jaw clenched, she held out her hand. "Give it."

Color shot to Colin's cheeks. He looked like a lad caught watching the milkmaids swimming. "I'm not going to—"

"You're drunk and it's more important that you survive."

Bea stiffened, wondering over the comment. "Why?" she asked, but they didn't even look her way. She tapped her foot on the reed mats, more than annoyed that no one seemed to be capable of answering a simple question. They stared at each other for one long moment, at an obvious impasse. Finally, Colin sighed and slapped the butt of the pistol into Ella's hand.

Confusion turned to fear. Bea pressed her palms to her chest and shook her head. Ella couldn't possibly think she was going to help Leo while Colin stood there doing nothing. "Wait a moment."

But Ella didn't wait. She rushed past Bea and into the hall without hesitation, like a Viking warrior on a mission. Colin started to follow. Bea reached out, grasping on to his bicep. He stopped, glaring down at her. For a moment, the muscle in his arm made her forget her next words. Dear Lord, the man was much stronger than she'd realized.

"What?" he snapped. Apparently he was still annoyed that she was related to Henry.

She tore her attention from his arm and met his gaze, refusing to quiver under his intense stare. "You're . . . you're just going to let Ella go?"

He shrugged, but curiosity flickered in his gaze, as if she were a puzzle he was trying to figure out. "She's a grown woman. She makes up her own mind." His interest gone, he pulled away from her and disappeared into the hall.

Shocked, Bea merely stood there, too stunned to move. Ella was going to confront the men. Ella. Sweet, cheerful, Ella. She'd be injured, or worse.

They were insane. Every single one of them. Frantically her gaze searched the room. She could hide, hide under the bed and hope they left . . . or she could help. She paced back and forth, her mind spinning.

Before she could make sense of what was happening, Leo's voice rang out in an angry snarl, spewing words she couldn't make sense of. Hindi, she realized by the lyrical tone. Blast it. They were mad. Every one of them. But they were family. Bea latched on to her small dagger and burst out the door before she could think twice.

Ella and Colin were huddled close together on the tiny landing that overlooked the hall below. Bea slipped her dagger into her dressing gown pocket. The house wasn't large. A kitchen, hall, and parlor made up the downstairs. While above the rickety steps was a medium-sized bedroom that Ella and Leo had claimed, Bea taking the small room that apparently doubled as a storage area. Not many places for a person to hide.

"You'll stay here," Ella whispered, starting down the steps. Colin nodded his consent. Bea's fingers curled as she resisted the urge to tell him what she thought of his cowardly behavior. She certainly didn't expect this from the infamous Colin Finch, a man Ella spoke so fondly of, Bea had thought perhaps he was a saint.

Saint, indeed. With a snort of disgust, Bea swept past the man. She couldn't let Ella go alone. She took a step down. A board groaned under her weight. Bea froze, her heart slamming against her chest. When no one came rushing her way, she knelt, peeking between the railings.

Over the roar of blood through her veins, she could hear murmured voices, but she couldn't make out the words. She leaned closer to the railings and spotted Ella, hidden in the shadows below. Bea inched farther down the steps.

"Wait!" Suddenly Colin was at her side. He latched on to her arm, his grip stinging. He was so close she could smell the scent of whiskey on his breath.

Bea fought the man's hold, stunned he'd try to stop her when he'd let Ella go so freely. "Release me at once. You might be a coward, but I'm not."

He jerked her closer, his face only inches from hers. Her soft breasts crushed to his hard chest, the contrast strangely enticing. His breath fanned hot across her lips, but she refused to cower. "You have no idea what I am."

The way he said the words made her pause. Her stomach clenched. She felt as if the conversation had evolved somehow into something she didn't understand. She shook off her unease. "We can't let her go alone."

"We can." His gaze was hard, uncompromising, uncaring.

Alarm shot through her. Who was this man? This man who'd let his own cousin rush to her possible death? Bea struggled to free herself, but the evidence of his strength was there, in his tight hold. "You're a coward."

"Damn it." He jerked her closer. Bea's hands flattened against his chest. "You go down there, you get shot, you may very well find out what I'm capable of."

She didn't understand his words, so why did fear tingle at the tips of her fingers? Slipping her hand into her pocket, she pulled the dagger free and shoved it between the two of them. "Let me go."

Slowly, his gaze dropped to the blade. Amusement flickered across his blue eyes. "Will you stab me?"

Of course she wouldn't stab him, but he didn't need to know that. She tilted her chin high. "Perhaps I will. I grew up in the wilds of Scotland, Mr. Finch. Don't tempt me." Actually, Scotland wasn't as wild as everyone seemed to think and she'd lived the first ten years of her life in England, but he didn't need to know that either.

The left corner of his lips lifted into a crooked grin. He wasn't afraid in the least. "Oh, I've heard about you, my dear."

Drat! She resisted the urge to cringe.

"You were born in the mild country of England, sent to a castle in Scotland when you were just a child, pampered, and protected. I highly doubt you could fight a kitten and come out the winner."

She pressed the point of her blade to his heart, forcing her hand not to tremble. "Try me."

After a long pause, he released his hold, but the amusement was still there. Bea stumbled back into the stone wall. How did he know about her childhood? Before he could grab her, she raced down the steps. She was terrified, the fear growing with each step she took, gnawing at her stomach until she thought she'd be sick. She didn't dare look back to see if Colin had stayed put. The man was a coward; surely he was still hiding upstairs.

By the time her bare feet hit the wooden planks of the floorboards, her knees were knocking together. Hidden by a wall, she crouched low, her gaze pinned on Ella, who stood across from her, the open doorway to the parlor dividing them.

"We want Colin," she heard one of the men say. Bea had to resist the urge to point Ella's cousin out to the intruders.

"Unfortunate for you," Leo growled.

Bea moved a step forward and peeked through the

doorway. Leo stood in the middle of the room, two men in front of him. He was outnumbered, and from the soft glow of the lamp sitting on a table in the far corner, she could see that the men were just as large as he. None seemed to be backing down.

Across the hallway, Ella stood hidden in the shadows, her gaze trained on Leo. "Ella!" Bea whispered, but the woman didn't turn. Blast her. She wouldn't leave until she made Ella see reason. She could not, in good conscience, let her cousin's wife get involved. It was a sound plan—drag Ella back up the stairs by her hair, if need be. Yes, it was sound until she saw the large black dog sitting at Ella's side.

The mutt glanced back at her, his tongue hanging limply from his mouth, and Bea froze. Would he attack? Or worse, bark and alert them to her presence? Bea backed up a step and hit a small table. She gasped and spun around, latching on to the vase just before it toppled to the ground.

"We don't want a fight, mate. Marco sent us to bring back Colin Finch," one man said in an Indian accent.

Bea turned back to Ella, but her friend had stepped into the sitting room, pistol trained on the men facing Leo. "Drop it." Ella's voice was hard, harder than Bea thought possible from the delicate woman.

The men fell silent, obviously weighing their options. Perhaps they'd relent and they could call the constable. Perhaps they'd not have to brawl after all. And perhaps she was a bloody idiot.

She craned her neck, attempting to decipher one shadowed man from another.

Movement flickered from the kitchen doorway across from Bea. Her heart lurched, and slowly she turned her head, hugging the cold, porcelain vase to her chest. The dog whimpered, lifting his paws. He'd seen it, too! Bea sucked in a gasp as the shadow emerged, morphing into a human shape.

Without thought or hesitation, she lifted her arms and

threw the vase toward the shadow just as Ella turned. The vase hit the man's head and shattered, pieces crumbling to the floor. He cried out and stumbled back, hitting the wall with a thud that shook the tiny house. With a groan, he slid to the floor. The dog lowered himself to the ground and growled, as if keeping watch over the stranger.

"Ella!" Leo called out for assistance.

Ella spun around and pulled the trigger. The blast rang through the room, leaving behind the acidic smell of gunpowder. Her aim was accurate. The intruder cried out, clasping on to his leg and hopping up and down.

Leo lunged for the other man. They fell to the ground with a thud that had Bea stumbling back. Leo had the man pinned to the floor within mere seconds. Ella kept her gaze trained on the other two intruders, one unconscious from the vase, the other moaning in pain as he held on to his bloodied leg.

It happened so fast, Bea's mind spun. Her gaze flickered from person to person. Ella had shot someone. Ella, dear sweet Ella, had shot a man. And Leo, well, Leo had hit a man so hard that he was currently unconscious on the floor.

"I am sorry," Ella was mumbling to the man with the bullet wound. "But really, you brought this on yourself."

"Get Colin," Leo demanded, turning to face Bea and interrupting Ella's apologies.

"I'm here." The deep voice slid over her like velvet.

Bea jumped, realizing he'd been behind her all along. Yet the bastard hadn't offered to help. Colin turned to move past her, his chest brushing her shoulder, his gaze pinned to her. Slow and unhurried, as if gunfire in his home was a common occurrence, he moved into the small parlor. "How many seriously injured?"

"Just him. Can you help?" Ella asked, nodding toward the man she'd shot.

A man who currently lay upon the ground, a pool of red blood beneath his body. Bea's stomach clenched.

Ella had shot a man.

Bea's wide gaze landed on her friend. But the woman wasn't nearly as unaffected as she first seemed. A fine sheen of sweat covered her face, and her arms were trembling.

Colin crossed his arms over his chest, looking thoroughly disgruntled. "Why should I help him?"

"Colin!" Ella reprimanded.

He rolled his eyes. "Fine." The man had stilled, his moans quieting.

"How?" Bea demanded. "He's practically dead! How will you possibly help him?"

Colin and Ella shared a glance.

"Not dead yet." Colin smirked.

Apparently finished with his tousle, Leo sauntered toward them and took the pistol from Ella's hands. Bea sank onto the bottom step, her knees too weak to hold her any longer.

"Well done," Leo said, glancing at Bea and nodding toward the vase that lay shattered next to the third intruder. She didn't know how to respond. He flashed her a grin as if he was proud of her. "Perhaps you'll fit in after all."

Fit in? She didn't want to fit in with this group! They were all bloody mad. "Would someone please explain what in blazes is going on?"

They ignored her. Of course.

"Did they give you any information?" Colin asked, kneeling down next to the bleeding man.

Leo rested his hands on his narrow hips. Blood was splattered across his chest, but she knew it wasn't his own. Still, the sight brought bile to her throat.

"Henry saw you with Marco. He knows you're here. Paid them generously to kill you."

"Henry?" Bea demanded, straightening. Her cousin Henry?

Leo shrugged, as if it was general knowledge that Henry was in India.

"We might have . . . omitted something, my dear," Ella

said, slipping her arm through Bea's and pulling her to her feet. "We didn't come to India merely to visit Colin."

"Why then?" Bea asked, not entirely sure she wanted to know the truth.

Ella looked away, fidgeting with the belt of her night dress. "Well, we came to find a murderer."

"A what?" Bea cried out. Surely she'd misheard, surely—

"A murderer, darlin'," Colin interjected, standing and smiling in that obnoxious way.

Bea shook her head. No. She wouldn't believe it. She couldn't believe it. Yet she could see the truth in their eyes. For once, they weren't lying.

"Who is this murderer?" she asked weakly.

Colin winked. The blasted man actually winked. "Why your lovely cousin Henry, of course."

Chapter 3

A dull ache thumped in his head, drowning out all sensations but his own pain. From somewhere, light poured into the room, seeping through his closed lids and demanding he wake. He should wake. He needed to wake. Hazy memories tapped at his mind, insisting he take note. *Something* had happened.

Yet Colin didn't want to wake. To wake would mean accepting the fact that he would feel like hell. No, sleep was good. Very, very good.

A long and loud sigh grated his nerves and tore him from the dredges of unconsciousness.

With a groan, he rolled onto his side. Something poked him in the ass. Something hard and sharp. Slowly, he lifted his lids. Light stabbed his irises, momentarily blinding him. Sand had been thrown into his eyes; it was the only way to explain the grainy feel. He groaned again and blinked until the ceiling came into focus. A stain marred the white plaster, threatening to leak water onto his head. He frowned. He was in the parlor, on the settee. Why wasn't he upstairs in his bed?

"Uh-hmmm," someone cleared her throat.

Yes, it was a her. The sound was too delicate for a man. He turned his head, although the movement sent the room

spinning. A woman stood next to him, wearing a soft blue
gown of the European style with a tight bodice and flared
skirt that ended at trim ankles securely strapped in black
boots. One boot, which was tapping annoyingly against the
floorboards. Pale, delicate hands were folded neatly in front
of a narrow waist.

Slowly, his gaze traveled up to her chest, barely noticeable under the high collar of her bodice. He frowned. Something was wrong with the way she was dressed . . . too
prim . . . too proper. Further still his attention moved to a
long, elegant neck, up to a pointed chin. Finally, he settled
on her lips, lips that hinted at lushness, but were currently
pressed into a tight line.

He blinked, taking in the entire picture of her. Dark tendrils hung around a pale Botticelli face. While eerie amber
eyes were surrounded by thick, black lashes. He sucked in a
breath. For a moment, he thought he stared at Sarah. But no,
Sarah's eyes were blue. Her body shorter, fuller. He shook
the unease from his mind.

This woman . . . well, she certainly wasn't his usual pick;
they often looked much more delighted the morning after.
Still, a woman was a woman, and with her hair loose about
her shoulders and her lips relaxed and soft, he knew she'd be
beautiful.

A smile tugged at his mouth but he could manage to lift
only one corner. "Morning, darlin'."

He didn't think it possible but her lips pressed even more
tightly, hiding them altogether. Who in God's name was she?
Perhaps she was the new maid he'd ordered last week, although he'd been expecting a native. Was she a captain's
wife down on her luck?

"Excuse me," she demanded, her English accent so sharp
it could have cracked the plaster.

He winked, trying to lighten the mood. "Sure, why?"

She sighed again and looked heavenward as if praying for
patience. "You're lying on my book. I'd like it back."

He lowered his gaze. From under his tan breeches, he could just see the top of a novel.

The Lifecycle of the Butterfly.

"Sounds delightful." The reason for the sharp pain. His confusion mounted, as did his interest. What sort of maid read about butterflies? "I wondered what that was." He rolled onto his side, his back to her, and looked over his shoulder. "Go on."

Her lips parted on a gasp of outrage. "You . . . you don't expect me . . ."

"What?" He glanced down.

She, apparently, didn't wish to go near him . . . backside or any other part. He frowned. Definitely not some chit he'd brought home last night. Her eyes narrowed and she snatched the book from the settee. He rolled onto his back and studied her, attempting to make sense of the situation.

Her eyes flashed with what he could only assume was anger. Who the hell was she and how had she gotten into his home? Slowly, his gaze traveled the sitting room, looking for answers. A chair was broken, a table overturned, and the remains of a vase lay in the corner. Something had obviously happened. He raked his brain, attempting to remember last night's events. He'd gotten word that Henry had been seen near a gambling hell. He'd gone there to get answers, only to be forced into playing cards with a very large, very bald man named Marco. After that, his memories seemed to blur.

The woman spun around and started toward the stairs. Then, apparently thinking otherwise, she paused and faced him. "I've endured months at sea to get here, only to realize that India is much hotter than I'd thought. I've been almost killed . . . twice. Once by you, I might add. And have recently uncovered that my cousin is a murderer. I only want to lose myself in a book."

He winked. "Why don't you lose yourself in me instead."

Like Queen Victoria preparing to behead a servant, her

face grew brilliant red. "You . . . you are a scoundrel and a coward."

He quirked a brow. If anyone else had called him a coward, he would have had the person's head on a platter. For some reason, he was amused by her outburst. Apparently, he'd offended her, which was rather typical where he was concerned. "I've killed men for such comments, you know."

Looking completely unimpressed, she hugged her book tightly. "Ha, I doubt you're capable of killing anyone. At least you weren't last night."

Last night? Colin's confusion mounted. "What was your name?"

"Ugh," she sighed and started toward the steps.

"Who are you?" he demanded before she could escape.

"Colin," Ella's calm voice interrupted their argument. She swept down the stairs in a light green dress in the gauzy native material. Her face was flushed, her golden hair long and wavy as it floated around her shoulders. She certainly looked better than she had a year ago, when he'd first met her and she'd been half-dead.

Suddenly, everything came back.

Marco.

The blasted man had suckered him into a game of cards and Colin had been only too happy to oblige, thinking he'd get some answers about Henry. But the only thing Marco wanted was Colin's money. Colin had barely escaped with his hide still attached.

He'd arrived home with Marco's thugs close behind him. And of course, he'd happened upon Leo's cousin. He should have remembered the moment he saw her. The same eerie amber eyes that Leo had, but on her, for some reason, they seemed more intense, different, sexy as hell. Of everything that had happened, kissing her was the most vivid of his memories.

"Do not be rude to Bea," Ella demanded.

His gaze jumped to the woman who stood on the stairs next to Ella. Was this the same person whose soft flesh he'd fondled only last night? A woman any man would want in bed? And now, damn, she looked like a nun about to slap him with a stick.

Standing next to Ella, he couldn't help noticing the difference between the two. Ella wore her traditional sari with ease, a scarf over her head, and in this heat, she'd be grateful for the clothing. Bea, on the other hand, looked as if she were still in England. Tall and thin, her hair a dark mahogany next to Ella's lighter locks. And whereas Ella was smiling, always smiling, this woman seemed to wear a permanent frown. Yet there was something about her that made him want to tease, to taunt until he broke her. He never could resist a challenge.

"Cousin." Ella swept forward and leaned down to kiss his cheek. "You need to shave." She wrinkled her pert nose. "And bathe."

He laughed and managed to sit up, even while his head pounded with the slightest movement. "And the compliments continue to arrive."

He wore the same clothes he'd worn last night. A white linen shirt with the sleeves rolled to the elbows and tan trousers. Perhaps not his finest look, but he was far from resembling a street urchin. But he supposed the clothes stank like smoke and stale beer. Hell, he did need a bath.

Bea was looking at him smugly. Apparently she agreed with Ella's comment.

"Who's she?" He said the words just to annoy her when he knew very well who she was.

Red bloomed to life across her cheeks and she looked away. Damn, if the color didn't heighten her attractiveness. He'd met women like her before, especially in England. Beautiful, but cold inside. Like Sarah. His jaw clenched and for a brief moment he had to look away.

"Colin," Ella admonished. "It's rude to speak about

someone as if they're not present when clearly they are. Besides, I introduced you last night but you were apparently too foxed to remember." She sighed and turned toward Bea. "Bea, this is my cousin Colin Finch. Beatrice Edmund, Leo's cousin."

He forced his thoughts from Sarah. One small reminder and she was back in his life. He stood and bowed low, a mocking movement. As punishment, pain shot through his skull. He cringed, pressing his fingers to his temples. "Let me get this straight. We're cousins, Leo and Bea are cousins, you're married to Leo. Does that mean Bea and I are related?"

"I should hope not," Bea muttered.

Her arrogance bothered him more than he let on. Colin quirked a brow. "My, doesn't she have a sharp tongue."

"Colin," Ella reprimanded. "Behave, please." She slowly turned, taking in the small parlor. "You have a lovely home."

He laughed. Typical Ella. Marriage and riches hadn't changed her. She was obviously being polite. "I wouldn't call two bedchambers, a parlor, and kitchen a lovely home." Hell, the walls weren't even plastered but still the same rough stone used to build the place. If he'd known they would be here so soon, he would have searched for better living quarters.

He sighed, stretching his arms over his head, his tight muscles relaxing. "Where is your beast of a husband?"

Ella smiled, truly smiled, her face lighting with a happiness he didn't understand, and frankly, didn't know if he wanted to. The cynical part of him wanted to roll his eyes, but a part, deep down, was mesmerized when they were together. How two people could feel such an intense affection was beyond him. Ridiculous. He wouldn't believe it if he hadn't witnessed their love himself.

"I'm here," Leo said, moving down the narrow steps past Bea. He ducked under the overhang and filled the room with his size and arrogance.

Really, it was getting much too crowded in his small

home. Alone, the two-story, two-bedroom abode had been plenty large, but with three others, he felt the pauper who could only afford a shack. It didn't help his pride knowing that his three guests typically resided in a castle. He was suddenly aware of how sparse his sitting room was.

Settee and chair occupied the room, no paintings, no flowers, no wallpaper on the stone walls. His only form of décor, a vase, lay shattered upon the floor. What would Sarah think of his home? The thought brought a wry smile to his face. Sarah wouldn't be caught dead here.

Leo didn't hesitate, but approached his wife and slung his arm around her waist, drawing her up hard against his body like the animal he was. Completely unconcerned with propriety, he pressed his mouth to hers.

"Christ," Colin snapped and turned away. "You could save that for the bedchamber, you know."

Bea swept to the only window in the parlor, drawing his attention to her. She brushed aside the beige linen curtains he'd nailed to the sill. Her back straight, she feigned interest in the scenery. So much like Sarah. Same chillness evident in her stiff bearing. Same ethereal beauty. Same dark hair. An odd pang stabbed him in the chest. Not heartache, no, he'd gotten over Sarah long ago. Regret, perhaps?

He swallowed hard. No. This Bea wasn't Sarah. Sarah was married to an earl, probably had a baby by now. Bea was Leo's cousin and he supposed he'd have to attempt a cordial politeness. He could pretend, at the least.

He spared a glance at Leo and Ella. They still embraced, whispering sweet, nauseating nothings to each other.

Curious and oddly drawn to Bea, Colin made his way across the room. "Not much for scenery."

She stiffened at his approach, but didn't bother to look at him. He wasn't sure what she was watching. The glass was covered with dust. He supposed he should have cleaned the place. But it was a rarity anyway to get a house with glass windows. With a sigh, he lifted the edge of his shirt and swiped at the window until a circle of clarity formed.

He followed her gaze, taking in the dirt road out front, the many stone buildings pressed tightly together. People scurried down the crowded streets, their feet stirring the dust, their voices and shouts muffled through the window. Different people, different-colored buildings, yet the hectic pace rather similar to any city anywhere in the world.

"'Tis odd," Bea said softly, drawing his attention to her. "It's so pale, the buildings, the sky, the roads, all shades of beige. Yet the people are so brilliantly dressed as if to make up for the lack of color."

He was surprised by her insight, even more surprised when she glanced up at him through those thick lashes as if judging his reaction. And why the hell was she suddenly being so nice? Something flickered across her gaze, an emotion she wrestled with. She smoothed her hands nervously down her skirt, her attention dropping to the floorboards. Perhaps she felt she needed to give him a chance for Ella's sake.

An olive branch he'd be forced to take.

"All right, answers, Colin," Leo demanded, apparently done pawing Ella.

Colin frowned, and reluctantly turned away from Bea. Leo always demanded things. Never asked, and he was the one being reprimanded for being rude?

Colin slumped into the only chair in the sparse room, annoyed and exhausted. "I was getting answers. To get answers from Marco, you need to play cards and drink."

Ella frowned and settled on the settee. She smoothed her Indian skirt primly around her, the golden bracelets on her wrists jingling with the movement. "And there's no other way to gather information from this man?"

He flashed her a brief grin. Women. They were so oblivious to the real world. "Not without losing your head . . . or worse."

Leo paced in front of him, the man's arms crossed against his chest like a lord holding court. He'd tied his long, dark hair back with a leather strap, not that it did any good. The man still looked like a heathen. "And what information did you procure?"

Hesitating, Colin glanced at Bea. She stood at full attention now, watching him through curious eyes. How much did she know? How much could he admit in front of her? Damn, he wished he could remember more of last night. But the moment the intruders had been taken care of, he'd passed out on the settee. What had Ella and Leo told her?

"It's all right, Bea knows that Henry stole my necklace." Ella gave him a tight smile. "I told her last night. I also told her about Henry. How he tried to kill not only Leo, but me as well."

The missing necklace. He didn't need to read minds to know that was all Bea knew. She had no clue what he and Ella really were, what they were capable of. He gave Ella a brief nod of understanding.

"I still don't understand." Bea started pacing, passing her cousin Leo, the book clutched to her chest. "Why didn't you tell Grandmother?"

"We did," Leo replied, stopping.

She paused, face-to-face with her cousin. The surprise evident in her eyes. "But . . . why didn't she tell me? Henry was a cad, truly, but a murderer? And all for some supposed necklace that leads to a treasure? It's ridiculous."

Ella shrugged, but there was no look of offense upon her face. "Who knows why she didn't tell you. As for the necklace, it might be ridiculous, but he believes it's true."

Bea looked at each of them in turn. "And this is the real reason why we're here?"

Neither Leo nor Ella offered her a response.

"Is that why we stopped in Italy? Did you think the necklace was there?" Her voice hitched slightly.

"Yes," Leo replied.

"You . . . lied?" She was hurt, obviously. He could see that in the trembling of her full bottom lip. But she didn't understand the direness of their situation.

"I did get something from Marco. Henry is supposedly heading south," Colin murmured, deciding to change the subject.

Leo frowned. "For?"

Colin shrugged, glancing toward the kitchen. He was hungry, tired, and his head ached, but he knew they would not relent until he answered their questions. "Bombay, most likely."

"We must find him, Colin." Ella's voice was soft, but he didn't miss the underlying desperation. She feared for their safety, but mostly he knew she wanted to end this for all their sakes. Henry had owned that necklace for over a year now. If he found a way to the statue, Colin and Ella would be as good as dead.

Colin gave Ella a brief nod. He of all people knew how important that necklace was. "Today we'll speak with a man who deals in antiquities. He was the last to see Henry and may be able to help."

"Wonderful," Ella beamed. "I'll fix you some breakfast. I assume you haven't a cook in this . . . fine establishment?"

"We aren't all earls, you know," Colin bit out, raking his hands through his hair.

"Be careful," Leo said, following his wife toward the kitchen. "Your voice reeks of bitterness."

Colin settled his hands on his hips. "Ha, bitterness. You can take your title and . . ." But Leo had disappeared into the kitchen.

Bea shifted and he was reminded she still stood there, book clasped in hand. How much, exactly, did she know? Perhaps he could catch a few minutes alone with Ella and find out.

She glanced hesitantly toward the kitchen. She was probably worried that if she followed, she'd find Ella and Leo in some embarrassing embrace. Cold Englishwoman who had probably never been kissed . . . before last night.

He smirked, amused by her innocence. "Never seen a man and woman embrace, *Queen Victoria*?"

Her eyes narrowed into mere slits, her contempt obvious, but she said not a word.

He winked. "Feel free to use my room to read, darlin'."

She tilted her chin and spun around, starting up the steps. "Wonderful and feel free to bathe while I do."

Colin's smile fell. So much for that olive branch.

Chapter 4

Feel free to bathe.

The comment still rankled Colin hours later. Who was she to come into his home uninvited and tell him he stank? The woman was enough to drive a man to drink. No wonder she wasn't married. Still, for Ella's sake, he'd bathed and put on clean clothes. It wasn't Ella's fault her husband's cousin was a snobbish prude. Cold and taunting, Sarah had been that way at first. She'd been a challenge, a challenge he thought he'd won. She'd had the last laugh.

He took in a deep breath. Yes, he'd try to be polite to Bea, but it was obvious the woman was just like Sarah. How would he stomach the cold bitch for days? More importantly, how would he stomach the memories she brought with her? As if sensing his attention, Bea slowly turned her head and slid him a glance through the thin veil that covered her face. Even though he'd made sure they didn't touch, he could feel the heat of her body as she sat next to him in the carriage.

He gave her a smirk, mostly because he didn't know how else to react to the woman. Smirking always seemed to work with a snob. Unfortunately, she didn't respond and his amusement fled.

She had to be uncomfortably warm in her European

clothing. Yet she didn't once complain. He didn't know whether to respect her, or think she was a damned idiot. She'd refused to wear the traditional sari Ella wore, or so Leo had said. He wanted to be annoyed with the chit; instead he found himself amused by her stubbornness. How long before she'd break? In this heat, not long.

The carriage swerved, turning a corner. Bea gasped and fell into Colin. He'd been crushed into the tiny vehicle with Bea at his side so Leo and Ella could sit together across from them. Now, he wished he'd begged off and taken his own mount. Colin didn't dare move as Bea looked up at him, her face pressed to his shoulder.

"I apologize." She settled a slim, gloved hand on his arm and pushed away.

"No need," he mumbled, shaking off the sudden heat that seeped through his body.

She rested her hands atop her bonnet, tilting the hat back into place and making sure the fine netting was hiding her features from view.

"Are so many weapons really necessary?" Bea asked, most likely speaking of the knife she'd seen strapped to his thigh earlier.

Colin narrowed his eyes. The woman just had to complain about something.

"Yes," Leo replied. "Henry tried to kill us."

She frowned and tightened the jaunty blue bow under her chin. "He was a rather obnoxious lad, but . . ." She sighed and shook her head. "But I never thought he'd do something so . . . heinous."

Ella reached forward and patted Bea's hand, always the one to comfort a lost soul. "He's a greedy man, Bea. He couldn't handle the fact that Leo had basically returned from the dead and taken his title. He'd been trained to run the estate and lost everything. They had no idea Leo still lived. When he returned, it sent not only Henry but your grandfather over the edge."

Leo remained hidden in the corner of the carriage. "To them, I was merely an animal out to ruin the family name and the family estate." To anyone who didn't know him, he looked at ease, but Colin recognized the steely glint that had entered his eyes. Ella settled back, her hand slipping into Leo's.

Bea looked away, but not before Colin caught the glimmer of something that almost looked like compassion in her eyes. No, it couldn't be.

"I didn't realize Grandfather, too, was mad. Why didn't Grandmother tell me any of this?"

Ella shrugged. "Protecting you, most likely."

Of course Bea didn't understand the situation. A rich, pampered Englishwoman who'd been sheltered her entire life. And she'd never truly understand the entire situation if Colin had anything to do with it. Ella had wanted to share everything with Bea, all their secrets. But he'd put his foot down. His secret was his to share with those he trusted. And he sure as hell didn't trust Beatrice Edmund.

The carriage slowed, drawing Colin's attention to the streets. People teemed down lanes, speaking in a language that was still difficult for him to understand even though this was his second visit and he'd always picked up languages quickly.

Eager to put distance between himself and Bea, Colin was the first to jump out of the tiny vehicle when it stopped. His feet landed with a splat in brown gunk he pretended was mud. With elephants, camels, and cows running amok, one wasn't sure what they'd find on the streets of Delhi. The stench was overwhelming. And if Bea thought *he* stank, wait until she stepped outside.

"They'll need to be carried," he said over his shoulder.

As if to back up his statement, a cow paused in the middle of the street, looking back at him. No one seemed to notice, the carriages swerving around the beast and going along their way. It still amused him how the animals were everywhere, given free rein to run the country.

Leo moved from the vehicle slowly, like a predator attempting to find his next meal, his eyes taking in every tiny detail. Apparently finding the area secure, he held out his arms for Ella. He lifted her easily and started toward the shop, leaving Colin with Bea.

Colin rubbed the back of his neck and slid Bea a sidelong glance. Queen Victoria sat in the corner of the small carriage, her eyes wide through the fine net of her bonnet. The contempt she felt toward him was written clearly across her face. Usually, he couldn't care less what people thought. For some reason, it bothered him that she believed he was a coward. But then how could she possibly understand? And he sure as hell wasn't about to attempt to explain his situation to someone like her.

"You can wait for Leo's return, or I can carry you." He paused. "If you can handle my scent, that is."

She frowned and glanced toward the shop, then around her, apparently trying to decide the lesser of two evils. Did she really find him so repulsive? Finally, she nodded and scooted toward him. Her body stiffened the moment he slipped his arm around her back and under her knees. He moved quickly across the road, weaving between people going to market or home. Close to the shop, he slowed. The sun was almost gone, but the remaining rays dappled her skin with gold, making her hair shine brilliantly.

She was softer than her demeanor, softer and suppler. The feel of her body pressed to his had his heart hammering a lusty tune. What the devil was the matter with him? He didn't have time for an infatuation, especially with this one. She was far too cold. Far too judgmental. Far too much like Sarah. Not to mention, she was far too related to Leo. The man would pummel him for stroking a single strand of her hair. And then Colin would have to hit him back and they didn't have time for fisticuffs over a woman.

Besides, most likely she was promised to some haughty earl back home. Yet he couldn't seem to stop himself from breathing in deep. The sweet scent of clover and heather tickled his senses. Even though it was an English scent, it was still more familiar than the spices here in this foreign city.

He paused there, next to a stall selling water, where monkeys hung from the poles, attempting to steal a drink . . . paused with a strange woman in his arms. He should have been shocked that he didn't want to let her go, shocked that her warmth seemed to seep into his body all the way down to his toes. But he wasn't. Damn, what was the appeal of this woman? Was he some glutton for punishment?

She glanced at him out of the corner of her eye. "Mr. Finch, they're waiting."

Her hard tone jerked him from his thoughts. He had to keep his mind on the mission. Leo and Ella would kill him if he dallied with Bea. He glanced toward the shop where they waited and watched with curious eyes. Besides, she obviously didn't feel the same about him, and for some reason that annoyed him more than he wanted to admit. Women found him endearing, charming. Even Sarah had. But this woman . . . Bea . . . looked at him with ill-disguised ire. Because she thought him a coward? Or because of that simple, pathetic excuse for a kiss?

"Call me Colin," he snapped and started forward.

So it wasn't exactly a simple kiss. There'd been tongue involved, yet if he remembered correctly, she hadn't exactly been stiff underneath him. No, she'd been a willing participant.

"I can't call you by your first name. That's hardly proper," she said haughtily.

He looked at her in disbelief. "I'm carrying you through the streets of Delhi, I think we're beyond the formal stage."

Her cheeks grew pink but the color only heightened her appeal. He was insane. Completely and utterly insane. "Obviously you don't care for me, Miss Edmund. But since we'll be together for a few days, can we not at least be civil? Besides, Leo and Ella would appreciate it."

She clenched her jaw. "Of course."

Colin resisted the urge to snort. "Really, you're too kind."

"What do you expect from me, *Mr. Finch*?" she hissed. "You pawed me in your bedroom last night, touching places . . ." Her face went from pink to a brilliant red. "Touching places I've never even touched."

Too bad for her. If she touched herself once in a while, perhaps she wouldn't be so stiff and cold. For some reason that thought made him chuckle. Bea grew even stiffer, if that was possible.

"Then, you refused to help Ella or Leo when the men arrived, men you brought to the house because of your sinful ways, I might add."

Colin's body stumbled, his amusement fading. "I told you, you can't possibly understand—"

"I understand you're a coward."

Colin froze, his anger flaring. How dare she! Their faces were so close together that he expected her to cower away. She didn't. He wasn't sure if he should be amused or annoyed by her bravado.

"Khana." A scrawny boy jerked on the back of Colin's shirt. He shoved dirty hands toward them.

Bea's eyes widened and she slipped her arms around his neck, tightening her hold. "What's he saying?"

Colin ignored the boy and ignored the strange surge of protection he felt toward her when she wrapped her arms around his neck. "Food."

She looked back. "Well, give him a coin, something. He's terribly thin."

"Darlin', if you haven't noticed, I'm not exactly sleeping in gold. Besides, you drop that lad a coin, you'll have a good hundred rushing over here for more. You got enough to feed all of Delhi?" He reached the steps and set her down.

She glared up at him. "How horrible! How wretchedly

horrible you are! The child is starving and if we can help just one—"

"What is it?" Ella asked, stepping closer, her brows furrowed with worry.

"I'm sorry, Ella," Bea said, tilting her chin high. "But your cousin is a lout."

She sighed. "Yes, he is at times."

"Excuse me?" Colin demanded.

Leo rolled his eyes. "Can we move inside? It's damn hot out here. Besides, you're attracting a crowd."

"No, not until I give that poor child a coin." Bea pulled her small bag from her wrist.

"Uh, Bea, my dear," Ella whispered, her eyes going wide as she focused beyond Bea and the swarm of needy coming their way.

"No, I insist." She rummaged through her reticule. The boy rushed forward, clawing at the skirt of her dress.

She stumbled back into Colin. "Oh, oh my. Yes, yes of course." She tried to rummage faster, but the boy tugged harder, until Colin was sure he'd rip the dress from her form, leaving her standing on the street in her bloomers. A smile quivered on his lips at that thought.

Shouts rang through the air and Colin cringed. From every corner, every lane, children were rushing toward them. Some just barely missed being struck by horses. As the shouting grew in volume, Bea finally looked up and the color drained from her face.

Leo grabbed Ella and tugged her into the store, the bell tinkling overhead. Bea screamed and tossed her bag into the air. It landed with a thud, a burst of dirt puffing above the ground. Children teemed over it like flies on a carcass. Colin reached into his pocket and tossed a handful of coins in the other direction. Half the children left the purse and rushed toward the coins. Spread out, at least there was less chance they'd kill each other. Not waiting for permission, he latched on to Bea's arm and jerked her into the shop.

The door closed and silence fell. Blessed silence.

"I didn't . . ." Bea stared out the window, her eyes wide, her face paler than normal. Any smugness he felt vanished.

Colin sighed. "I didn't know when I first arrived either."

She glanced up at him and he was shocked to see the gleam in her amber eyes, sparks of gold glistening under guileless tears. "Certainly, there must be something that can be done."

His shock gave way to wary resignation. "Miss Edmund, you have homeless children in England, yet your country hasn't been able to solve that problem. What makes you think they can here?"

She lifted her thin veil, her gaze flashing with annoyance. "Yes, but we don't have as many."

His ire grew and he threw his arms wide. "Are you insane, woman? Have you looked around London? Seen the poverty, the starvation in every city? I've had my pocket picked more times than I can count by children in London."

"Colin," Ella admonished, slipping her arm around Bea's waist. "Bea spent most of her time in Scotland, in the countryside. She rarely went to London."

Surprised, he fell silent. No spoiled wealthy woman? He knew she'd been banished to Scotland with her grandmother, but now he wondered what sort of life she'd lived. Bea looked away, a flush of obvious embarrassment highlighting her high cheekbones. She came from a wealthy, titled English family. She should have been visiting London, attending balls, flirting with titled gents. Hadn't she?

"Mr. Finch!" The deep voice boomed across the shop, interrupting Colin's confusing thoughts.

A short man with a long mustache came scurrying toward them, weaving around the many shelves that littered the shop.

"How lovely to see you." The man's dark eyes gleamed with interest, his eyes shifting around the group, no doubt looking for his most hopeful prey. Always looking for a sale.

Colin nodded in greeting. "Pickens."

Voices rose from outside, children arguing over their loot. Pickens tossed an annoyed glance out the windows, then snapped the curtains together, blocking any remaining light from entering the dingy place.

"Disgusting brats," the man mumbled. "But I suppose it could be worse." He smiled, revealing a gaping space between his front teeth. He looked like a tuskless walrus. "What can I do for you? This just came in only yesterday." He picked up a golden statue of a lion and dusted it with the handkerchief he'd pulled from his vest pocket.

Colin ignored the offer. "Mr. Pickens, this is my cousin Lady Roberts and her husband Lord Roberts, their cousin Miss Edmund."

"The earl?" Pickens said, his eyes going as wide as a child in front of a sweet shop.

"Just Leo," Leo muttered, throwing Colin a glare.

Well hell, what'd he expect? Of course he'd mentioned Leo. People were a lot more forthcoming when he tossed around the fact that his cousin was married to an earl.

"What did you mean when you said it could be worse?" Leo demanded, turning his attention back to Pickens.

Pickens took no offense to Leo's curt tone. "My lord, you haven't heard?" He replaced the lion, his gaze flickering between Leo and Colin, a thrilled gleam to his eyes.

Colin shook his head, wishing the man would get on with it. "We've been . . . preoccupied."

Bea shifted and Colin's gaze was immediately drawn to her. She moved slowly through the room, pausing in front of a brilliant green butterfly mounted behind glass. She was like that butterfly, brilliant and delicate.

Pickens cleared his throat, forcing Colin's attention to him. "Rioting erupted outside the city. They're saying it should reach Delhi by late tonight."

"Rioting?" Ella clutched Leo's arm, her face pale, while Bea turned toward them, looking just as shocked.

Colin resisted the urge to curse. As if they needed any more difficulty. He wasn't surprised. The animosity between the British soldiers and the natives was obvious the moment he'd stepped foot in the country.

Leo slipped his arm around Ella's waist and drew her close. His stoic face revealed nothing of what he was thinking. "We heard of rioting on the way here, but were told it would be quickly taken care of."

"And so it shall be," Pickens said, tugging at his waistcoat as if offended even by the thought. "The British will contain them soon enough and send them back to where they belong."

Colin couldn't ignore that ridiculous statement. "And where would that be? Here, in India? Their homeland?"

"Well . . . I . . ." As Pickens stuttered out a response, Bea moved closer to Ella.

"But Ella," she whispered, just loud enough for Colin to hear. "Your condition."

Ella's gaze snapped to her. "You know?"

"What condition?" Colin demanded, their situation momentarily forgotten as he elbowed his way past Pickens.

Leo's attention jerked to his wife. Ella's face turned a brilliant pink and she suddenly found interest in the gold bangles around her wrist. "Nothing, really."

Bea's gaze slid to Ella's waistline. It was a flicker of a glance, but Colin hadn't missed it. He stiffened, outrage coursing through his blood. Dear God! Ella was pregnant! How could she? How could she come here knowing—

"We're here about Henry," Ella interrupted.

Leo frowned. He was calm, too calm, and Colin knew without a doubt Leo hadn't a clue as to Ella's condition. The man may portray the coldness of a statue, but underneath, he was a volcano awaiting eruption.

Pickens clasped his pale hands together. "Henry, of

course. The man you asked about." He moved through the crowded shop, twisting around shelves heavy with antiquities, and disappeared through a back door.

"Should we be worried?" Ella asked, looking up at her husband, most likely trying to change the subject.

"No, my love. I'll protect you." Leo pressed his lips to the top of her head.

"Then why are you worried?" she demanded.

Leo rolled his eyes. "*Merda*, woman, stop reading my blasted mind."

Dear God, what the hell were they talking about? "Of course you should be worried," Colin snapped. "Damn you, Ella!"

Leo stiffened, his face going taut. Slowly, his hard gaze slid to Colin and he could read the warning there.

"Oh, don't look at me like you're going to kill me. Give over, man. Your wife's with child."

Bea sucked in a gasp, obviously shocked by his bluntness. Ella paled.

It took a moment for the words to sink into Leo's dense brain, a long moment that gave Colin time to regret his outburst. If possible, Leo's face grew even paler than Ella's. Shame crept through Colin's body like the black spider currently making its way across the floorboards. Well hell, maybe he shouldn't have yelled it out like that. He rubbed the back of his neck. Bea was glaring at him; Ella was glaring at him; Leo, at least, had the good sense to glare at his wife.

Leo gripped Ella's shoulders, forcing her to look him in the eyes. "You're . . . you're . . ."

"With child," she admitted, giving him an overly bright smile. "Surprise."

The man's nostrils flared slightly. "You never should have come here . . . to this place full of death and disease."

"And you think England isn't full of death and disease?"

He sighed and closed his eyes and Colin wondered if Leo

was attempting to count to ten before he blew up. He had no doubt Leo would explode.

"I will not discuss the merits of England versus India and you will not change the subject."

Ella's face fell, her lower lip quivering. Colin rolled his eyes, recognizing a female trying to get her way when he saw one.

Confirming his suspicions, she threw her arms around her husband's neck. "I didn't know until we'd arrived and I couldn't bear to be without you."

Leo breathed in deep, his arms slipping around her waist. "And you didn't think to tell me?" he whispered into her hair.

"I knew you'd turn back the moment we arrived and I needed to know Colin was well. We hadn't heard from him in months."

"Great," Colin muttered, crossing his arms over his chest. "Put the blame on me."

Leo cupped the sides of Ella's face. "*Merda*, Ella, don't you understand how important you are?"

Colin's gaze slid to Bea, wondering how the cold English-woman was reacting. She stared at the two as if watching a play. Suddenly, he found himself entranced, witnessing the slight race of emotion cross her face as Ella and Leo declared their undying love. He could see it, the shift in her eyes, the melting of her body and soul. Her hands were clasped tightly in front of her, her lower lip quivering. So, she was a typical romantic and emotional woman after all.

Bemused by her softness, a smile tugged at his lips.

"Here. He came for this," Pickens said, rushing forward and interrupting the play. "I didn't show him the statue. Man owes me quite a bit and I knew he'd want to purchase the piece." Pickens smiled and held the polished light green stone high, like a man admiring his first child. "I showed him a drawing only."

Colin moved closer. His heart slammed against his chest.

His fingers curled at his sides as he resisted the urge to grab the statue. So familiar, yet not at all what he'd expected.

"What is it?" Ella asked, her voice sounding muffled through the roar of blood to his ears.

Colin reached out, his hands trembling. Without hesitation, Pickens handed over the piece. The jade was cool and smooth. "Four."

"That can't be," Leo snapped, snatching the statue from Colin. "It's not right."

"Mad, isn't it?" Pickens said, his skin gleaming with a fine sheen of sweat. "There are supposed to be four separate statues. This throws the entire myth upon its head."

"The statue? *Our* statue?" Ella whispered.

Colin shook his head, confused. "It can't be." His gaze pierced Pickens. "Is it a reproduction of all four? There are supposed to be four. Legend says there are four separate pieces."

Pickens shrugged, latching on to the statue and cradling it close. "No one knows for sure."

"Or we were wrong all along." Leo stated what they were all thinking.

"I don't understand," Bea interrupted, her voice meek and confused. "What's going on?"

Ella turned toward the woman, apparently taking pity on her. "There is a legend that says there are four separate statues representing each major religion of the world. Statues with supposed power."

"Power?" Bea demanded. "And this"—she waved her hand toward the statue Pickens held—"this is what Henry attempted to murder you for? I thought he wanted a necklace?"

"The necklace shows the way to the statues."

"It's a mistake," Leo said.

Pickens shook his head, his dark gaze gleaming with excitement. "The man said he saw the statue and it looked exactly like this."

"A man? What man?" Colin demanded.

Pickens grinned, a greedy grin. He loved the fact that they were completely in the dark and he could provide them with answers. "A religious man, rather well known around the area, named Anish."

Colin glanced at Leo, then Ella, looking for someone to clear up the immense mistake that had apparently been made. Their faces looked as confused as he felt.

Colin rubbed the back of his neck and paced across the floor. "It can't be. There are supposed to be four. It's a mistake, or someone is misleading us."

"We came here for a statue?" Bea interrupted, her gloved fingers pressing to her temples. "I don't understand."

"Neither do we." Leo took hold of Ella's hand. "But it doesn't matter. We're leaving."

"What?" Ella demanded, pulling back. "No!"

"Yes," Leo said, his voice hard. "I'm taking you back to England, where a woman in your condition belongs."

She narrowed her eyes, looking annoyed and offended. "A woman in my condition?"

Leo ignored her hard tone and started for the front of the shop, taking her with him. "We're leaving."

The door burst open with such force, the bell overhead clanged to the ground. Everyone froze. A thin, young boy stumbled inside, his breathing ragged.

"Raj, what is it?" Pickens demanded.

The boy spoke rapidly in Hindi. So fast, Colin only understood one word. Without thought, Colin pulled the pistol from his waistband.

"Oh dear Lord," Pickens whispered, his face going pale. He set the statue on a shelf, the piece forgotten, and raced to the front door.

"What's happened?" Ella asked.

But Pickens didn't answer, merely threw the bolt across the door and slumped against the wooden panel. But then he didn't need to answer. Colin's jaw clenched tight. He didn't know much of the language, but he knew enough.

Colin's heart slammed against his rib cage. "He said the rioters are attacking."

"Jaldi bhaago!" the boy said, looking at them and shooing them with his hands.

"What's he saying now?" Bea demanded.

"Run," Colin replied.

Chapter 5

"Run?" Bea's voice came out as a squeak. But honestly, someone had to say something. The entire situation was ridiculous. With all the screaming and shouting, Colin's bizarre, guarded expression, and Pickens's constant babbling, she didn't know if she should be frightened or annoyed.

"Apparently, the British Army deemed it appropriate to use cow and pig grease on the rifles, which, of course, upset the locals," Leo said, as if that explained everything. "British are slaughtering the Indians. Indians are slaughtering the British. Men, women, children."

Pickens raced to the windows and drew the shutters, although Bea realized it would do little to keep out those who wanted entrance.

"Come. We must hurry." Leo pulled a pistol from his waistband.

Fear sliced through Bea, sending her insides aquiver. Dear Lord, they must hurry or they could die. She'd wanted adventure, not death! Colin moved to the windows and nudged the curtain aside. Leo was talking furiously fast in Hindi to the lad who'd barreled in telling them of the attack. Bea was left to stand in the middle of the shop, not knowing if she should run or hide.

She attempted to decipher the conversations flowing

around her, but could catch only words here and there. No one seemed to be making any sense. Confused and frantic for answers, she turned to Ella, the only person who'd listen to her . . . who'd explain. But the moment she caught sight of her friend, the words died on her lips.

Ella's hands were pressed to her belly as if that could protect her unborn child. For the first time since they'd met, Bea saw real fear in Ella's eyes. Sympathy and shame sank heavily in her gut. She was worried about herself, only herself, when Ella had a husband and baby to protect.

Bea slipped her arm around Ella's narrow waist, drawing her close. "We'll be all right." She had to force the words from her mouth and pretend to believe them for Ella's sake.

Ella nodded, lifting her lips into a strained smile. "Thank you, Bea."

And even though she wanted to stay calm for Ella, she couldn't stop the bombardment of questions from racing through her mind. "Ella, I don't under—"

Leo latched on to Ella's hand. "Come. Raj will take us through the back. His grandfather owns a boat and can escort us downriver, clear of the city, at least."

Before Bea could agree or disagree, Leo took her hand. Bea stumbled along, wishing, not for the first time, that she'd worn the traditional Indian garb that was lighter and easier to control. Damn her English propriety!

"We haven't a moment to spare," Leo said, confirming her worst fears.

"You coming?" Colin asked Pickens.

The storekeeper shook his head, pulling out a pistol from behind the counter. "I can't leave my shop."

"Suit yourself," Colin muttered.

Leo released his hold and Colin immediately took his place, settling a firm hand on Bea's upper arm. Automatically, she stiffened at his touch. Without breaking stride, he managed to lead her toward the back of the shop. She had just enough time to glance over her shoulder and see Pickens shoving his valuables under the counter before she was tossed into a dark alley.

The sun had set, sending the narrow corridor into dark shadows that sent chills over her skin despite the heat. Without the protection of the store, fear and panic swept through Bea, making her knees buckle. She reached out, the alley so narrow she could easily rest a hand on each rough, stucco wall. The buildings wavered, spinning around her.

Leo held up his hand for them to stop as he peered around the corner. "Wait."

"Surely they won't attack us over grease?" she managed to whisper.

Colin shook his head, his annoyed gaze flickering over her. "Darlin', this has nothing to do with grease and everything to do with the disrespect for the working society. The natives have been abused by the British government long enough. They've finally got reason to act."

"But . . . but . . ."

The blasted man pointed a finger at her. "But you're British, therefore you're the enemy."

"But I'm a woman!"

"And women aren't capable of disrespect?"

She knew the answer to that. Of course women were capable. How many times had she and Grandmother been snubbed by society when they'd dared to visit a village? It didn't matter that they came from a titled background, or they were wealthy and English . . . Grandfather had excommunicated them to Scotland because of Grandmother's supposed madness, and everyone knew the reason. Bea had suffered along with Grandmother even when she'd barely been able to realize why.

"I'm being persecuted for something I have no control over," she whispered. She'd left Britain for freedom and now she was merely in a different sort of prison. It was madness.

Colin shook his head. "And you think they haven't been all this time?"

She looked away, unable to hold his hard gaze. Why did she have the impression that he was trying to blame her for this situation? Blast it, she was tired of taking the brunt of everyone's bickering.

"Enough arguing, let's go," Leo demanded.

Colin latched on to her again, and although she wanted to push him away, she didn't dare for fear she'd lose sight of the group. They wove their way around crates. From the opening of the alley, shouts could be heard, the people already protesting. Angry snarls in a language she didn't understand roared over her harsh breathing. Leo slid his arm around Ella's waist, holding her close. How Bea wished she could find the same sense of comfort, anyone to make her feel not so alone and afraid.

The lad, Raj, glanced over his shoulder and spoke to Leo. She was too far away to hear his words. Such a young boy. He couldn't have been more than thirteen years. Yet they were following his directions. Would he lead them to the safety he claimed, or to their demise?

Leo glanced over his shoulder, his eyes glowing eerily in the moonlight. "Through this lane, go across the street and into the alley beyond. Don't slow, don't get caught."

Bea felt a manic bubble of laughter well within. He said the words as if they had a choice in the matter. As if they could do anything to prevent being captured.

Before she could question the rationality of his decision, Leo and Ella darted into the street, the crowds and the darkness swallowing them whole. She was left alone with Colin, the one man she didn't trust in the least.

He turned to her, so close she could smell that warm, spicy scent. She closed her eyes briefly and breathed deep, taking comfort in the way his scent warmed her insides. Without a word of encouragement, he jerked the netting back over her face.

"Go," he demanded, shoving her hard.

Instinct propelled her forward, but her foot caught on the

hem of her skirt and she stumbled. Bea stiffened, prepared to hit the ground. But Colin was there, his hand latching on to her upper arm. He didn't break his stride as he pulled her into the street.

Immediately, protesters surrounded them, men and boys yelling words she didn't understand. Torchlight hit their faces, masks of angry people under their brilliantly colored turbans. Bea's lungs seemed to shrivel, her breath coming out in harsh pants. A suffocating fear clawed within. She would have stopped, there, in the middle of the street, frozen in fear. Fortunately, Colin pushed her forward.

They made it into the alley before anyone truly realized who they were. Hidden in the dark shadows of the stone buildings, Bea was finally able to slow. But Colin continued to tug at her hand, urging her to run. She couldn't keep going!

"The river is just ahead. Raj's grandfather has a boat that can take us down the Yamuna and out of Delhi," Leo called out, his face indiscernible in the dark shadows, his voice hardly audible over the shouts.

Bea barely had time to take a deep breath before Colin was dragging her down an alley again. Dust, stirred by their feet, puffed around her, entering her throat and coating her body. The corset she wore dug into her ribs, making it difficult to draw air. She couldn't seem to take in a breath without heaving. Her lungs were shrinking, the air thin.

Her legs grew weak and Bea stumbled. "I . . . I can't . . ."

She'd die, here, in a dirty alley with no one she knew or trusted. Her breath came out in wheezing gasps, her body desperate for air. Tears of self-pity stung her eyes. Ahead, she could see Leo, Ella, and the boy, Raj, disappear around a corner. They'd left her alone with Colin, *Colin*, for God's sake!

Her grasp weakened and Colin's strong fingers slipped from hers like a wispy dream. He glanced back, his gaze questioning, but his body was fading, the light fading with him. Her lungs no longer burned as unconsciousness promised sweet relief from the turmoil.

"Bea?"

A deep hollow voice seemed to echo around her, vibrating her very soul. Bea tried to open her eyes, but couldn't seem to focus. Her body went limp and she started to slump toward the ground. Just when she thought she'd hit the hard dirt, she felt a strong arm wrap around her waist and jerk her upright. The familiar scent of spice, sandalwood, and male surrounded her, making her insides tingle. Colin.

"I . . . can't . . . breathe," she managed in soft gasps.

She was barely aware when he shoved her against the rough stone of a wall and her bonnet tipped to the side, pulling at her hair and scalp. Barely aware when his fingers moved down the buttons at the front of her bodice.

Even over the foggy reality that had become her life, she knew she should be outraged and needed to push his hands away. Yet she couldn't seem to gather the strength, couldn't seem to care. The netting on her bonnet tickled her skin, propelled into movement by the harsh intake of her breath.

The buttons gave way and her bodice parted like the Red Sea.

A small curl of warm air managed to slip down her throat. Enough air to bring Colin's face back into focus.

"Ridiculous," he snapped, his thick lashes lowered as he focused on the task of untangling the strings of her corset. He had lovely lashes, really, for a man. Lashes any woman would envy. She almost giggled, realizing the absurdity of her thoughts. Truly, the lack of air had made her mad.

She finally managed to raise her arms, her fingers weakly clasping on to his wrists. "Colin, what are you doing?"

"Saving your damn life." With a swoosh of metal against leather, he pulled the knife from the sheath on his thigh. The blade flashed under the moonlight. Bea's eyes widened, her fingers tightening around his wrists. Suddenly, the situation was no longer amusing.

"Trust me." The sharp tip of his blade pressed to her belly.

Bea sucked in her gut. Colin flipped his hand up and the screech of ripping material momentarily interrupted the chant of protesters. The binding fell to the ground. Air filled her shrunken lungs, stretching them almost painfully. Bea cried out, slumping forward into Colin's strong arms.

He slipped his knife into the sheath and merely held her. For one long moment, neither spoke. He'd saved her life. In a ridiculous and indecent way, but still . . . The realization left Bea feeling off balance.

"You . . . you should dress," he said.

Bea realized her breasts were crushed indecently to Colin's chest. Only her shift and his shirt protected her modesty. Slowly, she pulled back. The warm air beaded her nipples against the soft material. She didn't care. Dear God, she didn't care about propriety. All she cared about was the fact that she could breathe again!

Colin nudged her back and cupped the sides of her face with his rough hands. She was surprised to see concern in his gaze. The emotion set her negative opinion of the man hanging precariously by a thread. "Are you all right?"

Disconcerted, she could merely nod. Gently, he rested her against the wall and pulled her bodice together, working the buttons up her chest. "It won't fit without the corset."

"Leave it open," she said.

She didn't care that her collar hung indecently wide, revealing the tops of her pale breasts. And she didn't care that Colin was watching her, his intense gaze moving from her chest to her eyes, where they held. She certainly didn't care that her heart was pounding so hard, that Colin could probably hear the unsteady beat.

She didn't care because Colin had saved her life and was watching her with the oddest look in his eyes. An unidentifiable look that sent her already racing heart spinning. Something had changed between the two of them . . . something she couldn't quite identify . . .

"Colin?" Leo called out, his voice piercing the darkness.

There was one long moment before Colin answered.

"Coming," he finally replied.

Without a word, without another look, he latched on to Bea's hand and jerked her down the alley. She glanced back, her fear forgotten. Her corset lay pristine white against the brown dirt. This morning she would have never gone without a corset. She was leaving behind a part of her in Delhi, a part she never wanted back.

Her corset gone, she felt a renewed burst of energy. She hiked up her skirts until her white stockings showed. Her bonnet thumped annoyingly against her head as she kept pace with Colin, but she didn't pause to fix it—they didn't have time for such nonsense.

Stucco and stone homes gave way to shacks, and dirt gave way to soft mud. The land sloped into stiff brush that poked through her stockings and scratched her legs. Bea dropped her skirts, the hem dragging through the mud.

Like a group of soldiers defeating the enemy, they crushed down the stiff reeds lining the river. Under the pressure of her boots, mud slurped and gurgled. Not only would her shoes be ruined, but her dress as well. Grandmother would have an apoplexy. For once in her life, Bea didn't give a fig.

Leo shouted in Hindi and Bea tore her gaze from her ruined shoes. Barely visible in the deepening dusk, a tiny vessel rocked on waves of inky water. This was the boat that would take them to safety? The thing barely looked buoyant. Bea glanced to her cousin for confirmation, but over the maddening thump of her heart, she couldn't understand what Leo was saying.

All she could seem to focus on was the murmured cry of the rioters in the background.

"They're not coming this way," Colin said, as if sensing her thoughts. "They're headed in the opposite direction."

She managed to nod, but how could he be sure? She turned. In the distance, she could see the wavering torchlight of protesters. She jerked her attention back toward the water.

The river was wide, a mirror of darkness. Lights from

homes lined the water, glowing eerily, like demon eyes in the night. An old man shuffled forward, the boat rocking with his movement. His back was hunched, his face so wrinkled one could barely make out his eyes from his nose, from his mouth. An apple left in the sun too long. He glanced at them; at least she thought he did.

"Nahee." He shook his head, holding up his hands. *"Nahee."*

"What's he saying?" Bea whispered.

Colin didn't bother to look at her. "No. He's saying no."

Shock replaced her fear. Bea's legs threatened to give out. Leo was speaking rapidly to the man, his body fierce, tight. He pulled out a pouch and jiggled it, the coins clanking together. The man paused only a moment, then lured by the promise of gold, he nodded. Relieved, Bea could breathe again. Leo wasted no time and helped Ella into the tiny boat.

Then, he turned to Bea.

"Doh!" the old man said, holding up two fingers.

Leo paused, his hands fisting with momentary annoyance. *"Chaar."*

The man shook his head, his expression mulish.

"What is it?" Colin demanded.

Slowly, Leo turned toward them. "The river is low because of the dry season. He says his boat can only carry two, at the most. The weight . . ."

They all fell silent.

In the background the rioters' angry shouts seemed to be growing closer. A rustle drew Bea's attention downriver. A white crane stood on the edge of the water, so serene amid the turmoil.

"Bea?" Leo held out his hand.

"No!" Ella cried, desperation in her voice. Reaching out, she latched on to Leo's shirt. The boat tipped precariously with her movement, but Ella didn't seem to notice. "We'll stay here with you. We'll hide. We'll be fine."

Tears stung Bea's eyes, the fear on Ella's face almost her

undoing. Fear not for herself, but for the man she loved. Fear for her unborn child.

Leo pulled Ella up against him, holding her tight. "Ella, I can't let you stay here."

"Leo." Colin rested his hand on Leo's shoulder. "They can't go alone, two women. It's not safe."

Room for two. Only two. She'd die if she stayed here, Bea had no doubt. But if Leo stayed, he might die and never see Ella again, never see his unborn child . . .

"We'll find another boat," Ella insisted, tears trailing down her face and glistening like trails of ice in moonlight.

Leo shook his head. "We don't have time. You must leave now."

Bea knew what she needed to do. She tucked the netting atop her bonnet, resolve settling around her, calm and serene. "Go, Leo."

He didn't even glance at her. "No."

She latched on to his arm. It was the first time since they'd met that she'd touched him intimately and the muscle she felt reassured her. Leo would protect Ella. They'd make it to safety. She had to believe that. "You must."

"Bea," Ella called out, reaching for her.

Bea glanced at the crane one more time. He stood there, still at ease, still serene in the midst of turmoil. She could be that crane. Bea stepped back, out of arm's length, afraid if Ella comforted her at all, she'd break down and beg them to take her with them.

Colin raked his hands through his hair, the curls ruffling with the soft breeze. "Leo, we can't open the map without you."

"Without my family blood," Leo interjected.

"Which means . . ." Every set of eyes turned toward Bea. She didn't understand what was happening, but she knew suddenly she was involved. Frankly, at the moment, she didn't care. She only wanted to find somewhere safe where they could wait out the riots and hopefully survive.

"It's best if we divide up anyway. I'll protect her," Colin said, resting his hand on the small of her back.

As surprised as she was at his touch, Bea couldn't deny that the pressure of Colin's fingers made her feel better . . . momentarily. Last night's misadventure still rang in her mind. Colin had been a coward, leaving Ella and Leo to protect his home. How could he possibly keep her safe?

"Bea," Ella whispered, her lips quivering.

"Go, Leo," Bea demanded. "Protect Ella and your baby."

Leo looked at Bea, truly looked at her, and she saw the emotions in his gaze . . . appreciation, respect, and worry. Her heart clenched. For the first time in a long while, someone actually cared about her. "The boy will take you home. He'll help you."

Bea nodded, fighting her tears.

Leo's gaze shifted to Colin. "If you don't catch up to us soon, then meet near Bombay. You know where."

Without waiting for a response, Leo waded into the murky water and jumped atop the tiny vessel, the boat rocking under his weight.

Ella wrapped her arms around her husband's waist, holding him close. Before they disappeared, Leo tugged the ring from his finger. "It's yours now."

He tossed it toward them. The green emerald glistened and flashed in the rising moon. Colin reached out, snatching it from the air. Bea thought he was talking to Colin, but he was looking at her. She didn't understand. Why was he giving her his ring? But she didn't have time to ask.

The current took the boat downriver, and darkness swallowed Leo and Ella.

Chapter 6

"We go?" Raj asked, his large eyes oceans of inkiness in the moonlight.

Colin grasped on to Bea's arm and yanked her up the bank as if she weighed little more than a ragdoll. His tight grip stung, but she knew better than to protest. Her feet slipped on the wet grass, her fear mounting the farther they traveled from the water . . . farther from Leo and Ella.

Startled by their sudden movement, the crane cried out and took flight, his huge wings swooshing through the air. Bea watched the bird, watched him even as Colin pulled her onto the dirt path they'd followed to get to the river. Never had she wished to be a bird more than she did at the moment. When the crane disappeared into the night, she felt bereft, as if she'd lost the last link to her sanity . . . her soul.

"Bea, damn it, hurry."

She reluctantly focused her attention forward, forced back into the turmoil that had become her life. "Heavens, Colin, where are we going?"

"My home." He pulled her behind a row of mud huts, the occupants either fast asleep or participating in the riots, Bea didn't want to know which. Following Raj, they leapt over clay pots and cow droppings that had been left to dry in the heat.

"But the rioters," Bea said, pressing her bonnet to her head as the speed of their pace threatened to tear it from her scalp. Faster Colin went, so fast it was impossible for Bea to keep pace. Her skirts twisted around her legs, making her stumble.

"My money, more weapons, they're all there." He paused only a moment to jerk the netting down over her face. Then he was off again, running through the streets, darting from shadowy corner to shadowy corner, dragging her behind like a mutt on a rope.

Even though her corset was gone, the intense activity had her gasping only moments later. She couldn't keep running like this; she wasn't dressed for the exercise. Needing air, Bea sucked in another breath. The sensitive skin of her throat stung. Her nostrils flared as an acidic scent assaulted her senses. "I smell something."

"Yeah, that's the muck stuck to your boots, darlin'."

"No," she snapped, hitting his shoulder to gain his attention. "I smell smoke."

He paused and she ran into his back, her face flattening against his hard shoulder. "You're right." He shrugged, sending her stumbling to the side. "Well, I suppose it's not a real riot unless there's fire."

Bea didn't have time to respond to his ridiculous words. He took her hand and jerked her forward again. Through one narrow alley after another, he forced her to run. "Colin, I . . . I . . . can't go much further."

"It's here." They turned down a corridor lined with narrow stone homes molded side by side. Colin didn't bother to unlock his door but, with a low growl, kicked it open. Shattering wood was barely audible against the racket of rioting out front.

"I watch," Raj said over his shoulder as he sprinted to the end of the alley.

Colin rushed inside without a word. Bea hesitated only

a moment. Not wanting to be left alone, she followed. In the sitting room memories flitted through her mind.

Just hours ago, they'd all been here, in this plain room, planning their next course of action. Just hours ago, she'd been oblivious to the real reason as to why they were here. Now . . . now the only two people she knew were gone and she was at the mercy of a man she'd just met and didn't fully trust. This was what her life had become?

Colin disappeared into the kitchen, but she was too depressed to follow. She pulled her gloves from her hands and let them fall to the ground, useless pieces of protection from the elements. When they'd first arrived, she'd been shocked at how tiny the house was. Now, the place was a heaven within hell. But she knew that sense of comfort was only a façade. They were no safer here than they were in the streets. She pressed her hand to her heart, the thump so loud she feared it would burst from her chest. How had she gotten to this point?

The shatter of breaking glass came from the kitchen. On numb legs, Bea made her way toward Colin. He was shuffling through cupboards, tossing objects aside as if they meant nothing. A glass jar lay in pieces on the floorboards. Dishes lay haphazard across the table.

"Where the hell is it?" He slammed his fists against the wall, making Bea jump.

"Ah!" He pulled out another jar and unscrewed the lid. Without thought or hesitation, he poured dry beans upon the floor. They skittered and danced like rain across the reed mats. With a grin, Colin pulled free a thick wad of bills and stuffed them into his pockets.

"Here." He extended his arm, the paper money he'd clutched in his fist fluttering with the movement.

"What?"

He grabbed her hand and curled her fingers around a wad of cash. "In case we get separated or something happens to me, that should be enough to get you to Bombay."

Bea shook her head, wanting to drop the money as if it were poison. "No. No, don't say that. Nothing can happen to you." As much as she disliked Colin, the thought of being alone here, in this upheaval, was too much even to contemplate.

"Just in case."

"No!"

He grasped her shoulders, looking directly into her eyes, his gaze so intense, she couldn't look away. "Bea, you've had to put up with your damn, insane family. Cousins and grandfathers wanting to kill each other. You and your grandmother banished to Scotland. You must have some strength in you. You can do this."

His words chipped through the fear. The moment was oddly intimate. Yet he was right. She'd dealt with a ridiculous amount in her life. But that didn't mean she'd be able to travel through India alone. She looked reluctantly down at the money. Merely for safety's sake and to appease the man, she stuffed the bills into her skirt pocket. "Don't you dare leave me here alone."

He flashed her that angelic grin. "I won't. I meant it—"

The sound of breaking glass interrupted whatever it was Colin was about to say. Bea screamed. Colin started through the doorway, realized she wasn't with him, and paused. "Damn it. Come on." He grabbed her hand and pulled her into the sitting room.

The windows were broken, the curtains engulfed in flames that licked and danced their way up the drapes. Whether it had been done intentionally or by accident didn't matter. Bea could merely stand there staring.

Colin didn't pause to look back, nor try to put out the fire. He jerked Bea through the back door and into the alley. They had to leave. But go where? Frantic, Bea searched for Raj. The boy was gone.

"You think to escape with my money?" a deep voice rumbled.

Bea stiffened, her grasp on Colin's fingers tightening so

hard that surely it hurt. Yet he didn't flinch. Slowly, they turned as one. Three fierce giants stood not fifteen feet from them. Their features were barely visible in the darkness, but she didn't need a lantern to know they were angry. Danger pulsed from them in waves that had her stomach knotting.

"Colin, who are they?" she asked in a low, quivering whisper.

"Damn it all to hell," Colin snapped, not exactly answering her question.

The leader, the tallest of the three, braced his legs apart and crossed his arms over his massive chest like a pirate at the helm of a ship. He looked like a pirate. His bald head gleamed in the moonlight and she could just barely make out intricate, dark brown drawings that swirled across the dome of his pale head.

"Marco?" Bea whispered.

Colin let go of her hands and stepped in front of her. "Yep."

Bea stood on the tips of her toes to look over Colin's shoulder. Marco had moved closer and the two cads behind him followed, fanning out to block the alley. Fear pulsed beneath her skin, urging her to run. Bea glanced behind them. They could make a dash for it, but most likely the pistols would stop them dead . . . literally.

Anger replaced fear. This was all Colin's fault. Blast him! If he wasn't such a rake, they wouldn't be in this predicament.

Marco flashed a wicked grin, dark spaces where his front teeth should have been. "Well, my friend, we meet again."

By the sound of his accent, another American. Bea wasn't surprised. Apparently, all Americans were cads. With an angry nudge, Bea attempted to make Colin step aside so she could get a better view. The man didn't move. In fact, he looked rather calm for someone who was about to be killed. Did he not take anything seriously?

Outraged, she was just about to tell him exactly what she

thought, when she noticed the way his gaze flickered. In his eyes she could see his mind working, no doubt attempting to find a solution to their sudden problem. He'd better find a solution, damn him. What had Leo been thinking to leave her with him?

Could Colin fight as well as her cousin? Colin was as large, and the muscle in his body was evident through the fine linen of his shirt. Yes, she'd felt the state of his body when he'd landed on top of her the other night. But so far she'd barely seen him lift a finger.

A smile tilted the corner of Colin's mouth, those dimples flashing. "Come, can't we let go of the past? I gave you the money."

Marco lifted a dark brow. "Not enough." The two cads behind him didn't say a bloody word. But they didn't need to. Their threat was evident in the glare of their gazes.

Colin shrugged. "Yes, well, the money was enough before you changed the rules, after the game was over, I might add."

The man narrowed his eyes and started toward them, dust puffing around his heavy black boots. Each thud of his feet sent Bea's pulse racing faster and she had to resist the urge to scream and run.

Colin stepped back, his body nudging her off center. She squeaked and latched on to his waist. He tilted his head to the side, his mouth close to hers. "If I tell you to run, run."

Bea's back grew damp, sweat snaking down between her shoulder blades. "Without you?"

"Yes."

Marco and his friends moved closer.

Heavens, this could not be happening. Even if she survived and miraculously made it to Bombay, how would she tell Ella that Colin had died? No, no, Colin wouldn't die. Yes, he was a bastard, but he didn't deserve to die! Frantically, she glanced around the alley, looking for a weapon, anything to assist the idiotic man who'd gotten them into this mess. Someone would have to save them, and it looked as if that someone would be her.

"You are not going to get rid of me that easily," she muttered.

Colin glanced back at her, just long enough for her to read the amusement in his blue eyes.

Irate, she twisted the material of his shirt in her fists. "You think this is funny?"

He shrugged, indifferent. "Just remember to run, darlin'."

Bea stood on tiptoe, looking over his shoulder. Marco and his bastard friends were close. Too close. Big, burly men that Colin certainly couldn't fight alone and come out the winner. She glanced at the wooden crates stacked in the alley. There had to be something . . . anything she could use to help. But the only thing of any interest was a pile of cow droppings and she doubted that would do much damage to men like them.

"Now really, let's be honest," Colin called out to the men. "We know what this is really about."

Marco paused, his dark eyes narrowing. "And that is?"

"That English ass Henry."

Marco's bulbous nostrils flared ever so slightly, his only telling response. "Don't know what you're talking about."

"Admit it, he's paid you to keep me busy, hasn't he?"

A slight movement flickered across Bea's line of vision. Confused, she took a hesitant step back, her eyes narrowing. A small form sat huddled near a pile of crates. His head lifted and huge, dark eyes met hers. Bea sucked in a breath. *Raj!*

"Does it matter?" Marco asked. "Either way, you're a dead man."

Bea's heart slammed against her chest. Dash it! Raj hadn't left after all. It was one thing to be in danger, but to place a child in the middle of a brawl? She glanced at Colin, then back at the boy. Raj was so young, he couldn't be more than thirteen, and who knew what horrors he'd see. Before she could shoo him with a wave of her hands, he started trembling. The boxes he leaned against rattled.

"And if I pay you more than Henry is offering?"

Marco laughed. Bea wanted to laugh along with the man. It was ridiculous. Their situation preposterous. This was not happening!

Marco slammed his fist into his open palm, the thud crackling through the alley. "Let's face it, my friend, you don't have that kind of money."

Raj shifted. Bea snapped her gaze toward him. He was crouched low, like an animal about to spring. Her breath caught as she resisted the urge to yell out no! He couldn't flee. If he moved, she knew they'd start firing.

"Colin," she whispered, her eyes still pinned to the boy.

"Not now."

"Colin, Raj!" she said, ignoring his command.

He glanced at her. She nodded toward the crates.

Colin jerked his gaze that way. "Damn."

She didn't dare flinch, barely parted her lips to respond. "Perhaps we could call a moment's cease-fire?"

Colin rolled his eyes. "Darlin', this isn't one of your fancy British wars with rules and regulations. They see the lad, he's as good as dead. He's a witness."

"But he's just a—"

"Give us the money or your head," Marco ordered, stepping closer and lifting his lips into a snarl.

"Here," Bea whispered, slipping her hand into her pocket. "Take the money you gave me."

"It's not enough."

She knew it wasn't enough. She wasn't daft. But still, it might tide them over.

Colin gave the men in front of them a mocking smile. "And if we do, you won't shoot us?"

Bea resisted the urge to sigh in frustration. Their conversation was pointless. Bea hoped Colin was trying to buy time while he came up with a plan.

Marco shrugged. "Yes, we'll still shoot you, but I can promise a quicker death."

Bea's stomach churned, and not for the first time since arriving, she felt her last meal making its way up her throat. She gagged, the sound like a dying cat. She couldn't do it. She couldn't stand here and wait for death.

Colin shot her an irritated glance. "Don't you dare get sick on me."

She swallowed hard and gripped his wrist. "Colin, what will we do?"

"Give them the money." He stepped back and settled his hands on his waist. "All right, boys. Easy." He tilted his head closer to Bea, his lips only a breath from her ear. "The moment I bring my hands up, dive behind those crates," he whispered. "And remember. Run if something happens to me."

Bea couldn't breathe, couldn't agree to his ridiculous plan because she was too stunned and too bloody afraid to move.

"Bea," he snapped. His gaze had gone steely, the blue somehow turning gray. Gone was the laughing man she'd come to know. And for one brief moment, hope flared to life. Perhaps Colin could save her. "Do you understand?"

She gave a quick jerk of her head.

"Now!" He pulled his hands up. Bea dove to the side, stumbling into Raj's bony frame. She fell to the ground with a thud, the boy half under her weight. Blasts rang out, so loud her ears buzzed. Raj wiggled under her.

"No!" Bea cried, grasping on to his thin arm. She jerked him back. The lad fought her, his limbs flailing, elbows digging into her sides. "You must stay put!"

But the boy was heedless to her cries. Frantic with fear, he gave her one hard shove and she fell back into a crate. The edge of a box dug into her back, making her cry out in pain. She could just see the beige of his shirt as he darted down the alley. Bea stumbled to her feet, intending to go after him. Her foot caught on the hem of her gown. The dress pulled tight and she crumbled to the ground. Her elbows hit hard dirt, her cheek pressed to the cool earth.

Blasts burst again like thunder, so loud the ground shook. Then there was silence.

Colin. Dear God, Colin!

Terror pulsed through her body in a quick, steady rhythm. She pushed herself up to her elbows. Colin stood in the middle of the lane. A sob of relief caught in Bea's throat, tears burning her eyes. He wasn't dead. She jumped to her feet and rushed at him. Without hesitation, she threw her arms around his neck. He stumbled back a step, but she didn't let go. Honestly, she'd never been happier to see a person than she was at that moment.

"It's all right." His body was warm and she was cold, so cold. She couldn't seem to stop shaking. She didn't have to look to make sure the men had been taken care of. She knew. She could feel it in the relaxed stance of his body.

"I'm sorry," she was finally able to mutter moments later. "I'm not at all used to such—"

"I know. But we need to leave. Now."

She nodded, her head bumping his chin. Taking in a deep breath, for one brief moment she savored the scent of him. There was something warm, something oddly comforting in the man's scent. She realized, in that moment, that perhaps he wasn't as cowardly as she'd deduced. Her fingers curled against his hard chest, her heart skipping a beat. Finally, she stepped back. He was watching her, a curious look upon his face. Heat rose from her neck to her cheeks. How could she throw herself at him? It was childish, ridiculous.

She turned her head away, unable to look him in the eyes. "I . . . I . . ."

Bea caught sight of a bare foot peeking out from behind a pile of rubble. Her heart stopped before kicking into a mad pace. She thought he'd escaped. She hesitated only a moment, then burst forward.

"Please don't be Raj!"

The boy lay upon the ground, a pool of dark red blood soaking into the yellow dirt beneath him. Bea's heart squeezed.

"No!" She reached for him, but was jerked back. Bea spun around, her fists raised.

"Bea, calm yourself!" Colin snapped.

"He's dead! They killed him!" She struggled against his hold, feeling she should do something to help the poor boy, *anything*.

Colin shook her. "Calm down, damn it."

"Calm down?" She slammed her fists against his hard chest and glared up at him. How could he be so cruel? How could he not care? "He's just a child, a little boy, and he died because he was trying to help us."

Colin gripped her shoulders, forcing her to look directly at him. "Go up ahead. Keep watch and yell out if anyone comes near. I'll look him over."

His odd words gave her pause. Confused, Bea shook her head. "You? What in the bloody world can you do?" Didn't he understand, Raj was dead. *Dead.*

"Go," he demanded, pushing her forward. "You're wasting time."

She wanted to argue, but at the fierce look on his face, she turned and rushed down the lane, not daring to glance at the boy's body. Where two alleys intersected, she paused, making sure to stay against the wall, where the shadows and night kept her well hidden.

In the background she could hear the people still protesting. So many angry people, angry at her. Fear snaked its way through her body, clinging to her nerves. The desire to run overwhelmed her. She spun around. Down the lane she could just make out a man lying in the dirt. The same man who'd wanted them dead. Now he was dead. So much blood, so much death.

She grew dizzy, her stomach rolling. Bea swerved on her

feet, sinking back against the rough wall of some abode. She'd faint. She wanted to faint. She couldn't faint. She'd be of no help unconscious. Frantic, she searched for Colin, needing to see him.

He was just barely visible crouched down by the lad, half-hidden among the crates. What was he doing? The boy was dead. An innocent child who'd done no wrong. Guilt tore at her heart, dropping piece by piece into the hollow cavity of her chest. Her knees gave out and she slid down the wall, the rough texture of the plaster biting through her bodice. Did he have a mother or father who'd come looking for him? Bea's hands fisted and she slammed them back against the wall as tears burned her eyes with a painful sting.

"Bea." Colin's muffled voice floated to her and broke through her despair.

She blinked and suddenly he was standing in front of her, the boy cradled in his arms. "Bea, damn it, look at me."

Reality rushed in like a slap. She sucked in a breath. "What happened?"

Colin frowned, sweat gleaming across his tanned skin. He looked tired. Exhausted really. "I'd say you were about to faint."

"Not with me, you baboon, the boy!"

At the sound of her voice, Raj turned his head and looked directly at her. Bea gasped, stumbling back. His dark eyes were wide and full of life.

She shook her head, her gaze scanning his body, taking in the blood-soaked shirt where a rip was clearly visible from a bullet wound. "He was . . . he was dead."

"No. He wasn't," Colin said, brushing past her. He set the boy on his feet. "Now, come on. We have to get out of here before more men arrive."

"More? But . . . but . . ."

Raj took no time in scurrying down the lane, shouting something in his language and waving them forward. Colin started after him, then apparently realizing Bea still stood there, he paused and glanced back. There were dark circles under his eyes, and where he'd once been smiling, now his mouth was held in a tight, grim line. Exhausted. He looked exhausted. Something odd had happened and Bea had no rational explanation.

He placed his hands on his narrow hips and sighed. "Darlin', I'm going with the lad. You coming, or you staying here?"

Chapter 7

"Colin," Bea called out breathlessly. "Please. You must explain!"

He knew she'd follow. What choice did she have? But the thought of having to explain what had happened left him cold. He had to give some sort of explanation.

Reluctantly, he turned. She slammed into him, her hands flattening against his chest. A breath of air escaped her lips, a caress that whispered across his neck. Unwanted heat shimmered over his skin. A sane man would have jerked away from her. Obviously he'd lost control of his sanity. Even in his exhausted state, he found himself reacting to her touch. He shook aside the unsettling feeling and wrapped his arm around her waist to keep her from stepping back. She felt good under his fingers, her body soft and warm, and if only for a moment, he wanted to soak in her essence, to forget reality.

"Don't we need to run?"

"We're all right, for now. The trees will hide us and no one will think twice when they find the bodies in the alley." And he was too damn weak to move any faster, but he sure as hell wasn't going to admit that.

In the dim light, he could see the charming flush that had settled on her high cheekbones. Her bonnet had slipped back and her hair had long ago come loose from the tight bun, falling in cascades around her face. With the moonlight bathing her in silver, she looked . . . well . . . beautiful. And that thought was ridiculous considering they were running for their lives.

Needing something mundane to occupy his troubling thoughts, he untied the straw hat and tossed it aside.

"My bonnet!" She started to reach for it, but paused, as if realizing that her hat was the least of their problems. Taking in a deep breath, she stood on tiptoe and tilted her face up only inches from his. For one insane moment, he thought she might kiss him. Time ceased. His heart slammed against his ribs, begging her to move closer . . . closer . . .

"Where are we going?" she whispered against his ear.

Confused, he pulled back.

Her gaze was on Raj, and he realized with some disappointment that she'd stepped close to him so the lad wouldn't overhear.

Colin blinked away his lustful thoughts, annoyed with her, more annoyed with himself. "I haven't the slightest."

Without waiting for her response, he started forward again, dragging her down a dark alley, behind stone homes. He felt disappointed that she hadn't kissed him. Which was odd, considering he didn't even like her. But then, she was an attractive woman, he argued with himself. Plus, after saving the lad, his defenses were weak. And women were certainly his weakness.

"But . . . but . . ."

"You're stuttering, darlin'."

"Well, do you blame me?" Her steps caught up to him. "I'm basically placing my life in the hands of a boy who has risen from the dead and you. *You!*"

He quirked a brow and grinned, a grin that most women found quite disarming, or so he'd been told. She didn't seem disarmed. She seemed annoyed. For some reason he found that amusing.

"Well, really," she rasped. "I don't know you in the least, and if this night is any indication of the company you keep, maybe I don't want to remedy that."

"Yes," he said, tearing his gaze from her and studying the row of stone homes that branched out around them. He needed to focus on their surroundings, not an arrogant Englishwoman and her lush lips. "It's really very improper of you to keep company with me."

"I had no choice!" she cried.

Most of the people had fled to watch the protesting. He shrugged, peering into the shadows of the buildings that scattered around the outskirts of Delhi, looking for movement or anything of a suspicious nature. "Your reputation is surely ruined."

She slapped his arm. "You're not amusing, sir." She looked away, but not before he saw the gleam of tears glistening in her eyes.

Guilt tugged at his heart. Hell. She was a gently bred woman alone with a man she barely knew in a foreign country. Most females would be in hysterics by now. Perhaps she wasn't nearly as bad as he'd thought.

"Bea—"

"Miss Edmund," she snapped, giving a delicate sniff. But she wasn't done with her pout. She crossed her arms over her chest and refused to look at him.

Colin pinched the bridge of his nose, but secretly delighted that the stubborn woman he'd come to know had apparently returned. A strong, impossible woman he could handle, but one crying . . . he was looking for the easiest way to escape.

"*Miss* Edmund, no one will possibly care about your reputation here. And it is highly, highly unlikely anyone back home will hear about your little jaunts through the back alleys of Delhi."

She released a puff of air, which sent her dark strands to momentary flight. "You don't know my grandmother."

He clasped her shoulders in his hands, surprised by how delicate she felt. He was too used to being alone. She needed protection, and he'd vowed to protect her. He was the first to admit that he might have been a bastard at times, but he always kept his promises. "I swore to Leo I'd keep you safe, and that includes your reputation."

She sighed, her shoulders sinking with despair, a despair that darkened her amber eyes to a deeper gold. "You can't promise that. You have no control—"

"Just trust me, for God's sake."

She pressed her lips into a thin line, as if trying to keep from crying. Guilt knotted his stomach. Gone was the awestruck woman he'd seen this morning as they traveled the streets of Delhi. Gone was the dazzling smile she wore when she was in Ella and Leo's company. He'd give anything to see her eyes flash with anger or joy. But he couldn't see her like this, with fear lingering on her face. Fear he was powerless to remove.

"Come," Raj called out impatiently. The boy waved them forward, the blood on his beige shirt like a beacon for death, a sign to all of how close he'd come to the end of his short life. "Home."

He pointed ahead to a row of small buildings covered in yellowed plaster. Not a terribly poor neighborhood, but far from wealthy. The few people still out sweeping the streets didn't bother to look at them, bent over their tasks of menial servitude.

"Colin?" Bea whispered, fear heavy in her voice.

Reluctantly, he met her gaze.

"What if . . . what if we're walking into a trap?"

What if? He supposed that was always a possibility. But did they have a choice? "We're fine."

"But—"

"I told the boy we're married," he blurted out, mostly to stop her questions, partly because he wanted to see her reaction.

The shock on her face stung. Would it be so bad to be his bride? God, what was the matter with him? Why did he care?

"But that's a lie!"

He cursed. Even after he had almost died to save her life, she didn't trust that he knew what was best? There was only so much questioning a man could take. He flexed his jaw. She would trust him. He had a simple task to do. Escort Bea to Bombay. He would not have her questioning him every step. He wouldn't fail. No, he'd make sure she made it to the port city, so she could sail back to England and marry some dandy.

"Why?" Bea blinked up at him with wide, guileless eyes.

He lied, of course. He hadn't told the lad they were married, but the boy probably assumed it anyway. "It made sense. It's better for safety, and your reputation."

She frowned, but nodded slowly, and he released the breath he didn't realize he held. She believed him. Frankly, it was true. She would be better protected as his wife but he was certain she'd put up a fuss. Apparently, the woman had a sensible streak after all.

"Come," the boy said again, before darting into the doorway of a narrow one-story building.

"Married," Bea whispered.

Colin rubbed the back of his neck. The area was surprisingly quiet. Too quiet. Most of the natives had probably gone farther into the city to protest, the others asleep. Soon they'd be back, and she and Colin would be in danger. Bea glanced at him and he could see the hesitation, the uncertainty in her eyes. The urge to reassure her overwhelmed him.

"Hell." He took her hand and pulled her into the house.

It was a typical Indian abode, with one main room that had a fire pit in the middle. A large colorful rug was spread across the matted floor. In the air hung a mixture of spicy scents, cinnamon and others he couldn't identify. Two doors interrupted the beige plastered wall along the back. A small home, but suitable and clean.

The boy raced into one of the back rooms, leaving them to stand there awkwardly alone. Muffled voices whispered through the home, but he couldn't make sense of the words. Bea stepped up close to him, her body warm against his side. Her eyes were wide as her gaze traveled around the abode.

He could imagine what she thought. The house he'd leased hadn't been much better than this. Had her face worn the same look of scorn when she'd entered his home? No doubt she was used to tea in bed, a roaring fire in a marble hearth, servants to wait on her. Things he'd sure as hell never be able to afford.

"Not exactly a castle," he murmured, stepping away from her.

Her brows snapped together. He didn't know why he felt the need to bait her. Fortunately, the soft sound of shuffling interrupted what would probably escalate into an argument. The boy was back, and at his side stood a tiny woman wearing a brilliant pink sari. Her dark eyes were wide, her tanned face chalky as she stared unblinkingly at him, as if seeing him for the first time.

Finally, she bowed low and waved them in closer.

He hesitated, recognizing that look in her eyes, part shock, part horror, part disbelief. How many times had he seen that reaction before? His heart hammered painfully in his chest as he made his way toward the tiny woman.

Raj started speaking rapidly to his mother, tripping over his words in his haste to explain. Colin was able to pick out only a few meanings but enough to know he was telling his mother exactly what had happened in the alley . . . every last bit. Colin resisted the urge to slap his palm over the boy's mouth.

The woman's gaze jerked back to him. Too late. He felt the heat starting to make its way up his neck. He prayed to God that Bea didn't know any Hindi.

"Miracle," the mother whispered.

Colin cringed.

She didn't seem to notice his less than thrilled reaction, but started toward him. Without hesitation, she dropped to her knees, soft sobs vibrating around her.

The heat he'd been trying so desperately to keep at bay rushed to his cheeks. He grabbed the woman's shoulders and hauled her to her feet. "Please, no. You mustn't tell anyone." His gaze flashed to the boy. "You understand?"

Raj nodded, his eyes solemn. "No tell."

"Why can't they tell?" Bea whispered, edging up closer to him once more.

He sighed, not daring to look at her as he evaded the truth. "We don't want to draw attention to ourselves."

"Of course."

"Stay," the woman said, taking Colin's hand and pulling them farther into the room. "You stay."

Colin nodded, knowing it was the most logical thing to do. Hide, and in the early morning, before the sun rose, when the rioters had finally returned to their homes to sleep, they'd escape and meet up with Leo and Ella. How far had they made it down the river? Dear God, he hoped they'd made it, but that boat had looked barely buoyant.

Bea raced after him. "She wants us to stay . . . here?"

"Too good for it?" he snapped. Her question enraged his already frayed nerves. Why the hell did she always have to question his decisions? He knew what he was doing; he was in charge.

"No. I—"

"Listen, princess, they barely have enough money to feed themselves and she's offering to let us stay. I say we take what we can get."

Her lips pressed into that thin line, although he wasn't sure if she was angry or trying not to cry. Immediately, guilt shook its judgmental head. Damn. He shouldn't have been so harsh on her. But he was tired, he was worried about Leo and Ella, and he didn't know how the hell he was going to escort Bea to Bombay and keep her safe with what little money he had.

"We help," Raj said. "What you need?"

To rest. To sleep for two days straight. "We'll stay here." Colin pointed to the house. "Tomorrow we leave, early, before the sun rises. When it's safe."

The boy nodded in understanding. He *hoped* the boy understood.

"Come, come." The woman latched on to his arm and pulled him toward a back room.

"Where are you going?" Bea demanded, her voice hard with fear.

He glanced at her and shrugged. She stood in the middle of the room, looking so out of place he wasn't sure if he wanted to laugh or groan. They'd never make it across the country without being noticed.

"Baby. Sick," Raj said.

Colin resisted the urge to sigh. He should have known he wouldn't be able to rest.

Without a word of explanation to Bea, he ducked under the overhang and entered the room. It was dark and dank but he could just make out a tiny form huddled on a mat in the corner. A weak gasp disturbed the room, and then a hacking cough that belied the tininess of the child. His feet crunched over reed mats. Sickness hung heavy and bitter in the air, making his stomach churn. He moved aside a curtain to allow a shaft of moonlight to enter. Light didn't make the situation any better.

"What do we have here?" He knelt by the mat that made a tiny bed and studied the child's face, too gaunt for a baby. She should have been rosy and round. Her dark, wavy hair contrasted against the paleness of her skin. So small, so weak. Too weak for this world. She'd probably die from another illness a year or so from now, but at least he could give her a chance . . . a chance to cheat death.

He glanced over his shoulder. The mother and son hovered in the doorway. "Go," he demanded.

The boy scurried from the room. The mother hesitated only a moment then also turned, and in a swoosh of silky pink, she left. She knew she had no choice but to trust him. He was her only option, a stranger, a foreign man. He wasn't sure if he could do the same. But he supposed if it was his child and a stranger was his only choice . . .

The pale moonlight coming from the open window marked the floor with a mystical light that only added to the oddness of the situation. The adjoining room was silent. He could imagine Bea wondering over his sudden disappearance. Wondering what the hell he was doing.

With a sigh, he sank onto the dirt floor. The child opened her eyes as if she sensed him. She didn't whimper, she didn't smile, but looked at him with solemn eyes that said she'd accepted her fate long ago. Well, fate be damned.

He settled his palms on her frail body, one on the crown of her head and the other on her sunken belly. She grew still almost immediately, instinctively trusting. Her skin was warm, too warm to live. She'd not last the week if he didn't help her now.

"Come on, darlin', you can live." He closed his eyes and took in a deep breath. Silence settled around him, seeping deep inside . . . into his very soul. He used the silence to his advantage, a way to calm his racing heart. He knew enough to know the silence wouldn't last.

The hum started almost immediately, a hum that pulsed in his body and vibrated his soul. Heat spiraled in the core of his being, spreading its blistering fingers toward his limbs, farther to his palms until they buzzed. He knew what would come, but it didn't make it any easier.

White heat burst through his body, singeing his cells. Colin gritted his teeth to keep from crying out. His back arched of its own accord. It felt as if the entire universe poured through him, too much power, too much energy. He floated on a cloud of pain, unaware of anything but the white light and the heat.

Just as quickly as the power had come, in a roar it pulled back, sweeping from his form and taking with any strength he possessed. Colin collapsed onto the floor, the side of his face pressed to the reed mats. The child was more dead than he'd realized, practically gone, and healing her had taken more energy than he'd used in awhile. Not since last year when he'd saved Ella had he used his powers so thoroughly.

"Colin?" Bea's soft voice entered his muddled mind, a call from a siren he was unable to resist.

Slowly, his lashes lifted and he stared into her eerie amber eyes. How much had she seen? She knelt beside him, and settled a lamp at her feet, the light highlighting the worry etched across her pale face. Her hands lifted, she hesitated a moment, then swept her fingers up and down his body, apparently looking for signs of injury.

"Are you all right? What happened? Where are you hurt?" Her fingers were like heaven, soft and caring. When was the last time someone had cared about his well-being? Damn, but in his exhausted state, he liked her attention much more than he wanted to admit.

"I'm . . . I'm fine." He pushed himself onto his elbows. The room spun. "The girl, how is she?"

Bea turned her head toward the bed. "She . . . well, she's fine. Why?" Her gaze rested on him, her brows drawn together in confusion.

Colin turned his head, needing to see for himself. The child was sitting up, a mound of blankets around her tiny form, her wide eyes pinned to him. It had worked, but then, it usually did.

"Sir," Raj called from the door. "Good?"

Colin nodded him in. "Good."

The boy turned and spoke to his mother. The woman cried out and raced into the room, a blur of brilliant pink. She collapsed onto the bed and scooped the child into her arms. Great wrenching sobs broke from her lips, and damn, if his cold heart didn't melt slightly.

It was worth it, he supposed. Worth the pain and exhaustion even if the child didn't make it to her next birthday, worth it to see the mother so happy and to see the child so well.

"Colin," Bea whispered, slipping her arm around his waist and helping him to his feet.

The sweet scent of clover and heather tempted him, brought him back to the conscious world when all he wanted to do was fade from existence. Colin breathed deep and resisted the urge to sink into her, knowing she couldn't handle all of his weight.

"What's happened? I don't understand. They said she was sick."

"She was."

"And you . . ." She glanced back at the child. "You healed her somehow? Are you a doctor then?"

He laughed and slumped into her, his knees going weak. Damn, he shouldn't have drunk last night. That combined with the day's excitement and he needed rest and time to recuperate before he fainted like a debutant at her first ball.

"Rest," the boy said, as if reading his mind. "Come, rest."

The mother nodded, still holding her child so close, Colin was sure she wouldn't release her for hours. Colin and Bea followed the boy into the next room, where a typical native bed occupied most of the room.

"You stay here."

Colin nodded and slumped onto the bed, the bamboo frame groaning. "We need to leave in a few hours, you understand? Early, before the city wakes."

The boy nodded. "You safe. Here."

Colin closed his eyes, giving in to temptation. "I understand, right."

The soft retreat of footsteps told him the boy had left, but he knew Bea still stood there. He could smell her, sense her. The side of the bed sank. Why was it, despite his fatigue, his nerves sparked at her mere presence? He willed her to come to him. Pretending to be her husband could have its advantages.

"Colin, I . . ."

He rested his hand on hers, her fingers soft and warm. "Bea, get some sleep. You're going to need it for tomorrow."

"But . . ."

He opened his eyes and studied her drawn face. "I'm serious. No questions, no doubt. Just sleep. Tomorrow we travel."

"But what if the rioters come? What if they tell them we're here?"

His lashes weighed heavy and he closed his eyes. He supposed it could happen, but what choice did they have? "They won't. Now sleep."

She was silent for a moment. "Where?"

He patted the spot next to him, too exhausted to do more than that.

"I can't . . . I . . ."

He sighed long and loud. "Bea, just get in the damn bed."

He rolled onto his side, his back to her. How badly he wanted to drift off, but he couldn't until he knew she slept. Finally, the mat sank farther as she lay beside him. She was stiff, inches away. He could still feel her heat, though. Damn, the woman was starting to grow on him. Moments later, she wiggled back just enough so that her back pressed to his. For the first time in a long while, Colin fell asleep with a smile on his lips.

Chapter 8

The sound of movement and muffled voices interrupted the silence of dawn. But Colin didn't want to wake; his body screamed for more rest. His back was warm and the sweet scent of clover hovered in the air like an elusive, erotic dream. He nestled closer to that soft warmth, but the noise was persistent and sleep finally surrendered to life. Slowly, he turned. The moonlight filtered through the window, bathing Bea in its soft glow. A goddess dropped to earth.

For a moment he thought he dreamt. Her hands were tucked under her face, her lips parted, and her breathing deep and even. In slumber, she looked at peace, she looked young and innocent. She looked . . . ethereal.

He'd never really gotten a chance to study the woman. Always going, always running since they'd met. Now, in this moment, with gray dawn threatening through the wooden shutters, he had time to truly look at her.

A perfect goddess but for the slight bump on the bridge of her nose. An imperfection so insignificant that a passing stranger would never notice and, if he did, would probably only say it added character. But most likely a stranger would focus only on her lush lips. At ease and parted, those lips were full, and a deep rose in color. Perfect for kissing. Worthy of worship.

The thought of pressing his mouth to hers flitted through his mind. He pushed the thought aside just as quickly as it entered, and he continued to study her face, looking for something, anything, to dissuade his lusty thoughts. Her chin was pointed and her eyes, which were turned up ever so slightly at the ends, were surrounded by thick, dark lashes.

But it was her hair, really, her hair that he supposed most woman would envy. Dark in color, it fell in soft waves around her face, down her back, and over her shoulders. Giving in to temptation, he reached for one of those curls. Silky smooth.

A pot clanged in the next room and Colin paused, the lock still wrapped around his finger. Bea's brows drew together, and with a soft sigh, she turned her head slightly. A scar flashed across her lower cheek, back by her ear. So she wasn't perfect after all.

Briefly he wondered how she'd gotten the scar, and it wasn't the only thing he wanted to discover. It was a known truth, he was addicted to uncovering treasure, and his mind spun with the prospect of uncovering her secrets. Why now? After everything that had happened with Sarah? Bea annoyed him, this proper Englishwoman. Exhaustion and the magic of morning, it was the only explanation for his sudden fascination. That and the fact that sharing a bed with a beautiful woman had made his body as hard as the earth in India.

A dry cough escaped her lips. Colin frowned, pushing himself up on his elbows, his lust momentarily forgotten as a surge of concern flared through his body. Her lashes fluttered as her mind began to wake. He knew the moment she opened those eyes, a reserved wall would cover any of her innocence. Against his wishes, those thick lashes lifted. The color of her eyes still startled him so much so that he sucked in a sharp breath. Amber, mixed with melted gold, they practically glowed. Her gaze found him and the drowsiness fled.

The left corner of his lips lifted. "Morning, princess."

"I . . . I fell asleep." The huskiness of her tone sent heat through his body, making his already hard member pulse to life.

He sat up, cringing slightly, his body uncomfortably needy. "You didn't mean to?"

She bolted upright. Her brows drew together in confusion. She shook her head, her hair slipping back and forth like the waves of the ocean at night. "I . . . no, I didn't. I felt someone should keep watch."

Colin sighed and stood, more than annoyed with the woman. "I told you to sleep." Damn, she could grate on his nerves. He'd told her to get her rest—she needed it. Why the hell didn't she trust his advice?

He raked his hair back from his face and attempted to straighten his shirt. It didn't help. Nothing but a bath and new clothes would. Slowly, he rubbed his knuckles over his rough, unshaven chin. At least his head was finally clear. He glanced at Bea. She was as disheveled as he, but for some reason on her, the look was charming.

Frantically, she scraped her hair back from her head, attempting to make some order to her locks. He was just about to tell her to leave her hair alone when her bodice gaped open, revealing the tops of her pale, full breasts. He couldn't seem to look away, like a young lad mesmerized by the erotic temples of Khajuraho.

"A ribbon, anything?" she asked.

He shrugged and jerked his gaze away from her body. But it didn't stop the heat from shooting through his form. Hell, he should have visited Delilah the other day, but he'd been too busy searching for that damn statue.

"Colin." Bea paused, working her lower lip between her teeth.

"Hmm?" He tucked his shirt into the waistband.

"Who is Sarah?"

Colin froze. His heart jumped into his chest. Slowly, he lifted his gaze, meeting hers. "Excuse me?"

Bea shrugged with her left shoulder, looking suddenly uneasy. "Last night, you said her name. I just wondered—"

"Yeah, well, don't because it's none of your damn business. Fix your clothes and meet me out front." He stomped from the room before she could respond. His body trembled. He wasn't sure if he should be shocked or angry as hell. He'd said her name. Still, after years, he said her name.

Raj's mother straightened away from the pot she was stirring.

"Morning," Colin muttered.

She rushed at him and bowed low. *"Jaadoo,"* she whispered.

He knew what the word meant. He'd heard the word in just about every language. *Magic.*

"No, none of that," he said, gripping her shoulders and pulling her upright.

Tears shimmered in her eyes. She waved him over. *"Beti."* She pointed toward a blanket, where the child sat murmuring and smiling up at him. She looked a million times better than she had last night. Damn, if he didn't feel the warmth of accomplishment filter through the stone wall he'd built around his emotions. After seeing so many sick and injured miraculously recover, there was something about witnessing the life return to such innocent eyes that held him still for the briefest of moments. Seeing him, the child's dark eyes sparkled and she lifted her arms.

The woman swooped the baby up and pushed her toward him. Unwillingly, Colin wrapped his fingers around the child's tiny waist and held her at arm's length. She smiled, showing brilliant white teeth just peeking through dark gums. Reluctantly, his lips twitched. Damn it all, he didn't have time to play nursemaid.

He focused on the mother. "Listen, I need to ask you something. Do you understand?"

She nodded. "Understand."

He glanced at the door to make sure Bea was still in the

back room. "I'm looking for a man named Anish. Have you heard of him?"

Her eyes grew wide and she nodded. "Yes, Anish. We take you to Anish."

"No, no, I don't—"

"Beebee." She took the baby and pushed a mound of clothing into his hands, soft and gauzy pieces of a brilliant bronze material.

Colin shook his head, confused.

"For your woman, your wife," Raj said, coming in from outside and bringing the crisp scent of dawn with him.

The boy's mother nodded, settling the baby on her hip. "Wife."

Doubtfully, he glanced at the material. Surely Bea would refuse, yet he knew if she wore traditional clothing, she would blend in better and the heat wouldn't be as intense. He nodded his thanks and made his way into the room where Bea was attempting to brush the wrinkles from her skirt. "Here."

"What's this?"

He shrugged. "She said it was for you."

Bea frowned in confusion, and Colin took the opportunity to shove the clothes into her hands. "But . . ."

Colin left the room before she asked more questions. He had the intense desire to get away from women, babies, and clothes as soon as he could. And just as he thought the words, Raj's mother rushed toward him.

"Here," the woman said, shoving the baby into his arms again. Raj had disappeared. "I help." She moved into the room where he'd abandoned Bea. Colin was stuck holding the girl once again. She grinned up at him, slobber glistening down her chin.

"Jesus," Colin grumbled, rubbing the back of his neck with his free hand.

The dark was giving way to light. They needed to leave; he didn't have time to play nanny. The child wrapped her arms around his neck, her tiny body pressed warmly to his heart. Shaking his head, he finally gave in to the urge to smile. As if sensing her victory, the child giggled.

"You're going to break some hearts when you're older, aren't you?"

A cough came from the bedroom, a familiar cough he'd heard before. Damn, was Bea getting sick?

"It's here," Raj called from the doorway.

Colin shifted the child to his hip. "What?"

"Boat. I take you to Anish."

Anish? How the hell had that happened? He'd merely asked about the man. "I don't want to see Anish." Colin shoved the girl into her brother's arms.

He took the child, expertly cradling her on his hip. "You leave? Secret?"

Colin raked his fingers through his hair. "Well, yeah, I suppose." He hadn't expected them to take him to this Anish man. He glanced back at the room where Bea was dressing. Would she mind a quick detour? Of course she would. Did it matter?

"Boat here. I take you to Anish." The boy smiled.

Damn. He wanted to argue, to decline. Yet how could he when they were getting a free guide to the very man who may explain his father's death? Who could explain why he had the odd abilities he did? And more importantly, could tell him about the statue he'd been searching for his entire life?

"Bea," Colin called out.

The shuffle of feet against the reed mats whispered through the small dwelling, sending anticipation skittering over his skin.

"Yes?" She appeared in the doorway, a goddess draped in shimmering clothes.

The firelight highlighted the curves of her form. She was dressed in loose bronze pants that matched the color of her eyes. A shirt in gauzy material covered her chest and arms and hinted at the body underneath without showing a thing.

She looked exotic, she looked beautiful, and even with a scarf covering her head, she still looked like a damn English-woman. Lying there, against her chest, was Leo's ring, which she'd placed on a chain, for anyone to see.

"You . . ."

Her cheeks turned a brilliant red. "She made me put it on."

He clasped his hands behind the small of his back, swallowing over the sudden lump that clogged his throat. "Yeah, well, I suppose you'll fit in a little better."

She nodded but she didn't look any happier about it than he was. How the hell was he going to keep his hands to himself when she wore clothes that hinted at every curve?

"Come. Now," Raj said. "Boat."

"Right." Colin forced his gaze away from Bea. "The ring, tuck it under your shirt." He didn't wait to see if she listened, but followed the lad outside. The sound of dawn was over-ridden by the soft rumble of voices. The moment he stepped onto the dirt path out front, the murmuring ceased. Through the haze of dawn, he could see at least ten people standing in a cluster, all staring at him with wide, knowing eyes.

He rubbed his face with his hands. "Damn."

"Why are they here?" Bea whispered next to him.

A tall, thin man stepped forward. "Help and you take my boat." He waved someone closer. A young woman parted from the group, crippled over with some sort of ailment.

"You help his wife and we take his boat?" Raj said, nodding.

Colin gave them all a tight grin. "Do I have a choice?"

"What do they want?" Bea asked, nudging her way between Raj and Colin.

Colin sighed and raked his hair from his face. "Me. They want me."

Bea ducked under a low-hanging branch and darted a glance at Colin. She could barely read his face under the rim of his brown hat. But dark circles marred the area under his eyes and already he'd stumbled twice. He was beyond exhausted, although why, she wasn't sure. He'd seemed rested enough that morning.

When she'd woken and found his gaze on her, there had been something in his eyes . . . something that thrilled her, something that made her body ache in a way it never had before. Now, he barely gave her a glance. She sighed, brushing aside such thoughts. Perhaps she was coming down with an illness.

Truth was, she didn't feel much better than he looked, but with his dour expression, she didn't dare complain. A cough had settled in her chest a few days ago and refused to leave. The constant dust didn't help. It hovered around her in a cloud of yellow, dirtying the beautiful green slippers she'd been given and irritating her lungs. How much longer would they keep walking? Already the sun was high. She didn't think she could go on much farther.

The leaves next to her rattled, drawing her from her thoughts. With a wary eye on the underbrush, Bea edged closer to Colin.

"Soon," Raj said. "We there soon."

Bea frowned, studying their guide. He was so young, how could he possibly help? And Colin was certainly in no shape to ward off an attack, should someone feel so inclined to do so. Still, she had to admit that he was much more capable than she'd first thought. In fact, she was quite at a loss as to how to feel about Colin. The moment he'd cut her corset from her body, saving her life, she'd found her opinion of the man changing.

"Colin," she couldn't help but ask, "how do you feel?"

He slid her an annoyed glance that had her frown deepening.

Apparently, he was some sort of doctor. He'd gone from hut to hut, helping the sick, and she'd been left to sit aside and wait and wonder. Only once had she mentioned assisting him. The immediate rejection she'd received had left her flushing in embarrassment. Colin didn't want her underfoot. He'd made that perfectly clear. Her thoughts toward him might have changed for the better, but it was obvious he still thought of her as the pampered chit he'd first met.

"It was a mere question," she said.

"I'm fine," he muttered, not bothering to look at her.

She didn't believe him in the least, and apparently when he was tired, he was far from pleasant. She tilted her chin high and resisted the urge to let out a disgruntled huff. Well, then, let him pout on his own.

"Ahead." Raj pointed down the path with a machete, the blade flashing in the quickly rising sun.

He brought the weapon down and with a thunk he snapped a branch in half. The bush fell to the ground, sending dust into the air. Bea stepped through the cloud, waving the dust away, but coughing anyway. Colin glanced back at her as the coughing abated. There was concern in his gaze, but she was too hot to ponder it further.

The gauzy material of her clothing was a cool relief from the confining English dresses she owned. But still, it wasn't enough. One could be completely devoid of clothing and it wouldn't be enough in this wretched heat. And it wasn't just the heat that made her uncomfortable. Each time she set her foot upon the ground, her head seemed to vibrate, sending a deep ache through her skull.

She glanced at the sun. Although still low in the sky, the ground already shimmered with warmth. Sweat beaded between her shoulder blades, tickling her skin. What she wouldn't do for water . . . a river, a lake, rain. Bloody anything to cool her off and clean her dusty skin. As if answering her prayers, she swore she caught the whisper of rushing water. She stumbled in her haste and licked her dry lips. Was she imagining things?

"Water?" she asked Colin. "Is the river ahead?" Her throat was as dry as the ground they shuffled over. How desperately she wanted something to drink. To close her eyes and drift to sleep . . . She stumbled again and her lashes lifted.

"Yes," Colin muttered, his voice sounding as weak as she felt. "Water ahead."

"Oh, thank heavens."

He glanced down at her, amusement flickering in his eyes. For the first time that morning, she caught a glimpse of the man she'd met. The sort of man who found humor in everything. The sort of man who drove her mad half the time, while the other half piqued her curiosity. How could anyone who'd seen as much as he'd seen be so amused with the world? His father and mother had died when he'd been a lad; she knew that much, thanks to Ella. It was obvious he had barely two shillings to his name. What could he possibly be happy about?

"There it is." Colin nodded toward the right.

"We'll have time to wash, I hope?" She spotted the river weaving its way through the hills below. The water was a murky snake, far from the crystalline creeks in Scotland. Her heart fell.

Colin chuckled as if sensing her thoughts. "Jump on in, darlin'."

She had just enough energy to glare at him.

"Here," Raj called out, waving them over and handing Colin a clay jar.

But he didn't drink. Instead, he pushed the vessel into Bea's hands. "Water."

Nodding her thanks, she pulled open the lid and downed the warm liquid. Her dry throat cried out in protest. Just as quickly, the ache eased and the liquid swept through her body, bringing back life for one brief moment. Her thirst quenched, she handed the jar to Colin.

He settled the jar at his mouth and tilted the vessel back. She tried not to look at his lips, tried not to notice the way his tanned neck moved, the way his thick lashes fluttered down for a brief moment. A sudden heat crawled through her veins, warming her blood. Even exhausted and dirty, the man was beautiful.

Annoyed with her wayward thoughts, she tore her gaze from Colin and studied their surroundings. A boat rocked gently on the river. A boat that looked more raft than vessel.

"We're supposed to get on that?" Bea whispered, not wanting to offend Raj, who was currently climbing aboard, confirming her worst fears.

Colin merely nodded and started down the dirt bank. It was worse than the boat Leo and Ella had sailed off on. Thoughts of her cousin settled around her heavy and thick, like the fog currently hovering over the river. Had they made it to safety? Would she ever see them again?

Colin jumped onto the vessel and the boat rocked back and forth, threatening to tip. Without a word, he held out his hand. She hesitated only a moment and then slipped her fingers around his. He lifted her easily, his strong hands settling around her waist. The boat rocked with the movement and Bea sucked in a breath, preparing to hit the muddy water. Somehow Colin managed to keep them upright.

"How long will it take?"

Colin shrugged. "Not sure."

Exhausted, Bea slumped onto a wooden seat and gripped the sides. Water sloshed over the low edges, settling on the bottom of the boat like gravy.

With a shove, they were off, careening down the river. Bea's stomach churned with the rocking sensation. Sweat broke out on her forehead and the water wavered in a dizzying swirl before her.

"How long?" Colin asked Raj.

The boy lifted a long wooden stick from the bottom of the boat. With a grunt, he shoved the pole into the water and pushed off the bank. "Depends on current. We'll go as far as the Chambal."

The boat swept toward the middle of the river, weaving from side to side. Bea's stomach lurched. She tightened her hold on the small bench. She must have looked wretched, for Colin collapsed next to her, his attention scanning her face and the concern evident in his gaze.

"Are you all right?"

She nodded, swallowing the bile that threatened to make a fool of her. Dear Lord, she would not get sick in front of Colin. She didn't know what was wrong with her. She'd always loved the water, learned to swim at five years of age. So why, now, was she suddenly nauseous?

A slight breeze swept from the river and cooled Bea's damp strands. A caress from Heaven. Bea sighed in sweet relief. Her hair rose on the wind and tickled Colin's neck. He didn't seem to notice but stared vacantly ahead.

What he looked at, she wasn't sure. Low brush lined the wide, shallow river, above a pale sky without a cloud. Only a single, lone woman knelt on the bank, scooping up water in a large, clay pot, but Colin wasn't focused on her. What was he so intent upon?

"Colin, I'm worried."

His gaze slid to her, and arrogantly he lifted a brow, barely visible under the brim of his hat. "Really? I'm touched."

"I'm serious, Colin." She scooted closer to him, her thigh touching his. "You look just wretched."

"Gee, thanks, darlin'."

She ignored his wry tone and settled her hand on his, his fingers warm under her touch. She tried not to focus on the way his skin felt, warm and rough. "Colin, what happened? You seem drained of life."

He gave her a weak smile. "Maybe I am."

She couldn't respond because she didn't really understand what he meant. The boat turned a bend and Colin fell into her, his arm hitting hers.

"Sorry," he muttered, straightening himself.

Bea's worry escalated. This was the man who was supposed to keep her safe? Was he getting sick? Injured? But he remained quiet and reclusive, offering her no indication of what was wrong.

Swiftly, the river moved them along, taking them farther downstream. How many minutes passed as the sun beat down on them relentlessly, she wasn't sure. Bea pulled her scarf lower over her face, trying to keep her skin from burning, but she feared it was a moot movement. Grandmother would berate her when she came back with freckles.

"Water," Raj said, leaving his post at the oar and handing her a jar.

She glanced at Colin and handed him the vessel.

He blinked, as if confused, as if he'd never seen water before.

Bea pulled the lid and lifted it to his lips. His hands came up, covering hers with their warmth, and he tilted the jar. Water trickled from his lips, trailing down his tanned neck and disappearing under his shirt collar. He pulled back and pushed the jar toward her.

She took a deep drink and, over the rim of the vessel, watched Colin. In the sunlight, he practically glowed, his skin golden, while scruff marked his cheeks and chin. Her fingers curled as she resisted the urge to reach out and touch him. Slowly, she lowered the water jar to the seat.

And his eyes . . . blimey, she'd never seen eyes so beautiful. He was completely different from the pale, almost sickly-looking men back home. She could admit, if only to herself, that she found she preferred his tanned features.

He took off his hat, setting it on the seat next to him. The wind caught his curls and tossed them about his head, giving him a boyish look. Before she could think better, she reached out and slipped her fingers into his locks. Silky and cool, they begged to be touched. His gaze jerked to her, the surprise evident. Dear Lord! What was she thinking? Heat shot to her cheeks and she pulled her hand back.

"A . . . a leaf," she said and prayed he believed her. Without thought to her safety, she jumped to her feet and scurried to the other end of the boat. The vessel tipped precariously to the side.

"No!" Raj called out, waving his arm through the air.

Bea froze. The boat tipped farther, and caught off balance, she slammed against the side. The edge caught her in the gut, pushing the air from her lungs. In the dark, swirling waters below, her reflection shimmered back at her. Her stomach churned, threatening to heave up the bread Raj's mother had given her that morning.

"Damn it, Bea," Colin growled right before his fingers bit into her upper arms. He jerked her back. "Don't you know the dangers of these rivers? One slip and the current could easily pull you under." He pushed her gently toward the bench.

Without argument, Bea collapsed onto the seat, her cheeks burning with mortification. "I'm sorry, I wasn't thinking."

He raked his hands through his hair, standing before her with his legs braced apart like a Viking warrior at the helm of a ship. An angry Viking. "Damn right you weren't thinking. I don't have the time or the energy to fish you out of a river I wouldn't even bathe in."

"Sir!" Raj yelled. "Sir! No!"

Bea jerked her gaze toward their guide. The boy waved his hands through the air, attempting to hold on to the oar and latch on to Colin at the same time.

Colin's brows snapped together as he turned. "What?"

Bea raised her gaze just in time to see the branch coming straight at Colin.

"Colin!" But it was too late.

The tree hit him across the chest with a sickening thud. Colin flew backward, disappearing from sight.

Bea screamed.

"Sir!" Raj called.

Bea leapt across the boat, reaching out. But he was already gone, over the edge. A loud splash rent the air and water sprayed into the sky like sparkling jewels in the morning sun.

"Dear God! Colin!" Bea leaned over the edge and peered into the dingy water. Colin was nowhere to be seen. The boat continued to float, maintaining a steady pace down the river, farther away from where Colin had disappeared.

"Colin!" Bea cried out, tears of panic stinging her eyes. "No! You have to stop!" She spun around to face Raj.

"Cannot stop!" Raj was struggling against the current and losing.

Bea faced the water again. Upriver, Colin burst through the surface, his hair plastered to his head. He gasped for breath, the sound insanely welcome to Bea's ears. But he was tired, weak; she could see it in the strained lines on his face.

"Colin!"

He didn't look at her, but started to sink again. Without hesitation, Bea jumped. She hit the surface with barely a splash. She was a good swimmer, but the current was stronger than she'd perceived, tugging at her legs and arms. Darkness surrounded her, making it difficult to know top from bottom. But she'd swum in frigid water with a stronger current, unbeknownst to her grandmother.

Gritting her teeth, she kicked furiously, the gauze material of her sari floating around her like a lost spirit. Just as her lungs began to burn, she burst through the surface, sucking in a gulp of air. "Colin!"

She swiveled her head around, looking for the telltale sign of curly golden locks. "Colin! Oh God, please, please."

"Bea, what the hell are you doing?"

Bea spun around. Colin was swimming toward her, his face pulled in a wet mask of fury. She didn't care. Colin was alive!

"I couldn't let you drown, you daft man!" She tried to meet him halfway, but the water was dragging her downriver farther from him.

"Raj!" Bea cried out, turning for help, but the boat had disappeared around a bend. "Dash it."

"Grab something, Bea, anything."

She jerked her head right, then left. Her only salvation lay in a root sticking out from the bank. Pressing her lips together, she kicked her legs with as much strength as she possessed, striving for the bank. With a cry, she reached out. Her fingers wrapped around the rough bark, and she'd never felt anything so heavenly.

"Colin, here!"

He swept by, so close she could see the blue of his eyes.

Focusing on her hand, he swung his arm wide. His strong fingers clasped hers. But his weight and the current pulled until she thought her shoulder would dislocate. Bea bit her lower lip to keep from crying out.

"Hold on, Bea." Colin pulled himself up her arm until he could reach the root. His hand landed just above hers, their fingers touching around the limb. He wrapped his other arm around her waist, and pulled her close.

He paused like that, his wet, warm body pressed to her. His breathing harsh, he nestled his cheek against her head. Bea sank into his body, closing her eyes for the briefest of moments. She would have floated there for only God knew how long just to feel the comfort of his strong body, the safety she felt in his arms. Never had she been so close to a man.

All too soon, Colin pulled back. "Come on."

She didn't have time to read his face; moments later he was dragging her up the bank. Bea's hands and knees sank into soft dirt. With a cry, she fell back, gasping for air and staring up into the brilliant blue sky.

Suddenly Colin appeared over her. "You're all right?" Water trailed down his face and dripped from his nose and chin to her neck. His face was as white as the few clouds hovering overhead.

Bea could merely nod.

As soon as she made the comment, the concern in his eyes disappeared and anger flared to life. "Of all the stupid—"

"It wasn't my fault!"

His eyes narrowed, while a pulse ticked in the side of his neck. "Oh really? You didn't jump from your seat and nearly overturn the boat merely because you touched me and what . . . God forbid . . . felt something?"

"Of course not! You had a leaf in your hair!" She fumed even as heat shot to her face. Only a cad would discuss her obvious unease. "Felt something? The only feeling I have toward you is—"

With a low growl, Colin pressed his mouth to hers. Stunned, Bea merely lay there. Vaguely she was aware that this time he was kissing her because he *wanted* to, not because he thought she was some loose woman named Delilah who had snuck into his room.

His lips softened and his hard body sank into hers. In the back of her mind she knew she should push him away, yet she couldn't seem to. Instead, her traitorous arms wrapped around his broad shoulders and her fingers crept into his damp locks.

Colin groaned and slipped his tongue between her lips. Excitement flared through her body. He swallowed her gasp of surprise and slid his fingers into her hair, tilting her head to deepen the kiss. Heat shimmered through Bea, an ache settling low in her belly. She wanted more. For some strange reason she wanted more. More of what, she wasn't sure. He tasted of mint and tea; he tasted wonderfully delicious.

The soft rattle of leaves entered Bea's muddled mind. She would have kept kissing Colin, exploring his mouth, the texture of his tongue and lips, but he jerked back. The rattle became louder. Colin rolled off Bea, leaving her feeling oddly off balance.

Reality rushed in on a cold wave.

Bea lay there, her heart thundering in her chest. Her fingers curled, digging into the soft dirt. Colin had kissed her.

But why? He didn't even seem to like her. Was it merely to humiliate her? To shut her up? Dear Lord, how could she let him kiss her? How could she kiss him back? Grandmother would most definitely not approve.

"Damn," Colin snapped, sounding anything but pleased.

Embarrassment flushed through her body. Had she done it wrong? The kiss hadn't seemed wrong. Embarrassment gave way to anger. She hadn't asked to be kissed.

"Don't . . . don't you ever kiss me again!" Bea fumed, pushing up to her elbows.

"Don't worry, darlin', I won't." Colin's lips pulled into a sneer, as if just thinking of the act repulsed him.

Had her kissing been that bad?

The vegetation beside them parted. "I found you, thank the gods." Raj was back, Colin's hat in his hands. How much had their young guide seen?

Bea's face heated. She couldn't look at Colin, couldn't look at Raj. Perhaps she could just crawl back into the river and let the current take her under.

"Well, then," Colin mumbled as he stood. "We should . . ." He glanced at her, then just as quickly looked away. "We should go."

As if she had the plague, Colin rushed away. Raj took her hand and helped her to her feet. Her mind spun, her knees growing weak. She wasn't sure if her reaction was because of the kiss, or because of the heat.

"Come," Raj said. "We go see Anish."

Confused, Bea jerked her gaze away from Colin's retreating back and focused on the boy. "Who's Anish?"

But Raj, too, had started forward and Bea was left to wonder what in the bloody hell she'd gotten into.

Chapter 9

Two hours later Bea's clothes had dried, but her mind remained muddy. Her head ached something fierce and she knew most of the reason was Colin's confusing reaction and her own betraying emotions. Unable to resist, she tore her gaze from the dirt path and studied the man.

He'd kissed her. She'd kissed him back. The question was, why?

She pressed her fingertips to her lips where the skin still tingled with the memory. Lord, she was barely aware of her feet hitting the hard dirt, for her mind and body had grown numb with thoughts of the man who walked in front of her.

She was honest enough with herself to admit she liked the touch of his mouth. But his actions didn't make sense. Colin didn't like her. It was obvious in the growl of his voice, the way he sarcastically called her "darlin'," the way he constantly glared at her. So why had he kissed her? And she certainly didn't like him. She supposed he was all right, considering he was Ella's cousin and he had saved her after all. But would she actually want to converse with the man in a drawing room in Scotland?

An image flashed to mind, Colin wearing his trousers and white linen shirt, open at the collar, that tanned skin in marked contrast to her pale grandmother. Even now she could imagine the horror on Grandmother's face.

She laughed at the thought. Raj glanced back at her, a questioning look in his dark eyes. She shook her head and he returned his attention to Colin, following like a pup after its master. And that's what she was, merely a thing, being led on a rope by the whims of a man who found the need to throw her emotions into constant turmoil.

She pulled a heart-shaped leaf from a bush, studying the way the veins branched through the skin. Then again, having Colin in a drawing room would certainly be entertaining. Yes, she'd give him that much. He was different . . . and sometimes amusing.

However, not once had he glanced back to make sure if she still followed. The thought of stopping just to see how far he'd get before he realized he'd left her behind crossed her mind. But the idea of being alone in the scrub jungle terrified her.

So instead, she trudged on. With a weary sigh, Bea rubbed the back of her neck, attempting to ease the tension that knotted her muscles. Yes, she couldn't deny that her mind spun with thoughts of Colin. Or perhaps it was from the heat beating relentlessly through the branches above. Tilting her head back, she glanced into the sun. Blinding rays sliced through the leaves, unperturbed by the scraggly canopy of branches.

"Here," Raj called out. "Anish."

"Thank God," Bea murmured and forced her attention ahead.

The trail widened, and a large cleared circle appeared. It looked like nothing more than a pile of hay or some sort of medieval hut on an ancient fiefdom. She would have probably not associated the pile of sticks with a home if not for the smoking fire pit in the middle of the cleared site. This was the sweet relief she'd been expecting?

"Namaste," someone croaked.

Bea spun around, the movement sending her vision wavering, which was why, for a mere moment, she thought a mythical gnome had spoken. She pressed her hand to her forehead and forced her vision to focus. No gnome, but an old man half-hidden behind the enormous root of a banyan tree. He shuffled toward them, his long white beard swaying hypnotically back and forth across his green robes. His tanned face lifted into a wide grin, his dark eyes sparkling as if he knew something they didn't.

This was Anish? The holy man Colin had finally admitted they were going to visit? Shocked and a bit perturbed that she'd been dragged downriver for this, Bea glared at Colin's back. He was too busy bowing to notice.

"Welcome," the old man said in English, as if he'd been expecting them all along. "Welcome."

He moved toward the fire, not a speck of dust rising with the wavering hem of his robes. With an ease that belied his old age, he settled on a straw mat. When they continued to stand in indecision, he sighed and waved them over impatiently.

Colin and Raj didn't hesitate, but settled on their own straw mats near the man. Bea merely shook her head, completely confused and more than annoyed. She didn't understand why they were there, or why this man was so important. She was tired, exhausted really, and her stomach wasn't feeling quite right. But with no other alternative to the situation she found herself in, she settled down on the mat next to Colin.

"Anish," Colin started.

The old man nodded, still smiling.

"I'm looking . . ." For the first time since he'd kissed her, Colin glanced at Bea. But the look was guarded, weary, as if judging her reaction. "I'm looking for a statue."

Bea sucked in a breath, shock warring with annoyance. A statue. The statue they'd been discussing at the antiquities shop? She'd walked for hours through heat, nearly drowned, felt worse than she'd ever felt in her life, and all for a bloody statue? She wasn't sure if she wanted to laugh or cry.

Anish nodded merrily.

"A statue, with four men." Colin picked up a stick and, in the dirt, drew a replica of the statue they'd seen at the shop.

Anish's smile fell. "No, no statue."

"But . . . they said you'd seen it."

"No. No statue." The man lifted a stick and stirred the kettle hovering over the flames. Bea merely watched Colin, wondering what he'd do next. Without looking at her, he turned. Before she knew his intentions, he slipped his fingers down the top of her shirt.

Bea gasped, even as shivers of delight raced over her skin.

"This." Colin pulled the necklace and ring free. "This is why we need the statue."

Reluctantly, Anish turned his gaze to them. His hazy eyes focused on the ring, then blinked wide. He whispered something in his language, but Bea didn't need to understand Hindi to know that it was an exclamation of some sort.

Colin let the ring drop against her chest, a smug look upon his face. "Now, where is the statue?"

The old man stared at him with something akin to respect shining in his eyes. "Yes, yes." He nodded his agreement. "Statue of life."

Colin leaned closer. "Statue of life." His gaze was pinned to the man as if *his* life depended on it. Bea gritted her teeth and narrowed her eyes. Why were they here? Why weren't they on a raft headed to find Ella and Leo?

"Colin," she ground out.

"Shh." He dismissed her. "This statue. You've seen it?"

She'd never felt more annoyed in her life. Bea's fingers fisted, gripping the gauzy material of her sari. She'd jumped into a river, for God's sake, in order to save Colin. How dare he ignore her!

Anish nodded. "Yes. I've seen the statue."

"I don't understand." Colin raked his hands through his hair, leaving the curls ruffled.

Instinctively, Bea reached forward to smooth those curls back. A sharp pain sliced through her temple. She cringed, lowering her hand. Around her, the voices became muffled, dulled by the throbbing in her head. She couldn't seem to make sense of the words being spoken.

"When?" Colin demanded, his voice finally piercing her foggy reality, but it was too loud, too sudden.

"Many years ago." Anish lifted a clay tea kettle from the iron hook that hung over the fire.

"Where?"

"Temple. Temple of Brahma."

Colin shook his head. "There's no such temple."

The man grinned as he poured water into a clay cup. Steam rose from the surface, in ghostly whispers. "Yes, there is."

The old man met Bea's gaze and he handed her the cup.

She didn't hesitate, but eagerly reached out. The vessel was rough and crude between her fingers. Tea leaves floated in the water, like muddy foliage. She didn't care. And she didn't care that the liquid was hot and the day even hotter. Perhaps the tea would give her the strength she needed to tell Colin exactly what she thought of him, the dratted man!

"Where is this temple?" he asked.

Bea drank deep, the water bitter and strong. Her stomach clenched, her headache worsening.

"South."

"Colin," Bea persisted, attempting to focus on his handsome face.

"What?" He merely glanced at her.

She started to ask him what the hell was going on. Instead, her stomach cramped and she grimaced. Dash it, she didn't feel well.

His brows drew together. "What's wrong?"

She shook her head, afraid that if she opened her mouth, she'd get sick all over him.

Colin turned back to the old man, ignoring her, which was exactly what she wanted at the moment. "This temple, where is it exactly?"

Anish narrowed his eyes and pointed toward a cluster of fig trees. "That way."

Colin's gaze flickered in the direction. "That way?"

The old man nodded and smiled. "South. But you want the Statue of the Lost first. It will give you the answers you seek."

"Of course," Colin sighed. "And where is that?"

The old man shrugged. "Follow the river."

Colin cursed. Bea didn't understand why they were there, but at the moment she didn't care. She didn't feel right. Nothing felt right. For a fortnight she'd been on a downward spiral and she feared she was close to hitting the bottom.

She closed her eyes for the briefest moment. Vaguely, she was aware of the cup slipping from her fingers. Vaguely, she was aware of falling back. Vaguely, she was aware of the back of her head hitting the hard ground.

"Bea?" Colin's voice sounded so far away.

Desperately, she tried to focus on him, tried to open her eyes, but it felt as if she were in that river all over again. Something heavy settled over her forehead.

She tried to lift her hands, tried to push the heaviness away, but someone was holding her arm down.

"Bea."

Slowly, she opened her eyes and stared into a brilliant blue sky. Where was she? Her body felt numb, her limbs no longer attached. Dear God, had she died?

A man came into view, his beautiful face wavering in and out of focus. Who was he? An angel come to take her soul?

"Bea," he snapped, his voice rather surly for an angelic being. "What is it? What hurts? What's wrong?"

The man's name came to her as if whispered from heaven, a mere memory that clung to the back of her mind. "Colin?"

She parted her lips to say more, when her stomach

clenched. Sweat broke out on her forehead. She blinked her eyes rapidly as acid rose in her throat. "Oh God." With a groan, she pushed Colin out of the way and rolled onto her side, emptying her stomach in the dry dirt.

"Damn it, Bea. When did you start feeling sick?" Colin demanded, as if it was her fault she was ill. She slumped back onto the dirt and closed her eyes. It was just like him to blame her for being ill. A warm, soft hand covered her forehead.

"She sick," Anish said and she realized he was the one pressing his hand to her face.

"How? When?" Colin asked.

Bea opened her eyes again in time to see Anish shrug. "Water? White people not drink water. Make them sick and she get fever."

Colin's jaw clenched and unclenched, his gaze pinned to her. She couldn't decide if he was angry or not. "Will she be all right?"

The old man shrugged again.

"Bea, look at me."

Colin's strong hands cupped the sides of her face. He hovered over her, his face drawn tight with worry. For her? She let her lashes drift down and pushed aside the slight thrill that swept through her body. No. He was only worried because if she died, Leo would be furious and she'd put a damper on his plans.

Annoyance gave way to fear. Blimey. She might die.

She felt like it, too.

Her insides cramped once more and she groaned, rolling onto her side into a tight ball.

"Damn it," Colin snapped.

A muscled arm slipped under her back, another under her knees. She was lifted, then cradled against a hard chest. Her head rolled back, hitting his shoulder, and her mind began to hum. It was a strange sense of comfort that washed over her the moment his hands touched her body. Bea sank into

Colin, trusting he'd care for her. She had no other choice. She didn't know where they were going, but she didn't mind. She only wanted to be closer.

His heart beat strong and sure against the side of her face. She focused on that thump, the sound ethereal and beautiful, like nothing she'd ever heard. Like the streams in Scotland, the birds in morning, like the soft rain on a summer day. With a sigh, she nuzzled her face into the area where his neck met his shoulder. His scent swirled around her . . . heady, calming, and captivating.

"You'll be all right," he whispered and she believed him.

His hold loosened. Bea wanted to cling to the man, yet couldn't manage to open her eyes, let alone lift her arms. A soft mat cushioned her back. Colin's touch was gone, and with its absence, the pain returned. She whimpered. Nausea rolled in her gut, a deep ache flaring through her limbs.

"She needs help," Anish muttered from somewhere. "I go and get plants for medicine."

Bea managed to peer through her lashes. It was dark, the heat stifling and heavy in the abode. The only light came through an open doorway so small, you'd have to hunch low to enter.

"Will it work?" Colin knelt beside her, his face shadowed by the darkness.

She couldn't read his features and she desperately wanted to know what he was thinking. If only she could look into his eyes, she'd know if she was going to die.

"Sometimes it works, if the gods will it."

Colin leaned closer, his jaw clenched, a fierceness in his gaze. "Yeah, well, I can't leave it to the gods."

Bea's lips trembled, the words resting in her throat but refusing to move past her lips. How badly she wanted to ask what the hell was happening. But she was too tired to demand an explanation.

Heat flared through her body, slicing down her spine. Bea arched her back, whimpering. A hand pressed to her forehead. Instantly, the fire lessened, swept aside by cool relief. Bea reached up, her fingers grasping the wrist, keeping the hand in place.

"I've seen this in South America." Colin's voice. Colin's hand. Colin's touch. His fingers moved to the side of her face. "The symptoms. The fever, chills. You'll be all right, Bea. I promise."

She opened her eyes and stared into his brilliant blue gaze. She believed him. She actually believed him. There was a calmness on his face now that gave her hope.

"Leave us," Colin said, and although she knew he spoke to Raj and Anish, he kept his eyes locked on her.

"You're him, aren't you?" Anish whispered. "The one they speak of."

"Leave," Colin demanded.

Raj scampered from the dwelling. Anish paused only a moment. He bowed low, then shuffled from the building, leaving Colin and Bea alone.

"Close your eyes, Bea."

She nodded and let her lashes drift down. Colin's hand left her face only to press on her lower belly. Oddly, she wasn't embarrassed by his touch, but welcomed the sudden warmth that seeped from his fingertips and numbed her pain.

A surreal calm entered her being and poured through her veins, traveling to her limbs. Bea surrendered to the feeling, welcomed the sensation. Heat shimmered through her lower belly, and white light burst behind her eyelids. She no longer heard the birds outside, no longer felt the stifling heat of the day, only a heavenly weightless sensation.

She knew she smiled. Somewhere in the deep recesses of her mind, she knew she smiled although she couldn't feel her face. She felt as if she were floating, as if she could fly, yet at the same time, she felt his presence. Colin's anchoring presence there, just beyond. A soft thump beat around her, pulsing through her being. She tried to turn, tried to locate the vibration, but could see only brilliant white light.

"Bea," someone whispered, the voice heavenly and ethereal. "Come back to me."

Colin.

The thump grew louder, her body vibrating with the sound. Colin's heart, she suddenly realized. The feeling surrounded her, enveloped her, and she found she didn't want to leave wherever it was she'd entered.

"Come back to me, Bea," Colin whispered.

Just as quickly as it had come, the light started to fade. Coldness replaced the warmth and ice began to crystallize in her veins. She wanted to reach out, to cling to the warmth, but with a roar it was gone. Air filled Bea's lungs. She gasped, her eyes popping open. Her heart beat loud and fast in her ears. She didn't dare move for fear the action would be too intense.

Slowly, the thump faded and Bea became aware of her surroundings. There was a muskiness in the air, the smell of vegetation and dirt. The scent was strong, stronger than normal. She remained still, afraid to move. It was dark, the light dim. Where was she? She felt languid and heavy, as if she'd slept for days. It was difficult to move. How long had she slept? She pointed her toes, stretching her legs like a lazy cat.

"Colin," she whispered.

There was no response.

She moved her right hand, her fingers touching cool, silky strands. Someone lay next to her. She pushed herself upright. A large form lay sprawled upon the floor beside her cot, his face away from her. Bea's heart jumped into her throat. He wasn't moving, didn't seem to be breathing. Bea slipped from her bed and rested her fingers under his chin. Slowly, she turned his face toward her.

Colin.

Chapter 10

Low voices entered his muddled mind. He squirmed, straining to make out the words, even as each muttered oath sent a deep ache pulsing through his body, beating in time with his heart. With a groan, he dared to open his eyes. Instantly he knew where he was. The dimness, the musky scent of earth and reeds . . .

He was lying on the mat in Anish's hut. His fingers clenched, his heart skipping a beat as fear settled icy cold in his body. Where was Bea?

Something wet and cool settled against his forehead. Water trickled down the side of his face, pooling annoyingly in his ears.

"And this statue has magical powers?" Bea's voice drifted through the layers of haziness.

Relief sank into his gut. Bea was here. Alive. Well enough to talk.

The relief immediately gave way to panic.

Statue? Magic?

Hell, what had Anish told her and how much did she now know? Colin reached up and shoved the cloth away from his face. It fell with a thud to the dirt floor. "What happened?"

There was a rustle of clothing and then Bea was there, leaning over him. Her dark hair fell in waves down around her shoulders, the top of her chest exposed by an open collar of the men's shirt she wore. Even in his pathetic state, he found his body heating at the mere sight of her.

"You fainted."

He scoffed, pushing up onto his elbows. "Don't be ridiculous. I'm a man and an American, we don't faint."

She lifted one dark brow and leaned back on her heels. "Well, then you took a nap, a very deep, very long nap."

Damn. There was no point in arguing. He'd fainted. Like a corseted lass in an English drawing room. Warmth swept to his cheeks. He slid Bea a glance, trying to read her face. The sun shone through the open doorway, highlighting her body with a halo as if she were some damn angel come to offer him mercy . . . or take his soul.

"How long?" He gritted his teeth and pushed himself completely upright.

The movement sent his mind spinning. He pressed his fingers to his temple, but the pressure didn't help. There was no magical elixir that swept away his pain. He could merely wait as the room stopped blurring and Bea's face finally came into focus. Her brows were drawn together, her lips in a tight line. She looked worried. More than worried. Even in the dim light of dusk, he could see the dark shadows under her eyes, contrasting against the paleness of her face.

"How long? How long have I been out?"

She released a soft breath. "Two days, Colin. Two days."

Shock swept through him. "What . . ."

But she was serious; he could see that in the concern turning her amber eyes gold. He jerked his attention away from her, afraid she'd see the surprise. His heart hammered its protest against his rib cage, his body eager to bolt. He'd never meant to stay this long. He'd learned early in his life to keep afoot. When you were in one place too many days, they'd find you.

He tossed aside the thin blanket covering his legs, glad to see he was still dressed. "We need to leave soon." He'd needed the rest, whether he wanted it or not. Now that he was rested, they needed to move.

"Yes, soon," Anish croaked from the doorway of the hut. "They come. Soon."

"They? Who?" Bea demanded, standing. She'd changed. Gone was the traditional woman's garb and in its place were tan men's pants that hugged her backside indecently and a beige shirt that showed every damn curve. The stiff English-woman he'd met had disappeared. She looked like a damn adventurer. He didn't know whether to be amused or irritated. What else had happened in the past two days?

"Men are coming," Anish said, as if that explained everything.

Colin didn't need to know more. He'd seen enough of the unexplained to know to trust the man's eerie predictions.

Apparently, Bea did need to know more. "What do you mean?" she demanded.

"Bea, let's go." Colin settled his stocking feet on the ground and stood. Too fast. The top of his head slammed into the low, straw ceiling. He swayed, the room wavering. Bea was there, slipping her arm around his waist. It more than bothered him that he had to rely on a woman to hold him upright. And that damn sweet scent of hers wasn't helping to clear his thoughts.

"But . . . but now? You feel well enough?"

He moved away, collapsing onto the mat. "Of course I do." He pulled on his boots, annoyed she was treating him like some weak child, more annoyed that he felt like one. He was supposed to be protecting her. When had their positions changed? When he'd fainted like a weak . . . English-woman. He grabbed his hat and stuffed it onto his head.

Anish watched them from the shadows, his gaze too knowing.

Bea nodded, but he could see a flash of suspicion cross her eyes. The question was, how much did she know . . . about him . . . about the statue . . . about his abilities? How much did she remember of what he'd done? He'd rarely stuck around long enough after healing someone to find out what they remembered. But there was one person, one person he'd been able to ask. Ella.

He'd saved Ella.

"It was . . . wonderful." He could still picture her face that day he'd gotten the courage to ask her what she'd experienced. There was a strange happiness, an odd sense of knowing that had swept through his cousin's eyes. *"Warmth, love. I felt free, free of hurt, free of pain."*

Her answer had made him jealous. How he wished he could feel that way, just once. All he felt was a damn headache afterward.

A thump shook the ground, jerking him back into the present.

"What the hell was that?" Colin demanded.

Bea looked away, a telltale flush of guilt staining her cheeks. In two long strides, Colin swept outside. Brilliant light stabbed his eyes, making him blink rapidly. When he could finally focus, his mouth fell open. A monstrous gray beast munched vegetation on the edge of the camp, a wooden chair atop his back. Next to the animal Raj stood with a brilliant white smile against his tanned face.

"Good day!" he called out, waving, his excitement almost tangible.

The scent of clover and lavender alerted Colin to Bea's presence. He spun around to face her. "Is that . . . is that . . ."

"An elephant," Bea supplied.

He pinched the bridge of his nose and took in a long, deep breath, attempting to regain control of his temper. How dare she make plans while he was unconscious. "What the hell is an elephant doing here?"

"Elephant," Raj said. "You see elephant?"

"Of course," he snapped, knowing exactly why the beast was here. He closed his eyes briefly. The woman tried his patience. One moment she was a quivering mess, the next she was making plans and ordering him about as if she were in charge.

"An elephant for your travel. I'll be *Mahout*," Raj explained, puffing out his chest like a peacock.

The animal lifted its long trunk as if in greeting and gave a little snort. His cream-colored tusks gleamed wickedly in the sunlight. Colin wasn't sure what the beast found so amusing, Raj's vanity or his own obvious trepidation.

"Please tell me you're joking."

"No," Anish said, moving past them. "No jesting. You ride on elephant. He take you to temple."

Surprise gave him pause. "Temple?" Colin's attention flashed to Bea.

She shrugged and looked away, avoiding his gaze before he could read her emotions. "It's where you wish to travel, right?"

"I . . ." He didn't know how to respond. He wasn't sure if he should be irate that she'd planned their travels without his consent or if he should be apologizing for not telling her about his intention to research the temple in the first place. "Bea, I can explain."

She met his gaze, her eyes hard, her body stiff. "It's why you've been in India; it's why Leo and Ella came here. It must be important. Correct?"

If keeping unimaginable power and wealth from the hands of evil was important, then yes, it was. He rubbed the back of his neck, unsure how much to admit. "Well . . ."

She nodded and something shifted in her eyes, something subtle that he couldn't quite decipher. Gone was any softness and in its place stood a tall, cold woman. The type of woman he expected to find in the ballrooms of England. Suddenly, Sarah stood before him in all of her arrogant finery. Colin shook his head. Bea wasn't Sarah. He knew it wasn't fair to compare the two, but when Bea looked at him that way . . . with that coldness in her eyes . . . damned if he didn't remember his last encounter with his fiancée.

Bea swiped her hands on her trousers, as if ridding herself of any remaining emotion. "Right. Well then, shall we?"

He hesitated, confused and unsure if he wanted to know what she meant. "Shall we what?"

She nodded toward the elephant. "Shall we climb atop?"

He laughed. "Climb? You can't be serious."

But she wasn't listening to him. Bea moved toward the animal as if she wasn't afraid in the least. Hell, maybe she wasn't afraid. Before she could escape, he reached out, resting his hand on her arm. "Bea."

She paused and glanced back at him. Her eyes were flat, her bearing still stiff, and her lips set in that hard line. "Well?"

He didn't want to end things this way. He didn't like this cold Bea, and suddenly the truth spewed from his mouth. "I wasn't going to go look for the statue. That wasn't the plan. I was taking you to Leo and Ella."

There was a flash of surprise that crossed her eyes, but it was gone as quickly as it came. She smiled, a forced smile. "Colin, please. Raj explained that you asked about Anish. He was the one who'd seen the statue. I know you planned our visit."

He lifted his hat and raked his hair back in frustration. "Yes, I just asked. I was curious."

She shrugged. "Well then. Why not look? The temple is on the way. Half a day's ride south."

That realization made his heart race. So close. "Really?"

She nodded. "So, shall we?"

Surprise warred with guilt. There was Bea. Pale, delicate Bea who'd never even been out of Britain and now was here. She'd almost died, might again, and what if he didn't get to her in time to save her? "No. It's too dangerous. We need to find Leo."

Bea moved away from him. "Don't be ridiculous."

As a sign of respect, she bowed to Raj. His face shining with delight, the boy bowed back. With a flourish, Raj tapped the elephant's left leg. Immediately, the beast lifted his forearm, creating a natural ladder. Raj didn't hesitate but scurried up the animal and rested, at ease on the elephant's neck.

"Up," he said, glancing at Bea.

Finally, Bea showed some good sense and hesitated. Raj nodded his encouragement, waving her forward.

"Right, then," Bea whispered.

"Take his ear," Anish called out.

Exasperated, Colin looked at the old man. Anish shrugged and clasped his hands behind the small of his back, amusement flickering in his dark gaze. Bea couldn't possibly think she was going to climb onto an elephant. Colin crossed his arms over his chest and waited to see what she'd do next. Sure enough, the woman grasped the animal's ear and hauled herself up onto his leg. Son of a bitch, she was actually going to climb and he had no doubt it was mostly so she could thumb her nose at him.

"I need to know if the statues are four separate or together," Colin asked.

Raj leaned down and took Bea's hand, helping her onto the wooden chair atop the beast. Without the least bit of trouble, she reached her destination. Bea collapsed into the seat, releasing a breath of air that Colin could hear from where he stood. And she wasn't done. She turned her gaze to him and smiled an arrogant smirk.

Anish nodded. "Yes, four separate, but together."

Colin sighed. It made no sense.

"Are you coming?" Bea asked.

Anish slapped him on the back and chuckled. "The *mahout* knows the way to the temple."

"He's just a boy."

"No, he's been trained. He knows. The elephant knows."

This wasn't how it was supposed to be. Just two days ago, he was on his way to see Leo and Ella. Now, his life was suddenly planned out for him and by a pampered English-

woman, no less. He was in control, he'd had it mapped out.
Drop Bea off with Leo and leave them all to their lives so he
could find the statue alone, as it should be. He didn't need
someone else to muck up his plans, to worry about. "Anish,
I barely know what I'm looking for."

"The gods will lead you."

The gods? It sounded like a damn sound plan to him. He
resisted the urge to scoff. "But—"

"Go." The old man shoved him with more strength than
Colin thought possible. He stumbled forward, glaring over
his shoulder. Anish merely smiled wider and waved.

Shaking his head, Colin focused on the elephant, surprised to see the animal had moved closer.

"Whoa." Colin backed up a step and gazed wearily into
the elephant's large, dark eyes. The beast lifted his leg, urging
him to climb.

"Well?" Bea asked from above, her gaze mocking him.

Colin sighed. He'd have to do it. There was no other
choice. "Don't you move."

The beast released a low grumble. He wasn't sure if the
animal was agreeing or laughing. He hoped agreeing. Stealing his resolve, Colin grabbed the massive ear, small hairs
pricking his skin. His muscles burned with the movement, his
body still exhausted. Gritting his teeth, he pulled himself onto
the leathery hide. The animal didn't even flinch.

Sweat broke out on Colin's forehead. He wrapped his fingers around a bamboo pole of the chair and pulled himself
up. He didn't look down. Releasing a breath of air, he collapsed into position next to Bea. She was watching him with
something that looked decidedly like disappointment in her
eyes. Had she been hoping he'd fall on his ass? Probably.

The elephant gave a snort and lumbered forward. The
chair wavered back and forth. Bea sucked in a breath and
latched on to Colin's arm. Feeling rather smug, he grinned.
Perhaps this wasn't such a bad idea after all.

"Farewell and good luck, my friends!" Anish called out.

Bea waved to the old man until the trees hid him from view.

Colin waited until she'd turned back around. "Plan on telling me what's got your bloomers in a knot?"

Bea glanced at him and raised a brow. "Excuse me?"

"Why are you so annoyed, darlin'? What'd I do?"

She crossed her arms over her chest and dared to look him straight in the eyes. "Why do you think it's about you? That's a rather arrogant assumption."

"No, an educated guess. I've had the . . . *pleasure* of the company of many women, and if they're annoyed, there's a pretty good guess it has to do with men."

Bea laughed. "Well, that says a lot about you then."

"I'd say it says more about women in general."

She narrowed her eyes, her anger piercing.

"You could have left, you know. Jumped on the first raft to Bombay. You didn't have to stay and take care of me. Why did you stay?"

She tilted her chin high, refusing to look at him. "I had no choice, I couldn't go alone." There was something in the flush of her cheeks that made him want to question her further.

Colin inched closer. "Raj would have escorted you."

She folded her arms across her chest, the movement sending her breasts higher. She refused to look at him. "Why, he's merely a lad."

Colin's lips lifted into an arrogant grin. "You like me."

Her gaze jerked to him, her cheeks a brilliant pink. "Don't be ridiculous."

His grin deepened. "Admit it, darlin', you like me."

She released a harsh laugh. "Yes, as much as I liked almost dying. As much as I like the heat in India, as much as—"

"I think I've got the jist."

They moved onto a jungle path, the sun filtering through the leaves and sending a pattern of light and shadow across her face. He slipped his arm along the back of their chair and leaned closer, daring to tempt the lioness within. She inched away, but had little room to move and soon was backed against the side of the chair. She was trapped, trapped on the back of an elephant.

He couldn't ask for a better opportunity. "So then, if you hate me, why are you blushing?"

"It's the heat," she snapped. "Makes me flush."

Her skin was darkening, turning into an unfashionable pink thanks to the hot Indian sun. How horrified her English family would be. He picked up a lock of her hair, twining it around his finger. "This doesn't have to do with our kiss?"

Her face turned bright red, endearing really. "No," she hissed. "This has to do with the fact that you've all been keeping secrets from me."

He raised a brow. "Secrets?"

"Yes." She turned her face away, but not before he noticed the flash of hurt in her eyes. "The statue. Whatever it is you've concocted."

His amusement fled, guilt tugging at his heart. He knew what it felt like to be caught unaware, to be lost without a clue as to what was happening. Except he'd been a lad when it had happened. "The statue wasn't a secret, princess. Just . . . well, I wasn't planning on searching for it right now. I promise. Not with you here."

"Why do you all want it so badly?" She pierced him with her brilliant eyes.

He leaned back, away from her, suddenly not so eager to be close. "You'll think we're insane."

She shrugged. "I already do. Going through all this for a statue. It's mad. Ridiculous."

Leave it to her to be blunt. Should he be just as honest? Should he tell her? What would she think? How would she judge him? Belittle him? Laugh? "The statue has powers."

Her gaze widened. He kept his face serious but it didn't matter. Bea burst out laughing anyway. "Powers?"

He gritted his teeth as heat settled uncomfortably in his

cheeks. "Yes. Leo's ring and Ella's necklace will help lead us to the statue. Whether you believe it or not, many in this world do. Why do you think Henry and your grandfather went insane and tried to kill Leo? For the power."

Bea shook her head, the laughter fading from her eyes. "This . . . all of this . . . has to do with a statue that has supposed powers?"

Colin nodded, annoyed she laughed at him, more annoyed she didn't believe him. "So, darlin', still eager to visit the temple?"

Chapter 11

Their living quarters were becoming increasingly dire.
Bea had gone from a castle, to a tiny stone abode, and now
to a tent in the middle of the jungle. She sighed and surveyed their dwelling. The canvas flapped on the small
breeze, the material stained and dirty. Positively ghastly.
Yet . . . there was something about the sunset . . . about
the sounds of night insects chirping . . . about the brilliant
pink flowers blooming on the vines . . . that made it almost
worthwhile.

Still, she couldn't help noting that there was only one
tent. One. Where would Colin sleep? She shifted, the
trousers much too tight on her hips and backside. Oh, she'd
pretended confidence when she'd sashayed across the camp
in her men's clothing and climbed that elephant like she
knew what she was doing.

Inside, she was quivering.

Still, as much as she hated her sleeping quarters and
manly trousers, she'd grown rather fond of her beastly
carriage.

As if sensing the way of her thoughts, she felt a soft
shove to her right shoulder. Bea turned. A long, gray snout
brushed her arm.

She couldn't keep the smile from her face. She'd seen

drawings and paintings of elephants, but never imagined how amazing they could be. "Why, hello, my love."

She leaned against the animal's foreleg, taking comfort in his immense strength and feeling safe against the encroaching darkness. The elephant grunted and reached out for her with his trunk. Bea grinned and smoothed her hands over his soft snout, his large brown eyes on her.

"Why, you're just like Mac, my terrier back home, aren't you? Although most definitely a bit larger. No, I don't believe you'd be able to sit on my lap on cold Scottish evenings."

He wrapped his trunk around her waist in a tight embrace. For the first time in days, Bea found herself giggling. "I shall call you King Henry."

King Henry grunted his approval and Bea relaxed enough to survey their surroundings. Her gaze shifted to the tall neem trees that surrounded the site, farther to the millet fields just barely visible through the branches. The sun was gone, gray dusk lingering with the chirp of insects, and with dusk came the mystery of night.

"What say you, King Henry? If I hop on your back, will you take me on an adventure?" She plucked a leaf from a nearby bush. The elephant eagerly took the foliage in his snout. "Perhaps we can find butterflies. I've barely seen any since I've arrived, you know."

"Bea, come eat," Colin called out.

Bea gave the elephant one last pat and reluctantly made her way toward the crackling fire. She wasn't sure how she'd expected to feel camping at night, but the insatiable thrilling fear wasn't it. Flames leapt and popped, leering at her through the darkness. A shiver snaked across her spine. It was eerie here, on the outskirts of a jungle where anything could hide. Part of her welcomed the thrill of the unknown.

But with darkness came the animals. Snapping sticks, crunching leaves, and sounds she'd never heard before, sounds that raised the fine hairs on her body. A harsh scream rent the air. Bea sucked in a breath and quickly settled on the log next to Colin.

"I take it you've spent little time outside at night?" Colin asked, amusement flickering in his eyes.

Bea shook her head. "Not at night. Only the disreputable went out at night, or so Grandmother said. I feel . . . watched. Exposed in some way."

He took a swig of water from the clay jar. "You are." He leaned closer to her, his breath warm on her ear while his musky scent whispered seductively. "Out there in the darkness, beyond our circle of light, anyone, anything could be watching."

Instinctively, her gaze widened and Colin laughed.

With a frown, she crossed her arms over her chest. He was teasing her again. As he'd been teasing her when they'd left Anish, asking her horribly uncomfortable questions merely to make her cheeks flush.

"Admit it, darlin', you like me."

Colin's words taunted her memory. Ha. As if she'd ever like a man so . . . so . . . She slid him a glance, noting the way the firelight highlighted the planes of his face, the way the moonlight made his golden curls shine.

"You're staring," he said, not bothering to glance at her. "Do you see something you like?"

Heat shot directly to her cheeks. "So glad you're feeling better."

He didn't respond, merely grinned and glanced at her with those sparkling blue eyes. She couldn't imagine what he thought; most likely that she was a naïve chit, easily toyed with. How she wanted to be angry at him, yet with the firelight playing across the harsh planes of his face, she found she could think of nothing else but how handsome he looked. She sighed and focused on the fire.

Arrogant oaf.

At least, she'd thought him arrogant. But she wasn't entirely sure now. When he'd somehow saved Raj's sister,

Bea's heart had softened toward the man. And then he'd kissed her and she found she could think of little else but him. The way his eyes turned to crescent moons when he laughed. The way he looked almost boyishly endearing when the wind tossed about his curls. The way his gaze drilled into her as if he knew things about her that no one else did.

Who was this man? Oaf or angel? In the two days he'd been unconscious, she'd sat by his bedside, praying he'd wake up, fearing he wouldn't. She told herself she cared only for Ella's sake. But he'd saved her life. Somehow the man had taken away her pain. He'd saved her life, and when she'd awoken, only to find him collapsed at her side, something had shifted inside her.

Her feelings toward Colin had shifted. She didn't understand him, didn't understand the mystery that surrounded his abilities, and she wasn't sure she wanted to know. But she did know one thing: Colin Finch was a much more compassionate man than he let on.

He handed her a tin plate of mush and bread. Their fingers brushed and a shiver raced over her skin, her very being startled. Her gaze met his. He watched her, something in his eyes she couldn't quite identify. She wasn't sure how long they stared at each other, but she knew she couldn't quite breathe the entire time and was rather sure she was close to fainting.

Finally, he pulled back and turned away. Bea let out a breath of air. With hands that trembled, she tore the flat bread in half. Was she supposed to be hurt or relieved that Colin seemed intent on avoiding contact? He'd been distant ever since their kiss. Bea scooped up the brown mush with the bread, as Raj did, and stuffed the food into her mouth. What was Colin thinking?

"No, no," Raj said, shaking his head and interrupting her thoughts.

Confused, Bea glanced around the site, looking for the culprit, but the boy seemed to be upset with only her. "Pardon?"

"Right hand only. Only eat with right hand. Left hand dirty."

Her left fingers opened and the food fell to the dish with a thud. "Oh, so sorry."

Heat shot to her cheeks, horrified and humiliated she'd once again done something wrong and had to be reprimanded by a mere child. How she wished she could slink back into the shadows. Would she ever fit in anywhere?

Using her right hand, she lifted the bread and nibbled, watching Raj through her lashes to make sure she didn't offend the lad again. But Raj and Colin were deep in discussion, ignoring her once more. She didn't fit here or in Scotland. She certainly didn't belong in English drawing rooms. Where did she belong?

"By tomorrow midday?" Colin said.

Raj nodded, stuffing so much bread into his mouth that he would surely choke.

"What?" Bea demanded, tired of being ignored.

"The temple," Colin said, glancing at her briefly.

Reality sank heavily into her gut. Or was that the bread? They really were traveling to the temple. She set her plate on the hard dirt, completely uncaring if ants would attack her food. She was no longer hungry.

It was her fault. She'd pushed Colin into traveling to the temple, so why then did unease tickle the back of her neck like a whispered warning? Because she hadn't truly believed there was a temple, or that they would go out of their way to find the sacred place.

The small green leaves of the neem trees directly behind them rustled, yet there wasn't a breeze to ease the stifling heat. Colin stiffened, and glanced over his shoulder.

"A wild boar?" he asked quietly.

Raj didn't respond, but remained alert on his log seat.

She could see in the tightness of their faces that something was wrong. Slowly, Colin and Raj stood.

Bea jumped to her feet. "What is it?"

Colin didn't bother to look at her. "Shhh."

Silence settled as thick and suffocating as the heat. Besides the soft chirp of insects, no other sound could be heard, and Bea thought for a moment they'd overreacted.

"Hello, my friends," someone called out.

The sudden voice was like a slap to her overwrought senses. Her frantic gaze searched the brush, her attention jumping from shadowy tree to shadowy tree. Yet nothing moved. No one was there. The persons remained as elusive as water in the dry months of India.

"Did I just imagine that?" she whispered.

Colin glanced at Raj. "Hunters?"

Raj shrugged.

Hunters? Relief sank in her gut. Hunters were acceptable, so why were they still frowning? "Shall we invite them to dine with us?" she asked, searching the area for movement or any indication of their visitors. Why couldn't she see them? More importantly, why were they hidden?

Colin's gaze flashed to her. "Darlin', this isn't a British drawing room."

She was just about to respond when the bushes parted. Twigs snapped, leaves rustled. A bird squawked and took flight, its wings beating as frantically as Bea's heart.

Four human forms stepped into their clearing. The firelight hit their visitors, highlighting their faces with an eerie glow. While they were still too far away to truly see their features, Bea noticed that two had the darker skin of an Indian, while the other two possessed the pale complexions of a European. She'd heard stories before of Englishmen come to hunt in exotic lands. Surely, hunting wasn't an uncommon occurrence, so why were Raj and Colin still so uneasy? Colin stepped in front of her, confirming her suspicions.

No one said a word. Not Raj, not Colin. Nor any of

their new visitors. Bea stood on tiptoe and gazed around the clearing, from man to man, attempting to deduce some sort of explanation from their stoic features. Outside of a drawing room, she wasn't sure how to properly proceed. She didn't understand why they were standing there in silence, but her mind and body warned her to be on alert.

"My friends." One of the men finally stepped forward and pulled the hat from his head, revealing dark locks and an easy smile that lit his narrow face. He pushed aside the rifle hanging around his shoulder and glanced briefly at Bea before returning his gaze to Colin. "We were passing through. I'm Stephan." He nodded toward the other white man, whose face was hidden by the shadow of his wide-brimmed hat. "And this is my friend Demyan."

Still Colin said nothing. What was wrong with him? His gaze had jumped to the man named Demyan, and there his attention remained riveted. Friends or foes, by being rude they'd only be courting trouble.

Bea hesitated only a moment before deciding to take things into her own more than capable hands. "Welcome, sirs."

In a swoosh of air, everyone faced her, making Bea instantly regret her decision. Still, hearing her voice, Colin seemed to snap from his shock. Without even looking her way, Colin smiled, an obviously forced smile that didn't quite reach his eyes, then took her hand, pulling her close.

"Always the first to welcome guests." His grip was tight, too tight. "Please, come and sit. We were just settling down to dine. I'm Charlie and this is my wife, Catherine."

Unnerved, Bea slid Colin a glance. Why would he lie? She didn't understand. Biting her lip to keep from demanding answers, she warily watched the two European men stroll through the campsite and settle on logs across the fire from them. The remaining two Indian men fanned out, standing in the shadows. Keeping watch, or watching them?

Stephan set his rifle on the ground. It should have put her mind at ease. It didn't. "Allow our men to keep watch."

Colin helped her to their vacated seat. Perhaps this Stephan was being kind, but instead of protecting, Bea had the sudden feeling the men were actually surrounding them. Maybe Colin's paranoia was rubbing off on her.

Demyan nodded a greeting, keeping his face tilted down and his gaze focused on the ground. Was he timid, or hiding something? Blast it, but fear and unease were taking control.

Stephan pulled the water jar from his hip, where it rested on a leather strap. "You don't mind if we set up camp here? Safety in numbers and all that."

Colin returned the man's smile and slipped his arm around her waist, pulling her close. She didn't protest. "Of course not."

Bea rested one hand on his flat stomach. She was thankful for his touch, while at the same time she noticed the stiffness of his body and wondered over it. How desperately she wished for a moment alone with the man. Raj picked up plates of food and scurried across the clearing to hand each man a meal. Bea didn't miss the look he slid Colin, but she didn't understand their unspoken thoughts. Still, she didn't have to be a mind reader to know without a doubt that Colin and Raj were leery of the men. She was leery, too. But why? What could they possibly want from them?

"Hunting?" Colin asked, his gaze flashing to the man named Demyan.

Stephan scooped up the bread. "Yes, and you?"

Colin eased his legs out in front of him, feigning an ease Bea knew he didn't feel. "Just getting started. How's the game downriver?"

"Thick. You'll be sure not to leave empty-handed." The man took a bite, watching them through his lashes. Demyan still hadn't said a word, and with his face averted, Bea couldn't make out his features.

"And how long will you be here?" Colin crossed his arms over his chest. That pulse was beating furiously in the side of his neck, while his breath hitched with each intake.

Even if their guests didn't seem to notice Colin's odd state, Bea did.

Stephan scratched his neck, his gaze narrowing as if thinking over the answer. "Not quite sure. Until we bag a large one. I see you're traveling by elephant?"

Bea's gaze slid to King Henry. The animal was munching on leaves, looking so bloody adorable, she wondered if she could possibly get him on a boat back to England with her. The thought of seeing Grandmother's face when she appeared with the beast in tow almost made her forget their current situation.

"Yes, we are," Colin answered.

Balancing his plate on his knees, Stephan stretched his arms out, warming his hands by the fire. "Hunted elephants just a fortnight ago. You wouldn't be interested in selling him? Ivory goes for a bloody fortune."

Bea sucked in a breath, her gaze jumping to Colin. They couldn't possibly be serious!

Colin chuckled, but there was no mirth in his cold blue eyes. "Afraid not."

The man shrugged. "Well, couldn't hurt to ask." His gaze slid to Bea and she had to resist the urge to shrink back. "Your accent. Are you from the Lowlands?"

She glanced at Colin, seeking his permission to answer, but he was staring at Demyan again. Of course she couldn't very well ignore Stephan's question. "English, but lived in the Highlands for some time."

"Ah. From London myself."

She nodded, clasping her hands tightly in her lap, unsure what to say or do, but wishing the man would focus on someone else.

Finally, Colin turned to her. He was smiling, but she didn't miss the tightness of his expression. "Darlin', shall we go to the river and prepare for rest?"

Bea wasn't sure what he meant, but knew she'd rather follow Colin than stay here. He took her hand, his warm, calloused fingers slipping through hers. With a yank, she was on her feet. She had just enough time to give the men a nod of farewell before Colin had pulled her into the trees. Bea glanced over her shoulder. Raj continued to sit silently by, tending the fire, while the two visitors ate their meals.

Colin pulled her farther into the forest, until the firelight faded and they were surrounded by darkness. This time the lack of light was a welcome cloak of safety. Leaves, wet with dew, slapped against her legs, soaking through the material of her trousers. Her hair, which she'd pulled back into a bun, came loose, falling in waves down around her shoulders.

Colin curved through the brush, going this way and that until Bea grew dizzy. Finally, they paused. She rested her hands on his hard back, her breathing harsh, as she waited to see what he'd do next. But Colin didn't move, merely stared through the leaves toward the direction of the campsite, watching only God knew what.

She couldn't see a bloody thing. "Colin, what is it?"

"We have visitors." He didn't bother to look at her as he whispered this.

"Obviously, but why do I get a bad feeling from them?"

Finally, he looked at her. "Because you should."

Well, that didn't make her feel any better. "Do you think they're truly hunters?"

He latched on to her hand and pulled her farther into the trees. Just barely, over the snap of leaves and twigs, she could hear the sound of gurgling water.

"No," Colin murmured.

Shocked, Bea attempted to pull her hand away, but he refused to release his hold. "How do you know?"

He sighed. "When they called out, they called out in English."

"And?"

He paused long enough to look at her. "Why would they automatically call out in English?"

Her brows drew together. She didn't understand his line of questioning. "Well, they must have seen us and noticed we were Western."

"Exactly. They knew ahead of time because they were watching us. Why?"

She shrugged, unease whispering over her skin like a chill breeze. They were watching them? For how long? "Being careful?"

"Maybe." They paused near a small creek, the water glistening like a silver snake under the moonlight. "Wet your face and dampen your hair as if you've been washing and preparing for sleep."

Bea knelt by the stream and slipped her hands into the cool water.

"I don't trust them." Colin knelt beside her, only a breath away. "That man named Dem . . ." He swallowed hard and looked over his shoulder. He was trembling, she realized, his breath catching slightly. Bea's fear grew. She'd never seen him this way.

"There's something . . ."

Bea scooped up water and splashed it on her face. "What?"

But he didn't answer. Colin's gaze flickered around the woods as if looking for something or someone. Bea inched closer to him, her heart thundering in her chest. Before she could realize his intentions, he jerked her to her feet and smashed his lips to hers.

"Colin," she mumbled against his mouth.

He pulled back only slightly, his grip still tight on her upper arms. "Shhh, kiss me and look like you mean it."

"But Colin . . ."

He took advantage of her parted lips and slipped his tongue into her mouth.

Shock gave way to welcome warmth. He tasted like honey, like sunlight. Shimmers of delight tickled her spine. She sank into his hard body, taking comfort in his touch, in his strong arms wrapped around her waist, holding her close. Hesitantly, Bea moved her tongue against his, stroking, rubbing. A deep ache settled low in her gut. Giving in to temptation, Bea slipped her fingers into the cool, soft curls at the base of his neck.

Frantic for more, she met his tongue thrust for thrust. Colin's hands slid up her rib cage, hovering just below her breasts. Her nipples hardened, her breasts growing heavy for his touch. Colin groaned and tore his mouth from hers. He didn't pull back, but held her close, the harsh sound of their breathing drowning out the chirp of insects.

"Colin," Bea said softly, her lips brushing against his neck, not quite ready to stop touching him. Her knees had grown weak and she found it difficult to stand. She felt as if she were in a beautiful, wonderful dream. "Why'd you do that?"

"Because they're watching us."

Bea stiffened. "Who?"

Colin cupped the sides of her face, his lips only inches from hers. "One, two of their men, I'm not sure. I heard them follow."

Fear replaced lust. Without moving her head, she scanned the woods, but she could see nothing in the dark shadows. "Wh—what do we do?"

"Nothing." He released his hold, stepping back.

"Nothing?"

He took her hand, his expression firm. Had their kiss affected him at all? "We go back to the camp, we settle in for bed."

"But—"

"Trust me."

Exhaustion and fear got the better of her. "Trust you?" she hissed. "The same man who's been lying to me since I arrived? The same man who believes a bloody statue has powers?"

He started back to camp, dragging her with him. "What choice do you have?"

Chapter 12

She wasn't sleeping. Colin could tell by the stiffness of her body as she lay next to him on the small cot. What she was thinking, he couldn't imagine. Most likely she was worried about her hide, and he was, too. Damn, but he should have gone straight to Bombay. What the hell had he been thinking to drag her out here in the middle of nowhere?

The statue. He'd been thinking about that statue. And because of his obsession with uncovering answers, he'd never rest. He'd endanger everyone around him. Just as his father had. And look where the statue had gotten the man? Nowhere but dead.

Still, could he give up the idea of the statue? Give up the one thing he'd been searching for his entire life? Knowing what would happen if it got into the wrong hands? Guilt warred with need. Until he destroyed the piece, he'd never be free, never be free of the danger, never be able to rest in one place.

Colin's thoughts changed, the picture of Demyan flashing across his closed lids. The image sent his heart racing. There was something about the man . . . something familiar, something that taunted the back of his mind . . . He pressed his fingertips to his lids. What was it that caught his attention?

Bea shifted. Her lean, lovely body lay beside him like an offering from the gods. Hell, if the situation were not so dire, he'd take advantage of the gift. Even now, she tempted him. Those long legs clad only in trousers, the way her waist nipped in, only to flare out at her hips . . .

"Bea?" he whispered, his voice coming out gruff.

She rolled toward him, too close. A gasp escaped her lips and her hands flattened to his shoulders as her body pressed indecently to his. Her soft breasts were crushed to his chest so that he could feel every beat of her heart. They both froze, suspended in a fog of heady desire. How badly he wanted to run his hand down the curve of her hip, to cup her rounded bottom, to forget harsh reality in her beauty.

"I'm so sorry." She wiggled, attempting to move away, but only made things worse. Lightning shot through his body, centering in his groin. He fought to ignore his sudden desire.

"Stop," he finally demanded when he could take no more. She froze. "Yes?"

Her warm breath sent shivers over his skin. He wrapped his arm around her waist, holding her still. "It'll be light soon. We need to leave now."

She tilted her head back, her eyes wide and shimmering pools of trust. "What?"

"Shhhh." He pressed his finger to her soft lips and they both fell silent.

He strained to hear what lay beyond their tent. The camp seemed still, except for the occasional pop of the dying fire. Everyone slept, or so he hoped. Slowly . . . reluctantly, he moved away from her. The cot creaked and he paused, cringing. When no sound of waking voices came, he managed to make his way to the tent flap without further incident.

Quickly, he grabbed his hat and scooped up the bag that held their necessities. He didn't glance back as he waved Bea over. They had to leave now, before dawn broke, or it'd

be too late. He didn't hear Bea approach and resisted the
urge to sigh. He turned. She was right beside him.

Surprise held him silent for one long moment. "How'd
you . . . how'd you make it here without a sound?"

She shrugged her left shoulder. "As a child, I used to
sneak out of the house."

"Really?" He knew they should leave, but for some
reason he was frozen in place, wanting to know more about
this odd woman. "Why?"

She looked away, as if embarrassed. "I liked to search for
butterflies, and Grandmother wouldn't allow me to go into
the woods alone and dirty my gowns."

"Butterflies?"

She nodded.

He remembered the book that had been poking him as he
lay upon the settee that first day he'd met her. Bea was a
bluestocking and she didn't mind getting dirty. He was
ridiculously pleased. There was certainly more to this
woman than he'd realized and even more he wished to know.

"Colin," she whispered. "Shouldn't we go?"

"Right. Of course." He pulled open the flap and allowed
Bea outside. She moved silently past him, her sweet scent
lingering in the air. Before he could prevent himself, he
breathed in deep the perfume of clover and lavender. Just
her scent sent Colin's heart racing. From across the campsite, Raj nodded toward them, his body glowing eerily in the
waning flames of the campfire.

His gaze slid to the other two tents, where Demyan and
Stephan slept. His fingers curled at his sides and his heart
slammed against his chest. Something was wrong. He knew
he was missing some vital piece of information. Instinct told
him that much. How he wanted to demand answers, to test
his strength. But he and Raj were no match against four
grown men with guns. Bea came first. He needed to get her
to safety.

"Wait," Bea whispered. "What about King Henry?"

Reluctantly, he glanced at her. "Who?"

Bea looked over her shoulder toward the large pacaderm. "The elephant."

The massive, dark shadow shifted, as if he'd been waiting for them. Colin took her arm and started toward Raj. "What about him?"

"We can't leave him here."

"We have to."

She attempted to pull away, but he didn't dare release his hold. She'd make a fuss and wake the entire camp if he let her. "Colin, you heard them. They'll make sport of killing King Henry."

He paused in exasperation. "Bea, we can't escape on an elephant without them noticing. It's the elephant or us."

She pressed her palms to his chest and peered into his eyes, that amber gaze simmering with tears. In that moment, he could have sworn the woman had her own magical abilities and he'd completely fallen. "Please, Colin."

Damn her. Didn't she realize how dire their situation was? But her lower lip started quivering and he knew he'd cut off his own arm just to keep her from crying. What the hell was wrong with him? When had she gone from being Leo's cousin to more? With a grunt of annoyance, he led her across the campsite, hiding in the shadows along the perimeter.

"We need to take the elephant."

Raj looked at him as if he were insane. A thirteen-year-old boy, looking at him like he was crazy. Hell, maybe he was.

"Please, Raj," Bea whispered.

Raj shook his head. "Too loud."

"Please, Raj, we must." Bea stepped closer, those pleading eyes taking the lad under.

Raj swallowed, his throat working, but the poor sod immediately nodded. Colin rolled his eyes. All it took was a pretty woman to bat her lashes. Then again, he wasn't much better.

"Fine then," Colin snapped. "Let's go."

King Henry, aptly named, bent his leg as if he were as eager to escape as they. Raj scampered up the beast, settling behind his head, then held out his hand for Bea. She didn't hesitate, but clambered onto her wooden chair like a queen ruling over her domain. And she was a queen, in her own way, a titled lady too good to be sleeping in the jungle, too good to be riding a dirty elephant, and too good for him.

"Sir," Raj whispered. "Hurry."

Colin glanced behind him, his fingers curling. The camp still lay silent. Were they waiting for them? His mouth went dry. He latched on to the elephant's rough ear and pulled himself up onto the beast. "Let's go."

Raj tapped the elephant's side with a thin branch and the beast bolted forward. The ground shook, trees bouncing, their leaves rattling. Colin's teeth chattered with the jarring movement. If the thumping of the elephant didn't draw their attention, Bea's screech would. She grasped on to the side of the bamboo chair, her yelp lingering in the gray dawn.

"Dear God!"

"Hold tight." Colin slid his arm around her narrow waist, worried she'd bounce off the animal's back and break her neck in the fall.

Vegetation snapped and popped under King Henry's massive feet, the noise like cannon fire drowning out the soft sounds of waking birds. As the spiny black branches reached out, claws that snagged their hair and clothes, Colin prayed for the first time since he was a child. He prayed that Bea would be kept safe.

He hunched low, pulling Bea with him. "Hurry, Raj." He wasn't surprised when shouts rang out behind them. "Took them long enough."

"They're coming!" Raj cried.

Colin glanced over his shoulder, peering through the weave of the chair backing. The two Indian guides were stumbling down the trail after them. They were dressed and ready. They'd been waiting in the woods for their escape, but they hadn't expected them to take the elephant and that was where they had the upper hand. He supposed he owed Bea his appreciation.

"He's watching," Bea whispered.

She'd turned, too, her fingers grasping so tightly to the edges of the chair that her knuckles had grown white. Colin followed her gaze. Through the cloud of dust that King Henry stirred, the man named Demyan stood completely still. In the middle of the campsite as chaos swirled around him, the man merely watched them.

Unease whispered over his skin, a memory . . . a warning of something . . . but what?

"Colin?" A soft touch on his arm roused him.

Bea waiting for him . . . to what? Save her? And he knew, looking into her guiless eyes, that he couldn't endanger her by returning to the campsite for answers.

"Faster!" Raj yelled, nudging King Henry with a stick.

The elephant roared in complaint and shook his massive head, the movement sending the chair trembling. Bea gasped and threw her arms around Colin's waist. Damn, how he wished Ella was with them; she'd be able to control the animal like no other. But he was helpless. Completely helpless, and Bea's life was in the hands of an elephant and a thirteen-year-old boy.

A bony branch reached out, coming straight at them. Colin jerked Bea into his chest. Too late. She cried out, pressing her hand to her cheek. He was always too late.

He grasped her chin and turned her face toward him. "Are you all right?"

She nodded, but when she lowered her hand, he could see the dark slash across her cheek. Such a minor injury, yet an injury all the same. Failure sank into his gut, bitter and heavy. He should never have gone after the statue, not with Bea in his company. He should've taken her immediately to Bombay.

He cupped her shoulders, looking directly into her eyes. "Bea, I'm "

A blast rang out, echoing through the jungle. They both ducked low. A flock of birds burst from the trees, squawking and crying.

"They're shooting," Bea whispered, horror written across her ashen face.

"Stay down. Understand?"

She nodded, staring up at him with those trusting eyes. Damn it. If anything happened to her . . . If the shot was instantaneous and fatal . . . If his powers didn't work . . . Another blast rang out, jerking him from his thoughts.

King Henry lurched forward, throwing Bea's soft body into Colin. For a moment, he held her tight, savoring her warmth, savoring the feel of her safely in his arms.

"Sir, elephant shot," Raj called out.

"No!" Bea clung to Colin's arm. Tears glistened in her eyes, shimmering under the crescent moon just barely visible over the tops of the trees.

"Stay down." He turned and tugged the pistol from his waistband. His gaze honed in on one of the guides racing after them. King Henry stumbled at the same time Colin pulled the trigger. The shot went wide and nicked a tree. "Damn it."

Without breaking stride, the native man lifted his arm, the pistol gleaming in the moonlight. The blast ripped through the dawn. Colin ducked. A piece of the chair chipped away, flying through the air.

Bea gripped his knee. "Are you all right?"

Colin didn't bother to answer. He needed a clean shot, yet if he stayed atop the chair and next to Bea, she might be injured.

"Colin," Bea insisted. "Are you all right?"

He pulled the hat from his head and pushed it into her arms, then gripped the strap holding their chair in place. Taking in a deep breath, he flung himself onto the side of the elephant. His boots hit the animal's thick hide and Colin wavered. Like an acrobat he'd seen out West when he was but a lad, he stabilized himself, then focused on the man behind them. He pulled the trigger. The man tripped, then fell.

Wicked glee washed over him. "One down," he whispered.

King Henry stumbled, sending Colin off balance. He bounced across the animal's side. His wrist twisted painfully, but he didn't dare let go of the leather strap.

"Colin!" Bea was leaning over the edge of the chair, her hair in long, dark waves that fell toward him. She stretched out her hand. "Grab on."

"Damn it, Bea. Get down!"

She hesitated, but did as he said and hunkered behind the side of the chair.

Gritting his teeth, he lifted his right leg atop King Henry's back and hauled himself onto the animal once more. With a grunt, he fell back into the chair.

"Are you well?" Bea's warm hands swept over his shoulder, then his chest.

Her touch sent unwanted heat through his body. Colin nodded, brushing aside his hands. "Yes."

She shoved the hat back atop his head. King Henry roared and tripped, tossing Bea into the corner of the chair. The bamboo cracked, the side railings tumbling to the ground in splinters of wood. Bea's eyes widened. Colin's heart stopped beating.

"Colin!" She started to fall.

Frantic, Colin latched on to her hand, his fingers tight around hers. Sweat broke out on his forehead. Her legs slipped over the animal's bloated belly. Colin's grip was the only thing keeping her from crashing to the ground.

"Bea, don't you dare let go!" Colin tucked his foot under the strap that held the remains of the chair to King Henry's back.

"I'm pulling you up, hold tight." He gripped her wrist and jerked. Bea scrambled onto the animal's back. She didn't release her hold, but threw her arms around Colin's waist. She clung to him, and as pathetic as it was, he needed her touch, reveled in the fact that she was hugging him tightly. This was why knights saved damsels in distress.

His hands trembled with pent-up emotion. "It's all right."

The elephant stumbled again. Colin tightened his grip, his body taut as he fought to stay atop. If he could only hold her, he had the insane belief that everything would be all right.

"He's limping," Raj called out. "He won't last much longer."

Bea tilted her head and looked into his eyes. "Colin, help him."

Apprehension whispered through his mind . . . a warning that her plea was more than what was implied. "What do you mean?"

"You're . . . you're a doctor, right?" Confusion, wariness, and knowledge flashed across her eyes. She knew more than what she was admitting. How much did she remember of her recovery?

"No," he said, loosening his hold.

The elephant slowed.

Bea gripped his shirt, her hold tight. "Please, Colin, please help him."

The beast stopped and his massive legs folded under him like a building collapsing. Bea started to slip from his arms. Colin grasped on to her but he was helpless to keep them upright. Together, they slid to the ground, Colin taking the brunt of the fall. He hit the dirt, his hat toppling off his head. Bea hit him, pressing the air from his lungs. But they'd survived, at least he hoped.

Relief quickly gave way to desire. Bea lay sprawled across him, her lush body pressed to his. He wished he could enjoy the moment.

Suddenly, Raj was hovering over them, his eyes as large as saucers. "All right?"

Bea shifted, her knee coming dangerously close to his

manhood. Colin rested his hands on her waist, lifting her from him before she could do any damage.

"Fine," Colin gritted out.

Bea made quick work of scampering to her feet and grabbing Raj. "How is he? How's King Henry?"

Raj shook his head, his mouth set in a grim line. Bea sucked in a breath of air and rushed toward the animal, leaving Colin to fend for himself. He sat up and searched for his hat. He found it resting atop a bush. They needed to hide, but he knew Bea would never abandon the elephant. He raked his hair back and shoved the hat atop his head.

She turned toward him, and even in the dim light of dusk, he saw the unspoken plea in those amber eyes. Her hair hung wildly about her shoulders. Her shirt, partially untucked from the waistband of her trousers, was smudged with dirt . . . as was her face. He'd never seen her look more beautiful.

Damn it all, Ella was the one with the affinity for beasts. He'd always worked with humans. He didn't even know if he could save an animal. Warily, his gaze traveled the immense gray beast. It would drain him, saving something that large. But Bea was looking at him, waiting for him . . .

He briefly closed his eyes. "Go, watch for the men."

Raj didn't hesitate and raced farther down the trail. But then the lad knew what Colin was capable of and no longer found it shocking. Bea merely stood there as if suddenly unsure.

"Well?" he snapped, annoyed with the woman's indecision, more annoyed now that he realized he'd do practically anything for her, even risk his own life. "Do you want me to fix him?"

She took her lip between her teeth and scurried after Raj. They had little time, and if the healing drained him, they'd be easily caught. But damn it all, he couldn't let Bea down. Colin moved around the animal, surveying the wounds. The beast was breathing heavily, his large wary eyes following him. It was the left hind leg that dripped blood. Colin pressed his hands to the leathery thigh. The shot had gone through. He could do this. Human, elephant . . . they were made of the same thing, surely.

Taking in a deep breath, he pushed his fingertips into the animal's thick flesh and closed his eyes. Nothing happened. Refusing to surrender, he refocused. Damn, but he didn't want to disappoint Bea. He concentrated harder, imagining the animal's heart pulse beneath his fingertips.

"Come on," he whispered, pleaded, begged. His gaze slid to the heavens, taking in the gray skies of dawn. "Don't let me down now of all times."

Suddenly, the familiar warmth jolted through him, an answer from God. This time the power was faster, roaring through his body like a tropical storm. Fire shot through his arms to the tips of his fingers. Colin cringed, but refused to step back, refused to stop touching the animal. Bending his head, he concentrated harder.

Vaguely, he was aware of the elephant shifting under his hands. But Colin didn't move, didn't flinch as the energy burned through him. Sweat beaded on his forehead. His body swayed, his limbs shaking. The urge to sink to the ground overwhelmed him.

Just when he thought he'd collapse, with a roar, the heat receded, sucked back into the universe or wherever it resided and taking Colin's energy with it. Colin stumbled back, and too weak to stand, he slumped to the ground, his head hitting the dirt with a thud that made his skull bounce.

"Colin, are you all right?" Bea collapsed at his side, but he didn't have the strength to answer her plea. Her warm fingers cupped the sides of his face, forcing him to remain in the conscious world. "Colin, please, tell me you're well?"

The elephant rumbled, then shuffled to his feet, a temple rising from the earth and making the ground tremble.

"Hurry," Raj called out, suddenly appearing before them and hopping up and down in his haste. "You must hurry."

Colin laughed, a wry laugh. He felt as if he had no muscles, no bones. He could barely move, yet they wanted him to hurry? He stared unblinkingly at the purple sky. Dawn would be here soon, the seconds flying by.

"Colin, please, can you at least climb onto the elephant?" Bea asked, slipping her arm under his neck.

As much as he'd love to race off on an elephant, the most he could manage was to glance at the beast. King Henry seemed as tall as a mountain, an impassable mountain. Exhausted just thinking about moving, Colin gave in to his main desire and closed his eyes.

"We must leave," Raj said, rushing around him like an annoying gnat.

"Go," Bea said, giving the lad a gentle push. "Take the elephant and go. You'll have a chance."

Raj paused, as if thinking it over. "Yes. They follow me, but I'll outrun them." Raj nodded. "You stay here, you go to temple. Creek there, past trees. When it splits, you take creek toward sun."

Colin lifted his lashes just enough to see Bea's nod. How he wanted to argue, but he could barely part his lips to form a word. Raj slipped his arms under Colin's shoulders and dragged him back into the weeds. Leaves and branches snapped under his weight, scratching his back and neck.

"Enough!" he growled.

The boy nodded and dropped Colin. His head hit the ground again, barely cushioned by the hard earth. Bea followed, hunching down next to him, half-hidden by the foliage. The musky scent of earth surrounded them. She'd managed to grab their sack, and the bag hung down around her neck, bouncing against her hip.

Raj paused. "Stay here, hide while men pass by."

Bea nodded.

Without another word, Raj raced back to the trail and climbed the elephant. He stopped long enough to throw them a nod, then he was off. The forest floor vibrated with the steps of the elephant, until they faded into a soft hum. The raucous calls of birds seemed louder now that they were frozen still upon the forest floor alone.

"Colin," Bea whispered. "Colin, are you all right?"

"I'll be fine," he managed to mutter. And he would be fine, as long as they weren't discovered. It wouldn't take long to recover; he could feel himself slowly returning to normal. But still, he wouldn't be strong enough to fight for a good hour or two.

Shouts rang through the woods. Bea stiffened before sliding her arms around his shoulders. "They're coming."

Colin swallowed hard. How badly he wanted to fight, yet his weak body wouldn't allow such bravery. He could only lie there, like a helpless babe. "Stay still. No matter what, don't move."

She nodded, but he could see the fear in her eyes, feel the fear in the trembling of her body.

"Down here," someone shouted, running past them with a torch in hand.

"Stay still," Colin whispered again.

Two left. Stephan and Demyan. Where were they? The thud of pounding feet interrupted the chirping of birds. The pounding stopped. Stephan and Demyan paused on the path, only feet from them.

Stephan panted, sucking in great gulps of air. But Demyan remained motionless, as if he hadn't just raced down the trail, as if he'd been there all along.

Stephan spun around, the torch he carried splashing the trees with light. "The elephant went down the trail. They're fast, but they can't run long. The animal was hit."

Colin narrowed his gaze, tilting his head ever so slightly in order to get a better view. He had to see the man; he had to put a face to the voice.

Demyan turned and Stephan's torchlight hit his features, highlighting his angular profile. Colin's heart clenched.

There was familiarity in the hook of his nose, the prominence of his chin . . . Where the hell had he seen the man before?

"Unless they didn't go by elephant," Demyan said in a deep, surreal voice of an Eastern European . . . a voice Colin knew he'd heard before.

"Dem, it makes the most sense." Stephan stabbed himself in the chest with his finger. "I'm going after the beast."

"Then go." Dem's voice was calm, too calm.

Stephan paused only a moment, then spun around and rushed after King Henry, taking the torch with him. The forest fell silent and dark. Bea's arms tightened around Colin, her breath harsh in his ear. Demyan didn't move, merely stood there, a shadow among many in the dawn. Finally, the man turned . . . toward them.

Green eyes glowed eerily in the dark. Colin's gaze riveted on those eyes. Anger roared through his body. His heart pounded so hard he was sure the man could hear the beat. He knew those eyes. He knew that voice. He knew that man.

Bea's arms quivered around him. "Can we move now, please?" she whispered.

Chapter 13

In moments, the sun would spread its glowing rays through the trees, bringing the jungle to life. In moments, the light would hit Colin and Bea. In moments, they'd be killed.

Slowly, the man named Demyan turned. Eerie green eyes glowed in the dawn. Bea sucked in a breath, shock holding her immobile. But no, those couldn't be his eyes. It was a trick, a trick of dawn. The man took a step off the trail, a step toward them. Bea shrank back, attempting to hide farther in the foliage.

Don't move. No matter what. Colin's voice repeated over and over through her head.

"Bea," he said in a low, calm voice.

But she couldn't take her gaze away from Demyan. "Yes?"

"The pistol, in my waistband. Take it out."

Her heart skipped a beat. She knew, deep down, she knew what he wanted her to do. She finally looked at him. "Colin—"

"Do it." His voice was hard, but his gaze still tracked Demyan.

Bea swallowed her retort and slipped her hand under his shirt to his warm body. Her fingers trailed over the muscles on his stomach and around to this side, until she felt the pistol. She paused only a moment and then wrapped her fingers around the cool weapon.

Her hand trembled as she pulled the pistol free. Could she do it? Could she shoot a man if she had to? Ella had, that first night in Colin's home. But she wasn't Ella. Her cousin's wife was brave, fearless. Bea was a weak Englishwoman, just as Colin believed.

Demyan's lips lifted into a small, taunting smile, just barely visible in the dim light of dawn. "I know you're here."

Bea's heart practically leapt from her chest. How? How did he know they were here? She'd been quiet, so very quiet!

"Kill him, Bea," Colin demanded.

Although his tone was soft, a shiver of shock raced over her skin. "What?" He couldn't be serious.

"Pull. The. Trigger."

Apparently, he was serious. "I—I—I can't. He's done nothing wrong." Her hands were shaking so badly, she doubted she could do much of anything, let alone be a sure shot.

Colin snatched the gun from her hands, pointed, and pulled the trigger.

The blast echoed through the forest, ringing in her ears. It happened so quickly Bea didn't have time to gasp. A flock of bright yellow birds burst from the trees and disappeared into the pink sky. Demyan staggered back, then finally collapsed to the ground.

Bea's stomach clenched. Terror mixed with shock. "Colin," she cried out, latching on to his arm. "Are you insane? You just killed him. Killed him! And he'd done nothing but threaten us. He wasn't even holding a weapon, for God's sake!" They'd throw Colin in prison and Ella would blame her!

Colin pushed himself upright, his arms quivering like a newborn colt. "Go."

Bea stiffened beside him. "What?"

His face was furious, his jaw clenched, his eyes

gleaming with something odd that Bea didn't recognize. "Run, go."

She shook her head, frantic tears stinging. She didn't understand anything at all, but she knew she couldn't leave Colin. "No. I won't leave you."

He closed his eyes for the briefest of moments, but just as quickly, he was looking at her again and that odd gleam was still there. "You have to."

"Colin, I . . ."

A rustle of leaves broke through the forest. Demyan stood like a tree sprouting from the earth. He paused for just a moment, shook his head, then stumbled toward them. Horrified, Bea could merely stare wide-eyed. He'd been shot . . . he should be dead . . . .yet he was moving forward, not a speck of blood on his body.

"Oh, dear God, he still lives," she whispered.

"Go, Bea, damn you, go!" Colin lifted his arm and pulled the trigger again. The blast exploded. Bea pressed her palms to her ringing ears, cringing. The man stumbled back, then fell to the ground. Colin must have missed the first time, but this time . . . he'd killed the man.

Tears of frustration trailed down her cheeks, stinging the scratch that had been left by the branch. But the pain was barely noticeable over the fear pumping through her veins. "Colin, please stop! You must stop!"

From the corner of her eye, she noticed something move. Bea stilled. Swallowing hard, she slowly turned her attention to Demyan. The man was standing again. Standing, as if he'd never fallen. Never been shot.

Was she dreaming? Hallucinating?

"I . . . I don't understand."

With his free hand, Colin latched on to Bea's wrist, his grip so tight it stung. "You don't understand what you're dealing with, Bea. Trust me, for God's sake, trust me. I can hold him off, at least long enough for you to escape."

He was serious, completely and utterly serious. Yet

underneath that hard gaze was something more, something that sent her pulse racing. Fear? Colin was afraid?

"Escape? No." She shook her head, frantic he'd leave her alone. Colin was the only familiar, normal thing at the moment. "No, I can't. I can't leave you. You're coming with me." She slipped her arms around Colin's chest and pulled back. He managed to tuck his feet underneath him and struggled upright.

The river. She needed to get to the river. The surge of hope gave her strength. She shuffled toward the right, remembering the direction Raj had pointed. Before she made any headway, Colin burst forward so quickly, she didn't have time to stop him. Stunned, she merely watched as the man made his way toward Demyan. Weak, he didn't get far. Only steps ahead, he collapsed, his knees hitting the ground with a thud.

"Colin! Are you insane?" As she reached for him, she glanced up. Demyan was moving toward them now . . . his wicked, glowing gaze piercing her very soul. Colin jerked forward again, nearly sending Bea to the ground.

Regaining her balance, she latched on to his arm and gave him a good shake. "Damn you! Stop! It's madness. You can't go after him. Not in your state."

Hunched over, his breathing heavy, Colin seemed deaf to her pleas. His gaze remained pinned to Demyan like a wolf after its next meal. He'd gone feral, mad, and Bea didn't know how to bring him back to sanity. Where was the laughing, obnoxious man she'd met? The man who'd do anything to keep her safe. Hadn't he whispered as much that night in Anish's hut, when she'd been half-dead?

"Blast it, Colin, what the hell do you think you're doing?" She tightened her grip and stepped in front of him, blocking Demyan from view. But Colin wasn't there in those blue eyes. Something primitive had replaced those laughing orbs. Fear shivered through her being.

"Colin?" She wrapped her arms around his neck, and

pressed her cheek to his. "Please, Colin, please. If we don't leave now, we'll die."

Breathing heavily, he slumped into her, his weight so intense that Bea stumbled back. Sweat broke out on her forehead, but she managed to keep him upright. She didn't understand why, but he wanted to fight. He was in no shape to fight. And if they stayed, if they didn't leave soon, they'd die.

Leaves rustled a warning. Demyan was moving again. Fear clawed its way into Bea's throat. She latched on to Colin's shirt, balling the material in her fist. "Please! Colin, please! I'll die if we stay. Do you want me to die?" Her voice broke as tears spilled from her eyes.

The words worked, or perhaps it was her tears. He jerked his head toward her, but his eyes were still wide and wild.

"Please, Colin. The river." She cupped his chin, forcing him to remain focused on her. "I'm taking you to the river."

She talked slowly and purposefully, as she'd seen mothers do with children. As if giving in to defeat or perhaps exhaustion, he slumped into her, the fight seeming to drain from him.

"And what do you plan on doing there?" he whispered.

He moved his legs, trying to keep up with her, but his feet were hitting hers, hindering her more than helping. His voice was normal once more; her Colin had returned.

"Stop asking questions," she grunted, tightening her arm around his waist. "Save your energy."

"You . . . don't . . ." He swallowed hard. "Want me to ask." He took in a deep, trembling breath. "Because you don't know what the . . . hell you're doing."

He was right, of course, but she couldn't just sit there and allow them to die. "I won't leave you behind, Colin. And I sure as bloody hell won't give up without a fight."

The words seemed to inspire him. With a low growl, Colin pulled away from her. Without his weight, Bea suddenly felt off balance, alone. He hunched over, his breathing rigid, a fine sheen of sweat covering his forehead. It was obvious merely standing was draining him of energy. But they didn't have time for him to recuperate.

With a sigh of frustration, she focused on Demyan. He was moving closer, crunching through the dry vegetation like King Henry. Nothing would stop the man. "Colin, please! We must hurry!"

Colin turned and pulled the trigger. Demyan staggered back and collapsed to the ground, his body hidden by weeds. But he was still there. And apparently, he'd regain his feet. Somehow . . . God, she didn't understand. Her mind spun, her vision growing blurry with confusion. Only fear and instinct urged her to run.

Colin grabbed her arm and pushed her forward. "Go."

Bea stumbled through the forest, having just enough time to glance back and make sure Colin followed.

"Go!" he demanded, catching up to move beside her.

She ignored his surly tone and burst through the brush, the bag thumping against her hip. Branches snagged her clothing before snapping like bones breaking. Heat shimmered off the leaves, dew evaporating into the brilliant morning. There was enough light to see now, enough light to easily find them. Colin panted beside her, tripping more than he was running. He couldn't go much farther. She couldn't last much longer. Her lungs already burned with the need for rest.

Bea glanced back. Demyan was gone. Her heart jumped in her chest. Where was he?

She latched on to Colin's arm and pulled, urging him forward. "The river. We'll go to the river." She knew, just knew the water was ahead. Over their panting, she swore she could hear the soft gurgle of a river whispering through the air, calling out safety.

The ground suddenly gave way. Bea's ankles twisted and a yelp escaped. Their bottoms hit the slope and then they bounced into the air. Bea felt as if she floated, and for a mere second, no ground was underfoot. Then Colin's hand ripped from hers and she was falling, falling into the gray dawn. A scream slipped from her lips. She had only a moment to notice the brown water below before her body hit the surface with a splash.

Bea.

Dear God, he had to get to Bea before the monster did.

Colin flung his arms above his head, but he felt like he was swimming through mud. Every slight movement pulled at his muscles, stretching, aching. The current tugged at his body, dragging him down farther . . . farther . . .

He would not drown. Damn it. He would not drown and leave Bea to fight on her own. He would not abandon her as he'd abandoned his mother. With a growl, he fought against the pull, against his weakness, one monster's face spurring him upward.

Just above the water, sunlight glinted like gold, precious and surreal . . . so close. He jerked his head left, then right. Bea. Where the hell was Bea? Fear pulsed through his body. The water was murky, the light barely adding to the visibility. What if she'd drowned? What if Demyan had gotten to her . . .

Gritting his teeth, he moved his legs, struggling to reach the top. Bea was a great swimmer. She'd be there, waiting for him. He had to believe that. He burst through the surface, immediately sucking in a gulp of air. Frantic, he spun around, looking for her. His hat floated on the water next to him. No Bea.

The sound of sputtering came from behind. A sound as beautiful as angels singing. He turned. She was there, only feet away, coughing and flailing her arms, trying to fight the current and reach him at the same time.

"Colin!" Bea cried out.

Relief sank into his gut, nearly dragging him back down into the water. "Bea."

Smart girl that she was, she'd latched on to a branch and was reaching out for him. Colin gripped her hand, her fingers cold, her grip slippery. It was the second time she'd pulled him to safety. Clumps of wet hair fell around her face. She looked beautiful. He looped his arm around her narrow waist and pulled her close. Part of him wanted to hold her forever.

His heart slammed against hers. He took only a moment to savor the feel of her safe in his arms. Finally, he pulled back and scanned the bank. Just through the branches, across the river, a shadow shifted. Demyan on the cliff, looking down at them. Anger scalded Colin's insides, burning a path up through his body. He closed his eyes and took in a deep breath. How badly Colin wanted to go after him. How badly Colin wanted to kill the man.

"Who is he?"

Forced back into reality, Colin opened his eyes. Bea was watching him, but how the hell did he explain? "Let's get on dry land."

He glanced back. Demyan was gone.

"Colin?"

It would take the man some time to find a way across the river. Still, they had only moments to rest. Colin took Bea's hand and pulled her toward the shore. Deep down he'd known. He'd known Demyan was the man he'd been searching for, but dear God, he had no idea what the man was capable of.

Colin's feet sank into thick, brown mud, slowing their progress. His hat had caught on a branch. He grabbed it, then latched on to Bea's arm and helped her up the bank. Reaching solid ground, they collapsed onto a carpet of wet leaves, lying side by side.

He couldn't close his eyes without seeing Demyan's face. Colin's entire body trembled, his heart racing so fast he feared it might explode. All the while, his mind warred with his emotions. Even now, more than ever, he knew he had to get Bea away from Demyan. He needed to get her to safety. But guilt and sorrow demanded retribution. He pounded his fists against the damp earth. He wanted to find the man. He wanted to put a bullet through his black heart. To see him suffer . . .

"I lost the bag. It was too heavy, I couldn't hold on to it."

He glanced at Bea. He'd almost forgotten she was there. "It was nothing."

She turned on her side to look at him. "It was everything we had!"

"It was nothing," he yelled.

Bea flinched and fell silent.

He closed his eyes and pinched the bridge of his nose. He shouldn't have yelled at her, but damn it, didn't she realize the bag was nothing compared to what they could lose? Didn't she realize what kind of danger they were in?

"We can't stay long. He'll find a way across the river."

Bea nodded as she sat upright. Her white shirt clung indecently to her chest. Her hair, wet and dripping, made muddy puddles on the dirt. Christ, he was an idiot for even noticing her state of undress when they were in such dire circumstances.

"Who is he?" she whispered.

Colin raked his wet hair back and shook the excess water from his fingers. He hated the fear he heard in her voice. Hated that he hadn't a clue as to how to protect her. Silently, he stared up into the green canopy above. He didn't want to talk about the man. Talking would only bring back painful memories he'd worked so hard to bury. But he knew he had to give her something.

"The man who killed my mother."

Stillness stretched taut until Colin wondered if Bea had heard him. He turned his head toward her. Shock and disbelief warred in her gaze. She'd heard him; she was merely too horrified to respond.

"He what?" she finally replied.

Colin looked away, taking in a deep, calming breath. Even now, the memories were too fresh, too painful. "He killed my mother. I was ten when he appeared. He wanted me. My mother held him off as long as she could. Enough time for me to escape. I haven't seen him since. But it's him. I'd never forget those eyes."

He was proud of himself for keeping his voice so calm. Bea wouldn't have to know how afraid he'd been as a lad, how angry he was even now. How every night, he dreamt . . .

He felt her fingers slip around his, her hand soft and warm and comforting in a way he would have never expected. Colin stiffened. He swallowed hard, unsure if he wanted her touch or not. He was so damn used to being alone.

"He came for Ella, too," he whispered, wanting to take the attention away from him. As much as he craved her touch, it felt awkward, unjustified. He hadn't been comforted in years; he didn't need it now.

"Why?" Bea shook her head. "Why does he want you?"

He pulled his hand away. "Bea." Struggling upright, he looked directly into her amber eyes. "You know. Deep down, you know there's something . . . *different* about me and Ella."

Her brows snapped together as she frowned. "I don't understand."

"You do." He couldn't believe the woman didn't know. She wouldn't have asked him to heal the elephant, and she couldn't have spent months with Ella and not have noticed.

But Bea stood and squeezed the water from her hair, avoiding his gaze. "No. I don't. We should follow the river. Raj said to follow the river." She started downstream.

"Bea." Colin stumbled to his feet. "Bea, wait." What was wrong with her? Why did he have the feeling she was trying to escape? She'd been the one to ask about Demyan, after all. She needed to know what the man was capable of.

"Colin, we must hurry. You said as much just moments ago." She didn't bother to look back as she said this. Haughty, cold Bea was in charge once more.

Angry and annoyed, Colin hurried his steps and latched on to her arm. "Look at me."

She turned, her lips tight with annoyance. "What?"

"You saw him, you saw him regain his feet after I'd shot him."

She shrugged. "You missed."

He shook her with just enough force to get her attention. "No, Bea, I never miss." That was a lie, but really, he'd never met a more stubborn woman.

She jerked her arm away and started picking through the scraggly brush that grew thick along the river. "So you're saying he's immune to bullets?"

Colin stomped after her, his boots crushing thick fronds. "He's immune to death."

She stopped, but didn't look back. Sunlight pierced the thick canopy above and highlighted her hair, making it glow. "Impossible." It was a whispered word, barely audible over the rustle of leaves. One word and it embedded deep in his skin like a burr.

Colin scanned the woods, his heart jumping with each slight snap of a branch. "Is it?"

She turned, and surprisingly, her face was emotionless. He'd been expecting fear, perhaps even anger, but not calm. "Colin, I don't have time for such nonsense. In fact, I've been thinking, and we should go straight to Leo and Ella, forget the statue."

Colin gripped her arm, just above the elbow. He didn't give a damn about the statue. "Damn it, Bea. I know this is difficult to understand, but—"

She tried to pull away, but he wouldn't let her go. "Difficult? You're being ridiculous. A man who doesn't die, a statue that has powers? Do you even hear yourself speaking? It's mad. Completely and utterly mad."

"I know."

He'd let his feelings sway his emotions before, but he wouldn't now. Bea would hear the truth whether she could handle it or not. She seemed flustered and surprised by his honest response. Her brows snapped together and she shook her head. "Fine, if you wish to find this temple, then we shall. But I won't believe in this nonsense."

"Bea, I'm not telling you this so you'll agree to travel to the temple. You have to believe."

She sighed, her shoulders sinking. "Why?"

There was an exhaustion, a frustration in her eyes that tugged at his heart. "Because if you don't believe, you underestimate your enemy."

She laughed and tucked a wet lock behind her ear. "My enemy? I have no enemies." She frowned. "At least, I didn't until I arrived here."

He started forward, dragging her along. They needed space, space between them and Demyan. "You've always had enemies, but until now they were focused on Leo."

Her face paled as she tripped beside him. "What do you mean?"

Finally, she was listening. Finally, she'd grown serious. "Whether you believe in these strange powers or not, your family has always been deeply involved in the recovery of the statues. That ring around your neck . . ."

Hesitantly, she reached up, touching the ribbon that held Leo's ring.

He used her attention to press the subject further. "That ring is supposed to open a map, a map in Ella's stolen necklace. That ring has been in your family for God knows how long."

She was silent for one long moment, but in her eyes he could see her mind working, attempting to process a ridiculous situation. "The boat," she whispered. "It's what you were discussing at the boat when Leo and Ella left."

He nodded.

"But you spoke about blood. What did you mean?"

He cupped her elbow and drew her to the left, finding a natural path through the vegetation, made by animals. "Myth says you have to be of a certain family, a certain blood."

"And Leo is?"

Grimly, he glanced at her. "And *you* are."

She shook her head, stumbling beside him. "I . . . I have no power. I'm just . . . me."

"The power's in your blood, your heritage. Mine and Ella's powers are on the surface, but yours and Leo's . . . its underneath, hidden, silent. You're more powerful than you realize, Bea."

"No." She shook her head, her face growing pinched again. "If you want my help, that's fine. But enough of this nonsense. I'll go with you to this temple, I'll even let you use the ring, but I will not believe that a statue holds power."

She jerked away from him and started forward on her own. With each step she took, Colin's frustration mounted. "And what about me?"

She paused under a banyan tree, its sprawling roots surrounding her as if she were merely a tiny fairy, easily crushed in the palm of a hand. "What about you?"

He settled his hands on his waist. How badly he'd love to crawl under the shade of one of those roots and rest. "You know, Bea. You've seen it, you've felt it. You asked me to help the elephant, for God's sake."

She swallowed hard.

He jumped over a root and started toward her, annoyance spurring him forward and giving him strength. How long he'd tried to keep his secret, and now that he was admitting his powers, she didn't believe him. "The way I can heal."

She climbed over a tree root with an elegance that grudgingly impressed him. She was running away from him and from the truth he was forcing her to deal with.

Before she could escape, he latched on to her arm, tighter than he meant to, feeling the insane need for her to believe. She glanced at him, the surprise evident in her gaze. "I can heal, Bea. You know it as well as I or you wouldn't have asked me to heal King Henry."

She jerked away.

He moved forward. She stepped back. "And what about Ella? Have you never noticed how well she can control animals?"

She shrugged, her gaze darting around the area, as if she was frantically looking for an escape. "So? She's good with animals. Many are."

He chuckled, a harsh sound. "Right."

She slipped past him, moving around the tree and finding the path. "We have more important things to discuss."

"Unbelievable," Colin snapped. He followed her, hurrying to catch up. "Ella can control animals, sense their emotions."

She shook her head, but didn't look back. "That's . . . that's . . ."

He grabbed her arm and spun her around to face him. Her dark locks spread out, flinging water droplets through the air. "It's the truth. And the truth is, I can heal people. I don't know how, or why, but there it is. And more importantly, the truth is there is a man hunting us right now who wants nothing more than to see us dead."

Chapter 14

Heal people? Speak to animals? Utterly and completely ridiculous. Grandmother had taught her to be a rational person. Rationality had saved her many times in the past; why should she start believing in nonsense now? She would not, *could* not believe that there were actually people with strange, mythical powers. Yet how could she deny the possibility?

Colin held a branch high and Bea ducked underneath, barely aware of the narrow dirt path she followed. Barely aware of the dried vines and limbs that clung to her trousers and scratched at her legs as if they were begging for reprieve from their dreary, horrifyingly hot life. Through her lashes, she watched Colin. His gaze was partially blocked underneath the brim of his hat, but his lips were set into a grim line that spoke of worry and annoyance. Guilt washed through her. He'd wanted her to admit the truth, but she hadn't been able to. Who was she to question the very man who had saved her life more than once?

He killed my mother.

Those softly spoken words whispered through her mind. She'd had no idea. How could she? A shiver traveled across her skin. Was it possible? Could Demyan truly be such a monster? Could he truly have such powers? And was he hunting them even now?

Bea dropped her gaze as unwanted memories flashed to mind. Ella and her affinity with animals. Why, on the boat from England to France, the gulls literally perched on her shoulders. When they'd ridden the camels through India, even though she'd never seen one, Ella had seemed at ease on the bizarre creatures while Bea had barely been able to stay atop.

And then there was Demyan. She shivered just thinking about the man and his eerie green eyes. Perhaps it was a trick of dawn? And Colin . . . surely he must have missed when he'd pulled the trigger. Yes, Ella and Demyan were easy to explain away. But Colin and his abilities to heal . . . he was a mystery that she wasn't sure she wanted to solve. How could she possibly explain the situation with Raj? The boy had been covered in blood, yet hadn't a scratch. And King Henry had a bullet wound, yet miraculously regained his feet. It didn't make sense.

Colin paused in the middle of the trail, just at the forest's edge, where the trees met a field. There, still in shade, he placed his hands on his slim hips. "I don't see it." Even with a frown marring his face, he was ridiculously handsome. Bea looked away, annoyed with the way her heart fluttered at the mere sight of him.

They were surrounded by brush. Scraggly brush that pulled and caught her clothing and tore her hair from the twine she'd used to tie her damp locks back. Yes, she'd focus on her discomfort instead of the man before her. The heat, so incredibly hot that it actually felt heavy.

Bea's clothing had dried, but the material was becoming damp all over again. Sweat slipped down her back, between her shoulder blades until it soaked her shirt and made the material cling to her torso. With a long sigh, she swiped her forehead with the back of her hand. Never, in her entire life, had she ever experienced such intensity. Everything about India was intense. The food, the weather, the colors. Compared to Britain, where everything was gray, it was overwhelming.

"A needle in a haystack," Colin grumbled. "We need to find shelter, find somewhere to hide and rest."

His shirt was as dirty as hers. His hair, damp with sweat, curled at the ends. Yet with his hands on his hips, he looked like a warlord. There, even under the protection of the trees, the sun beat down relentlessly, the heat almost visible, shimmering up from the dry ground. But he didn't seem affected by the weather. Certainly not as affected as she.

Bea's stomach growled, clenching with hunger. She cringed, pressing her hands to her midsection. Frankly, she wanted to do nothing more than sit for a good hour or two . . . or three. She shifted, the boots Anish had given her rubbing against the raw skin on her heels, stinging. How she wished for the soft slippers she'd first worn.

"Colin, please, I can't take another step."

He sighed and turned toward her. "I know. Come, get out of the brush before you're eaten by fire ants."

She didn't bother to check, but scurried through the leaves until she burst into the open field. Cool air swept across the plain, a sweet and welcome relief from the humidity that seemed to hover in the jungle, trapped by the foliage. Bea closed her eyes and took in a deep breath.

"Are you all right?"

She nodded, focusing on him. "I suppose I will be when we find shade and water." At least, she hoped she'd be all right. But as the trees wavered before her and her head pounded with each thump of her heart, she began to wonder.

Colin took off his hat and placed it atop her head. The brim blocked the midafternoon sun, but it wasn't enough.

"Good, because we . . ." His gaze focused over her shoulder, his voice trailing off.

Fear tingled along her spine, and for a moment she wondered if the fire ants had found her. What was he looking at?

A jackal? A tiger? Dear Lord, she wasn't sure she wanted to know what was behind her. "Colin, what is it?"

He didn't respond.

Slowly, she turned, her gaze quickly scanning the wavering wheat. She was so intent on finding a threat that she almost missed the massive stone temple that jutted from the field and rose into the blue sky.

"Heavens," she whispered. "We found it. Anish was right."

A heady sense of relief and shock swept through her, as heavy as the heat in the air. Her mind spun, unable to process the structure before her. It was the most amazing thing she'd ever seen. A piece of Heaven in the midst of a dirt field. The castles in Scotland were nothing compared to the artistic splendor before her.

Yellow sandstone spires inlaid with brilliant white marble reached for the sky. A few columns had fallen and crumbled to their demise, pulled down by time and the brown vines that twisted and curled, snaking around the temple. Still, it was a beautiful building, fit for a king.

"Am I imagining it?"

Colin didn't laugh as she'd expected. "No."

Just as quickly as the awe came, it was replaced with a sense of overwhelming despair. "It's . . . it's massive. It'll take days to search. How will we find anything?"

"I don't know, but I suppose we should start." Colin didn't wait for her, but moved through the field, sending grasshoppers flittering into the sky.

Bea sighed loud and long. With no other choice, she trudged after him. Who knew what beastly animals would be lurking inside the shadows of the building. It'd take days to go through the entire place. They didn't have days. Still, perhaps the stone walls would keep them cool. It certainly couldn't be hotter in there than out here. But really, what did Colin expect to find? She feared he'd once again be gravely disappointed.

A grasshopper landed on her shirt. Bea took off Colin's

hat and swatted at the tiny beast. The air practically vibrated with their buzzing cry. Unfortunately, she'd seen few butterflies since she'd arrived. Most likely it was too bloody hot for the delicate beauties. But the grasshoppers were everywhere.

"Colin, we must be reasonable about this," she shouted over the cry of insects.

He chuckled, but didn't look back. "Of course. Reasonable Bea. A person can't possibly have powers."

She rolled her eyes heavenward and replaced the hat. "I thought we were no longer discussing that subject?"

He held his arms wide. "You were sick, I made you better."

She hastened her steps, attempting to catch up to him. "You're saying you can cure people? Bring them back from death? You realize how mad that sounds?" It was ridiculous, so why then was she actually eager to hear his answer?

"No, I can't bring people back to life. Once they're dead, they're dead." He finally stopped and faced her. His gaze pierced hers, stealing her breath with its intensity. "Come, Bea. Surely you've noticed."

She brushed past him, ignoring the unease that tingled up her spine. "I don't want to discuss it."

"Why? Why does it frighten you?"

She forced herself to laugh. "It doesn't frighten me."

She could hear his hurried steps crunching the weeds as he came after her. "I think it does."

She had to resist the urge to run, to cover her ears with her hands like a child not wishing to hear that fairies weren't real. "Don't be ridiculous."

"Bea." Colin's fingers bit into her arm, drawing her to a stop. "Why does it scare you?"

Why? Why did it scare her? Because he was right, it did. Hesitating only a moment, she turned and looked into his eyes, truly looked for signs of madness. Could it be true? Could Ella and Colin have powers? Could Demyan? She couldn't . . . she wouldn't believe he could . . .

Colin's thumb rubbed the sensitive skin of her wrist. "Why, Bea? Why are you so afraid?"

She pulled away, unable to think when he touched her like that. "Demyan, my grandfather, my cousin Henry, men so evil they'd kill their own families. If I believe you have powers, then I have to believe they do as well. I can't believe that. I can't. It's too much, Colin."

He sighed and pulled her close and blast it all if she didn't sink into his hard body. She needed his comfort, if only for a moment, and even the stifling heat couldn't keep her away from his warm embrace.

"My own grandfather, my own cousin . . . they tried to kill Leo. Would they have come for me next?"

He didn't respond, but he didn't need to. She knew the answer. Bea turned her head, pressing her face beneath his chin, the place that held his scent. "And all for a statue that has supposed powers."

He rubbed her back in slow, circular motions as if they had all the time in the world. As if they weren't standing out in the open, in the middle of a field, being chased by demons.

"All right," he said, his voice rumbling through his chest. "We won't speak of it again."

She sniffed, feeling the sting of tears, but grateful for his understanding. "Thank you."

All too soon, he clasped her upper arms and drew back. "Now, shall we search that temple, or would you rather just leave?"

She looked up into his tanned face, trying to read the truth behind his question. Did he want to stay? Would he resent her if she said no? Her gaze slid to the temple, sitting there like a diamond amid a mound of coal, just waiting to be plucked.

Blast, if a thrill of adventure didn't sweep through her. The same sensation that had propelled her into saying yes to the trip to India and look where that had gotten her. What was wrong with her? Why couldn't she be happy with what she had instead of always wanting more?

Still, she couldn't seem to stop herself from responding, "No, of course not. We're already here, we should at least look."

"You're sure?"

No. She wasn't. Yet she nodded.

He released his hold. "All right. Let's get this over with."

They started through the weeds once more, but this time together. For the few minutes it took to reach the temple, Colin didn't say a word. Bea slid him a glance under the brim of her hat. Was he eager to reach the temple? To find answers? Would he put her safety on the line in order to find the treasure? Why not, everyone else had. Her grandfather, her cousin Henry, even Leo and Ella. If Demyan found them once more, would Colin forget his revenge for the good of their safety?

Colin paused at the bottom of the shallow steps leading to the main building. "It's even more impressive than I realized." His intense gaze scanned every inch. Bea couldn't imagine him being impressed with anything, but he seemed genuinely interested in this old building. "Doesn't look like many looters have gotten to it. Amazing."

Bea tilted her head back to take in the enormity of the monument. Banyan trees wrapped around the building, clasping on to the yellow stone like lovers embracing. Inlaid into the stone was pure white marble, forming a variety of swirling designs that sparkled and glowed in the setting sun. A large round temple stood in the middle, while plateaus of columns were scattered around the perimeter. Who would believe that it had once been even more impressive than it was now?

Colin snatched his hat from Bea's head, plopped it on his own, and climbed the shallow steps. Bea hesitated, glancing around her. She felt as if they were invading someone's home. But the field lay empty and barren. Only statues of gods long forgotten were there to glare down at them.

"You coming?" Colin glanced back.

"Of course."

He pulled the knife from the sheath attached to his thigh and hacked through the thick vines covering a dark doorway. As Bea reached the top step, he disappeared inside.

"Colin! Wait." Bea stepped cautiously into the building.

The musky scent of dust and age tickled her nose. Bea sneezed, the sound echoing against the stone walls. Just barely visible through the dim light that managed to filter through the cracks, she could make out Colin's form ahead.

Bea sniffled and stepped over a thick vine that had found its way through the walls and lay dormant, like a sleeping python across the stone floor. A soft squeak rent the air. Bea froze, her heart jumping into her throat.

"What was—"

The squeak sounded again.

She spun around, but could see nothing. With her heart thundering in her chest, Bea turned back toward the tunnel where she'd last seen Colin. Freshly disturbed dust floated on a beam of sunlight that sliced through the open doorway, but Colin was nowhere to be seen.

"Colin?" her soft voice whispered down the corridor.

No response came. Frantic fear clawed at her lungs, choking the air from her throat.

"Colin?" she cried out louder.

High-pitched screeches answered her call. Dark shadows darted toward her, wings beating against the air. Bea gasped and dropped to the floor as the bats disappeared into a cloud of black outside.

"Oh dear God," she whispered, stumbling to her feet. A warm promising whisper caressed her skin, an odd sensation that set her mind at ease.

"What is it?" Colin asked.

Bea spun around. Colin stood in the corridor. Tears of

relief sprang to her eyes and she had to resist the urge to throw her arms around him. He hadn't disappeared, he hadn't left her. "Nothing. I . . . I thought you'd . . ."

He took a step forward, looking so bloody beautiful she wanted to memorize every inch of his face. "What?"

She clasped her hands tightly together. "I thought you'd left me." It was an honest mistake. After all, it was obvious the man cared more about the damn treasure he hoped to find than some woman he considered a spoiled lady.

He sighed and moved toward her, his boots thumping against the floor and sending puffs of dust into the air. "Bea, I swore I'd protect you. That includes not leaving you alone in an abandoned temple in the middle of nowhere."

"I know," she whispered, glancing up at him through her lashes. Of course he wouldn't leave her. Leo would murder him.

He held out his hand. "Come on."

She hesitated only a moment then rushed forward and grabbed his fingers. In his defense, he didn't smile at her obvious unease. He merely led her down the hall.

"It's not funny," she mumbled.

He slid her a glance. "Of course not."

But there was definite amusement in his gaze and she was thrilled to see it there, even if it was at her expense. Their shoes tapped against stone, echoing mournfully like the heartbeat of lost souls. Bea shivered and moved closer to Colin's warmth. "Who do you suppose lived here?"

Colin shrugged. "A king or commander. It's built to their gods."

"The castles back home are nothing compared to this," she whispered.

The amazing detail of scrolls, plants, animals, and gods carved into the rock had to have been done by the most delicate of hands. She reached out, trailing her fingers along a wall, rough stone weathered with age. Tiny pieces crumbled to the floor.

"It's beautiful and a bit frightening," she admitted. "Why do you think Anish sent us here? What does he want us to find?"

Colin shook his head. "I haven't the slightest."

The tunnel flared into an open room. Colin swept inside like he owned the place, like they'd been invited to bloody tea. Bea followed more hesitantly, her wide eyes scanning the large room. If he wasn't going to be cautious, she would.

A high dome rose into the darkness above. A curved window pierced the stone on each side of the room, lending enough light to see the mystical beasts carved in the pale walls. Bea followed the trail of animals up to the ceiling.

"Heavens," she whispered.

But Colin ignored the artwork and moved to the middle. With his gaze pinned to the ceiling, he slowly turned. "I don't get it. What are we missing? What are we supposed to find?"

Bea shrugged, wishing she could help, but more interested in the statues that lined the perimeter of the room. Naked, marble women stood on pedestals. Lots of naked women. Their arms were turned in delicate positions as if they'd been dancing when they'd been frozen in time.

"Talk about a needle in a haystack." Colin clasped his hands behind his head and sighed, staring at the ceiling as if looking for answers.

But Bea could barely take her gaze from the feminine statues. She wanted to be embarrassed, yet she couldn't find anything wrong with the amazing detail in their frozen faces. There was something magical about those women, something lifelike in the way they stood around the room, the way they were posed, as if pausing in action.

She started toward one of the statues when something small fluttered across her vision. A familiar movement that sent her heart racing. Bea jerked her head toward the right. An orange and black butterfly floated on the still breeze, his long, narrow wings softly moving up and down, barely moving yet he stayed aloft. She'd never seen the species before.

"Oh my," she whispered.

"What?"

Bea didn't bother answering but raced across the room, following the insect. This was why she'd traveled to India. Why she'd risked her life and reputation. The butterfly landed on a vine that sprouted from the walls. What was he doing here, of all places, in a dim and dusty cavern of a temple? Bea paused, afraid if she moved, he'd fly away. Instead, he crawled farther into those thick vines, disappearing from sight. Her heart fluttering nervously, she reached out to brush aside the vegetation when she caught sight of something blue. She moved a leaf. Blue paint on stone wall.

"Colin," she called out.

Not willing to wait, Bea wrapped her fingers around the thick, heavy vines and pulled. A painting emerged. A man sat cross-legged on a lotus, barely visible, the painting so old and faded. Her butterfly was nowhere to be seen.

"Brahma," Colin said softly from just behind her.

The god that Anish had spoken about. Bea spun around. Colin was close, so close her breasts touched his chest, but Colin was staring at the painting, completely unaware of their intimate position.

"Who is—"

Colin reached over her shoulder, his fingers brushing softly against the stone, as if he were caressing a woman. "A god. One of the gods on the statue. God of creation. The same god on Ella's necklace that Henry stole."

Her heart thundered in her ears. What he was saying, it meant something, didn't it? So why wasn't he more excited? "What does it mean? Have we found the treasure?"

The left corner of his mouth rose into a crooked grin, and finally, he looked at her. "No, it's not here, but it means we're damn close."

His happiness was contagious and she found the insane

desire to laugh. His lips only inches from hers, he finally seemed to notice their precarious position. Slowly, Bea lifted her gaze from his mouth, to his eyes.

He was staring at her so intensely that she felt the heat to her toes. He was going to kiss her. She knew it, in that moment she knew without a doubt he was going to lower his head to hers. Giving in to temptation, she allowed her lashes to drift down and leaned up on tiptoe.

A soft neigh broke through the heady sensual cloud Colin had spun. Bea sucked in a breath as her eyes opened. Had she imagined the noise? Colin turned, his back to her. Apparently, she hadn't.

"What was that?" Bea asked, peeking over his shoulder.

"Horses." He took a few steps forward, pulling the knife from the sheath on his thigh. "Looks like we've got company."

Bea's shoulders sank. Their attackers had bloody bad timing. "Not again," Bea complained, slumping back against the stone wall.

A soft groan rent the air, then the patter of pebbles falling against stones. Suddenly, the wall was gone. Bea tensed, but it was too late. There was nothing to support her weight. She swiped her arms wide, attempting to latch on to the vines, but missed.

With a yelp, she fell backward into the darkness.

Chapter 15

Colin shifted the knife from hand to hand, taking comfort in the feel of the hard, bone hilt. The need for retribution coursed through his body sweet and hot. This was what he'd been waiting for. This was why he'd traveled the world. This was the fantasy that had kept him up at night. "Come on, you bastards."

He started forward when a scream interrupted his progress. Colin spun around. The wall was gone, Bea was gone. A dark, gaping hole remained. He paused for one brief moment, shock holding him immobile.

"Son of a . . ." He rushed forward and placed his hands on either side of the crumbling wall. Peering into the darkness, he could see nothing. Revenge forgotten, his heart slammed against his chest, so loud it practically echoed against the dark cavern. "Bea?"

"In here, Colin," she called out from somewhere slightly below.

"Are you hurt?"

"No, I'm fine."

Relief made his knees weak. "Stay there, I'm coming." He latched on to a vine hanging from the ceiling and gave it a quick jerk to see if it would hold.

"Please hurry," Bea said in a steady voice that sent an unwanted grin to his lips.

Always feigning courage, but she had to be cringing in there. She was brave in a way even she didn't realize. She didn't deserve this life, the kind of life he'd led since he was a child, the kind of life he would always lead. On the go, running, hiding, killing before they killed you.

His mind was set in that moment. He'd get her out of there, drop her off in Leo's capable hands, and leave her in peace. "I'm coming, keep quiet, we don't know—"

"Stay where you are," a familiar English voice echoed down the corridor.

Colin resisted the urge to curse. His fingers tightened on the vine, anger and frustration boiling beneath his skin. Too damn late. Always too damn late. Flashes of light danced across the walls, illuminating faded paintings of gods and goddesses from long ago. The light wasn't close enough to find Bea, but it was enough to get a peek of the hidden room. High ceiling, stone walls, broken columns. Bea would have plenty of places to hide.

Please hide, Bea.

"Turn slowly, arms up," the familiar voice snapped out.

Colin slipped the dagger into his shirtsleeve and turned. The tip of the blade slid down his forearm, slicing open the skin, but he didn't dare flinch. Five men stood in front of him, torches in hand, the light highlighting their lean, fierce faces. Only one man was familiar. He wasn't surprised to see Stephan again. He was surprised that Demyan wasn't with him. Where the hell was the Demon?

Forcing down his disgust, Colin smiled a slow, easy grin, feigning an ease he sure as hell didn't feel. "Well, we meet again, how lovely and serendipitous."

"Quiet," Stephan demanded, shuffling forward and separating himself from the four natives he'd either hired or forced into working for him. Most likely forced.

Colin's gaze slid to the man he needed to worry about.

Stephan's steps were slow and unhurried but not because of
arrogant assuredness. No, it was obvious the man was near
exhaustion. Gone was the charming gent they'd met at camp.
This man looked beaten down, his clothing torn and dirty,
his energy dissipated. It would have been amusing if Colin
hadn't been outnumbered. Although Stephan looked half-
dead, the other men were fit and young.

Even as he kept Stephan's gaze, Colin searched for a
nearby weapon, something other than the damn knife he had
in his shirtsleeve. "Really, there was no reason to track us
down merely to thank us for our hospitality."

Stephan narrowed those beady eyes. "You are quite annoying. Like a fly . . . sneaky, but once caught, easy to kill."

Colin sighed. "Well, that's no way to show your appreciation."

His guests didn't respond, merely edged closer, jackals
after a sure kill. Colin's entire body stiffened, preparing for
the attack. He was outnumbered, but it didn't matter as long
as he kept them occupied until Bea found a way to escape.

"Where is he?" Colin asked, lowering his arm so the knife
slid down his sleeve, the hilt coming to rest in the palm of
his hand. If he took out Stephan, most likely the natives would
run. He could tell by the shifting of their eyes and the hesitancy in their steps they didn't want to be here any more than
he wanted them here. No, they were here for the money. Take
out their source of income and they'd leave.

Stephan paused for a brief moment, the torch highlighting his grim features. "Who?"

"The evil bastard you work for. Demyan, I believe you
called him."

Stephan tilted his chin high, recognition and annoyance
working across his face. "I haven't the slightest idea what
you're talking about."

So, there was dissention in the ranks. If they were fighting among themselves, he might be able to use that to his
advantage. Still, he had to know where Demyan was. He

didn't believe for a moment the bastard had let Stephan escape his clutches. No, the devil's spawn was lurking somewhere nearby. He could feel it in his bones . . . the evilness heavy and as suffocating as the heat.

"Now it's my turn. Where is it?" Stephan asked.

Colin curled his fingers, moving the knife down his hand. Inch, by wretched inch. "What would that be?"

"Playing dumb?" Stephan gave the natives a quick nod. Immediately, they lifted their arms, wicked pistols gleaming in the torchlight.

Well, hell.

Colin's relief faded as quickly as it had come.

Pistols against a damn knife. Not exactly a fair fight. He'd be dead before he could release the dagger. He should have known they'd be at least smart enough to come prepared. But still, if his eyes hadn't deceived him, their arms were trembling.

Stephan handed one of the men the torch and crossed his arms over his chest. "You know exactly what we're looking for."

Colin tilted his head ever so slightly, straining to hear movement beyond. Where the hell was Bea? He prayed she was hiding, or at the very least trying to find a way to escape.

A slow smirk worked its way across Stephan's face. "Where is she?"

Colin blinked his eyes wide with innocence. "Who?"

Stephan chuckled. "The girl." Stephan started an easy, unhurried pace down the narrow corridor. "You think we don't know who she is?"

Colin stiffened, panic flaring bitterly cold through his body. He'd been right. Leo and Ella had been right. Bea had been in danger all along and they'd brought her here, where the danger was worse, more real. He'd brought her here. Into the lion's den.

The men moved closer. "We know what family she belongs to. We know what she's capable of. Now, hand me the girl and you can go. We don't need you."

Colin's fingers fisted, his lip curling into a snarl. He had to resist the urge to reach for the arrogant bastard. Shit. They knew. They knew they needed Leo or Bea to open the map. But how? How had they uncovered the truth? His father had been the only person to know and he'd taken the truth to his grave.

"We don't need you."

Stephan's words flitted through Colin's mind. If they didn't need him, that meant they had someone else with an ability like him and Ella. Who? Demyan?

Stephan shook his head, holding his arms wide. The man's confidence was coming back fast, perhaps knowing he suddenly had the upper hand. "Come now, we know she's here."

Of course they were going to go after Bea. She'd be easier to catch. Hell, maybe they hadn't been after Leo at all. Perhaps all this time it'd been Bea they wanted.

Bea.

She was in more danger than they'd realized. His heart stopped. His mind screamed for her to run. *Run!* Damn it, if only she could read his mind as Ella could read Leo's.

Swallowing hard, Colin forced the words to come out calm and unhurried. "Don't know where she is, I'm afraid. She became a nuisance, I left her behind."

Stephan chuckled, an annoying sound that grated on his already frayed nerves. "Really, then who were you talking to when we arrived?"

"Myself?"

The man frowned. Growing impatient, he tapped his booted foot. "Hand her to me now, or you die."

Colin shrugged. "I've heard that before, and as you can see, I still live. The threat has sort of lost its meaning."

Stephan started forward in a flurry of irritated movements. "Well, allow me to make it more meaningful." He nodded toward the natives. They stepped closer, their pistols trained on Colin's head. He had only a split second to act.

Colin shoved his dagger into the sheath on his thigh and,

at the same moment, jumped through the black hole where
Bea had disappeared. A blast rang out, hitting the wall only
inches from his head. A piece of rock flew through the air
and landed on the floor, right before Colin hit the ground
with a thud. His hat fell away, rolling across the floor like
tumbleweed. He jumped to his feet.

"Bea!" Colin whispered furiously into the dark.

There was no response.

"Damn you, Bea! Where are you?" He moved through
the inkiness, his arms outstretched like a blind person.

"Bea, where—" His foot hit something hard, propelling
him forward.

His arms swung wide as he attempted to regain his balance. Unable to hold himself upright, he fell to his knees, his
palms flattened to the ground. His muscles flexed, the cut
on his arm throbbing. He had no time for an injury. Colin
gritted his teeth, and stumbled upright.

"Bea, where the hell are you?"

Torchlight filled the room, shimmering across the yellowed stone and bringing the walls to life. A variety of
marble statues were scattered around the place as if to keep
guard. Some had toppled over, their heads and arms missing. Colin darted behind one of those gods, his mind spinning furiously fast. It wasn't the first dire situation he'd
found himself, but it was the first time he'd had to worry
about someone else.

"Come, do you truly think you can hide?" Stephan called.

"I can try," Colin muttered softly.

The light came closer as they stepped into the room. In
the soft orb of light they provided, he could see high stone
walls disappearing into a ceiling of darkness. The area was
large, but not that large. They'd find him soon enough. And
unless she'd found a way out, they'd eventually locate Bea.
Colin bolted forward, diving from dark shadow to dark
shadow, where the light couldn't reach. To hell with the
statue. To hell with the treasure. He needed to find Bea.

"You see," Stephan called out, his voice calm and even. He thought he'd won. "It's silly, really, to run. There is no way out. We knew you'd come here and we were waiting."

Colin leaned back against a statue, the marble cooling his fevered skin. Damn it. He had to think of something and fast. Shuffling feet whispered closer . . . closer. He hoped to God that Bea had found an escape. As silently as possible, he moved to the wall and inched his way around the perimeter of the room. The walls were rough under his fingers, rough, but solid, there was no opening, no sign of outside light through cracks. No way out.

"Mr. Finch," Stephan said.

Colin held his arm close to his chest, trying to stop the trickle of blood. He didn't want to leave behind any trail. He was already making it too easy for them. He wasn't surprised they knew his name. Were they working with Bea's cousin Henry? It would make the most sense. But then, why not use Henry to open the map? After all, Henry had the same blood as Bea and Leo. Why would they need Bea?

"You can't hide and you are only prolonging the inevitable."

Colin paused, his heart hammering in his chest. The bastard was right. He wouldn't be able to escape, but he could fight. Surprise would be his weapon. Slowly, he slid the knife from the sheath on his thigh, gripping the hilt. He could fight, and damn it all, he'd take that bastard Stephan with him to hell.

He moved his right foot forward.

Fingers clasped around his left ankle. Colin stiffened in shock, resisting the urge to yell out a curse. It took only a moment to realize the grip belonged to Bea. He slipped the knife into the sheath as Bea tugged on his trouser leg. He hesitated only a moment. Finally, trusting her, he dropped to the floor, lying flat on his stomach. The dust puffed around him, tickling his lungs, but he refused to cough.

"Here," she said next to his ear, her sweet breath whispering against the side of his face.

"Where?"

She didn't respond, but tugged on his shirt, pulling the hem from his waistband. Colin rolled to his side, and suddenly, there was nothing but air underneath him.

"Damn it," he hissed as he fell to the ground with a thud.

"Are you all right?" Bea crawled atop him, her warm body covering his. Heat shot through his veins, the attraction immediate and ridiculous, given their circumstances. Even in the middle of a dire situation, his body reacted to the woman. Bea's soft hands slid up his chest, her lips close to his.

"You could have warned me."

"No time," she whispered, and her legs fell open so she straddled his waist.

His member stirred to life. Hell. Did she even understand what she was doing to him?

"Spread out, find him. He couldn't have disappeared." Stephan's voice echoed from the room above like cold water to his overheated senses. Footsteps pounded, sending tiny pieces of debris and rocks pattering onto Colin's face.

He swiped his features clean. "Where are we?"

Not waiting for a response, Colin wrapped his right arm around Bea's waist, keeping her on top of him, while he reached out with his left hand, feeling the rough stone above. More stone. A coffin. They were in a damn coffin.

Chapter 16

"It's a tunnel of sorts," Bea answered.

Colin couldn't deny the relief he felt. They were safe for now, but Stephan's men would locate the tunnel soon enough. "How'd you find it?"

"A butterfly."

He paused, confused. "A what?"

"Nothing. I'll explain later." Bea was breathing heavily, her high voice edged with panic. A lesser woman would have succumbed to fainting by now. "I think it was under one of the statues. One that had fallen over."

A quiver trembled through her body. He reached up and cupped the sides of her face, knowing she was close to losing control. He didn't blame her. "It's all right, Bea."

She took in a deep, shuddering breath. "Colin, I'm frightened."

His heart warmed, realizing she trusted enough to tell him the truth. He wouldn't destroy that trust. He'd find a way out. "I know. Come on. We might as well follow the tunnel. It has to lead out."

Bea sniffled as she crawled off him. "You think so?"

"Sure," he managed.

Side by side, they inched their way forward. Tiny pebbles dug into the injury on his arm, but he didn't dare curse.

He could hear Bea beside him, whimpering in her own discomfort, but keeping quiet for the most part. He felt oddly proud of her.

"Colin," she whispered. "How much farther?"

"Until we're safe." He realized how ridiculous that sounded, but she didn't point that out, merely continued to crawl beside him like a solider going into battle. Truth was, he didn't know where the hell they were going. Didn't know if this damn tunnel would lead them to safety or death.

"Colin," she said some minutes later.

Sweat beaded on his forehead, his muscles beginning to quiver like a newborn pup. Damn it, his strength hadn't fully returned and he was quickly draining. "Hmm?" He glanced back.

The gray light from the opening they'd fallen through had disappeared. They were in complete and utter blackness. He couldn't be positive, but it felt as if they were going downhill. The air had grown colder, the rock damp.

He felt Bea's warm hand on his forearm. "Colin, I just . . . I wanted to let you know . . ."

He paused, noting the seriousness of her voice.

"I . . . thank you."

Just like that his annoyance fled. She couldn't see him and he knew it was safe to smile. She liked him. She might not admit it, but she liked him. She was close, her soft body pressed next to his, so close he could almost forgive Stephan for their situation. He turned, knowing she was facing him for her breath fanned across his lips.

"Sounds like a farewell speech," he said.

There was a telling quiet and he could imagine the endearing flush on her face.

"Just . . . in case," she finally whispered.

"Well then, darlin', that's not how you say farewell. This is." He reached out and cupped the back of her head, his fingers slipping between her cool, silky strands.

Before she could inch back, he pulled her toward him. By instinct, his lips found hers. She tasted like the berries they'd eaten only an hour ago . . . sweet and tangy. So incredibly good. Heat shot through his body, an almost painful need to hold her close, to make her his.

Heedless to the men searching above, he tilted her head and deepened the kiss. Bea looped her arm around his neck, pressing her chest to his. Dear God, he was insane, completely insane to be doing this now. Yet when Bea sighed, Colin took full advantage and slipped his tongue between her lips. He didn't know why, but he felt the need to taste her. To kiss her thoroughly, completely.

Muffled voices echoed down the tunnel, shattering through their lovely cocoon of seduction. Reluctantly, Colin drew back. "We've been found."

She didn't respond, but he could feel the frantic beat of her heart against his chest, feel her harsh breathing fan across his face, so hot that for a second he thought about kissing her again. They'd been found and he could hardly care.

"We . . . we should go," she whispered, the voice of reason. Apparently she wasn't as affected by his kisses as he was with hers.

"Come on," he mumbled, sounding more annoyed than he wanted.

Had his kiss confused her? Hell, he didn't have time to deal with perplexing virgins at the moment. He started forward, forcing sexual thoughts of Bea from his mind. Something sticky and fine caught against his face. Colin grimaced, reached up, and pulled the web from his skin. The tunnel had to end eventually. Then what?

"Colin," Bea whispered beside him.

Were they crawling into a trap? Did they have any other choice? Damn, he should have stayed in the room. He should have attacked. He could have taken—

"Colin!" Bea snapped.

He jerked his head toward her. "What?"

"I believe the tunnel has widened."

Colin paused. Carefully, he extended his arm up. No rock

met his fingers. Cool air brushed across his skin . . . open air. He slipped his feet underneath him and stood hesitantly, his hands above his head to feel for a ceiling. No ceiling came. The room was tall, wide, but how tall, how wide?

"Find the wall," he said into the darkness. "See if you can locate any other rooms, doorways, tunnels."

"Colin, light!" Bea whispered furiously.

He turned. There, on the far wall, a pinpoint of light so small it allowed only a faded ray of sun into the room. A ray so faded that it did nothing to show the details of their location. With his gaze, he followed the ray as it sliced weakly through the darkness. At the end of the beam, something . . . sparkled . . . something across the room.

"Stay here." He moved toward that tiny window, his heart thundering with each shuffled step. Was it a keyhole? A way out? But the closer he got, the more the window took shape. A flower. A lotus, he realized, about as large as the palm of his hand. At the wall, he gently ran his fingers up the rough surface. There was no crease, no line that suggested a door or escape. Just above his head, too far to look out, the tiny window beckoned. Why the hell would there be an opening here?

"They're coming!"

He spun around, searching for Bea. But it was impossible to see her in the dark. With his arms outstretched, he started back toward her. His foot hit something hard. It skittered across the floor before landing with a soft splash.

Colin froze. "Bea, stop."

"What is it?" She sounded out of reach.

"Don't move, there's water."

Muffled words echoed from the tunnel, growing louder with every moment that passed. Their enemies were getting closer; they were running out of time.

"Bea, come toward me, follow my voice. Slowly."

Her shuffled feet drew nearer and he prayed she made it to his side in time. They had only moments before Stephan arrived and then what? Hell, why pretend he had a plan? He hadn't a damn clue what to do.

"Colin?" Her warm breath whispered to him.

"Here. Keep coming." He started forward, frantic to reach her.

Torchlight bounced down the tunnel, flaring into the room, warning of Stephan's imminent arrival. "It's open," he called, his voice high with excitement.

Too late. They'd arrived.

"Colin," Bea whispered.

She was close, so close, he could smell her . . . clover and lavender. He reached out and found her warm shoulders. His heart hammered in his chest, his body prepared to fight for this woman. He didn't have a sure plan, but he knew he wouldn't let anyone harm her. They would get out alive. He slid his hand down her arms and wrapped his fingers around hers, then jerked her down into the shadows.

"Stay low," he whispered. Outnumbered, surprise would be their only advantage.

He squeezed her hand, an unspoken command to keep quiet. Light danced across the top of the cavern, a smooth, rounded ceiling of the same sandstone that made the walls. Each tiny piece of quartz sparkled. Gods morphed from the rock, crawling from their tomb to glare down at them as if wondering how they'd dared to find their place of worship. At the sight, Bea gasped, her eyes as wide as a child's in front of a toy shop. Colin clasped a hand over her mouth, containing her excitement.

He had only moments, brief moments in which to study their prison. Flowery designs were made with pieces of gold and brilliant colored jewels swirled up to the top of the ceiling. Colin started to pull his gaze away when he caught the faded color spread upon the dome. Escape momentarily forgotten, he dropped his arms from Bea. With narrowed eyes, he attempted to make out the painting. A triangular shape of some sort. He turned and the shape took purpose.

India. It was a painting of India. Done in colors of blue and green, it was barely visible stretched across the ceiling. Never had he seen anything like the mural.

"Colin." Bea nudged him in the side.

He dropped his gaze. "What?"

Bea pointed ahead. Torchlight had found the middle of the room, and with it was highlighted a statue of pure gold that rose from the middle of a murky pond. A god, at least ten feet tall, sitting on a lotus. This was the small sparkle he'd seen at the end of the ray. This was why Anish had sent them here. This statue was another clue that would lead them to the treasure.

"Blimey," Stephan whispered, shuffling closer, the torch in his hand highlighting his stunned features.

The natives who stumbled after him paused, gasping in a universal language of shock. For one odd moment, they were all bonded in awe. With their gazes fastened to the riches covering the room, it was the perfect time to escape. Colin tore his attention from the statue, taking Bea's hand more firmly in his.

"Get ready."

She nodded, although her gaze remained pinned to the statue.

"What is it?" Stephan asked, his voice a breathless whisper.

"It's Brahma," a strong, familiar voice called out from the opposite side of the room.

Bea sucked in a breath, her hand tightening in Colin's.

There, barely visible under the torchlight, half-hidden in the shadows, stood Demyan. The man who should have been dead five times over. Anger flared through Colin, a blistering heat that boiled his blood and made him see red.

"Dem," Stephan said, his voice shaky. "I . . . You see . . ."

Demyan's gaze was focused on Stephan as if he didn't notice Bea and Colin crouched on the floor in front of him. "Silence." The man's voice was as hard as the stone walls surrounding them. Stephan jumped.

Bea fell back into Colin, her body trembling. His grip on her upper arms tightened. He hated that she was afraid, hated that he couldn't protect her. But he could try. He jerked her behind him, hiding her as much as he could with his own body. All the while, his gaze scanned the room. How had Demyan gotten inside? Was there another entrance, or had he been here, waiting all this time?

"We found the statue," Stephan persisted, yet his voice was hesitant, unsure.

Demyan didn't move. "Yes, I see that."

Stephan followed the edge of the small pond, spreading his arms wide. "Of course, we were going to tell you."

Demyan cocked his head to the side, as if in deep contemplation. "Really?"

Stephan nodded, his frantic gaze flickering around the room. Most likely he was looking for an escape route. Demyan lifted his arm. There was no word or warning. Colin recognized the glint of metal a split second before the pistol went off. The shot echoed through the room. Bea gasped and flung her arms around Colin's waist, her face pressed to his back. The natives dove to the floor, their torches still in hand, highlighting the fear on their faces.

"Why?" Stephan stumbled forward. Dark red blood soaked his white shirt. With wide eyes and ashen face, he crumpled forward, into the water. A soft splash sent droplets into the air. Bea sucked in a breath, latching on to his shirt.

No one else moved. No one said a word as they watched the body float facedown in the murky depths.

"Get them," Demyan said calmly.

The natives rushed toward Colin, their faces set in determination. The torchlight fluttered over the walls like demons making sport of their plight. The Indians had seen what would happen if they disobeyed Demyan, and they weren't about to die.

"Right. Well then, here we go." Colin jerked the blade from the sheath on his thigh.

The men slowed, circling like vultures. He'd been in fights before. Colin had the scars to prove it. But he'd never had to protect someone and watch his own back. An odd need welled within. Like a man out to secure what was his, Bea was under his protection. With a growl, Colin lashed out with his knife, catching one man across the gut. The man stumbled back, his hand going to his wound. One down, four to go.

"Colin!" Bea cried out, her fingers digging into his shirt.

He glanced over his shoulder. One of the natives was coming directly toward her.

"Do whatever you can. He won't hurt you. They need you." He prayed they needed Bea as much as he thought they did.

The man lunged for Bea. She lifted her leg, kicking him in the shin. He cried out, grasping his leg. Bea, smart girl, darted into the shadows.

"Go, Bea!" Colin demanded, focusing once more on the three men surrounding him. "Now then, my friends, shall we?"

One man dared to shuffle forward, lifting his pistol high. Colin flung the knife. The blade flashed, spinning over and over until it landed with a thunk, half-imbedded in the man's chest. The native dropped his torch, his scream echoing through the room. His light went out, throwing the room into darkness. A soft thud told Colin the man had collapsed to the floor.

Colin wasted no time and dove toward Bea. She reached out at the same moment and their bodies hit. He pulled her to him, keeping his balance. Bea wrapped her arms around his waist, holding him close, her breath harsh against his neck.

"Find them!" Demyan snapped over the shuffle of feet.

"There has to be an exit somewhere," Colin whispered. "When I step out, go the opposite way. Blend into the darkness, find an escape."

"But . . ."

He cupped the sides of her face. "No, just go. Demyan won't harm you. He wants you."

"Because of the ridiculous ring?"

"Because of your bloodline. Now stay quiet."

He felt her nod, but she didn't release her hold. A smile curved his mouth, and he couldn't stop himself from pressing a quick kiss to her soft lips.

"Ready?" He didn't wait for her response but gently pushed her away. Stealing his resolve, he stepped out of the shadows and stared directly into the green eyes of the demon who'd killed his mother.

Chapter 17

Bea stumbled forward, her feet tripping over each other in her haste to run. But she had to keep moving, must keep moving. Her heart slammed against her chest, threatening to explode all over the cavern walls. Surely Demyan could hear the thundering beat. Finally, the darkness swallowed her whole. Here she was safe. Here she could think.

A sudden swoosh of light bounced against the cave walls. Bea hunkered low, keeping still in the shadows. But Colin, oh God, he stood in the torchlight, his arms raised in the air as if he was surrendering. Her insides twisted.

He'd be murdered, shot dead where he stood. She shook her head, reaching backward until she felt the rough stone of the wall. The native man she'd kicked had regained his feet and held the torch high, his gaze scanning the cavern, no doubt looking for her. Demyan merely stood there as if he had all the time in the world. A rich lord, hunting down prey. She shivered at the comparison.

Briefly, she closed her eyes. She must be rational, gather the facts. The facts were, they wanted her. They wouldn't kill her. But Colin hadn't said they wouldn't kill him. She moved as softly as her trembling legs would carry her, quietly following the wall with her fingertips, looking for what, she wasn't sure, but knowing she couldn't keep still.

"Where is she?" the monster asked in a calm, serene voice.

"Who?"

Demyan strolled forward, three of the natives following. "She can't escape. You know that. It's fruitless and ridiculous. I grow tired of these games."

Bea stepped closer to the wall, practically hugging the cool stone. With bated breath, she waited. Would Colin give in and tell them where she was? What other choice did he have?

Colin shrugged. "Sorry, but I can't help you."

Tears stung Bea's eyes. Standing there so strong and sure, Colin took her breath away with his bravery. If only she could be that brave!

"Oh, I think you can." Demyan lifted his arm, pointing the pistol at Colin's head. Bea froze, her heart stopping for a moment. She felt as if she were watching a play, as if she were the audience, there in the darkness. "Miss Edmund, please do not make me search. Either come forward now, or he dies."

"Don't, Bea." Colin's voice was hard, demanding. "He'll kill me anyway. Don't listen to him."

Indecision held her captive. Demyan would kill him anyway. Just the thought made her knees buckle. No. No, they couldn't kill Colin. That was unacceptable.

"You have no choice but to trust me, Beatrice," Demyan said, his voice almost lyrical.

She shivered at the use of her given name on the monster's lips. He knew her name; what else did he know about her? Part of her didn't want to uncover the truth. Part of her wanted to close her eyes and pretend none of this was happening. But it was happening and she had to make a decision and fast.

"You have until I count to five." He barely paused after he said this. "One."

Bea's heart slammed against her chest, panic edging out fear.

"Two."

She took a hesitant step forward, her knees knocking together. There must be some way she could save both herself and Colin!

"Three."

He stepped closer to Colin.

Colin tilted his chin high, daring the man to shoot him. Dear God, he'd shoot Colin!

"Four."

"All right!" Bea burst forward, not stopping until she reached them. She threw her arms around Colin's waist, taking comfort in his warmth, his scent, his solidness. Colin closed his eyes, but not before she saw the disappointment in those blue depths.

"Damn you, Bea," he whispered.

But she didn't care if she'd disappointed him. She didn't bloody well care. She'd had no choice!

The monster smiled, a slow grin that spread across his pale face. "Very good." He tossed the pistol to a native and started toward them. Colin stiffened, an animal preparing to attack.

"Don't," she whispered, tightening her hold. She was unwilling to come so close to losing him again. Colin's jaw clenched, but for once, he listened to her. He didn't move, but he didn't relax either.

Demyan latched on to her arm, his long, thin fingers biting into her flesh. She sucked in her gasp as he jerked her forward. His touch was cold, his fingers like steel manacles over her warm flesh. She shuddered. He was surprisingly strong for someone so thin. Glancing over her shoulder, Bea begged Colin with her eyes to stay still. His furious gaze followed them, his hands clenched at his sides. She prayed the man wouldn't try anything heroic.

Bea jerked her head forward as Demyan quickened his steps, pulling her past a native. "Kill him."

"What? No! No!" Bea struggled against his hold but the man's fingers were tenacious. He stopped only when they stood in the shadows. With a cry, Bea glanced back at Colin. He was watching her, merely standing there watching her as if he'd accepted his fate.

"Colin," she whispered, but knew he heard her by the way he flinched.

The Indian man moved forward, his gun pointed directly at Colin's chest. His hand was shaking, the hesitancy obvious in this shuffled footsteps. He didn't want to shoot Colin. Perhaps he wouldn't. It couldn't end this way. She couldn't let it end this way. She would think of something, some way to—

The blast rang through the cavern, sending tiny pieces of debris pattering to the floor. Colin stumbled back and fell to the ground.

Panic pulsed through Bea, a pain so acute that it felt as if she'd been the one shot. She screamed, the high-pitched wail echoing eerily through the cavern. "Let me go! Now!"

Demyan released her, only to latch on to her neck. Those long fingers dug into her throat, and with a growl, he shoved her hard against the stone wall. Her skull hit rock and stars danced in front of her eyes, momentarily stunning her.

"I grow very, very weary of your dramatics." His breath was ice cold, whispering across her skin like a snake. Bea didn't care, didn't look into his eerie glowing eyes, but continued to watch Colin.

Colin unmoving.

Colin on the ground.

Colin dead.

Demyan's fingers dug into Bea's throat, his eyes producing a green glow that highlighted the harsh planes of his face. Fear and desperation held her immobile. Bea's lungs burned, her throat constricting. But she didn't care. Didn't care that she couldn't breathe or that Colin had been wrong and Demyan would kill her. She didn't care. Colin was dead. Gone. And she knew she was about to die, too. Tears stung her eyes, blurring her vision, and she was glad she could no longer make out the Demon's features.

"What's this?" She was barely aware of Demyan's voice. Barely aware when he pulled on the chain that hung around her neck. When his hold loosened and her lungs automatically expanded, sucking in a great gulp of air, she was forced back into the present.

"It's here. It's been here all along," Demyan whispered.

Bea gasped for air, her hands going to her aching throat. Reluctantly, she looked at the man, but he wasn't focused on her. He'd lifted the necklace, and was staring at Leo's ring. The emerald glistened and sparkled under his scrutiny, a brilliant green, a calming green that belied the intensity in Demyan's mad eyes.

The ring? That's all he cared about? She should have known.

"Take it!" she cried out, ripping the chain from her throat. "Take it!"

She didn't care, nothing mattered anymore. She shoved the ring into his hand and pushed at his bony chest. The piece of jewelry bounced across the floor and rolled into the shadows.

"No!" he roared, dropping to his knees.

Bea ignored the man and burst forward. "Colin!"

He didn't move. Merely lay there, his eyes closed, his body still.

"Colin!"

She fell, her knees hitting the hard stone. Cupping his broad shoulders, she shook him. He didn't even flinch. Unheeded tears slipped down her cheeks, dropping to his chest.

"Colin, please. Oh God, please." Frantic to find the wound, she ripped open his shirt, the buttons pattering across the floor. Under the light of the torch the native still held, his golden skin was pure, intact. Not a mark marred his muscled torso. Unease whispered across her skin. She didn't understand.

Suddenly, Colin latched on to her wrist. His eyes opened and a soft grin lifted his lips. "Trust me." He winked.

Bea's mouth dropped open. She wasn't sure if she wanted to hit him or throw her arms around his neck and never let go.

"How?" she whispered. "You were dead!" She moved back, horrified and amazed. "You can heal yourself, too?"

He sat upright. The native man holding the torch mumbled something in his language, his narrow face going pale. He shook his head and dropped the torch. Their only light source went out, throwing the room into darkness.

Colin reached out into the inkiness, his fingers taking Bea's hand. His palm was warm and comforting. "Wasn't dead, just pretending. He missed. But glad to know you finally believe in my abilities."

"I . . . I . . ." Bea sputtered, her ire growing. "You cur!" Blindly, she reached out, feeling some sense of satisfaction when she hit his shoulder with her fist.

"Hey." Colin wrapped his arm around her waist and pulled her close, so close his warm breath brushed across the side of her face, momentarily stunning her. "It worked, didn't it? Now be quiet before Demyan finds us."

"Too late," the man's voice whispered through the darkness, a snake hissing in hunger.

Bea froze, shrinking back against Colin. There was a soft swoosh and then a flare of light as Demyan relit the torch. Bea's eyes protested the sudden brightness. All too quickly her gaze adjusted. Demyan stood before them, a torch in his left hand and a pistol in his right. Three natives stood behind him, ready to do his bidding.

"You're going to stand up slowly now."

Colin paused, but did as he was told and stood, pulling Bea with him. She thanked God for Colin's strength, for her legs were shaking so badly she had to lean against him for support. Frantic, she scanned the area. Surely there was something they could do, something they could use to fight the men.

"Take it." With his free hand, Demyan held out the ring, his gaze pinned to her.

"What?" She was confused, her mind muddled. She didn't understand what he was asking or why he was focused on her. He wanted the ring, so why was he now giving it back? For one naïve moment she thought perhaps he'd had a change of heart.

"The ring. Take it."

She glanced up at Colin. He gave a brief jerk of his head. Bea swallowed hard and pulled away from him. Her legs had gone to melted butter and she wasn't sure she could stay upright. But she had to. She stumbled across the room, shortening the distance between her and the very man who would kill her just as soon as look at her. Feet from Demyan, she paused, her heart slamming wildly against her chest.

He stretched out his bony hand, the ring nestled in his pale palm.

Slowly, she reached out, making sure not to touch him as she scooped up the jewelry. The ring was warm, surprisingly hot against her skin. Part of her hated it, hated that the simple piece of jewelry had been the reason for so much evil. And another part of her wanted to hide it, to keep it safe like a mother with her child.

"Hurry." Demyan jerked his head toward the right. "Go to the statue."

Bea paused, shocked. Of course he wasn't giving it back. Hadn't Colin said only Bea's blood could use the ring? They were still after the treasure. It would never end. "In the water?"

"Of course. Now go." He shoved the heel of his hand into her back.

Two things happened at once. Bea stumbled forward, which made Colin bolt toward her. Demyan swung his arm wide, the pistol only inches from Colin's chest. There was a soft click, click, click as the three natives cocked their pistols and focused on Colin.

"Colin, no!" Bea cried out. "It's merely water."

Water, with a body floating on the surface. Oh, dear God. Bea swallowed down the bile threatening to come up. She wouldn't get a case of the vapors, not now of all times.

Colin stood still, his wide chest rising and falling with each harsh intake of breath. His hands were fisted, his eyes nearly red with fury.

"It's all right," she whispered, praying he'd stay put.

Before he could respond, she slipped the ring onto her thumb and jumped. The cool water enveloped her body, covering her head and dragging her under. Bea opened her eyes and looked up. Above the surface, the golden god loomed, wavering in and out of focus, a small smile upon his face as if he realized the insanity of the situation.

Bea started to move when she caught something from the corner of her eye. Heart hammering against her chest, she spun around. Stephan's body floated near, his glassy eyes open as he stared down at her. Bea held her scream and kicked her feet, pushing herself up to the surface.

"There," Demyan said the moment she broke through. "There, in the lotus atop his head."

Bea glanced back, sucking in a great gulp of air. "What?" Water was filling her boots, dragging her down. She kicked harder, determined not to drown.

Demyan growled, obviously annoyed. "Climb up. Now." Bea barely had the energy to keep afloat and he wanted her to climb a bloody statue?

Colin merely stood there, his hands fisted, his hard gaze flitting from Demyan to Bea. He was thinking, planning, but what?

"Climb," Demyan demanded again.

Tearing her gaze from Colin, Bea wrapped her arms around the golden base and pulled herself up. Her wet clothing hung on her body, adding extra weight she didn't need. Even though the cavern and water were cool, sweat broke out on her forehead.

She hugged the precious metal, pausing for a moment to calm her racing heart. She was so tired. So tired of running, hiding, and worrying. Her harsh breathing made a foggy circle on the golden statue, her reflection momentarily blocked from view. That last night in Scotland, as her grandmother had warned her not to leave with Leo and Ella, she'd been standing at her bedroom window, the air so cold and her face so close to the pane that a foggy circle had formed on the glass.

"Proper young ladies do not travel the world!"

She spun around to face the old woman. "And what would you have me do? Stay here for the rest of my life, rotting in a moldy castle like you?"

Grandmother stumbled back as if she'd been slapped.

Realizing immediately the harshness of her words, Bea reached out. "Grandmother, I didn't mean . . . I'm so sorry."

She tilted her chin high. "Go then. But know that you're dead to me."

"The lotus, there. Place the ring in the symbol," Demyan demanded, his gaze dancing with anticipation.

Would Grandmother mourn her death now? Or was the old woman still too bitter to care? Bea tilted her head back, looking directly into the statue's eyes. Atop his head, a golden crown perched. In the middle of the crown was carved a flower-shaped symbol, about the size of a half-penny. A keyhole, of some sort. Between his eyebrows, that same flower shape was mirrored in a panel that flared with light. Light?

Bea narrowed her eyes, confused. Where was the light coming from? She turned. Over the people standing below, across the room, she followed the ray as it came through that small window that Colin had gone to when they'd first entered the cavern. Bea sucked in a breath, pulling back slightly. The setting sun was shining directly through the window. Directly onto the statue. Perfect timing.

"Do it now," Demyan snapped.

Her heart hammered against her chest. What would happen if she did as Demyan demanded? Bea pushed the wet strands of hair from her eyes, her hands shaking so badly the task proved almost impossible. Taking in a deep, trembling breath, she pulled the ring from her thumb. For a moment she paused, staring at the piece of jewelry. If she dropped it . . . the water would swallow the ring whole. Gone. It'd take days for Demyan to find it, if he ever did.

"Drop it and he dies," Demyan snapped.

Bea jerked her gaze toward him. The pistol was pointed at Colin's head. Demyan had known her thoughts. Did he read minds as well? She shivered and turned back around to face the statue.

Swallowing hard, she pressed the emerald into the carved lotus. It fit perfectly. As she'd assumed, it was a keyhole.

"Turn it."

Bea glanced at Colin for confirmation. His jaw clenched, he nodded. Taking her bottom lip between her teeth, she turned the ring. The golden panel between his eyebrows slid back, revealing a perfect, pure diamond embedded in his forehead. Bea sucked in a breath. The light hit the jewel, sending a blinding ray upward from the top of the crown.

"Get down, Bea," Colin demanded.

Without hesitation, she jumped. Her feet hit the water, sending droplets into the air before swallowing her whole. Hovering suspended in the cool liquid, she almost didn't want to return to the surface. Suddenly, Colin was beside her, his curly strands floating like a halo around his head. He wrapped his arms around her waist and pulled her upward.

Together they burst through the water and sucked in the crisp air.

"I don't . . . I don't understand," Bea whispered, clinging to the man's sodden chest. "What is it? What's happening?"

"I don't know." Colin moved toward the water's edge, his gaze on Demyan. "But I'm betting he does."

Bea reached out, taking hold of the pond ledge. Demyan merely stood there with his gaze pinned to the ceiling. Using her remaining strength, Bea managed to pull herself to dry land. Immediately her gaze went above. A beam of light pierced the painting, highlighting the coast of India. Pinpointing a location?

"Colin," she whispered as he settled on the stone floor beside her. "What is it?"

He didn't answer. Instead, he jumped to his feet and bolted forward, hitting Demyan with a thud. Caught off guard, the thin man crumpled under Colin's weight and they both fell to the ground with a force that surely should have broken a bone or two. Unable to hold on to the torch, it fell to the floor and went out, throwing the room into darkness, but for that one beam of light on the ceiling.

"Colin!" Bea cried, jumping to her feet.

"You knew all along, didn't you, you bastard?" Colin growled in the darkness.

"Of course I did," Demyan replied.

There was a thud, then a grunt, as if someone had hit someone. The remaining natives shuffled back, wanting no part in the dispute.

"Colin! Please!" Bea shot out. Through the dim light the beam provided, she could just make out their shadows, wrestling on the floor like two street urchins fighting over a coin.

"Go." Colin turned as he said this and she knew he was talking to her.

Bea stumbled back. "What?"

Colin stood, his arm lifted. A pistol gleamed at the end

of his hand. He took a step back, then another. "Go now. The tunnel."

Indecision held Bea captive. "But the ring."

He dared to glance at the statue where the ring was still embedded. And she saw it there, that brief moment of hesitation. He was giving it up, his life, what he'd been searching for, giving it up to protect her.

"Doesn't matter. Let's go." He latched on to her hand and pulled her toward the opening of the tunnel, their only possible means of escape. Bea's elbows hit the stone with a thud that vibrated her bones. No time for pain, with a grunt, she pushed herself to her hands and knees and raced up the corridor.

"He knew," she panted. "He knew what would happen, what the ring could do? Where that map was?"

"Yes," Colin said from behind her.

"He was waiting for us?" She focused on the floor, focused on the darkness, urging her body to keep going.

"Seems so."

Bea dug the tips of her toes into the stone floor, urging her legs to move faster. No matter how hard she tried, she couldn't seem to crawl with enough speed. Was Demyan coming after them? She strained to hear movement, but over her own harsh breathing she could make out nothing. She bit her lip, resisting the urge to look back. Looking back would only waste valuable time.

"How'd he know?" she asked, mostly to hear Colin's voice. "How'd he know it was here and how'd he know we would come?"

"I don't know," Colin grunted, the exhaustion evident in his tone. He hadn't fully recovered from saving King Henry. She'd been selfish, so bloody selfish demanding he save the animal, but she couldn't stand to see the beast hunted for sport!

Shouts rang from behind, the voices echoing after them.

"They're coming!" Panic pushed her onward.

"It's there, just ahead. I can see the light."

She lifted her head. Colin was right. There, just out of reach, was that gray square that hinted at escape. Sweat beaded on her back, and with a completely unladylike grunt, Bea jumped through that opening. The moment she hit the floor, she rolled to her side. Colin landed beside her, panting.

"Come, Colin, hurry." She took his hand and helped him to his feet.

He stumbled. Bea slid her arm around his waist and together, they navigated the room, darting around the broken statues.

"The sun," Colin explained, pushing away from her. She knew he hated the fact that he had to lean on her; she could see the shame in his eyes. Talking was obviously his way of ignoring his lack of strength. "The light from the sun came through, it hit the statue. He knew it would pierce that window at a certain time."

He pushed aside the vines and they climbed through the opening, into the main corridor.

Together they burst down the hall. There, at the end, the setting sun allowed light to pour into the temple. Their escape. Their freedom. "The sunlight, that ray, produced the beam that lit the map?"

They made it to the opening and stumbled down the steps, jumping over the last few. The sun was a fiery ball that hovered on the horizon. Once it dipped below, they would be harder to find.

Colin took her elbow, steering her toward a clump of trees. "Yes, the light pointed to the map."

There, tethered to the branch of a fig tree, was a brown mare. Demyan's or Stephan's, it didn't matter. Relief was immediate and sweet. Never had a horse been such a blessing. Colin pulled himself into the saddle and reached for Bea. With what strength he had left, he pulled her up behind him. Bea wrapped her legs around the beast's sides and clung to Colin's waist.

"But the ring," she whispered.

"Forget it."

She could forget the ring, but could Colin? They both knew that with Demyan holding the ring, they were as good as dead. She wanted to argue, but she couldn't because she was a coward. With a cry, Colin dug his heels into the horse's sides. They burst across the field, the thud jarring Bea. She gripped Colin's shirt and buried her face into his back. She didn't dare look behind them.

Chapter 18

They'd escaped. Even now, hours later, Colin was shocked by that realization. They'd escaped, they still lived, but without the ring, for how long?

"Are you going to tell me what it meant?"

Bea's soft voice broke through Colin's numb mind. Her grip tightened around his waist, and she shifted her face so her warm breath fanned against the back of his neck. He glanced over his shoulder and met her gaze. Those eerie amber eyes had turned into melted gold under the light of the moon. If he wasn't careful, a man could drown in her gaze.

He was surprised she'd been quiet as long as she had. Hell, after what they'd experienced, he was stunned. They'd been riding for hours and he'd fully expected her to ask him questions the moment the temple was out of sight. Perhaps fear, or shock, had kept her unusually silent, the soft thump of the horse's hooves and the turmoil of his mind Colin's only companion for the past hours.

"What *what* meant?" he asked, knowing full well what she asked, but hoping she'd drop the subject.

"The map on the ceiling, the statue. All of it." She tilted her head farther, her lush lips parted, so close that if he turned, he could press his mouth to hers.

He jerked his gaze forward, ignoring the tendrils of excitement that swirled through his body. How easy it would be to lose himself in her, to forget everything.

"How should I know?"

She frowned and shifted again so her soft breasts crushed to his back. Colin gritted his teeth as heat shot straight to his groin. How much was a man supposed to endure?

"You know," she said in a sure voice. "You wouldn't have left so quickly if you didn't know."

It annoyed him that she thought he was so interested in the statue he'd chance her safety. He wasn't a greedy monster, for God's sake. Then again, both her grandfather and cousin Henry would have tossed her to the very devil for a penny. Perhaps she thought all men were alike. "I would have left for your safety."

"Perhaps. But you do know what it meant?"

She was certainly persistent. And she was right.

Colin sighed as he nudged the horse left. He'd kept to the fields so they wouldn't be seen. But it was time to find a place to bunk down and rest. They couldn't go on any farther. *He* couldn't go on any farther. His hands stiff from lack of use, he stretched his fingers around the reins. His limbs buzzed with the vibration of the horse's movement, and he itched to leave his mount, to walk and move his legs.

"Colin?" Bea audaciously reached around and rested her hand on his. "What was in that temple?"

He sighed, long and loud. He'd have to explain. She wouldn't let up until he did. He pulled back on the reins and turned in the saddle to look at her. Her hair hung in waves around her face, dark half moons covered the area under her eyes, those lush lips were pressed tense with worry. How different she looked from the pampered, perfect miss he'd met in Delhi.

Could she handle much more? Did she have a choice?

"Colin?"

He didn't miss the way her voice quivered. She needed

the truth. She deserved the truth. "A map of India, and I have no doubt the bastard knew it was there. But he couldn't do a damn thing until we arrived with the ring and opened the statue to the sun."

"The light shone on something, off the coast. What was it?"

"I don't know." He hated admitting that. Hated admitting that he hadn't a clue. "It's obviously pointing to something, some place." Was it the location of the statue he searched for? Could he really finally have answers?

Bea didn't respond, either deep in thought, or realizing he was a damn idiot and it was pointless to ask anymore. "Now, come. We need to set up a camp."

She looked dubiously around the field. "Where, exactly?"

Colin nodded toward the scraggly trees that followed the creek. "There. Along the river."

"What if they travel by water?" Bea asked.

He faced forward and tapped his heels against the mare's sides, urging her forward. "It's a tributary. They'll be following the main river."

At least he hoped. Hell, what choice did he have? He couldn't keep this pace much longer . . . he couldn't keep pretending he knew how to protect her, or pretending to know what he'd do if they were attacked. His body ached with the need to sleep and his mind had grown numb long ago. But how could he sleep and protect Bea at the same time?

He shook his head, focusing instead on the temple and the ring, substituting one impossible problem for another. It had killed him to leave that ring behind, and if he was honest with himself, he'd had his doubts about doing so. But then he'd thought about Bea.

He couldn't endanger her life. He'd had a chance to escape and he'd taken it. And now . . . Hell, now they could lose everything because of his soft heart. The worst of it was, he knew he'd do it all over again. But perhaps they didn't need the ring any longer.

The map led somewhere. No doubt Demyan knew where.
Demyan.

Thoughts of the Demon sent his stomach churning. He
finally had a name for the bastard who'd killed his mother.
How many years had he imagined meeting the man? The
man who had ruined his life. Destroyed everyone he loved.
He swallowed over the lump in his throat, his fingers tightening around the reins. When the man had touched Bea . . .
How badly he wanted to wrap his hands around Demyan's
throat . . .

He forced himself to relax his grip. It wouldn't help to
focus on the impossible. And killing Demyan was impossible at the moment. But the man had to have a weak spot. No
one was invincible. Everyone's power had limitations. What
were his?

"Colin?" Bea interrupted his musings. "Will this do?"

With disinterest, he glanced around the small grouping
of trees that formed a half circle near the river. "Yeah. Sure."

Almost of its own accord, his body slid from the mount,
his feet landing with a thud that stirred the dry dirt into the
air. He'd had just enough energy to keep from whacking Bea
in the head with his boots. Bea, fortunately, didn't wait for
his help, but slid from the animal.

Colin flipped the lid of the leather bag strapped to the
mount. There had to be something they could use . . . food,
a weapon. "Search the bags on the other side, Bea."

Without argument, she moved around the beast. She
didn't complain, although she had to be nearly as exhausted
as he. She really was a daisy, the way she fought, the way
she stood up for what she believed in, the way she gave him
hell. A reluctant grin tugged at the corners of Colin's mouth.
Certainly not the prim, proper woman he'd thought. Not
Sarah. He knew that now. How ironic that when he'd asked
Sarah to travel to India with him, she'd scoffed.

Only three months ago, when he'd arrived, he'd met her
on the streets of Bombay. They'd paused, neither speaking.

Both shocked. Never, in his life, had he thought to meet her again, in India of all places. But he knew she wouldn't have traveled here alone.

"You married him, then?" Colin had asked.

"Yes," Sarah had said, tilting her chin high and daring him to comment.

He hadn't spoken another word to her, merely moved past. And he sure as hell hadn't looked back. She hadn't wanted to travel with him, a poor American, but she would with a wealthy Brit.

"Netting," Bea called out, interrupting his musings. "I have netting and a reed mat."

He nodded, stuffing his hand in the bag on his side. Bea had seemed to hate India, too, at first. Oddly, she seemed to thrive now. In the sun and nature, she was in her element. Paper crinkled under his fingertips. Carefully, Colin pulled the rolled missive free. With his brows drawn together, he moved to a stump and settled down, unrolling the waxed paper.

"What is it?" Bea asked, edging closer.

"A map. Europe and Asia."

She frowned and settled next to him. "It's marked." She leaned closer, her scent whispering to him . . . that sweet clover, heady lavender. Lifting her arm, she pointed to the X'ed spots. England, France, Spain. He frowned, trying to connect, but nothing made sense. With a sigh, he rerolled the map.

Exhausted. He was damn exhausted. The soft buzz of insects hummed in the distance, mixing with the buzz in his brain.

"It's the route we traveled."

Colin jerked his head toward Bea. "What?"

She grabbed the map and unrolled it again. Her long delicate finger pointed toward the first spot. "Here. We were here." She pointed to the next. "And here."

There was a long moment of silence. Finally, she handed it to him. "I thought it odd that we didn't sail the entire way."

Colin rubbed his jaw, rough with whiskers. "Leo knew they'd look for you on the waters. He took another route. But they knew anyway. They were following you."

Bea shivered and crossed her arms over her chest. "Just waiting for the right opportunity to get the ring. And now he probably has it, or will soon."

"He still needs blood, family blood." But he knew that wasn't true. Henry was most likely working with Demyan, and if so, they'd use Henry's blood.

The question was, how had the man known their route? Leo would have realized if someone was following them. Colin's jaw clenched tight, his mind spinning. His gaze slid to India, that triangular shape. Where had the light been pointing? Using his finger, he found Bombay, then moved upward and out. The Seven Islands?

"Why?" she finally asked. "Why'd he bring me here?"

Colin tore his gaze from the map. "Leo?"

She nodded.

He shrugged and rerolled the map. "I told you, he thought you'd be safer with us. He worried they'd come after you. He was right."

"He was protecting me?"

Colin nodded, but she said no more. Was she angry? Annoyed? She looked merely thoughtful but her silence unnerved him so he decided to change the subject. "We should set up camp."

She nodded and jumped to her feet. Too fast, too soon. She wavered, pressing her hand to her head. Colin slipped his arm around her waist, holding her upright.

Slowly, her gaze lifted to his. For one long moment they merely looked at each other. He wasn't sure what she was searching for and he wasn't sure he wanted her to uncover the truth. His heart beat frantically against his chest. His body begging him to pull her closer, his mind warning him that getting closer would only court trouble. This was no woman to dally with. So why, then, couldn't he leave her in peace?

His fingers tightened on her arms, his gaze dropping to her lips. Her hands flattened against his chest. She wanted him to kiss her. He felt it in his soul. He wanted to kiss her. So why didn't he? Because he wanted more than just a kiss. He'd had a taste of her luscious lips and it had driven him mad for days.

His blood roared with need. There was no ring to remind him she was Leo's cousin. There was no stuffy English clothing to remind him she was a titled lady. There was only them, in the wilds of a foreign country where no one knew them and their only link was each other.

"I'm sorry," Bea whispered. "I guess I'm rather exhausted." All too soon, she stepped away and brushed her hands against her trousers as if to rid herself of his touch. "What should I do?"

Colin dropped his arms, his fingers stretching as he resisted the urge to bring her back. "Go, clean."

She flushed. "Do I smell that bad?"

A smile flittered across his lips. "No. You smell . . . lovely."

She blinked, surprise evident in her wide gaze. Even in the moonlight, he could see her blush deepen, and her attention dropped to the ground as if she wasn't used to compliments. "Thank you."

"It's a fact, Bea. You're beautiful." Was he really such a beast that she hadn't expected a compliment from him? "The heat, it's stifling. I thought you'd enjoy the time to cool off."

"Of course." She hesitated only a moment, wringing her hands together as if in indecision, then without another word she spun around and broke through the brush toward the river.

"Be careful of animals," he called out but she didn't respond.

Colin watched her go, knowing he should take the time to secure their camp, yet unable to focus on anything but those long, dark strands that swayed above her backside. Or the way her trousers hugged her ass. Or the way that damn shirt was taut over her . . .

He took in a deep, trembling breath and tore his attention from Bea, ignoring the heat that shot straight to his groin.

"Focus, you damn idiot."

He started to gather pieces of wood in order to make a fire. As many enemies as they had, the elements would be their worst. So many things to worry about yet he mostly worried about Bea. How much longer could she last? Still, she'd proven herself to be much stronger than he could have ever imagined. He admired her, he realized. Admired her strength, her caring nature, her passion for those she believed in. Would she be as passionate in bed?

His gaze traveled to the scraggly brush where Bea had disappeared into the shadows of the trees. As if a sailor drawn to a siren, he moved. He couldn't take it anymore, being away from her, not touching her. Slowly, he traveled toward the sound of gurgling water, pulled by the exotic force that was Bea.

He admired the way her lips quivered when she wasn't sure how to respond to some ridiculous statement he'd made. He pushed aside a branch, allowing the moon to light his steps.

He admired the way, when the light hit her eyes just right, they glowed like melted gold.

A soft *hmm* reached his ears, a sweet song from the lips of a seductive nymph.

Hell, he even admired the way her voice was soft and husky in the morning. He lifted a branch and ducked underneath.

Spotting Bea kneeling at the water's edge, her profile to him, Colin froze. She'd tied her hair atop her head, leaving her long, slender neck exposed to the kiss of the silver moonlight. Her shirt hung open, the tails wavering in the soft breeze, revealing her flat stomach, yet unfortunately still covering those soft breasts. She stood and tipped her cupped hands.

Colin's body flared to life. Lightning shot through his veins. He was a damn pervert, standing there watching her, yet he couldn't seem to move.

Water snaked down her skin, disappearing under the collar of her shirt. She turned toward him, her eyes closed. Colin sucked in a breath. The buttons undone, her shirt lay open, showing the valley between her lovely breasts. Her pale skin was painted silver under the light of the moon; she was like an ethereal statue come to life. A Greek goddess. Dear God, he couldn't take much more. His fingers curled at his sides and he knew, he knew he had to have her.

Bea's lashes lifted and her piercing eyes met his. He expected her to gasp, to scream, to curse him to hell. She didn't. This woman wasn't Leo's cousin or Ella's friend. This wasn't the cold Englishwoman he'd first met. This wasn't Sarah come to crush his soul.

He started forward. Bea met him halfway. They paused when they were only a breath away. Colin reached out, hesitated, then cupped the back of her head, his fingers slipping into the silky strands.

There was an unspoken agreement that flickered between them. An unspoken acceptance in her eyes. Colin didn't need any more. He tilted Bea's head back and crushed his mouth to hers. He was gone. Perhaps it was the moonlight. Perhaps it was the fact that they'd just escaped a dire situation. Perhaps it was because of Bea. But the moment they touched, any sensibility fled, leaving him a tangle of pulsing desire.

Boldly, Bea's tongue traced his lips. Heat shot straight to Colin's groin. With a growl, he pulled her closer, hugging her lush curves to him. His hands slipped underneath the material of her shirt, his fingers spreading over her warm flesh.

He didn't pause, didn't hesitate to take what he wanted, what he'd been aching to have for days now. Colin slid his hands around her waist and cupped her bottom, bringing her up hard against his arousal. A shudder crept over her body; he could feel it in her muscles, in her soul. She wanted him just as much and the thought made him heady with desire. His lips found her neck, still damp with water.

"I was so afraid, Colin, so afraid you were dead," she whimpered against his mouth. "Don't ever do that to me again."

He nodded. He would have agreed to anything. But mostly, his mind centered on the fact that she cared. She cared about him. She cared if he lived or died. She cared.

His hands slid forward, up over her ribs, hesitating briefly at the underside of her breasts and prolonging the moment. How his fingers itched to touch her, to brand her. Finally, he gave in to temptation and cupped the soft mounds. They fit perfectly in his palms, slightly overflowing his grasp. Colin's shaft pulsed against her lower belly. Too much, it was all too damn much for even him.

He moaned into her mouth, his tongue rubbing against her own, while his thumbs flicked over her hard nipples. Bea's fingers bit into his shoulders, her body trembling from lust. He knew she wanted him; he could smell it on her, the desire, sweet and shocking. The realization thrilled his already overheated body. His lips moved to the column of her throat, needing to taste more of her, all of her.

"Colin, please, don't stop."

Sweet relief nearly made his knees buckle. Dear Lord, she'd kill him with her words. He spun her around, her back pressed to his chest, his hands resting against her warm, lower belly. Before she could object, he slid his tongue along her neck. Bea sighed, sinking into him.

"Damn, you smell good," he mumbled against her skin.

Colin moved his hand lower over her flat belly, his other arm wrapped around her waist, holding her upright. Bea's stomach muscles quivered as he drew his finger along the band of her trousers.

"Colin?" she whispered, her voice unsure.

He didn't respond, merely flipped open the button on her trousers and slipped his hand inside, cupping the soft curls at the junction of her thighs.

Bea sucked in a gasp, her back arching.

"Colin, what . . ."

He slid one finger between her slick folds.

"Oh my, yes," Bea whispered, sinking into him once more.

She was wet, wet for him. The realization sent his pulse pounding. As his finger slid in and out of her folds, he brushed his mouth against her neck, reveling in the taste and feel of this woman. Bea's breath came out in harsh pants. Her eyes were closed, her head thrown back in ecstasy. He knew, even as his shaft pulsed hard against his trousers, he knew he needed to stop. Yet he couldn't. He couldn't stop kissing her, couldn't stop touching her, couldn't stop breathing in her scent.

"Colin, oh, Colin." She tilted her head, so her lips pressed to his jaw.

Her fingers wrapped tightly around his arms, her nails piercing his forearms. Her body quivered and he knew she was close to finding her release. Her reaction was devastating to his already tormented soul. His erection begged for mercy, urging him to remove his fingers and find release with her. Colin resisted. The tiny part of him that clung to reality resisted. Bea would find her release, but he wouldn't. He wouldn't ruin her completely.

He pressed his face into her hair, breathing in her scent. Yes, he'd make sure she found her release. His hand moved to that spot, that tiny bud. Bea cried out, her voice echoing through the trees. Her body pulsed, contracting in blissful waves that tightened around his finger.

Colin gritted his teeth, holding still as the silence settled around them. Sweat dotted his forehead. His shaft pulsed, hard and hot against her backside. How badly he wanted to push himself inside her tight warmth. To taste every inch of her body. To make slow, torturous love to her the entire night. It would be so easy, she was so incredibly ready for him . . .

Shit. What the hell was he thinking? This was Bea. Leo's cousin. He dropped his hold and stumbled back.

Bea didn't turn to look at him, merely stood there, her shoulders rising and falling with each harsh breath.

"I suppose I should apologize," he said, his voice gruff with emotion.

At his words, her shoulders stiffened.

"But I won't."

She spun around to face him. Her eyes wide, her lush lips parted in surprise.

Colin stepped up close to her, his chest pressing to her breasts. He slid an arm around her waist, holding her tight against him, then pressed his lips lightly to hers. She remained stiff in his arms. Did she already regret what had happened? Or did she fear what he would do next?

"I can't say I'm sorry," he whispered against her mouth, "because I'd do it all over again."

He released his hold and turned, leaving her.

Thirty minutes. At least thirty bloody minutes Bea had remained rooted in place in that scrub brush near the creek, unable to move. How could she look the man in the eyes after what she'd let him do? How he'd touched her, what he'd said . . . And she'd liked it, damn her soul to hell. More than liked it. His touch had been purely . . . *amazing*.

Her heart skipped a beat, her body warming just at the memory. Through the brush, she could see him relaxing near the fire. She knew he couldn't spot her beyond the light, but still, his gaze was pinned to her, as if he could. The scent of cooking meat made her stomach clench, momentarily replacing her anxiety with the need for nourishment.

"Blast it," she said, taking a hesitant step forward. She stumbled, her legs long ago having grown numb with lack of movement. Colin most likely would find her embarrassment amusing. Bea, the arrogant English virgin. Still, she had to confront him sooner or later. Might as well get it over with and hope for a decent meal.

The smell of smoke stung her nostrils right before the path widened and she found herself within the campsite. Bea hesitated. His attention had fallen to the fire, as he stoked the flames. Light flickered over the hard planes of his face, drawing deep shadows beneath his cheekbones and dark fans from lashes much too thick for any decent man. Even now she could picture him peering through those lashes, that half smile that made her heart flutter. Yes, the man was much too ruggedly handsome for his own good.

"There's food, if you're hungry," he said, not bothering to look up.

How should one respond after being intimate with a man one barely knew? Perhaps she should pretend it hadn't happened, even if her body still thrummed from his touch. He didn't need to know.

She cleared her throat and started forward. "Will a fire not draw their attention?"

He shrugged. "I refuse to eat raw meat. Besides, there are, no doubt, a multitude of fires throughout the countryside. We'll hope they find ours last."

He flashed her a dimpled grin, his teeth gleaming white in the darkness. He was acting as if it hadn't happened. He was acting as if he hadn't touched her most intimate of spots. Perhaps he wasn't acting. Perhaps he wasn't embarrassed at all. Was it such a normal action for him? Had he not thought she was some whore the first night they'd met? Perhaps he frequented whores so often that taking a woman in the middle of a scrub jungle was an everyday occurrence.

The thought spurred her forward, her footsteps loud with anger.

He lifted his plate and began to eat, not bothering to wait for her. Back home she would have found his lack of manners insulting. She had more important things to worry about now. Like . . . hell, like Colin and the way he made her feel. Those brilliant blue eyes flickered to her, as if he could read her mind.

Color shot to Bea's cheeks. A warm tendril of heat swirled within her gut. She looked away, fearful he'd read the attraction she felt, the way she wanted to touch him, to lean into him just to breathe in his musky scent. Across the fire, she settled on a log, the warm flames the only barrier between them. She tried to focus on those flames, but found her attention rising, just above the dancing fire, to stare at him.

He met and held her gaze, but she could read nothing in his features, nothing of his thoughts or desires. Did he want her the way she wanted him? Frantic for something to occupy her thoughts, she lifted a stick and poked at the flames. Sparks rose into the night air, drifting across the brush. Sparks that reminded her of the heat he'd produced deep within. She'd never known . . . had no idea it could be this way between a man and a woman. No wonder her grandmother never left her alone with a man.

"They'd have fires at night back home," she said, wanting to fill the silence but her voice sounding high-pitched and odd. Did he notice?

"In Scotland?"

She nodded, feeling he should know *something* about her after being so intimate. "The villagers, they'd huddle around the flames, gossiping, laughing. I'd watch from the window of my chamber."

"Did you never join them?" He was watching her with a mild curiosity.

She hesitated only a moment, unsure if she wanted to relive her lonely childhood. "Once. And was told quite thoroughly that I was not to befriend the help." She forced herself to laugh and dared to look up at him then. He wasn't smiling. Her laughter faded and she dropped the stick and wrapped her arms around her. "It's gotten rather cold."

Colin lifted a metal pan from the fire and stood. Bea stiffened, watching him make his way toward her, her heart pounding with every step closer.

"Move over." His voice was gruff and demanding.

She scooted immediately, part of her cursing him for tormenting her with his nearness, and the other part thrilled to be so close. He settled next to her, sitting on the tails of her shirt, which she hadn't bothered to tuck in after her short bathing experience. She frowned and pulled on the shirt until she was free.

"Here, eat." He shoved a metal dish into her hands. The pan was warm, as if he'd been keeping the food hot for her. It was a generous gesture that didn't go unnoticed. On the plate were small chunks of gray meat, lying in puddles of grease. Not exactly appetizing, yet that didn't matter.

As there were no forks, she lifted a chunk with her fingers. Her stomach growled. She stuffed the meat between her lips. The flavor was soft and mild. She swallowed and took another piece, her stomach clenching, begging for more.

"You'll need to keep up your strength."

She nodded her agreement, and stuffed another piece into her mouth. "This is quite good. Why type of bird is it? Tastes rather like chicken."

Before Colin could answer, she'd managed to fill her mouth yet again. Ridiculous, she knew, but dear Lord, she was hungry. She looked around for a napkin, realized there was none, and swiped her greasy hands on her trousers.

"It's not a bird," Colin answered.

She glanced at him, curious now, and stuffed another piece into her mouth. There was something in his eyes, something that set her on edge. She swallowed the lump of meat. "Then what is it?"

He leaned closer, the sparkle of amusement in his eyes making her nervous. "Snake."

Her fingers unclenched and the dish clattered to the ground. "What?"

He scooped up the plate with a frown. "Snake. No reason to waste it." He took a bite and grinned, showing those blasted dimples.

Bea's stomach rumbled, bile rising in her throat. "Please tell me you jest."

"Nope." He stuffed another piece between his lips.

"Oh dear Lord." She pressed one hand to her stomach and another to her mouth. "I'm going to be sick."

His head jerked toward her. "Don't you dare. Took me forever to skin the damn thing."

The visual those words produced was not pleasant. "Oh God." She jumped to her feet.

"Bea." Colin's voice was so sharp, she actually paused. "Sit down." He stood, glaring at her.

She wanted to refuse. She wanted to run to those bushes and vomit up her meal. Instead, she slowly lowered herself onto the log, forcing her small dinner to remain firmly in her gut.

"You will keep that damn food in your stomach, understand?"

She barely had the energy to nod.

He pointed at her like a father reprimanding his child. "We need our strength. *You* need your strength. I will not drag your unconscious, weak body across India."

She knew she should be offended, yet couldn't get over the fact that she'd eaten . . . oh dear Lord . . . she'd eaten snake! She gagged. Her stomach clenched. She gagged again.

"You sound like a cat with a hairball." He flipped open a bag and pulled out an oblong, yellowish fruit. With the small machete lying at his feet, he whacked the melon in two. It fell apart with a thud, revealing a pale yellow flesh.

"Here." He shoved half into her hands.

The skin was smooth, the scent crisp and sweet. "What is it?" she asked warily.

"Fruit. Mango. You'll like it. Focus on that, not"—he waved the machete through the air—"what you ate before."

She swallowed hard and forced images of snake from her mind. Slowly, she lifted the fruit to her mouth. Her tongue darted out and touched the fruit hesitantly. It was sweet. She dug her teeth into the flesh. Juice trickled down her throat.

"Mmm," she muttered. "Tastes rather like honey."

Colin grinned. "Figured you'd like it."

She took another healthy bite, the greasy snake meat forgotten. "Delicious." She closed her eyes, allowing the sweet taste to invade her senses. This, she could appreciate. This, she could enjoy. The warm night, the brilliant stars twinkling above, the sweet fruit, this she could admire about India. And she could almost forget what she'd allowed Colin to do to her body . . . almost.

The silence finally invaded her heavenly dream. Slowly, she lifted her lashes. The campsite was quiet, still. She turned her head ever so slightly and met Colin's gaze. There was a hardness in his eyes. They'd gone from the soft blue of a summer sky to the brittleness of snow on a moonlit night. She swallowed hard, her heart racing, knowing what he thought about. It was there, written on his face. His desire for her.

"What?" she finally whispered, unable to take the silence any longer.

He reached out.

Bea stiffened, sucking in a breath. His calloused hand cupped the side of her face. He stared at her mouth and slowly brushed his thumb across her lips. She couldn't seem to breathe. Couldn't seem to think logically. All she knew was that Colin was going to kiss her and she wanted him to.

He leaned toward her and she allowed her lashes to drift

down. His warm breath brushed across her lips right before his mouth pressed to hers. Bea sank into his touch. His lips were warm, firm, perfect. He tilted his face, his hand cupping the back of her head and drawing her closer.

"You taste so sweet," he whispered.

His words sent her pulse racing. Bea's hands slid around his shoulders and she molded her chest to his. That place between her thighs ached as heat flooded her body. Wearing only the thin shirt, and trousers made for men, she felt exposed to the elements, exposed to him. God help her, she wanted him to touch her again.

Softly, his lips pressed to hers, his teeth nipping the sensitive skin over and over as she'd done with the fruit. Finally, Bea could take no more. Boldly she slipped her tongue into his mouth. He seemed surprised by her move. But just as quickly, Colin took control. With a low growl, his tongue met hers thrust for thrust.

Bea knew she was getting in deep, murky waters but she couldn't seem to care. Colin's hand slipped from her hair to her collar. Before she could even realize his intentions, he'd opened three of her buttons. Part of her mind screamed for him to stop. She silenced that part, pushed it to the farthest recesses of her mind.

Her shirt gaped enough for him to slip his warm hand inside. His palm cupped her left breast. Bea's nipples instantly hardened, growing heavy with his touch. She wanted him, all of him, so much so that she'd sell her very soul. He tore his mouth from hers and lowered his head, pressing his lips to her neck. Lower. His mouth rested in the valley between her breasts.

Bea sighed, tilting her head back. Her hair tumbled in waves down her back. Somehow he'd managed to untie the ribbon holding the locks in place. Overhead, stars twinkled in the darkening sky, diamonds on dark velvet. The night was magical, Colin was magical. The things he was doing to her, the way she felt, were magical.

"Lovely," she thought she heard him whisper. She wasn't sure. It didn't matter if he'd said the word or not, for she felt lovely under his attention. The way he looked at her, the way he touched her, she'd never felt so attractive, never felt so heady with power.

Suddenly, Colin stiffened and pulled away. She felt his absence like the winter in Scotland, cold and piercing.

"What—"

He pressed his finger to her lips. "Shhh."

His gaze narrowed, his breathing coming out in short, sharp pants.

The fine hairs on Bea's neck stood on end. "Colin?" she whispered.

He shook his head, his gaze scanning the scrub beyond the light of their fire. She froze, her heart slamming against her chest as she waited for an explanation. Then she heard it. The snap of a branch.

Bea sucked in a breath, her skin crawling. Colin surged to his feet while Bea fumbled with the buttons on her shirt.

"Show yourself," Colin demanded, his voice hard and sure, so sure that for one blessed moment Bea thought they had nothing to worry about. Perhaps Raj had found them?

"Damn," Colin whispered just loud enough for her to hear.

Fear spurred her into action. Bea jumped to her feet and peeked around his shoulder.

Five men stood before them, wearing only trousers, their thin, tanned chests bare. But the state of their undress didn't attract Bea's attention. No, the rifles did.

Chapter 19

The moon hung low in the sky, its round, merry face mocking her plight. Bea leaned back against Colin, giving in to her exhaustion. For at least two hours they'd ridden. She hadn't protested when Colin had placed her on the horse, then settled behind her. And she'd known better than to open her mouth and ask any of the many questions swirling through her head. There were some instances when keeping your mouth shut was the best possible response. This was one of those instances.

Immediately, the men had surrounded them, two riding on mounts in front, the other three walking behind. They were a silent group, giving no indication of where they were going or why. Did they work with Demyan, or someone else? How she wished she could ask Colin *something*!

As if sensing her thoughts, Colin tightened his grip around her waist. She was thankful for his presence, truly she was. Thankful she could feel the strong beat of his heart against her back, for it meant he still lived. As frantic as she was for answers, she didn't exactly want their trek to end. She knew the end would only bring more fighting . . . perhaps death. He might be a dunce at times, but there was no doubt Colin was brave and strong. He'd try to free them. He'd try. But he couldn't possibly win against so many men.

Perhaps that was how it was supposed to be. After all, death had been nipping at their heels for days now. Perhaps they were fighting a losing battle. She closed her eyes as tears stung the backs of her lids. She didn't want to die, and for now, she'd be a coward about the possibility. But when it happened, she'd be strong. She'd make Leo and Ella proud. She'd make Colin proud.

She might have slept. She wasn't sure. But suddenly, Colin shifted and she was torn from the dredges of the semi-unconscious.

"Bea." His voice was soft and warm against her ear. Her lashes fluttered up. The side of his face was pressed to hers, his whiskers rough, his skin warm. For a moment, with Colin so close, Bea thought she was in the middle of an erotic dream.

"We've arrived."

Confused, she focused ahead. The silent men trudging along beside them brought the situation rushing back. Gone were the fields. Instead, a small village of dark huts spread out before them.

"Where are we?" she whispered.

Colin merely shook his head, but his hard gaze was taking in every detail. Exhaustion hadn't dulled his protective instincts. While she'd been drifting to sleep, he'd been keeping watch.

They moved into a single line as the streets narrowed between houses of white plaster. Although a few homes had lights that twinkled, the village was quiet and still. Not a soul stirred. Their horses trotted slowly, the thump of their hooves against the dirt echoing down the narrow lanes. There was something rather eerie about the place, something she couldn't put her finger on. It was as if the occupants were waiting . . . for them?

Bea shivered at the thought.

"Are you cold?" Colin asked, misinterpreting her reaction.

His hands settled at her waist, the warmth of his touch scooping through the fine linen of her shirt.

She gave him a soft, sad smile. As if being cold mattered when they'd probably die soon. She shook her head, but he still looked worried. Bea swallowed hard and looked away. She'd been so wrong about Colin. How she'd wanted to despise him when they'd first met, wanted to despise the sinful feelings he stirred within. Another man focused on seeking adventure. Hadn't she enough men like that in her life? But as day after day swept by, she found she couldn't hate Colin after all. And now . . . well, now they were most likely walking to their demise.

Their abductors turned down a narrow alley, the ground underfoot changing from dirt to stone of some sort, and the clomp of horses' hooves grew louder. Bea tilted her head slightly, narrowing her gaze. Was there something ahead? Between the rows of homes? The dark shape emerged, forming a large building. Bea latched on to Colin's hands, her heart hammering against her ribs. This was it, the end.

"Do you have a plan?" she whispered.

"Not a one," Colin replied.

She frowned, unsure if she wanted to laugh or cry. Surely, maybe, hopefully they could think of something before . . . before it was too late. Oh, what did it matter? They were outnumbered.

She turned, frantic to make a connection with the man one last time. "Colin, I . . ."

He raised a golden brow. "Yes?"

"I . . . I do like you."

He blinked, obviously stunned by her emotional outburst.

She tilted her chin high as heat raced up her neck and into her cheeks. "I do. Yes, you're rather obnoxious and annoying at times." She twisted her hands together. "And a day doesn't go by when I don't imagine, with glee, punching you in the face . . ."

His other brow lifted.

"Oh, dash it. What I'm saying is . . . it's just that . . . if we're going to die, I thought I'd let you know that . . . well"—she looked down—"you're not entirely terrible."

They paused outside an iron gate. Someone shouted from the darkness and metal screeched against metal as the gates were thrown inward. Still, Colin said nothing and it was too blasted dark to read his eyes.

He cleared his throat and pulled Bea close, forcing her to turn forward, her back pressed to his chest. That was it? He wouldn't respond? No words or acknowledgment?

"Well?" she hissed under her breath as they started through the gates and into a courtyard.

"Well, what?" His breath was a warm caress across the side of her face, and unwillingly her body responded. She ignored the shivers, focusing instead on her annoyance.

"Well, what?" That was all he had to say? She'd just told him she liked him and that was his response? Her fingers tightened on his wrists. *"Well,"* she drawled out through gritted teeth. "Have you nothing to say in return?"

"Not particularly."

"Not," Bea sputtered, barely able to get the words out, "particularly?" She jerked her head to the side, attempting to make eye contact. He looked down at her, his gaze twinkling. Bea's mouth fell open. He was making jest of her admittance and when they were going to die, no less? *The cad!* She'd been right all along. She faced forward again, anger pushing aside her fear.

"Down," one of the men next to them said, pointing his rifle at Bea's chest.

She sucked in a breath and leaned back. Colin didn't hesitate as he slid off the mount. Looking into her eyes, she could read the message clear. Stay quiet, keep close by. He rested his hands on her waist and set her upon the ground. Her legs gave out. She didn't seem to have any muscles left and slumped toward the ground. Colin was there, slipping his arm around her waist and holding her close.

"I'm not used to riding," she whispered, taking a moment to relearn the use of her limbs.

"Follow." The guide jerked his head toward the building.

A lantern glowed on either side of a massive wooden door. Colin escorted Bea up the shallow marble steps to the entrance. Her legs tingled with each movement, slowly coming back to life, but fear was making her weak.

She wasn't sure what she'd been expecting, but it hadn't been this, a home of massive riches. Surely Demyan didn't live here. The place was too beautiful, as stunning as any English manor but with the rich detail only India could provide. Made out of white stone, the front façade was covered with windows that lined the top and bottom. Each window was covered with intricately carved shutters of dark wood.

As they reached the top step, the double wooden doors swung wide. A man wearing a white shirt and trousers stood just inside, a turban twisted atop his head. He bowed low. A show of respect and welcome. The bow threw Bea off balance, played with her emotions. She'd been expecting a fight to the death, not this decent reception.

"Colin, I don't understand," Bea whispered.

His grip tightened on her arm. "Shhh, not now."

Somewhat annoyed, she turned to face him. "Are we in danger or not?"

He looked down at her, the exasperation evident in his eyes. "I'm not sure."

"I'd like to know," she shot back as they made their way up the shallow steps.

"Why is that, princess?" he asked, looking truly curious.

"Well, so I can prepare and know how to behave."

They paused in the foyer, the area cool, the marble under their feet hard. Great wooden arches rose above, while heavy metal chandeliers hung from the ceiling, throwing shadows and light across the walls. The doors shut with a thud that echoed down the long corridor. Bea's heart leapt in her throat, but she didn't dare turn, too afraid to move. The beauty of the place belied their dreary situation.

Colin's hand rested on her lower back. "Really? You have different protocols for different situations?"

"Of course," she answered, her fear momentarily forgotten.

"And do you need to change your outfit, too, that is, if you're marching toward your death?" He chuckled, a deep, low chuckle that warmed her insides as much as it annoyed her. "You amaze me, Bea, truly." It wasn't exactly the compliment she'd been wanting earlier when she'd admitted she liked him.

"Am I to be worried or not, 'tis a simple question, Colin."

He sighed, pausing when the man leading them stopped. A large open doorway loomed before them, and Bea realized that whoever it was who'd brought them here would soon be revealed. Yet she found more interest in what Colin's response would be than their kidnapper's identity.

"Well?" Bea demanded in a harsh whisper, eager to hear his answer and for a brief moment focus on something other than whether they were strolling toward their demise.

"I find worrying to be a worthless emotion, don't you?"

Bea's lips parted to respond, but she wasn't quite sure what to say. It wasn't the first time Colin had rendered her speechless. She could only hope it wouldn't be the last time.

The man in the white turban bowed to someone in the room, then stepped aside. Just through the doorway, Bea noted high ceilings and more marble flooring. With his hand on her lower back, Colin nudged Bea inside. The lighting was dim and it took a few moments for Bea's eyes to adjust. A sweet, earthy scent lingered in the air, something almost overwhelming, something that made her dizzy and unable to focus.

It wasn't until they'd paused in the middle of the room that Bea noticed the others. Settled on a mound of brilliant blue pillows, an Indian man reclined near the far wall, his young, handsome face passive and at ease. At his side, a woman lay with her arms wrapped around his neck, her body pressed indecently to his. They were so still that, for a moment, she thought perhaps they were one of the statues scattered about the room.

Then the man shifted ever so slightly. His long legs were clad in white trousers, but his dark chest was bare. Between slim fingers he idly held a sort of long pipe that let drift a thin trail of smoke. Stunned and confused, Bea found herself staring wide-eyed at the small group. They were beautiful, in an exotic and foreign way. The woman with her curvy body and shiny black hair, her face half-covered with a wisp of brilliant pink material that matched the color of her trousers and blouse.

"Welcome." The man gave them an unhurried smile, revealing brilliant white teeth.

"Why are we here?" Colin demanded immediately.

Like a panther sunning himself, the man lazily looked Colin up and down, then slid his gaze to Bea. His attention felt odd, warm, yet somewhat uncomfortable. She wasn't sure if she should feel flattered or offended by his perusal. Colin shifted, stepping in front with a warrior stance that blocked the man's view. Was he jealous? The thought thrilled her more than she wished.

"Come, my friends. Sit. I am Shiva Krishna."

Two servants swept forward, setting cushions near the man and his woman. Colin didn't move. "Why are we here?"

Insatiably curious, Bea rested her hands on Colin's broad back and stood on tiptoe, peeking over his right shoulder.

Shiva Krishna chuckled, a light airy sound. "You white men, so difficult." He handed his pipe to the woman.

Then slowly, he stood. He reminded Bea of a birch tree, elegant and lean. With short, unhurried strides, Shiva walked toward them. He paused only feet from Colin and smiled again as if they were long-lost friends. He was shorter than Colin and half his bulk, yet the man showed no fear under

Colin's intense scrutiny. But then, why should he be afraid? They were in his home, surrounded by his guards.

"I know of you, my friend."

The room grew silent, and for a moment Bea thought she'd misunderstood Shiva's words. To an outsider, Colin seem impassive to the man's statement. Bea knew otherwise. That pulse in the side of his neck jumped to life and his back muscles grew tense under her palms. Her frantic gaze jumped from Colin to Shiva. Colin's anxiety was hers. What, exactly, did the man know?

Their host held his arms wide. "You are the miracle they speak of."

Bea's heart skipped a beat and suddenly she understood. They knew. Already they knew what Colin was capable of. Did the entire country know? According to Ella, he'd been in India only a few months. Colin remained mute, not uttering a single word of protest or affirmation.

The man started around them, his hands on his hips. "They say you saved a child on her deathbed. You made a crippled woman walk again. You've snatched hundreds from the grasp of death."

Bea slid Colin a glance. He merely remained frozen in place. Was it true? Had he really saved that many? Once again Colin said nothing, neither confirming nor refuting the statement. But then, she knew Colin, or at least she felt she did, and Colin would never discuss the particulars.

Shiva paused beside them, this time his gaze pinned to Bea as if to read her response. That same sweet scent that hovered in the room seemed to follow him, confusing her already troubled mind. "They say you can even heal animals."

He said the words to Colin, yet continued to watch her. Bea's lips parted on a gasp of surprise. Even if Colin hadn't showed his shock, she couldn't seem to contain hers. How did Shiva know about King Henry so soon? She looked away, feigning interest in the dark veins in the marble floor. Who had told him? Stephan or Demyan?

"What do you want?" Colin finally demanded, his voice showing his impatience.

From the corner of her eyes, Bea saw the man flash that brilliant smile again, easy and sure. "*Want?* Why, nothing. Merely for you to be our honored guest."

Bea didn't believe the man and apparently neither did Colin. His legs shifted, braced apart like a pirate at the helm of a ship, preparing for attack. "How'd you find us?"

"You were easy to track, my friend. Your coloring." He slid Bea another glance. "The description of your woman."

"My wife," Colin shot back.

Bea attempted to hide her surprise, trying to keep her face as expressionless as Colin's, but she could feel the heat rising to her cheeks in a telling flush.

The man raised his dark brows, his gaze still pinned to her. "I hadn't realized. You are a fortunate man."

Bea dropped to the heels of her feet, using Colin's broad shoulders to hide behind. Colin, apparently, wasn't as unaffected as she'd believed. His long fingers curled at his sides. She rested her palms on his lower back, hoping her touch might ease his tension. Responding to the man would only court trouble. There had to be some way to escape. Bea took the time to examine their surroundings, her gaze slipping serendipitously around the room, looking for, at the very least, a weapon.

Hardly anything was visible in the dimly lit area. A few lanterns glowed in the corners. The dark shutters covering the windows kept any light from entering the dwelling. She could only decipher a few large statues of humans scattered here and there. Frustration welled within.

Bloody nothing to help! The door whispered open. Bea spun around. Two women floated into the room, the gauzy material of their trousers and bodices portraying every curve. They glanced only once toward Bea and Colin, but showed little interest in their guests.

"Come, my friends," Shiva said, sliding an arm around

each lass and leading them toward the mound of cushions, away from Colin and Bea.

The small group settled, stretching out onto their makeshift bed as if Bea and Colin weren't even present. Horrified and enthralled, Bea watched as one of those women leaned down and pressed her red lips to Shiva's chest. Another woman, as if taking her cue, slid down Shiva's body and pressed her mouth to his flat stomach.

Heat shot to Bea's cheeks and flared through her body, intense and rather uncomfortable. She tore her gaze away, deciding to focus on the room. Through the haze, the marble statues morphed into men and women. *Naked* men and women. Bea's mouth fell open, only just now realizing what those statues were. One man lay upon the ground, his shaft buried into a woman's stone mouth.

"You enjoy my art?"

Bea had to resist the urge to press her hands to her face. The heat was so unbearable she thought for sure she'd burst into flames. "I've . . . seen nothing like it," she managed in a horrified gurgle.

Shiva merely grinned. "You'll grow used to them. In fact, I'm sure you'll come to enjoy them, as I do."

"I doubt it," Bea muttered.

Colin took her hand, his grip tight, but his face surprisingly passive.

"Come." Shiva waved them over. "Rest."

Bea glanced at Colin to judge his reaction. A small smile lifted the left corner of his lips. Surprised, Bea nearly stumbled when he pulled her forward. His gait was unhurried but confident as they made their way to the unused pillows. Bea had to resist the urge to dig her heels into the marble floor and pull back. What the bloody hell was he doing? Colin settled on the cushions and jerked Bea down. She landed on his lap with a yelp.

Before she could escape, he wrapped his arm around her waist and held her tight to his chest. His gaze slid to her, a quick acknowledgment, but enough time for her to read his thoughts. Don't move. Shut up. Bea clenched her jaw and focused on the shutters covering the windows, the only safe place in the room to look. She didn't know what Colin's game was, but she refused to participate.

Slowly, his fingers trailed through her long locks, almost as if he didn't realize he did it, but she did. Damn it all if shivers didn't race over her skin. She took in a deep breath, telling herself she would not react to his touch. Above, a large fan that was attached to the ceiling swung back and forth, providing them with a soft breeze that cooled her flushed skin.

Shiva gave a discreet wave of his fingers. "You travel far from home, my friend."

A woman swept forward and handed Colin a drink. She didn't ask Bea if she was thirsty. Bea shifted, half on Colin's lap, half off. Stiff and nervous, she was uncomfortably perched on his hard thighs, but too afraid to move.

Colin didn't seem to notice, merely sipped his drink, his attention on Shiva.

"I'm thrilled you're here. Why, already your talents have traveled far. Many wish to seek your assistance. You are very valuable, my friend." Shiva's hand settled on the thigh of one of the women.

Valuable? As if Colin were a thing, instead of a person. Bea frowned, the words not sitting right with her. Colin, though, didn't seem to mind but continued to stare passively at the group.

He set his glass on a low table made of dark wood. "Honestly, I don't give a damn what anyone wants."

"Of course not," Shiver replied, steepling his long fingers together. "You're a man who has a purpose, yes?"

"I'm looking for a statue," Colin said. "But then you already knew that."

Bea stiffened, waiting with bated breath for Shiva's response. The man didn't deny, didn't lie, but merely smiled.

Colin drummed his fingers against Bea's thigh, his face bored. "How long do we have, before he arrives?"

One of the women handed Shiva a pipe. The man gave her a grateful smile and sucked in a deep puff, then released the gray smoke into a cloud that hovered overhead until the movement of the fan sent it forward. Bea couldn't tell if she liked the sweet scent or not. It left her feeling odd, light-headed and off balance.

Finished, Shiva handed the woman the pipe. "Not long, I'm afraid."

Bea forced her mind to concentrate, surging through the numbing sensation that had settled in her body. She'd known all along that Shiva must be working with Demyan, yet the man's words shocked her all the same. Had he just admitted he was in league with the monster? Just admitted the Demon would be here soon?

"How soon?" Colin asked.

One of the women straddled Shiver's hips and pressed her mouth to his neck. Shiva sighed, closing his eyes in ecstasy. "A day, perhaps two."

Bea attempted to focus on Shiva's words, truly she did. But instead, she found utter fascination in the way the woman was rocking against the man, completely uncaring that strangers were in their midst.

After a few moments and a few moans, Shiva patted her on her bottom and set her aside. "I've decided you and I shall be friends, yes?" He looked at Colin. "With your talents and my money, there is no need for anyone else. This suits you?"

No! No, it didn't suit Bea.

Colin didn't respond.

Shiva merely watched, waiting for a response. Bea was no ninny. She knew enough to know they had no choice. Work with Shiva or work with Demyan. But could Shiva truly keep Demyan away if the man wanted them? And what would Shiva do if he realized Demyan didn't want Colin at all, but wanted Bea? Would he toss her to the wolves?

The woman who'd straddled Shiva's waist was at it again, tearing Bea from thoughts of Demyan. She slid her hands down Shiva's flat stomach to the waistband of his silky trousers. Bea sucked in a breath and froze. The woman wouldn't dare.

She did. Turning her dark gaze in Colin's direction, the woman slipped her hand underneath Shiva's waistband. Bea's heart slammed against her chest. Shiva's lids drifted down, the pleasure evident on his face. Bea jerked her gaze away, staring at the far, dark corner of the room. Her heart thundered in her chest. How? How could this happen, here, now? People just didn't do these sort of things in front of others, did they?

"We shall enjoy ourselves now, yes?"

No! Bea wanted to scream. No! Colin's hand moved slowly up and down her arm. The touch should have been comforting, yet it felt wrong, here and now, and she had to resist the urge to jerk away.

"You know how white women are," Colin murmured, apparently using Bea as an excuse. Well, that was fine with her!

The woman whose hand was down Shiva's trousers grinned behind her veil. Shiva, too, smiled slow and wicked. "Of course. Go then. Make your own merriment and think over my proposition. With your abilities, we could have power together, my friend."

Colin nodded. Before Bea could guess his intentions, he scooped her up into his arms and carried her toward the door. She clung to him, her body trembling, her heart racing as she resisted the urge to shout at him to move faster.

"My friend," Shiva called and Bea resisted the urge to curse.

Colin paused and turned, the doorway just out of reach. Shiva still lay upon the bed, looking relaxed and at ease as the three women crawled over him like butterflies on a flower.

His arm wrapped around one woman, bringing her close. "It's the dry season, you know."

Colin let Bea slide down his body.

Shiva nuzzled his face into the woman's neck. "In India, more than anywhere else, we value water."

Colin didn't move and Bea was left to stand there, wondering what the hell Shiva was speaking of. Oh, she knew he was telling them something important—that much was obvious—but what?

Shiva looked at them again. "Water is life, purification." A knowing smile slipped across his lips. "You understand, my friend?"

Colin nodded slowly.

They were silent for one long moment.

Shiva clapped his hands, the sound unnaturally loud in the silence. "Now, I'm sure you'd like to rest. You'll stay, as my honored guests, yes?" Servants scurried into the room, bowing low. "Show them to their quarters."

One of the women jumped to her feet and sashayed forward, swinging her hips from side to side in a way that most men would find mesmerizing. Bea didn't miss the flirtatious smile she threw Colin's way, visible through the gauzy material covering her full lips. The flare of jealousy that coursed through her body felt odd and unnatural. All she knew was that she wanted to do nothing more than to tear the hair from the woman's scalp.

Colin, though, didn't seem to notice the woman's attention. No, his mind was probably centered on the odd words Shiva had spoken. Bea dared to glance back. Their host stood in the center of the room, watching her as if he knew more than he was letting on. A shiver of unease tickled her spine. She jerked her gaze forward, scurrying after Colin up a flight of marble stairs. How badly she wanted to demand answers, but knew better than to ask now. They stopped outside a dark wooden door. The woman pushed it wide and bowed.

"Thank you." Colin pulled Bea inside.

As soon as the door shut, Bea faced him. "We can't possibly stay here. It's ridi—"

Colin moved past her, his hands brushing up and down the walls.

"What are you doing?"

"Looking for peepholes," he murmured, continuing his progress around the room.

"Rubbish." Bea's lips curled in disgust. He couldn't be serious, yet he obviously was as he continued his search. Bea took the time to survey their surroundings. Her ire and confusion were momentarily forgotten. Curtains hung around the room, brilliant blues and greens that covered the windows and bed. Already, a fire roared in a marble hearth. And it was clean! Wonderfully clean without a speck of dirt or sand in sight.

Bea's breath caught. "Oh my."

Colin lifted a brow, returning to her side. "You were saying?"

She slowly shook her head, unable to tear her gaze from the room long enough to look at him. It was beautiful. So clean, so stunning. Tears welled in her eyes. After days of camping outside, days of dirt, it was heaven. And she was supposed to stay in this sensual room, as a married couple, with Colin. It was too intimate, too much. Heat traveled through her body, making her skin tingle.

"It's . . . lovely," she finally managed. "So, does this mean we aren't in danger here?" She couldn't keep the hope from her voice. How wonderful it would be if they could stay in this room for a day, two, a lifetime.

Colin sighed softly. "No, it doesn't. Damn it, Bea, if I thought you'd learned anything so far, it's that you're always in danger."

She ignored his dire words and settled her hand on one of the cushions of the bed. So incredibly soft, it was like cream. The dirt under her fingernails caught her attention. Horrified, she drew back.

"Obviously they were expecting us." Colin nodded toward the tub that lay half-hidden behind a curtain of brilliant blue.

Like a child drawn to sweets, Bea made her way toward the water. The scent of roses hovered in the air, the oil swirling atop the surface tempting. Her body ached with just the thought of settling into the warm liquid.

"Get in."

Bea spun around, pressing her hands to her chest. "What?"

Colin's eyes twinkled with amusement. "I said get in."

"But . . . I can't . . . you're . . ."

He started unbuttoning his shirt. "I'm not leaving you here alone and unprotected, but there's no reason why you can't bathe."

She wasn't sure which was more tempting, watching Colin undress, or taking a bath. Oh, how wonderful it would be to bathe, to be clean once more.

Colin nodded. "Go on then."

She couldn't resist. "You won't look?"

He grinned a slow, completely lovely smile that showed off his dimples and warmed her heart. "Of course not. Don't you trust me?"

Chapter 20

Colin kept his eyes closed, focusing on the darkness and attempting to make sense of what had happened with Shiva. But each slight splash of water sent fire pulsing through his veins, centering his thoughts on Bea. Always Bea. He tried to control his breathing, tried to control his thoughts. Then Bea sighed. It was the tenth time she'd sighed. It was also the same way she sighed when he kissed her, touched her . . .

His hands fisted into the satin duvet covering the bed as sweat beaded on his bare chest. How badly he wanted to haul her out of that water, to show her how loudly he could make her sigh. Slowly, he lifted his lashes and studied her through the green, gauzy material covering the bed. Only one lone lantern sat on a stool near the tub, but it was enough light to highlight her creamy bare shoulders.

With a growl of frustration, he flung the curtains wide and stood.

"Colin, what . . ." Bea's protest died as he moved toward the balcony.

Yes, he'd promised to lie upon the bed with his eyes closed, but hell, how much could a man take? Not much, apparently. And if he had to hear one more sigh part her lips, he'd . . .

The marble was cool under his bare feet. He took in a

deep breath, trying to calm his racing heart. The night air hung heavy with the scent of jasmine, so sweet and intoxicating that it was almost overwhelming. The scent reminded him of Bea. Mysterious, complicated, addictive. His fingers tightened around the stone railing as heat pounded through his body in a force that could kill a lesser man.

He should be focused on Shiva. The man had given him a choice, work for him, or Demyan. But if Shiva knew Demyan, then he knew what the man was capable of. How could he possibly think he could defeat a man who wouldn't die?

Water splashed, reminding him of Shiva's cryptic message. *Water is life, purification. You understand, my friend?*

No. He didn't understand. But the overall message was clear: Shiva knew something and he'd most likely share it with Colin if he relented and joined Shiva's little army of the insane.

Water splashed once more, sending a jolt of passion flaring through his body and tearing his mind from dark thoughts to more pleasant ones. He knew she stood, could hear the rustle of cloth as she dried. He knew she stood there naked and it took everything he had not to turn, haul her sleek, warm body up against his, and . . . and . . .

"Colin?" Her English accent moved over him like warm honey.

He breathed deep and swallowed hard. He didn't dare answer for fear she'd hear the tremor of his voice.

There was a whisper of clothing as she walked toward him. "Are you well?"

His fingers tightened on the railing. "Yeah, fine."

The scent of roses wafted through the air and he knew she was close. He could feel her indecision, heavy and suffocating, as she paused just behind him. She didn't say a word, merely stood behind him. Damn her, why didn't she return to the room? Why didn't she retire to bed? Gritting his teeth, he finally turned.

She looked better than he could have imagined. Her wet hair hung in loose waves down her back. Her face was flushed pink from the warm water. Wearing a long robe of a gauzy green material that showed every dip and curve of her glorious form. Did she realize that with the lantern shining behind her, he could see the outline of her body? Did she realize how badly he wanted to rip that robe from her?

"Well then," she finally whispered, her gaze lowering to take in his bare chest. "I should . . ."

Leave? Go to bed? Take off that damn robe and let him touch every inch of her?

She took her bottom lip between her teeth, her gaze flickering with indecision. "Colin."

"Yeah?" His voice came out husky, breathless.

"Did I . . . are you . . . are you angry with me?"

He released a wry laugh. Far from angry. No, he was angry with himself for falling for the impossible once again. And Bea was certainly an impossibility. "No. Of course not."

She frowned. "Then why are you snapping at me?"

"I'm tired, Bea." His voice came out in a low growl. Damn her, why didn't she leave him in peace?

"I'm sorry." She turned and started back toward the room.

Insanity spurred him toward her. Colin latched on to her wrist and spun her around. The moment he touched her, rational thought vanished. Bea's lips parted as she met his gaze. There was confusion there, shimmering in those golden orbs. Confusion and surprise.

He supposed he should have apologized. He didn't. Instead, he jerked her forward. Her hands flattened against his chest, her body falling into his. Before she could offer any protest, he crushed his mouth to hers. This was what he wanted, what he *needed,* what he'd been dreaming about since she'd entered that damn bath.

Colin slid his fingers into her damp locks, the silky strands clinging to his hands. His lips molded to hers and his body practically groaned in sweet relief. Bea sank into him, her warm, soft breasts crushing to his chest. She didn't fight, didn't argue, merely tasted him like a woman starved. Her reaction thrilled and delighted him.

He tilted her head, deepening the kiss. As his tongue slipped between her lips, his arousal flared to life, pulsing hard against her lower belly. She didn't step back like some simpering virgin. No, she groaned and pressed closer to him as if she knew exactly what she was doing. Her obvious desire only heightened his.

Colin moved to her neck, her smooth, slender neck, while his hands parted her robe. She sucked in a breath as his fingers moved to her backside, cupping her round bottom and pulling her up hard against him.

"Colin," she whispered.

It was all he needed to hear. He slipped his arm under her knees and around her back, cradling her to his chest. Bea stared up into his eyes, a dreamy look to her gaze. Pink stained her cheeks, whether from embarrassment or desire, he wasn't sure. But she didn't simper. She didn't resist. She only stared up at him with those amber eyes like she wanted him. Needed him. And that thought drove him mad with desire.

He paused at the bed, allowing her to slide down his body. *She* wanted *him*. And in this moment, with a soft, clean bed and only the two of them, he knew she'd allow him to take her innocence. Could he? Could he ruin her to satisfy his own animalistic need?

"Colin?"

His hands fisted at his sides. He should step back. He should move to that settee along the far wall and give her the bed. He should leave before something happened. Dredging up what little self-control he had left, Colin started to move.

Something strange flashed across Bea's eyes, something indecipherable, something completely unlike her, something that made him pause. Slowly, she settled her hands on his chest. Colin sucked in a breath. Almost tauntingly, she drew her hands up, slipping her fingers through the crisp hair on his chest. Her fingers settled at his hips and paused.

"A scar?" She slid her finger over the pale line of puckered skin near his right hip and lifted her eyes questioningly to him.

"Bea." He pressed his hands over hers, staying the action. "Stop. For your own damn good."

"Just one." Her dark lashes lowered. "Just one . . ." She stood on tiptoe and closed her eyes.

He knew what she wanted. She wanted him to kiss her. But he couldn't kiss her and stop. He couldn't. It was too much to ask.

"Bea, I—"

She crushed her mouth to his. Stunned, Colin merely stood there. Bea slipped her fingers into the hair at the base of his neck, caressing the strands. It was a primal kiss. A hard, heated kiss. She'd learned quickly. She drew her tongue along his lower lip, slow and torturous.

Heat pumped through Colin's veins. With a growl, he scooped her up and laid her upon the soft cushions that made their bed. The edges of her green robe trailed over her nipples and that spot between her legs, hiding her very heat, but hinting at that treasure. Her hair, loose and dark, fanned across the brilliant blue pillows. Damn, she was beautiful.

"Colin, please," she whispered, reaching out to him.

It was all she needed to say. Suddenly it didn't matter that they were running for their lives. It didn't matter that this very home Bea thought was a castle was really a prison and they were most likely trapped. Nothing mattered but her.

He settled beside her on the soft cushions. His hands found the seam of her robe. Slowly, he drew the material wide, the gauze whispering over her pale skin. She was naked. Completely and utterly naked. She was obviously trying to torment him to hell.

He closed his eyes for the briefest of moments, attempting to regain control of his thundering heart. This was Leo's cousin. Ella's friend, he tried to remember. But it didn't help. He opened his eyes and slid his hands up her smooth thighs, farther to her flat stomach, to her breasts. Soft mounds with tight rose-colored nipples begging to be touched. Her skin was flushed, a charming pink that spread from her upper chest to her cheeks. She was embarrassed, he realized, yet she met his gaze boldly, daringly. She wasn't one to back down from a challenge.

"Dear God, Bea, you're beautiful."

She looked away then, the pink on her cheeks deepening.

Colin frowned. "Has no one ever called you beautiful?"

She shook her head and he knew she meant it. The realization tore at his heart. She wasn't fishing for compliments. Sarah had known from the very moment she was born that she was beautiful, Colin had no doubt. And she'd used that knowledge to lure men to her side like a siren with sailors.

But Bea . . . Colin found Bea's innocence rather refreshing and almost sad really. How could she not know? He gave in to temptation and lay next to her. She rolled into him, her body pressing to his. Suddenly meek, she nestled into his neck. Slowly, her fingers trailed through the crisp hair on his chest.

He cupped the back of her head, breathing in her scent. "You were quite alone in that castle, weren't you?"

She nodded and tilted her head back, looking up at him. There was an unspoken acknowledgment in their gaze, a flash of recognition. Kindred souls. The realization left him feeling odd, off balance. He was so used to being alone, thinking only about himself.

"You understand, don't you?" she whispered, her pleading eyes peering into his soul.

She needed the truth. He swallowed hard. He'd had so

few close acquaintances. How could he with his abilities? She cupped the side of his face and pressed her lips to his in a gentle kiss. A kiss that spoke of emotion. Damn it all, if his heart didn't warm. Somehow, at some point, Bea had pushed aside the stone wall he'd built.

He nudged her back into the satin pillows, deepening the kiss, wishing to forget the turmoil of his mind and soul. As if sensing his need, Bea wrapped her arms around his neck, drawing him closer to her warm, soft body. Frantic for more, he slid his hands down her thighs, shifting his body so he could touch the sensitive skin of her inner legs. She sucked in a breath, the sound like music. Then he touched her there, in the silky folds of her femininity. Bea nipped at his lower lip with a sweet growl.

She was wet, warm, waiting for him.

"Colin." Bea arched her back, moaning against his mouth, her legs tightening against his hand. "Oh God, Colin, please."

When he slipped his finger inside her, his cock hardened and pulsed almost painfully against his trousers. Bea's fingernails bit into his back. Her pleasure was his. His body roared to life with a predatory need to make her his own. But he would not take her. He was an ass, but he held tight to a tiny bit of salvation.

"Come for me, Bea." He moved to her neck, pressing his mouth to her skin. Lower to her collarbone, still lower to the top of her right breast. Her harsh breath fanned through his hair and her nails dug deeper into his skin. She was close, so close.

With his thumb, he rubbed the sensitive bud that would be her undoing. Bea cried out, arching her back. At the same time, he felt her body tremble, her tight sheath convulsing around his fingers. Sweat broke out on Colin's forehead as he resisted the urge to replace his fingers with his shaft. His own body grew taut, boiling heat thrumming under her skin. He wanted to drive into her, to take her, to make her his.

Pure bliss crossed Bea's face and she slumped back into the bed. Her lashes fluttered up, her eyes misty with a sexual haze. She looked lovely, and Colin's heart melted a little more. Trembling slightly, Colin moved up her body and pressed his mouth to hers.

"I like you, too, Bea," he whispered against her lips.

Warm light bathed Bea's eyes, making her lids glow with the gold of morning. Slowly, she became aware of the silky bed beneath her, so soft and clean. At her back, something incredibly warm pressed to her flesh. She resisted the urge to sigh and snuggle closer. She felt odd. As if her entire body hummed, as if she floated. Had she died and this was heaven? She couldn't seem to find the strength to care about an answer.

That was until a heavy weight suddenly rested across her waist. Reality burst to the forefront and Bea's lids lifted. A green haze hovered in front of her. It took a moment for her to realize it was material and not something incredibly amiss with her eyesight. Slowly, she glanced down toward her waist where the heavy weight lay. An arm. A muscled, hairy arm.

Colin.

Dear God.

Everything came rushing back on a wave of emotion. Last night. Colin touching her. *Naked.* She was still naked! Her breath came out in harsh pants as her panic flared. She'd fallen asleep in Colin's arms . . . completely, utterly naked. Frantic, she searched for something to cover her form. Her green robe lay at the end of the bed. With a trembling hand, she reached out and slowly drew the material toward her, inch by wretched inch. Every moment of last night flitted through her memory. Every touch, every kiss, every sigh.

Granted, she'd been more than happy to instigate, but now . . . Heat shot to her cheeks. She crept her way across the bed, away from Colin. Dawn had yet to make an appearance, but she knew morning would soon arrive, and with it, Colin would wake. Then she'd have to avoid eye contact and feel embarrassed all over again. Colin's arm fell with a soft thud to the pillows. Free, Bea, dashed through the gauze and punched her arms through the sleeves of her robe.

Oh dear Lord, how could she let him do those things? She turned into a complete and utter nit the moment the man looked at her. Ella would be horrified. Leo would kill him. Grandmother would disown her . . . again. She paced the large room, wringing her hands tightly. No. They couldn't know. No one must know. Bea made it to the wall and spun around to pace to the other side when she caught sight of a silver tray and a glowing fire. A variety of fruits and nuts lay upon the platter, a platter that had not been there when they'd fallen asleep.

"Breakfast?" Bea whispered.

Someone had entered while they slept? Someone had brought them food and stoked the flames. Someone had seen them! Was her shame to know no boundaries?

Her stomach clenched, growling, and her embarrassment was momentarily forgotten. Bea recognized some of the fruit. Things she'd tasted before. Mango, Colin had called the yellowish piece. She lifted a chunk and slipped it between her lips. The flavor was just as sweet as she'd remembered. On the chair next to the table lay the traditional sari in a brilliant pink. Her own clothing was nowhere to be found. She drifted her fingers across the shimmering material.

"I could get used to living like this," she mumbled around a mouthful.

"And I could get used to seeing you like this." Colin's deep voice washed over her like a lover's caress.

Heat shot to Bea's face and she paused, the fruit still in her mouth. Slowly, she turned to face him. Colin was sitting up, his form blurry behind the gauzy curtains, but she could see that his hair was mussed and his chest bare. It was an intimate look. The sort of look Bea could imagine seeing Colin wear every morning. The kind of look that should have been reserved for his wife. The thought sent her heart racing. She looked away, afraid he'd read the thoughts in her gaze. She dropped the fruit to the plate with a clatter and pulled her robe tighter. Marriage to Colin? Ridiculous!

"I . . . are you hungry?" she said, desperate to think of anything other than Colin, every morning, for the rest of her life.

He pulled aside the curtain and stood, the dark blue sheet tied around his waist. Bea watched him move across the room, almost predator-like. His muscles bunched and flexed, his skin golden from the Indian sun. His hair was rumpled, the curls lying haphazardly across his forehead. How badly she wanted to slip her fingers into those strands.

"Good morning," he said softly.

"Is it morning?"

He glanced toward the windows. "In an hour or two." There was something in his eyes, something warm and lovely. Something intimate. Something she found she liked. Mesmerized, she couldn't seem to tear her gaze away.

"Well, then, good morning," she whispered.

He paused only when he reached her side. His scent swirled around her, musky, male, and something else spicy. It must have been in the soap he used. He reached out and took an orange slice, popping it into his mouth. She tried not to stare at his mouth, tried not to remember the way his lips had moved over her body, but not trying was impossible. She looked away, ignoring the tremble of her breath.

"Colin," she said. "What is the plan exactly?"

He reached for an almond. "Plan?"

She tucked a lock of hair behind her ear. "Yes. Shall we stay here for long?"

"We shall stay, I'm afraid, until we can either escape, or he allows us to leave." He popped another piece of fruit into his mouth.

Her brows drew together. "But . . . you mean he's keeping us here?"

"He, and the men surrounding the walls outside."

Bea's eyes grew wide. "Men?"

Colin settled in a chair, easing back as if he hadn't a worry in the world. He crossed his arms over his chest, the movement sending his muscles bulging. "Of course. Who do you think keeps the poor out?"

Bea hesitated, unsure, then moved to the double doors that led out onto the patio. A tall wall surrounded the home, much like the castle she'd grown up in. But this one was solid, not crumbling and uncared for. He was right. They were trapped, for only the Lord knew how long.

A soft scratch whispered through the room. So soft, that at first Bea thought she'd imagined it. Confused, she spun around.

Colin stood.

"Did I imagine that?" Bea asked, rushing to his side.

Slowly, the door creaked open. A small woman in a dark blue sari moved silently into the room. The silver threads through her dark hair were the only indication of her age. Her hands were clasped tightly together, her dark eyes wide and white in the murky darkness. Bea remembered the woman, one of many who'd brought food for them last night. What was her name? Ashwini?

"Come." She didn't wait for their response, but swept back through the door from which she'd just entered.

Colin dropped the sheet, his bare backside exposed. Bea was speechless. He dressed quickly, but like a man unconcerned with modesty. Clothed, he rushed to the door, and Bea finally regained the use of her tongue.

"Colin, you can't possibly be thinking of . . ."

He paused, glancing back. "You coming?"

"But we don't know what she wants."

He shrugged.

Knowing he'd leave her, Bea grabbed the loose trousers

and shirt left by the servants and turned her back to him. Giving him a taste of his own medicine, she dropped her robe. He didn't say a word, but she could feel him staring, feel his gaze burning into her back. A smile of success quirked her lips. Quickly she dressed in the traditional woman's garb. When she turned, he was watching her, his gaze hard. She'd seen that look before. She'd seen that look last night.

Chin high, she swept past him and out the door. "Well, you coming?"

She didn't look back after baiting him. Sashaying as she'd seen the native women do, Bea followed Ashwini down the dark hall. But her glee at putting Colin in his place faded. The palace was quiet, the people asleep. What was this woman doing awake? Colin fell in step beside Bea and latched on to her arm.

"Are you sure we can trust her?" Bea whispered.

"No," Colin replied.

Bea frowned. Was he being intentionally evasive? They turned a sharp corner and the woman was gone. Colin paused.

Bea turned, searching the darkness. "Where . . ."

The woman peeked her head out from behind a curtain. "Come." She held the curtain wide. Colin wasted no time, but followed, taking Bea with him. The curtain fell into place with a soft whisper, enclosing them in a false safety. There, in the small alcove, Bea could make out another woman, holding something . . .

A soft mew whispered through the darkness. A child, Bea realized, stiffening. Immediately, she knew what they wanted. Apparently, Colin did, too.

"Damn," he snapped. "Should have stayed put."

She knew he didn't mean the words. The child wasn't more than two. He was pale, sweating, lifeless in his mother's arms. Bea pressed her hands to her aching heart.

"Help my sister," the woman whispered, peering up at Colin, her eyes pleading.

Colin hesitated. "What do I get in return?"

The woman glanced at the baby, the desperation apparent in the tight lines of her face. She didn't seem offended by Colin's response. In fact, she seemed to assume he'd ask.

"I know nothing."

Colin crossed his arms over his chest, his face passive. "Liar."

Bea resisted the urge to flinch at Colin's harshness. The baby gave a deep wheezing breath that sounded so incredibly close to death, Bea had to resist the urge to demand Colin help the child.

"He comes tonight," Ashwini blurted out. "Tonight the man with the green eyes comes." The woman latched on to Colin's arm, any sense of hesitancy gone. "Please. Help. Shiva will keep you to himself. He will not use you to help others as he says. You will be a prisoner. We can help you."

Colin had been right all along. Shiva was no friend. Another greedy monster. But how could they possibly trust this woman?

Colin shifted. "You'll help us escape?"

The woman nodded. "Anything."

They were quiet for one long moment; the only sound was the soft, whimpering murmur of the lad. She knew he'd help, she knew Colin would help no matter what, yet she couldn't seem to keep her heart from clenching as she waited with bated breath. The child's head lolled back and he met Bea's gaze. Bea's soul ached, breaking into tiny pieces.

She could resist no longer. Bea rested her hand on Colin's shoulder. "Colin, please—"

"Give him to me." Colin held out his hands, ignoring her. The child was pushed into his arms. Such a small boy, wasted thin by disease. "Bea." Colin was looking at her. He didn't say anything, but she understood. She could see the unspoken plea in his gaze. He needed privacy.

She nodded, tears stinging her eyes. She'd known Colin wouldn't disappoint her.

Colin went to a far, dark corner of the small alcove, settling on a chair, the baby lying limply in his arms.

"Go," Bea said, shooing the women back.

The women hesitated, shifting uneasily and murmuring to each other in their language. Bea put on her fiercest face and stood in front of Colin, attempting as best as she could to hide him. Apparently, it worked. The women stepped back, clinging to each other, their wide eyes watching, terrified . . . of her? Bea almost laughed. Never had anyone found her intimidating. Most people on the estate in Scotland merely ignored her.

The whimpering behind her ceased, then soft gurgles whispered through the air. A giggle? Bea spun around. The boy was sitting up, smiling.

Ashwini's sister rushed forward, bumping Bea aside. Colin got to his feet, barely acknowledging them as they tore the boy from his arms. Bea pressed her hands to her mouth, shocked to her core. She'd seen it so many times, seen what Colin could do. But here, now . . . for some reason it was all becoming too real. Sudden tears stung her eyes.

"Bea," Colin muttered.

She faced him just as he fell into her body. She stumbled back, gasping under his sudden weight.

"Help," he whispered.

Chapter 21

He didn't know how long he'd slept.

Hours? Perhaps even days? Damn, he was too exhausted to open his eyes and find out. Colin curled his fingers into the satiny bedspread, his muscles tingling with the movement. He'd saved too many too close together. It was sapping his strength and he wasn't getting enough time to restore. As much as he wanted to succumb to the unconscious once more, he knew he had to open his eyes. Urgency pounded under his skin, a warning.

Slowly, he lifted his lids, his thoughts going immediately to Bea. Where was she? Had she finally had enough and abandoned him to his own demise? Or had Shiva taken her? The thought sent anger pounding through his veins. He swallowed the dry lump that had lodged in his throat and forced his gaze to travel the room. He found her almost immediately. Bea sat on the bed, huddled in the corner with her knees to her chest and her gaze pinned to him. Relief had him closing his eyes for the briefest of moments. She was here. She was safe. For now.

"You're awake," she whispered.

He pushed his hands underneath him, clenched his teeth, and managed to sit up. His mind spun with the movement.

But he had to keep going, must get up. He pressed the heels of his palms to his temple. "What time is it?"

"Past midnight."

A shiver of unease raced down his spine. Past midnight. "Shit." He tossed aside the light coverlet.

Bea straightened, her gaze alert, like a doe sensing a hunter. "You can rest more, if you'd like. I sent a message to Shiva that you weren't feeling well, that you were sick."

Colin laughed, a weak chuckle. "He knows of my powers. I doubt he'll believe you. He'll know immediately that something's off. When did you send the message?"

Bea shrugged. "But a few minutes ago." She fell silent, merely watching him with a weariness that set him on edge. She'd seen too much, seen him at his worst. She knew more about his abilities than even Ella.

"Can you . . . can you get sick?"

He closed his eyes, pressing his fingers to his lids as weariness washed over him in a sickening wave. She wanted more, more secrets unveiled. Didn't she know enough?

"Colin?"

He wanted to laugh at the question, laugh at the absurdity of it all. Could he get sick? That was the irony that came with his abilities.

"Yes," he said softly, settling his bare feet on the cold marble floor. "I can. I was injured when my mother was murdered and I very nearly died with her." He pushed the memory aside. He didn't want to think about his mother; he didn't want to think about the knife wound he'd received; he didn't want to think about almost dying. There was no point in morose thoughts.

"The scar, on your side."

He didn't respond to her statement, and silence settled heavy around them.

"The woman, Ashwini," Bea shifted. "She came asking after you. She brought a knapsack with food."

Colin stood. His mind spun, the room a dizzying whirl of

blues, pinks, and greens as his body protested. Swallowing hard, he closed his eyes and attempted to regain his balance. Ashwini had brought a knapsack. She was going to keep her promise and help them escape after all.

"Why do you not want people to watch you?" Bea asked.

Colin gritted his teeth, rolling his eyes heavenward. Christ. The woman wouldn't stop until she had his soul on a platter. He glanced over his shoulder. Had she been pondering the question all day? How did he answer her without revealing everything?

Her brows were drawn together; she was waiting for a response. "Why . . . why did you want me to hide you? When you . . . you do . . . you know."

Colin sighed and brushed aside the gauze surrounding the bed. She had no idea what his life was like. How could she possibly understand? "I'm not something to gawk over. Some oddity to be put on display." He dared to glance back.

She nodded slowly, as if she understood. But how could she? No one but Ella could possibly understand how it felt when people pointed and condemned.

She dropped her chin to her chest, using her finger to follow the swirling, gold-threaded designs on the bedspread. "They'd stare at me." Her voice was so soft, he thought he'd misunderstood at first.

"When I'd leave the castle to go to the village, they'd all stare at me. Twice, we went to visit Grandfather when I was a child." She glanced up at him briefly, as if judging his reaction. "They stared worse there. The pathetic child who was forced to stay hidden in a castle in Scotland with her mad grandmother."

He found her honesty refreshing. He was so tired of hiding. He craved her openness and suddenly wanted more. "Why were you hidden away?"

She shrugged, giving him a wry smile that lifted only the left side of her mouth. "Grandmother was too vocal. Grandfather banished her to Scotland and told everyone she'd gone mad. When my parents died, he wanted nothing to do with a female and he sent me there as well. Perhaps he thought he was being kind, giving Grandmother someone to keep her company."

He doubted her grandfather had thought of anyone but himself. The bastard had condemned a child to loneliness. He'd died in a fire after attempting to kill Leo and Ella, and not for the first time, Colin hoped the old man was rotting in hell. Did Bea know? Did she have any clue what her grandfather had been capable of?

Bea plucked at the fringe on a pillow. "Grandmother didn't let me befriend the servants, and they ignored me." She shrugged. "Wasn't really their fault."

It was difficult not to blame adults for ostracizing a child, but he knew how the British nobility worked and it wasn't uncommon for servants to have nothing to do with the family they worked for.

Slowly, Colin rubbed his chin, the short whiskers scratching against his knuckles. How odd that they should have a similar childhood, two people seemingly so different. A bit disconcerted, Colin went to the water bowl and splashed the tepid liquid onto his face, trying to shake off the memory of her eyes. Sad eyes. Eyes that seemed to peer into his very soul.

A bizarre mixture of guilt and the urge to protect her welled through him. He turned, daring to look at Bea once more. She still sat there, watching him, expecting what? An apology for the way he'd judged her so harshly when they'd first met? For thinking the worst of her? He'd been wrong. Completely wrong. He was an ass. A complete and utter ass.

"Bea, I'm—"

The door whispered open and Ashwini peeked inside. One look at her pale face and Colin's heart skipped a beat.

"Here. They're here," she whispered.

"Demyan," Bea whispered.

Colin didn't need to respond.

Bea pushed aside the gauze and jumped from the bed. Her gaze was on him, waiting for him to do something. Shit, he didn't know what the hell to do. His heart thundered madly in his chest as he scanned the room. The balcony. Could they escape there? Highly unlikely. Men were in the gardens, on posts around the wall.

"Come," Ashwini demanded, waving them forward. "I help you escape, but we must leave now."

Bea snatched up the bag lying on the floor and raced after the woman. It was only at the door that she paused and glanced back at him. "You coming?"

He didn't miss the irony in her words, the same words he'd said to her when they'd first met. Somehow they'd switched places. Bea had become the adventurer, ready to dive headfirst into the unknown. The thought terrified and thrilled him. "Don't really have a choice, do I, darlin'."

A ghost of a smile flickered across Bea's lips. She held out her hand. He slipped his fingers around hers, and together, they followed Ashwini into the hall. For a moment, for one brief moment, he felt at peace.

Softly murmured words floated up the stairs. The peace fled as quickly as it had come. *His* voice. Demyan had arrived. Colin's hand tightened on Bea's. The urge for revenge flared to life, always there, waiting. How badly he wanted to walk down those steps and confront the monster. Why was Demyan here? They didn't have the ring. If he was working with Henry, they didn't need Bea.

"This way." Ashwini darted into the room across the hall.

Colin paused, his gaze pinned to those steps. Obviously, they weren't working with Henry, or they wouldn't have come for Bea.

"Colin?" Bea whispered, the urgency in her voice his undoing. He jerked his head toward them and followed, pulling Bea inside and shutting the door softly behind them. He had only a brief moment to take in the richly decorated bedchamber. Ashwini was merely a dark shadow against the far wall, her movements hidden by night. What was she doing?

"Here." A soft groan rent the air. From behind the massive marble fireplace, a gaping hole appeared. "Through here."

Ashwini darted into that darkness. Colin ducked under the mantel and followed, pulling Bea with him. He could tell by the echo of his own harsh breath that the walls were close. He dropped Bea's hand briefly and reached out. Cold, hard stone met his fingertips, so close he felt like he was in a coffin. Bea inched closer to him, her warm body nestled to his back.

"Hurry," Ashwini whispered through the darkness.

Shiva was smart, and the man knew they'd try to escape. Was this merely a trap? Or maybe Demyan had gotten the woman's cooperation. He slammed his fists against the stone walls, the skin on his knuckles ripping sharply. He had no other alternative but to trust this woman, this stranger. He only prayed he was right. Colin tightened his hold on Bea's hand, pulling her closer. If something happened to Bea, he was the only one to blame. Slowly, he stroked the inside of her wrist, attempting to give her a bit of comfort.

"Here, turn," Ashwini said.

Colin dropped Bea's hand. Her grasp went immediately to his waist, where her hands settled, tightening around his shirt. She wasn't about to let go. The thought made him smile. She needed him. Maybe she didn't like to admit it, but she did.

He held his arms wide, feeling his way down the corridor. The stone had grown rough, as if servant hands had stopped smoothing the texture. A forgotten escape route? He lifted his arms. There, just above his head, his fingertips met the damp ceiling.

The tunnel sloped, the trail going slightly downhill. The movement pulled on his leg muscles and sent Bea tumbling into his back, her warm body pressed tightly to his. The air grew thin, damp, and Bea's soft breath whispered warmly across his neck.

"Colin?" Bea's voice quivered.

"It's all right," he replied. "I think we're going underground. Perhaps under the wall."

Ahead, Ashwini's soft footsteps stopped. Colin paused. Bea merely remained pinned to his back, her arms tight around his waist.

"Ashwini?" Colin whispered. Where the hell was the woman?

"Up, push open," she said, her voice merely a few feet away. He shuffled closer. "Up?"

He didn't understand what she was asking, until she latched on to his arms and shoved them into the air. His fingertips hit smooth wood. A door? He hoped. "Right, got it."

She stepped aside. Colin used the heels of his palms to push on the wooden panel above. The weight groaned and screeched, resisting before allowing only the smallest sliver of moonlight to filter through the crack. His muscles strained, he let go and the door fell back into place with a thud. Gritting his teeth, he slammed his palms into the wood again. This time there was only a soft groan of protest and then the flap lifted, falling back and sending dirt into the air.

"Up." Ashwini raised her hands, shooing them forward. "You'll go, hurry now." She pushed Bea until she stumbled into Colin's body. "There's a horse waiting outside for you. South, follow the river south. When the river splits, there will be a path through a forest, follow that trail. There's a temple. You'll be safe there for a bit."

Colin's fuzzy brain attempted to make sense of her words. "How long will it take?"

"A day. Now go," she urged, her eyes wide in the murky light. "May the gods bless you."

"But won't you get in trouble for helping us?" Bea asked.

The woman smiled, her white teeth flashing in the darkness.

"No one will expect me. I'm Shiva's sister. Now go." Her feet whispered across the floor as she raced down the tunnel and then the sound disappeared, leaving them in silence.

Colin wasted no more time. He reached out on tiptoe and grabbed on to the sides of the portal. Gritting his teeth, he hauled himself up through the opening.

Bea's head ached with each pound of the mare's hooves. Her lips were cracked with thirst and her shirt clung to her sweaty back. She could barely feel her fingers to know if she still held on to Colin or not. The only thing preventing her from crying out in frustration was the spinning of her thoughts. Ashwini was Shiva's sister? Just thinking the words brought a sense of bitter dread into her gut.

"She'll tell him, Colin," she muttered against his back. "She's his sister, for God's sake." She couldn't keep quiet any longer. For hours they'd ridden until the sun was high, and for hours she's mulled over the fact that Shiva's own sister had helped them escape. Didn't siblings tell each other everything? Not that she would know. No, Bea had grown up alone.

"She won't."

Bea tugged the scarf she'd found in the knapsack lower over her face, protecting her skin from the harsh rays, beating through the canopy of leaves above. "How do you know?" As far as she knew, Colin didn't have a sibling, so he knew about as much as she did on the subject.

"Have faith, Bea."

She wanted to snort with laughter. Faith? Have faith? That was his response?

He sighed and flicked an annoyed glance back at her. The wind had tousled his hair, making him look boyishly endearing. She grudgingly admitted, if only to herself, how bloody handsome the man looked no matter what the elements.

"People respond one of three ways when I save a loved

one." He turned back around, facing forward. "One of those ways is to be completely indebted to you. Ashwini fits that category."

Bea nibbled her lower lip and stared blankly at the muddy river weaving through the hard dirt. Ashwini. If the woman hadn't been lying, they'd be at the temple soon. Perhaps Colin was right. After all, wouldn't she feel indebted to the person who'd saved her loved one? "So, what's the second and third?"

He stiffened, his back growing taut under her touch. "Excuse me?"

She hesitated, wondering if she'd imagined his harsh reaction to her question. Yet as the silence grew, she realized she had to say something. "You . . . you said people react in three different ways. I was merely wondering what the other two were."

He didn't respond. She thought he would ignore her question and she shifted, uneasy with his lack of response. After all, how well did they truly know each other? Why would he share with her? Still, he was the one who had started the subject of conversation.

He continued to stare ahead, and she could read nothing in the even tone of his voice. "Or second, they look at you like you're a monster."

The way she'd looked at Demyan. But Demyan had been there to murder them. Demyan *was* a monster. Colin only helped people.

"You're saving their lives," she said.

He shrugged. "Sometimes it doesn't matter."

"You are not the same as Demyan," she whispered furiously as she rested the side of her face against his warm back, feeling depressed and annoyed with everything. "And this happens to you often?"

She saw the side of his face lift briefly, as if he smiled. "More than you'd think."

What he must have gone through. To have people condemn

you, be afraid of you. Had she actually compared her life to his? She wanted to laugh at the ridiculousness of it all. Had she actually thought she could possibly understand him just because a few people stared when she went to town?

She closed her eyes, feeling ashamed. "And the third?"

Colin shifted, nudging his heels into the horse's flanks and urging the animal faster. The mount took off in a gallop that rattled Bea's teeth.

"The third? They try to use you."

"Like Shiva?"

He didn't respond. For some reason she had the odd feeling that this third option was the worst. Had someone else tried to use Colin? A friend? A family member?

"Something's wrong." Colin pulled back on the reins, there, hidden among the trees.

"What is it?" Bea peeked around his shoulder, peering through the brush, then up to the canopy above. "I don't understand. What's—"

It was only then that she realized somehow the sun had faded. There was a hazy dullness to the sky. She pulled away from Colin's back, her spine stiffening. An odd hum buzzed through the air, a lack of noise. Birds didn't chirp. Even the insects had grown silent. When had it started? She wasn't sure. It could have been ten minutes ago, or an hour. She'd been so bloody tired, she hadn't noticed.

"Cloud," Colin said, pointing ahead.

Just barely visible through the trees a low, dark cloud hovered over the land, coming toward them. A cloud like none she'd ever seen before . . . menacing, expanding. "I don't understand." Her voice hitched, fear making the words stick in her throat.

The wind suddenly swooshed through the brush, sending twigs and sand through the air. Bea screeched and ducked her head down against Colin's back. An eerie howl erupted, swirling around them as if they were surrounded by wolves.

"Sandstorm," Colin shouted. He nudged his heels into the

mount's sides. The horse burst forward, following the path as it led through scrub brush. "Pull the scarf over your nose and mouth."

Bea did as she was told, keeping her head bent and clinging to Colin's waist as the wind pulled and tugged at her hair. He'd said the word "sandstorm" as if she should know what he was talking about. Her mind spun, her heart racing.

"Hold tight," Colin said, the wind taking his words so she could barely hear even though he sat directly in front of her. "Almost there."

Bea dared to peek over his shoulder. The trees kept some of the dirt and sand from getting into her eyes, but not enough. She lowered her lashes, narrowing her eyes to slits. The path flared, and there, among the tangle of brush and trees, erupted a stone temple. Ashwini had been right.

"How long will we stay here?"

"Long enough to hide from the storm." Colin pulled back on the reins. Trees grew up the temple, roots and branches interlacing throughout the carvings of beasts and people so that one could barely tell stone from vegetation. A low rumble of thunder shook the ground.

Colin leapt from the mount and jerked Bea down before she had a chance to prepare. "Are you sure it's the right temple?" she asked.

"Don't know, but for now, it is."

He took her hand and pulled her toward the building. She could barely think, barely remember to use her legs with the sand stinging her skin. Rubble littered the area, produced by the wind and age. Colin jumped atop a column that blocked their path and lifted Bea. She jumped down, her breath coming out in soft pants. Sand got in her eyes, blinding her momentarily. She stumbled. Colin slipped his arm around her waist, pulling her close.

"The storm will keep them from following and will cover our tracks," Colin yelled over the howl of the wind.

Leaves swirled through the air in a whirlwind that

taunted and pulled at her hair and clothing. Branches snapped, popping like dried bones before being tossed about by the wind. They started up the shallow flight of steps and burst through the open door. Inside, they were met with blessed silence.

Bea sank against the cold stone wall, her chest rising and falling with each harsh breath. "How long will it last?"

Colin shrugged, resting his hands on his narrow hips. "No idea. I'm getting the horse. You stay put."

Bea pushed away from the wall. "But Colin . . ."

He raced back out into the wind, ignoring her. Bea sighed, her shoulders sinking. Through the swirling debris and sand, she could barely see him. Slowly, her gaze began to adjust to the gloom. Statues morphed from the walls, the bodies bent in odd poses. Curious, Bea stepped farther into the temple. There, into the tunnel, the wind produced an eerie howl that set Bea's nerves on edge. But the noise was pushed in the background of her subconscious as she studied the carvings on the walls.

Bea brushed the sand and dirt from her face. From the statues, people emerged. People embracing and kissing. Bea stepped closer.

Oh my.

Heat shot to Bea's cheeks. Hesitant, she glanced back. Colin was just coming up the steps with the reins in hand, leading their mount to safety. He wasn't paying her the least bit of attention. She reached out, running her fingers over two figures, the man bent over a woman. Confused, she tilted her head to the left, then right.

"Colin, what . . ."

Realization came swift and embarrassing. Colin let the mount wander and made his way toward her. Pausing near the statues, he took one glance and lifted a brow. Of course, he found her embarrassment amusing.

The heat in Bea's cheeks intensified. "I . . . It . . . Never mind." She moved away, avoiding his gaze.

"Come, we'll go farther back where the winds can't find us." Colin took her hand and pulled her into the dark doorway, the knapsack over his left shoulder.

Bea followed, eager to be anywhere but near the confusing statues. Farther back they moved, until the tunnel flared into another open room. In the center of the room was a small pond that had once been an impressive temple fountain. Clear water filled the hole, not green or brown, but oddly pristine. Bea leaned over, staring at her reflection. She was dirty, her nose and cheeks reddened by the sun. For a moment she didn't recognize herself. She wasn't sure if she should be horrified, but oddly wasn't.

She pulled back and studied their surroundings. An area that was clean of debris, but filled with more caressing figurines. Someone had come here and come here often.

"It's clean," Bea whispered, clasping her upper arms. "Shouldn't there be debris and creepy-crawly beasties?"

Colin dropped the bag, the soft thud echoing through the room. "Yes, if no one knew about it, or visited."

Ashwini knew about the place.

"The statues, do they look familiar?" Colin asked.

Bea frowned and moved closer, studying the stone people. A man and woman kissing arched from the wall. A man standing with a woman's bare legs wrapped around his waist was in front of her. She peeked around the statue and came face-to-face with a woman, kissing a man's . . . Her eyes widened.

She'd seen that statue before. "Shiva."

"Yep," Colin replied. "He must have gotten the ideas for his unusual artwork here."

Fear clenched her gut, momentarily replacing her embarrassment. "But then, he could come back." She spun around and faced Colin. "Ashwini lied!"

"No, I'd say his sister knew exactly what she was doing. No one would ever think to look for us here, and with the sandstorm, we're in luck."

Colin flipped open the knapsack. Bea stood frozen in indecision. Could they trust Ashwini? Hadn't Colin told her to trust no one?

His gaze lifted to her. "We can trust her."

Had he read her mind? It left her feeling uneasy. She laughed, the sound echoing through the large room. "Is that one of your special gifts, too? You know who you can and can't trust."

She shouldn't have said the words, especially not in such a biting way. But she was frightened and confused. And when he didn't respond, merely continued to stare at her, her guilt flared.

Bea sighed. "Colin, I'm—"

"I knew enough to trust you."

She froze, her heart slamming erratically in her chest.

He stood and swept past her. "We'll rest here. Put down your bedding. I'll keep watch."

He moved toward the entrance, away from her, and Bea was left to wonder if she'd just imagined his intimate words.

Chapter 22

Bea couldn't sleep. It wasn't that the temple was too cold, which it was. Nor was it that the ground was too hard, which it was. It was that fact that Colin sat only feet from her, his body outlined by the lone torch they'd lit.

Outside, the winds still howled, an eerie sound that raised the fine hairs on the back of her neck. But the storm was the least of their worries. No, Colin remained the thorn in her side, the constant thought in her tumultuous mind. She should be sleeping while she had the chance. But she couldn't stop looking at Colin, thinking about him, remembering.

I knew enough to trust you.

The words echoed through her head over and over again.

She felt the importance of that statement, deep and penetrating. Colin didn't trust easily. She'd known that the moment she met the man. He trusted her. He'd trusted her the moment they met. Warmth seeped through her very being. There, under the knowingly seductive gazes of the statues, all in ridiculously sensual positions, she couldn't help thinking of Colin. In those statues of men with their shirts off, she saw Colin, his chest bare, his muscles hard and smooth like marble. Those mountains and valleys that traveled his stomach . . .

In the women, whose faces were hazy with bliss, she saw

herself, knowing that was how she looked when he touched her, when he kissed her, when he merely looked at her. And remembering sent heat through her body, made the ache in her lower belly intensify so that she thought she couldn't bear the need.

Biting her lower lip to keep from groaning, she pulled her gaze from his still form and clenched her knees to her chest. But not looking at him only left the statues. In the safety of the shadows, she studied those still forms unabashedly. She'd seen statues of naked people but those were considered art. Those statues didn't make her body flush with a heated desire. Those statues didn't make her want to do sinful things with a man she'd just met.

If only she hadn't let him kiss her. If only she hadn't let him touch her, then she wouldn't know, would never know what his caress felt like. Never know what it felt like to see the stars, to feel such intense pleasure that nothing could compare.

She licked her dry lips and focused on the statue closest to her. A male stood behind a woman, his hands covering her breasts, his lips on her neck. It was simple and tame compared to the others. It didn't matter. To Bea's aching body, it only added fuel.

Her heart skipped a beat before taking off into a wild gallop. Her body flared with passion, a need she barely understood, but she knew that need was for Colin. Never had she felt this way and the sensations left her confused. Slowly, she inched her blanket away, feeling confined under its weight. The cool air swept over her skin like a cold caress. It didn't help. She squirmed, a sigh escaping her lips.

"Bea, you can sleep. They can't find us now, not in this storm." Colin's voice was soft.

Bea rolled her eyes. As if that were why she couldn't sleep. She sat up, staring directly at him. With the movement, the trousers she wore tightened around her thighs and only heightened the ache. The material clung to places no one but

Colin had touched. There were no layers of crinoline to guard her virtue.

She could kiss him. Stand, walk over to him, and press her lips to his. He liked her, didn't he? He'd kissed her more than once.

Ridiculous. She wasn't that bold.

"It's hot. Are you hot?" She didn't wait for his response but crawled to the edge of the pond. Without pause, she dipped her hands into the water and poured the cool liquid down the front of her shirt. She didn't want Colin. Of course not. She was a refined lady, and refined ladies did not do things like . . . touch . . . kiss . . .

With a sigh, she settled back on her heels. Did he really like her? Or was she just another woman to him? Did he remember the way he touched her? The way she moaned his name? Heat flushed her cheeks. Slowly, she glanced back, her chin to her shoulder as she peeked at him. His face was turned away from her. There, seated against the sandstone wall with his shirt hanging open, the man looked like a statue come to life.

As if pulled by some unknown force, Bea started forward on her hands and knees. Her gaze pinned to him, she suddenly felt like a hunter and he her prey. She had no idea what she planned to do when she reached his side. Shove him backward, press her mouth to his, tear off his clothes. How shocked he'd be. The thought almost made her giggle. Only a few feet from him, she paused in indecision.

"What do you want, Bea?" he asked, his gaze still focused on the far wall.

What did she want? *You. You to touch me. To make me moan your name.*

"How did you see me approach?" she asked, more to fill the silence than to satisfy any curiosity.

He turned his head, looking directly at her. "I could smell you."

That gave her pause. She wasn't quite sure if she should be embarrassed or not. "Do I smell that horrible?"

She thought the corner of his mouth lifted, but with the lack of light, she wasn't quite sure. "No. Quite the opposite. Your scent is . . . refreshing, clean, unique. Sometimes I think I could pick up your scent from a million others."

Her heart hammered in her chest, his words taunting her already flared desire. She crawled closer to him, her hands on the cool stone floor. "Do you know what you smell like?"

He laughed, lowering his thick lashes as he looked at the ground. "I can imagine."

She didn't pause until her face was only a breath from his. "Sunlight. Warmth."

His jaw clenched, his throat working as he swallowed. She didn't wait for him to kiss her, but leaned forward and pressed her lips to his. Mad. She was completely and utterly mad. She didn't know how she'd become so bold. Perhaps it was the statues. Perhaps the fact that she was experienced now. Or perhaps because she ached fiercely and knew only Colin could ease that pain.

Bea wrapped her arms around his neck as his fingers slid into her hair.

"Colin," she whispered against his mouth. "How terribly I've wanted to kiss you."

He growled low in his throat. They both came up on their knees, desperate to touch body to body. Colin tugged on her hair, tilting her head back. "Do you realize what words like that can do to a man?"

He pressed his lips to her neck. Shivers raced over her skin, heated tremors that shook in her core.

"Such words can drive a man insane, Bea."

But she wanted him mad, mad with desire. Mad with wanting her.

Colin stood, lifting Bea with him. She wrapped her legs around his waist as he pressed her back against the cold sandstone. Trapped between the wall and the hard man holding her, a thrill coursed through her body. This was what she'd wanted, what she'd dreamt about while lying there. Colin cupped her backside, while his mouth found hers. Slow and torturous, he nipped at her bottom lip.

Bea slipped her fingers into the soft curls at the base of his neck. She was frantic. Frantic to have more of him, all of him. His lips moved to her jawline, lower to her neck. Tingles raced over her skin, the rough scrape of scruff on his face only increasing the pleasure. His lips moved lower, to that valley between her breasts.

"Dear God, Bea, I've never tasted anything so sweet."

With her legs still wrapped around his waist, he carried her toward the small bed. Finally, she loosened her hold and slid down his hard body. Her feet landed with a soft thud, her knees trembling so hard they nearly gave out. Bea had to lean against Colin merely to keep standing. He cupped the sides of her face and stared into her eyes as if looking for something. What? She didn't want him to pause. She didn't want him to think. She didn't want him to stop touching her. She was tired of waiting for life, waiting for things to happen to her.

She placed her hands over his. "I want you, Colin, please."

He closed his eyes briefly, as if fighting a battle. A battle he was obviously losing. Bea had to resist the urge to grin and instead pressed her body to his, tempting him in a way she didn't realize she could. The passion in Colin's gaze flared to life. His hands slid down her neck, over her shoulders, to the open collar of her shirt. He flipped open her top button and rested his hand there, in the valley between her breasts, over her heart. Slowly, he drew his knuckles up and down her sensitive skin.

Bea grew light-headed. Her breasts felt heavy, her nipples hard against the material of her shirt. Colin's attention left her eyes, pausing at her lips, traveling lower. She couldn't seem to breathe. Her chest rose and fell with shallow pants. He flipped open the next button, and the next, until her shirt hung wide, whispering around her waist. His hands slipped to her belly, his fingers warm against her skin.

"You don't wear a corset any longer," he whispered the obvious.

"It was too confining."

He smiled, a rakish smile that showed his dimples and made her heart skip a beat. "Your hair is loose." He picked up the long braid that hung down her back.

"When it was up, it was too tight. It made my head ache."

He smiled again. She wasn't sure why he found her discomfort amusing.

"I . . . I can put it back up." She started to reach for the braid, but he shook his head.

"No," he whispered, his hands going to her braid. He pulled at the ribbon, and the blue satin fluttered to the floor. Slowly, he raked his fingers through her hair until the strands fell in waves down her back.

"You are so lovely," he said softly, so softly that she wondered if she'd heard him correctly or merely hoped for the words.

His hands settled at her waist once more and he pressed his lips to hers in a soft, gentle kiss that stopped her thoughts and questions. She slipped her fingers through his hair, stroking the strands and urging him to continue. When his tongue boldly entered her mouth, she met him thrust for thrust.

This was what a kiss was supposed to be like. This was what a kiss was *always* supposed to be like. Bea finally understood what the poets wrote about. Why women gave up everything, even their own innocence, for a man. She finally understood passion.

With an ease that belied her weight, he slipped his arm beneath her legs and swept her up into his arms. Just as quickly, he laid her gently upon the blanket that formed her bed. Her shirt fell open, her nipples just barely concealed.

Colin followed her, stretching his long, lean body out on

top of hers. Bea welcomed the feel of his weight, reveled in it. She didn't want to think about family or anything to do with her old life. She merely wanted to *feel*. Colin lowered his face, brushing his lips across her cheek, his short whiskers tickling.

"How long I've wished for this," she whispered, closing her eyes and savoring the touch of his hands on her skin.

"Be careful what you wish for," Colin said, his lips brushing the shell of her ear.

Bea shivered, whether from his words or his touch, she wasn't sure. He drew back and jerked the shirt from his chest. He was glorious. Perfect. She reached out, tracing the dips and valleys of his muscles. Better than a statue, for he was warmth and life.

"Too much time, Bea," Colin said as he lowered himself once more, his lips finding her neck. "I've had to wait much too long to touch you."

He moved farther down her body, his mouth finding the hollow at her throat. "Waited so long that I thought I'd go insane with want."

Bea rested her hands on his bare shoulders, trailing her fingers over the bulge of muscles and tendons. His body was hard, his muscles stiff, his skin quivering with her touch. A powerful rush of reality washed over her. He was trying to hold back. The thought made her feel exotic, powerful.

She felt the warmth of his breath across her nipple right before his mouth found her breast. Desire shot through Bea. She gasped, her fingers curling into his hair. All thoughts of power vanished. She held no power over the man; if anything, it was quite the opposite.

She arched her back, moaning. "Colin, please, you drive me mad."

He released a harsh chuckle and trailed kisses down her body. "And you don't drive me insane?" He slid his arms under her back and pulled the shirt from her torso. "Every damn thing you do drives me insane." He pressed his mouth to her stomach.

Bea's muscles quivered, the ache between her legs flaring to life. She slid her hands over his shoulder, wanting to touch all of him.

"The way your hips move when you walk. The way your backside fills out those damn trousers." His fingers found the button at her waistband. "The way you draw your bottom lip between your teeth and suckle." His body shook under her fingertips. He wanted her.

He flipped open the button on the waistband and tugged. Bea lifted her hips, allowing him to pull the clothing free. He pressed his lips lower, to the area directly above the soft mound of curls.

"The way you smell, the way you taste . . ." His hands rested on her thighs, his fingers rough against her smooth skin. "The way you moan my name in your sleep."

Bea's eyes burst open. Surely not. He must be jesting.

Colin nudged her legs wide and pressed his mouth to her inner thighs. She quivered. Any embarrassment fled.

"Damn it, Bea, you keep me up at night, dreaming about doing this to you. Dreaming about touching you, doing things to you that would make you scream in pleasure."

She felt his warm breath right before his tongue darted out, slipping between her sleek folds. Bea gasped, clutching the blanket. Wrong. It was so wrong the way he was kissing her, licking her, sucking. Yet she couldn't stop him.

"Dear God, you taste wonderful," Colin murmured.

They were the words she needed to hear. She felt powerful with Colin, she felt wanted and needed. For so many years she'd been ignored. Colin never ignored her. No, he looked at her as if he wanted to devour her. As if she were the only woman in the world. As if she mattered.

His hands slid under her bottom, cupping her and lifting her higher. His tongue thrust deeper. A heated flush spread over Bea's body, almost uncomfortable in its intensity. She squirmed underneath him, moaning as the ache in her lower belly tightened. She wanted to pull away, didn't want to find fulfillment this way, yet Colin held her tight. And then, it was too late.

"Colin!" she cried out as wave after wave of ecstasy pulsed through her core.

Floating in an oblivion of fulfillment, she was barely aware when Colin moved up her body, pausing only when his mouth reached her neck. There, he hesitated, pressing his lips to her pulse, while his hands rested at her hips. His tongue darted out, tasting her skin. The touch was too soon, too intimate. Bea moaned, drawing her hands through his hair, the soft curls entwining around her fingers. In a heady bliss, she held him close, savoring the feel of his body against hers.

He shifted. His erection pressed warm and hard between her thighs. At some point, he'd unbuttoned his trousers. Bea moved, wiggling and arching her back. He was close, so close, and she wanted him, all of him.

"Damn it, Bea, stop moving."

She froze, tossed back into reality. Her breath came out in sharp pants as she waited. But Colin didn't move, merely lowered his head to her chest and rested on his elbows.

She tried to remain still, truly she did, but as the minutes past, she grew impatient. Bea wiggled beneath him, urging him to continue. "Colin?" she asked, confused.

He lifted his head, his gaze meeting hers. His eyes were heated, fierce. "What will I do with you?"

He didn't give her time to answer, but pressed his mouth to hers. As their tongues met, his thick erection slipped between the folds, driving her mad. She could feel him there, the tip of his arousal pressed to her, so close. Bea arched her back, trying to draw him in farther, but he wouldn't allow such action. Instead, he moved his hips, keeping outside of her body as he slid between her folds over and over.

Even as she released a frustrated groan, a delicious ache

settled low in her body, spreading through her like a fire across a dry, summer field. Bea's breathing grew harsher, so harsh she could barely seem to draw breath through her shallow lungs. Her entire body tightened with a need she didn't truly understand. With a whimper, she turned her head. Two stone figures met her gaze. They were frozen in pleasure, their faces showing pure delight as the man arched into her from behind. A shiver raked Bea's skin.

Desire took control. Wave after wave of pleasure burst through her body, holding her captive in a storm of erotic desire. Colin's arms tightened around her body. No longer was she aware of the earth, no longer was she aware of anything but her own pleasure and Colin, holding her close.

Colin rolled away, leaving her body exposed to the cold. He lay beside her, his eyes closed and a soft moan escaping his lips.

The cold fingers of reality scraped across her skin. "Colin?" She drew her shirt together and rolled onto her side, pressing close to his warmth.

He kept his eyes closed and didn't respond.

She hesitated only a moment, then reached toward him. His hand shot out, his fingers wrapped tightly around her wrist. "No."

It was one simple word, but said so harshly that she didn't deny his request. His hold loosened and she drew back, resting on her side and watching him. She waited, waited until his harsh breathing settled into some normalcy. Waited for an explanation. Was he angry? Had she done something wrong? Reality washed over her like a snowstorm. She suddenly understood his anger. Colin hadn't wanted to do this; she'd practically forced him.

With her, he held back. Always held back, and she knew the reason why. If Colin took her virginity, he'd be tied to her, and Colin was tied to no one.

Chapter 23

In the early morning, before the sun had even risen, Bea blamed herself for what had happened. If she hadn't seduced Colin like an animal in heat, he never would have touched her that way, she never would have reacted that way, and he never would have rolled away from her that way, leaving her cold and humiliated. Aye, it was her own bloody fault.

By midafternoon, with the sun high and beating down on them furiously as they followed the western coast of India, Bea blamed Colin. After all, he'd attacked her that first night in his home. As if that wasn't enough, he'd practically mauled her on their way to see Anish. If he hadn't kissed her, he never would have awoken that insatiable desire deep within. Aye, it was Colin's bloody fault.

By evening, with the sun slipping below the horizon, giving them blessed relief from the heat, Bea blamed the statues. She'd never liked art anyway. Ridiculous water-colors and drawing classes she'd never been talented enough for. What sort of person produced statues like that anyway? Heathens, that's who. Aye, it was the artist's bloody fault.

And by nightfall, as the first star burst to life, she came to the very depressing realization that it was no one's fault. After all, she couldn't quite blame herself, nor could she blame Colin for the ridiculous feelings that had stirred to life the moment they kissed in Delhi. Fate. The gods. Whatever one wanted to call it, Bea had been oddly attracted to Colin from the moment they locked lips.

With a sigh, she leaned forward, resting the side of her face against his warm back, and attempting desperately not to notice his scent, nor the way his muscles felt underneath her cheek. No, the attraction she felt for Colin was otherworldly, was confusing, tormenting, and she couldn't do a bloody thing to make it go away. Feelings he didn't seem to share in the least. Or did he?

She supposed one could say the first kiss they'd shared had been an accident. He'd thought she was some loose woman who'd invaded his quarters. But the second time, after they'd nearly drowned, well, he'd certainly known her identity then. He hadn't mistaken her for some past lover. Bea took her bottom lip between her teeth, mulling over the possibilities. Surely there was some attraction upon his part, wasn't there? She sighed once more. Being on a bloody horse all day gave a person much too much time to think.

"Do you feel it?" Colin asked, breaking into her thoughts.

Bea pushed away from him, stiffening in surprise. She wasn't sure what shocked her more, his words after hours of silence, or the actual question itself. She shrank down behind his shoulders, horrified he could read her emotions. Feel *what*, exactly? The way her body heated at the mere sound of his voice? The way her pulse raced when he was near? Dear Lord, could he feel her heart thundering against his back? Or could it be . . . was it actually possible the man was going to admit his attraction for her?

"Yes," she whispered tentatively.

He turned in the saddle and glanced over his shoulder, smiling that dimpled smile she so adored. Bea's body flushed with pleasure. It was true. He was going to admit his feelings. He liked her. He'd said he liked her. And she'd been such a silly nit, thinking he didn't care about what they'd experienced. A million possibilities tumbled through her mind. Perhaps he'd say the words she so desperately longed to hear. Perhaps their journey wouldn't end. Perhaps . . . perhaps . . .

"Colin," she started, lowering her lashes and feeling suddenly shy. "I—"

"The ocean," he interrupted, turning back around. "We're close. You can feel the salt in the air."

Reality came crashing down, crushing her soul as if she'd just been hit by one of the perverted statues from Shiva's home.

"Salt?" she choked, unable to keep the anger from her voice.

But Colin didn't notice. Of course not, he was a man, and men, apparently, didn't notice a bloody thing.

"We're almost there. We'll rest soon, then tomorrow, we'll head into Bombay."

She should have known! The blasted man. Of course he wasn't about to admit his feelings, because he was a toad, and toads had no feelings. Annoyed, Bea didn't feel like sharing in the excitement. No, she'd rather be contrary and scatter his happiness. "How do you know you can trust this man anyway?"

Colin darted her an annoyed glance over his shoulder, and she felt a grim sense of satisfaction. "Akshay was Leo's friend. They survived the jungle together, survived their families' murders, they survived your grandfather when he tried to kill them. We can trust him."

Colin focused forward once more, and chagrined, Bea was left to mull over her thoughts. It was still difficult to believe her grandfather had been such an evil man. She didn't particularly remember him, and what she did remember was a man who ignored her for the most part. But a murderer? Grandmother wasn't the kindest soul, but she'd never harm a person. Did she have any clue what her husband was capable of?

Had they been happy once, a long time back? They certainly weren't later in life when greed and obsession got in the way. Was every love destined for a horrible ending? No, Leo and Ella seemed happy and she couldn't imagine either destroying their marriage. But would she ever be so lucky as to find someone to share her life?

It was obvious Colin was more interested in the bloody statue than her. *Once a cad, always a cad.* Hadn't Grandmother whispered that one evening after receiving a letter from Grandfather? Not that Bea was thinking of Colin as someone she could spend her life with. Of course not. They were friends . . . friends who kissed, and touched . . . and . . . Oh, who the bloody hell was she kidding?

Their horse mounted a small hill and a village came into view. They were close, so close to ending their mission. She was happy to be near Bombay. Wasn't she? She'd been eager to arrive when they'd started the trip. Eager to get away from Colin, to get away from the foreignness of India. But now . . .

Once they reached civilization, Bea would be swept back into the world of wealth and titles. Would she see Colin again? Or would he be off on another grand adventure and she'd be sent back to that castle in Scotland? She swallowed hard and closed her eyes, resting the side of her face against his broad back and taking comfort, once more, in his strength and scent. No, she couldn't go back to Scotland. Grandmother had made it clear she wasn't welcome, and Bea wouldn't beg.

Misery weighed heavily upon her soul. Overhead, a star flared across the sky, before fading like an unfulfilled promise from the heavens. Blast them all, she'd traveled through India, she could survive whatever life decided to dump upon her.

Dry fields had given way to huts with straw roofs. Mushrooms alongside the road, just waiting to be picked by a giant. As much as she wished to be contrary, she couldn't help feeling there was magic in the air, as her father used to say when she was a little girl.

"On an evening like this, anything can happen, Bea, my love."

How odd that she should remember his words now. She'd been so young when he'd died, she barely remembered him at all. Why now, of all places, was she thinking of the man she had hardly known? As silly as her father had been, he was the one person who had followed his desires. He hadn't let responsibilities nor his title keep him from running wild. Of course, he'd ended up dead for it, a broken neck racing carelessly through Hyde Park. But he'd enjoyed life, hadn't he? What would he think of his daughter? Traveling through the wilds of India?

A little girl in a pink sari raced from a cottage. She squealed, bursting into giggles as a young boy caught hold of her hand. Their laughter invaded the night and lifted Bea's heart. Too young for romance, they were merely playing, enjoying. All around her, life was beginning, circling, evolving. Women were lighting lanterns and fires threw dancing lights across the hut walls, a merry dance of shadows.

It was almost welcoming, the warm flames, the brilliant saris and turbans. Even Hindi, a language she didn't understand a word of, sounded lyrical and beautiful, a soft lulling music in the background of what had become her life. This was why she'd left Scotland, this was why she'd risked everything, even her relationship with her grandmother . . . to *experience*.

"They don't seem to care," Bea said.

"What's that?"

She hadn't realized she'd spoken aloud until Colin asked. "The people. Even in Delhi they stared, but they don't here."

"Because they're used to seeing Europeans, being so near the port."

But Bea knew it was more than that. Although they glanced their way, no one came running, no one watched for more than a few seconds. Two dirty, obviously poor Europeans were no threat. Without her titled family, she finally fit in, as much as she could. And oddly she liked it this way.

She rather appreciated the stigma of being just another European adventurer.

And she was an adventurer, no matter what anyone else believed. For the first time in her life, she was sure of who she was. She was English, she was a woman, she was brave. Most likely it wouldn't work between her and Colin, and when Colin left her, she would lift her chin high and continue.

But continue where? Her shoulders slumped, darkness sinking heavy in her gut. Just the thought of returning to Scotland left a bitter taste in her mouth. And if she was honest with herself, the possibility of never seeing Colin again couldn't even bear thought.

Colin clicked his tongue, urging their mount forward. The poor beast was ready to collapse, but fortunately the huts had given way to buildings made of white stucco and gray rocks. Side by side, the homes formed a small village where cows roamed the streets and children played.

With their journey coming to a close, a new sense of depression overwhelmed her. "How much longer?" Bea asked.

She shifted on her saddle, like a child during Sunday's service. Next to Colin, with his scent swirling around her, she couldn't think, couldn't rationalize, and she suddenly found herself at odds. Part of her wanted to move far away from the man in order to preserve what little control she had left over her emotions; the other half couldn't stand the thought.

"So eager to be rid of me?" he asked casually.

Was there a hard edge to his voice, or had she imagined the tone? She certainly hadn't imagined the slight stiffening of his back under her hands. "Eager to rest."

He didn't relax. "We'll be there soon." Colin pulled his mount to a stop next to a man shuffling down the road. *"Kshama keejeeae."*

The man paused, glancing up at them through narrowed, suspicious eyes. *"Haan?"*

"Akshay Patel?"

He smiled briefly, setting Bea at ease. His low bow was a

show of respect. Would Colin be as respected in England, among her peers? Would he fit in as he did here? No, he was too wild, too sure of himself, too uncaring of what others thought. Colin would go mad, confined by English rules, and he'd offend more than a few. The thought almost made her laugh.

"Haan." The old man pointed toward a road that curved toward the left.

Colin bowed his head, mirroring the man's respect. *"Shukriya."* He nudged his heels into the horse's sides and they rambled forward. The movement sent Bea backward. She wrapped her fingers around the fine linen of Colin's shirt, linen that was still warm from his body, and held him close. She breathed in his scent before she could stop herself.

"What'd he say? What'd you say?" She probably shouldn't have demanded so harshly, but found herself in a suddenly foul mood and she wasn't quite sure why.

He rubbed the scruff along his jawline, flicking a hooded glance her way. "I asked for directions. Akshay lives just down the road. Don't worry, princess, you'll soon be rid of me."

His foul mood matched hers. She bit back her tart response. *Just down the road.* So close. "Wonderful," Bea whispered. Her stomach clenched. Would Leo and Ella greet them? Would she be immediately swept away to her own room? Perhaps they'd put her on a ship, deciding it was too dangerous, and send her back to Scotland. Oh God, she couldn't go back to Scotland!

"Just remember, his place may not be what you're used to." There was a warning note to Colin's voice. Apparently, he still thought of her as the rich, spoiled woman he'd first met.

She arched a brow, her ire flaring to life. She'd proven more than once that she was neither spoiled nor a princess. "Used to? Such as a hut? The dirt ground? Because at the moment, Colin, that's what I'm used to."

Surprisingly, his shoulders seemed to release. He threw a grin her way. *"Touché,* darlin'."

Just like that, her ire dissipated and she found herself returning his smile. She'd miss their verbal taunting, she'd miss his dimples, bloody hell, she'd even miss the way he called her "darlin'." With a sigh, she tried to focus on their surroundings and not her depressing contemplations.

Two-story stone buildings lined the streets, yet nothing else seemed out of the ordinary. Nevertheless, Colin's gaze darted from shadow to shadow, his instincts on alert. Demyan had found them before; there was no reason why he couldn't find them now. If she was going to be an adventurer, a *true* adventurer, she supposed she, too, should learn to keep watch.

At the end of the lane a white, two-story home sat surrounded by glowing lanterns. A welcoming sight that pained Bea when it should have brought relief. So close to the end, she could feel it. Yet why did her heart ache with the knowledge? Why did she have the sudden desire to beg Colin to stop the horse and turn around? Because her adventure was over. But even as she thought the words, she knew it wasn't true. No, truth was, her heart ached because her time with Colin was over.

"Doesn't look terrible," Colin said as they started down the lane.

But it did. It looked absolutely wretched. Bea bit her lower lip, refusing to give in to the sting of tears. Ridiculous rubbish. She was being a ninny. Exhausted and hungry, that was what the problem was. She swiped at her damp eyes as Colin turned in the saddle to look at her.

"Listen, I want you to wait outside while I go through the gates."

She frowned. "Wouldn't I be safer with you?"

"No, you'll be fine here. Just keep your eyes open."

Bea nodded and looked away. She knew what he was thinking. Demyan may have already gotten to this Akshay. They could very well be walking into a trap. Colin slid from the mount, his boots softly hitting the ground. He rested one hand on her thigh, the other on the horse's reins, and studied her for one impossibly long minute. "Bea, if something happens on that doorstep, kick the horse and run south, got it?"

They both knew the mount wouldn't make it far. She'd be caught outside the city. Still, she could try to hide. She nodded, attempting to keep her face stoic. Would she leave him if he cried the alarm? No. She knew before she'd even thought the question. She'd never abandon Colin. He apparently knew, too. He sighed, shaking his head before giving her a stern look. "I mean it. Run."

Without another word, he made his way through the open iron gates.

He paused only a moment to glance back. Bea gave him a jaunty wave. She couldn't see his expression, but was rather sure he rolled his eyes. Past potted ferns, he made his way up the steps. Bea's shoulders slumped, her attention focusing on her surroundings. Waiting for Colin outside the stone walls, she felt so very alone, so unprotected.

Out here, anything could happen to her. Her heart skipped a beat before taking off into a wild gallop. She nudged the mount, making her shift sideways, farther into the shadows. As frightened as she was, she could admit, as ridiculous as it sounded, that the danger thrilled her . . . made her feel alive in a way she'd never felt before.

Colin knocked, the sound hollow against the thick teak wood. Almost immediately the tall doors pulled inward. A man appeared, a white turban upon his head. Bea could read nothing in his blank expression, neither welcome nor unwelcome. If it wasn't for his clothing and darker skin, he'd resemble the typical cold English butler.

"I'm looking for Akshay Patel."

The man looked Colin up and down, then scanned the front garden. Bea stiffened, her instincts on alert. Looking for her? Had he been expecting them all along?

"Who shall I say is calling?" he asked in perfect English.

"Colin Finch. I'm a friend of Leo's."

The man bowed, yet still showed no signs of recognition. "A moment, if you please." The doors closed.

Colin glanced back, most likely to make sure she was still where he'd left her, then just as quickly, faced the door. Bea took the opportunity to nudge her heels into the mount, urging the beast forward. The door creaked open and masked the soft thud of the horse's hooves against the cobbled stone of the front garden. A gangly man appeared on the stoop. Even though Bea couldn't see his face, she could tell by his clothing and accent that he was Indian.

"Colin?"

"Akshay, my friend!"

They hugged, in the silly way only men could, with laughter and slapping of each other's backs. As much as she wanted to be contrary, Bea's lips lifted, their reunion almost endearing. She hesitated only a moment, then slid from the horse so quietly, that still no one noticed her.

"We've been worried," Akshay exclaimed.

"We? Leo and Ella made it then?"

Akshay nodded. "Although they went to the city on a lead."

Relief snaked through Bea, making her knees weak. Leo and Ella had made it to Bombay, just as they said they would. And with that relief for their well-being, something else niggled at the back of her mind . . . relief that her time with Colin wouldn't end immediately. Giddy, she started toward them, timid, yet eager to hear news of her cousin and his wife.

"Come! You must be exhausted." Akshay's gaze moved past Colin and his warm brown eyes met Bea's. There was curiosity on his face, an openness that pulled her in and set her at ease. This close, she was surprised by how handsome he was, with his thick, wavy black hair and dark, mysterious eyes. And he was young, around the same age as they were. As Leo's best mate, she'd been expecting someone more brooding than this cheerful-looking man.

"They made it?" she asked, returning the man's smile.

Colin sighed as he slid her a glance. "I thought I told you to stay behind."

She shrugged. "He's smiling, he looks kind enough."

"I have no response to that ridiculous piece of logic."

Akshay laughed, a deep, rich chuckle that made Bea want to laugh in kind. "You must be Leo's cousin?"

Bea nodded, feeling suddenly shy. She looked a horrid mess, with her wrinkled sari and dusty skin. What must the man think?

"Come, surely you're hungry. Come, come!" He stepped aside and waved them in.

But Colin merely stood there, pinning her with a glare. Bea hesitated only a moment, resisting the urge to flinch, then swept up the steps past him. No longer was she under Colin's thumb. Aye, she could do what she pleased now that she would be under Leo's protection.

Her slippers whispered over the marble floors, the area refreshingly cool. The hall was impressive. Elegant in marble and teak, yet not overly done. Whereas Shiva's home had been slightly intimidating, this one was homey.

"Colin!" A woman with brilliant red hair swept down the steps. "Oh, Colin, you're well?" Her voice was decidedly English, yet her brilliant green sari spoke of India.

She didn't pause once she reached the hall but threw her arms around Colin's neck in a manner that spoke of kinship, of familiarity. Bea winced as if she'd been kicked in the gut. Who the hell was she? Feeling suddenly as if it was difficult to breathe, Bea shifted into the shadows. Had one in every port, did he? The sting of jealousy mixed with a deep, aching hurt. Had he abandoned this woman as he would her?

Colin kissed the woman's pale cheek, only adding confirmation to Bea's conclusion. Her stomach churned, and for a brief moment, she thought she might get sick all over the marble floor. He could, at least, look sheepish, the dratted man! No wonder he'd been so intent on ending their intimacy!

"Fran, you look wonderful."

The Fran woman grinned, a toothy grin. Tears of anger stung Bea's eyes. She looked away, feigning interest in the décor. She supposed Fran was pretty, in a boring and wholesome way. Unable to prevent herself, Bea slid Colin and Fran a glance. They were holding hands now as if they were the closest of lovers. She resisted the urge to gag. How much longer must she endure their courtship? How could Colin do this, after what they'd experienced?

"Thanks to you, I look wonderful," Fran whispered.

Bea almost snorted. Could the woman fawn any more than she already was? It was disgusting, ridic—

The woman's words gave Bea pause. *Thanks to Colin?*

Colin flushed, rubbing the back of his neck in that way he did when he was embarrassed. Embarrassed about what? Had she missed something? How, exactly, were Colin and this Fran woman connected?

Colin slid Fran's arm through his. "Indian weather must agree with you."

Fran looked up at him with large, adoring, calflike eyes. "It does. I never thought I'd take to a country so different." She glanced toward Bea, her gaze shy, yet welcoming. "We're being rude, though. You're Beatrice?"

Bea hesitated, unsure how to respond. Finally, she gave a curt nod. Fran moved from Colin's side, taking Bea's hands in hers. Bea stiffened, confused and surprised by the woman's friendly touch. If this Fran was in love with Colin, shouldn't she be jealous of Bea? Unless, Bea realized, she looked so horrible that Fran figured she was no threat.

"Oh, how lovely! Ella was correct, you're stunning."

Bea flushed, resisting the urge to pull away. "I look a terrible mess."

"Of course not." Fran slipped her arm around Bea's waist. It was almost comical; the woman was a good head shorter than she, yet was leading her toward the stairs like a mother would a child. Blast it all, as much as she wanted to hate her, she couldn't, for Fran's eyes spoke only of sincerity.

"You *are* beautiful."

Akshay sighed long and loud. "Enough, my wife, you're both beautiful."

Stunned speechless, Bea's steps faltered. Fran? Akshay? Married? But . . . but he was Indian and she was . . . *not*.

Fran laughed, a merry giggle, and gave her husband a wink before turning back to Bea. "Of course, a bath and rest?"

Bea nodded dumbly, realizing that Colin and Fran weren't together at all. But then . . . what had they been talking about? *Thanks to you* . . . Realization dawned hot and heavy with humiliation. Colin had saved Fran, obviously, but Bea had been too stupid with jealousy to realize it. She slid Fran, then Colin, a glance. Adoration, but not love. No, Fran only looked at her husband with love in her eyes. Bea felt utterly and completely stupid. Had her feelings for Colin truly made her so daft?

Fran led her up the steps but not before glancing one last time toward her husband. "My dear, you'll see to Colin?"

"But of course," Akshay called out. "A bit of Scotch and he'll be good as new."

Bea didn't dare look at Colin, too worried he'd read the stunned humiliation upon her face and know her thoughts. Her mind spun with the possibilities, so much so, she was barely aware of where Fran led her. As much as she wanted to push the ridiculous notion aside . . . as much as she wanted to deny and ignore her feelings . . . Bea couldn't help pondering the insane.

If an English woman and an Indian man could make a loving relationship work during the reign of Queen Victoria, what could she and Colin accomplish?

What in the world was she thinking? What could she and Colin accomplish? Nothing, that's what. A relationship with Colin. Bea snorted. Even if it could work, he wouldn't want one . . . it was obvious Colin had no designs to settle down.

Perhaps he'd stay a month, maybe two, but a man like Colin, a man always on the move, always looking for adventure . . . a man like that would get bored with one woman, wouldn't he? Besides, he never actually said he wanted a relationship. No, he said he liked her and that could mean one of many things, none of which meant he wanted to spend the rest of his life with her.

"The gardens are quite lovely," Fran said.

Bea turned away from the open doors that led onto a stone terrace. The woman was watching her closely, too closely. Could everyone in this blasted country read minds? With Fran's eyes piercing her, it felt as if she could.

"Wear this. It's too warm to sleep in night clothing." Fran held out a silky blue robe.

Bea relented and dropped her towel, allowing Fran to slip the robe over her bare shoulders. Fran's hair had come loose and hung down her back in rich curls. Bea could see why Akshay had fallen for this woman. She was honest, open, and beautiful. Her home was just as lovely. The bedchamber Bea had been led to was large, comfortable, and clean.

Fran moved to the bed. "The gardens are quite lovely at night and quite safe, fenced in."

Bea nodded, confused. There was an odd twinkle in her new friend's eyes, a twinkle that hinted at something more to come. Bea brushed aside the woman's odd comment. As she'd helped Bea bathe, they'd become fast friends. Bea didn't need to ask why Fran and Akshay had left England; she could guess that society had not been accepting of their marriage. But Fran didn't seem to care; she looked truly happy here. Could Bea find such happiness in a foreign land?

Fran hummed as she folded a drying cloth.

"You like it here?" Bea blurted out. "I mean, you're English, and living in a world of foreigners." She knew her question was forward, but the woman didn't seem to mind.

Fran smiled, her eyes lighting up. "I 'ad my reservations at first, as I'm sure you understand. It's completely different than England. But I suppose sometimes different is good. Don't you agree?"

Bea nodded slowly, her thoughts in turmoil. The problem was, living the same life, day in and day out, had been . . . well . . . easy.

"And you?" Fran was watching her again, as if trying to uncover her secrets.

Bea tightened the belt of her robe, giving her hands something to do as she was unsure how to respond. Her feelings had changed so drastically from the start of their journey. "At first, I thought the place wretched."

Fran nodded with a knowing grin. "The dirt, dust, and insects as big as your bloody 'and. That, combined with a language I still 'ave trouble with, and I completely understand."

Bea laughed. "But now?" She turned toward those gardens once more. White jasmine hung heavy in the warm air and whispered sweet promises of seduction. She felt clean, so clean and good. She'd scrubbed herself twice, washed her hair twice, feasted upon a platter of fruits and nuts. She felt fresh and languid. She finally felt alive. How could she hate this place now, of all times?

She turned to face Fran. "Well, I suppose I like different, too. The colors, the sights, everything . . . it's rather amazing and there's always something new to see."

Fran nodded and came to stand beside her, gazing out upon her gardens with a satisfied look of pride. "Yes, there is. I wonder if I shall ever grow tired of the sights. In England, well, we never would 'ave owned this." She nodded toward the expansive grounds.

They were both quiet for some time, Fran studying her flowers, while Bea's mind spun with confusing and contradictory thoughts. Thoughts of Colin and thoughts of her and Colin. He'd been so bloody silent at dinner, so unlike him. More than once she caught him looking at her, yet she could read nothing on his stoic face.

"Fran . . ." Bea flushed, struggling to find the right words.

"Yes?" Fran tilted her head to the side, studying her in that knowing way.

Heat boiled under Bea's skin. What was she thinking? She couldn't ask Fran about her relationship. "No, nothing, really."

Fran lifted a brow and waited patiently.

Bea shrugged and toyed with her belt. "'Tis nothing really, it's just . . . well . . ." Oh, blast it, she might as well go through with it now. "Did you know immediately that you loved Akshay?"

Fran laughed. "Blimey, no. The dear man was an oddity to me. But, well, he grew on me and now"—Fran blushed, bringing her freckles to life—"I'd follow 'im to the ends of the earth, I would."

Bea nodded knowingly. She felt as if she'd been following Colin to the ends of the earth for a week now. Oddly, although she thought it would be hell, she found she craved the adventure . . . she craved *him*. After living the same blasted day over and over again in Scotland, she loved not knowing what was to come. But mostly, she loved experiencing each adventure with Colin.

Fran slipped her arm around Bea's waist and gave her a quick squeeze as if she realized the direction of her thoughts. "Well, I should leave you to rest. But please, if you ever feel the need to visit 'ere, know that you're always welcome." Fran pulled back and looked directly into her eyes. "I mean it, Bea, you don't 'ave to go back to Scotland."

Surprised, Bea wasn't sure how to respond. Of course she had to go back, didn't she?

Fran winked, then started toward the door. "I can see it in your eyes, me dear." She paused at the door. "And your eyes say you're not ready to return."

Bea stiffened, her mind in turmoil. Was it so obvious?

"Good night, Bea." The woman pulled open the door. "And really, try a stroll through the gardens. Perhaps you'll find the answer to your questions there."

The door shut, leaving Bea to her thoughts. Answers to

what questions? Curious, she glanced toward the gardens. A stroll would be quite welcome and the grass looked so soft and inviting, compared to the dry dirt they'd been traveling over for days. Taking in a deep breath, she moved outside, pausing on the terrace, the stone cool through her thin slippers. Yes, she supposed the fresh air did help to clear her mind.

Beyond the wall, the village was quiet, the house dark but for her own bedchamber lantern throwing a pattern of gold across the rosebushes below. In the middle of the garden, a barely visible arbor was covered with white jasmine, promising repose.

Bea's body felt restless, eager to move. She rested her hand on the marble railing, intent on going down the steps, but froze as a shiver raced over her skin. She sensed him before she actually saw him, the same heated shimmer she'd felt before when he was near.

Her breath hitched, her heart slamming wildly against her chest. Slowly she turned her head and met his gaze. Only a stone's throw away, Colin stood at the bottom of the shallow steps. Call it instinct, call it desire, but she couldn't seem to stop her feet from moving. She started down the stairs, pausing only when her feet sank into the damp grass.

"You should be abed."

She wanted to laugh at his ridiculous comment. Abed? As if she could sleep with him so near. He'd bathed. His hair curled damply against his neck in a way that taunted her fingers. His white linen shirt hung lose, unbuttoned at the neck. Had he been waiting for her? He looked relaxed and completely unconcerned. For some reason, that annoyed her. She wanted him restless. She wanted him anxious . . . anxious for her.

"I'm not tired." And it was the truth. Suddenly, exhaustion seemed to have disappeared. She tilted her chin high and feigned interest in a nearby rosebush. Blast him! Why couldn't he even pretend to be interested in her? Had he gotten over her so easily? Had their time spent together meant so little that—

"Please, Bea, go to bed."

His soft voice surprised her and her attention jumped to him. "Why?"

"Because if you don't . . ." His throat worked, as if he wasn't quite sure how to go on.

Her heart thundered madly in her chest. "If I don't . . . what will happen?"

He turned his back to her, his hands fisted at his sides. She knew everything, *everything*, hinged on his next words.

"Damn it, Bea, don't tempt me to be the rake."

Bea felt dizzy, her mind spinning, her emotions in turmoil. He wanted her. The realization thrilled her in a way she couldn't begin to describe. He wanted her. But it was obvious by the stiff line of his back that he didn't *want* to want her. Bea took in a deep, shuddering breath.

"Nonsense. I tempt no one," Bea whispered, surprised she could speak. "Besides, you're the one lurking beneath my window."

She started toward him, her slippers resisting softly against grass blades, knowing that every step closer brought her to her goal. Knowing that every step closer brought her to her demise.

With his back still to her, he rested his palms on the wall of the home, his head hung low, as if ashamed. "You're right. I'm to blame. But do you have any idea how hard it is to say no to you?" He turned to face her, his gaze pleading, and at the same time he looked almost angry. "How you tempt me, yet never fulfill?"

Bea couldn't seem to catch her breath. He was blaming her? Anger warred with frustration. "I've never stopped you."

He blinked, surprised by her answer.

Emboldened, Bea stepped closer, so close she could feel his harsh breath across her forehead. "Never once have I told you to stop."

"You don't know what you're saying."

"I'm not an idiot, Colin. I know what I want. I want you."
Dear God, had the words really slipped from her lips? Bea
resisted the urge to blush. Resisted the urge to take the words
back. Resisted the urge to flee to her room. Too late. She'd
spoken the truth and she wouldn't recant.

Instead of surprise, the only thing that seemed to flash
behind Colin's gaze was anger. Without a glance her way,
Colin stalked toward the gardens, his hands fisted. "You're
a virgin, for God's sake. An innocent virgin and you don't
understand the repercussions of your actions."

She laughed, a taunting sound. She was tired of people
controlling her life. Tired of people telling her what she
wanted and didn't want. She wanted Colin, and damn it, she
was going to make sure he knew. If their relationship didn't
work, it wouldn't be because of her. She lifted the hem of her
robe and started after him.

"Just because I want you doesn't make me a fool."

He spun around to face her. "Then what does it make you?"

Bea stumbled to a halt. She wasn't sure what he implied,
but she knew it couldn't be good. There was a hardness in
his eyes that she didn't like, an accusation that bothered her.
Without another word, he started past her, headed no doubt
to his own chamber, where he would lock the door on his
emotions. He'd left her before; he wouldn't do so again.
Angry, Bea reached out, latching on to his hand, hoping he
didn't notice the tremble of her fingers.

He froze as if her touch were poison. "If you don't . . ."

"What?" Bea taunted with a confidence she didn't exactly feel. "If I don't let go, what will you do, Colin?"

His free hand settled on her waist and he jerked her forward. Bea's palms flattened to his hard chest, a gasp parting her lips.

"This, Bea. I'll do this." His mouth crushed to hers. This
was no sweet, innocent kiss. Colin's mouth was demanding,
just as Bea wanted him. He tasted sweet, of fruits and wine.

His muscled arms tightened around her waist, pulling her so close, she could feel every wild beat of his heart against her breasts. When he thrust his tongue into her mouth, any little resistance Bea held shattered. She sank into his body, giving in to her desires. That was when he pulled back.

With his steely gaze on hers, his hands fell to the belt around her waist. "You want me? You shall have me."

Chapter 24

His words worried as much as they excited her. Even though she attempted to take a step back, her body shivered in anticipation of the thought of Colin's hands on her.

"Colin, I . . ."

He reached for the knife on his thigh. Bea sucked in a sharp breath. Before she could protest, he'd cut the belt of her robe and brushed the silky material from her body. The gown fluttered to the ground, pooling around her ankles and leaving her naked and exposed.

"Colin," Bea whispered, flustered, her gaze jumping around the dark corners of the garden, making sure they were truly alone. "You don't have to . . ."

He tossed his knife to the ground and cupped the sides of her face. Without pause, he was kissing her again. It wasn't right. He was angry. She was naked, in someone else's garden. It wasn't right, yet she couldn't seem to dredge up the energy to explain that to Colin.

The pressure of his body leaning into hers tilted her backward, but instead of hitting the ground, she was suddenly scooped up into Colin's arms. He didn't look at her as their kiss broke, but remained focused ahead, focused on his apparent goal. Confused and feeling timid, Bea wrapped her arms around his neck and peeked up at him through her lashes.

His gaze was set forward, his jaw locked in determination as he stomped toward the jasmine-covered arbor. Noting the fierce look in his eyes, she didn't dare demand an explanation. No, she knew exactly what he was going to do, and even though she knew she should tell him to stop, she didn't really want to.

Charming, laughing, taunting Colin was gone. Yet she still wanted him. He laid her down upon a cushioned fainting couch that had been placed romantically under the arbor. Laid out like an offering to the night, she was exposed, completely naked, but Colin didn't say a word. There was no compliment, no gentle words to ease her worries. There was merely a man and a woman, giving in to their baser needs.

Slowly, he undressed, his gaze pinned to her the entire time. Moonlight filtered through the vines, highlighting the muscled planes of his chest. Buttons undone, he pulled his shirt loose and tossed it aside, his chest gloriously unveiled.

And just when she had decided to enjoy his touch, Bea grew nervous. Her breath hitched, her heart racing madly. His hands fell to his waistband and her nerves grew frayed. His feet were already bare, and with a quick flick of his fingers, his trousers fell to the ground. He was naked. Completely naked. Like one of Shiva's marble statues come to life. Bea couldn't seem to breathe, couldn't seem to catch hold of a rational thought. Her gaze slid down his chest to that erection jutting out hard and large.

"Is this what you want, Bea?" He settled on the couch, looming over her, a hand on each side of her hips, trapping her. Slowly, he crawled upward, inch by inch. An animal about to pounce. The heat in his gaze held her captive, even as she felt, what could only be, his hard erection brush between her thighs.

"Is it?" he demanded, pausing when his face was only inches from hers.

She swallowed and gave a quick nod of her head, realizing there was no going back now.

"Then you shall have me." He lowered his body, his muscled form molding to hers as his mouth crushed to her lips.

Roughly, his knee nudged between her legs, parting her thighs. Hips to hips, his erection nestled heavy and hard against that aching spot. Frozen, Bea merely lay there while he nibbled her lips. She didn't know what to do, what to say. Didn't even know if she really wanted this.

Colin's thumb rested on her chin, and with a little pressure, he opened her mouth. His tongue swept inside, making quick work of seduction. Heat shot through Bea's core. Any reluctance fled. Her tongue met his, rubbing and thrusting until the ache between her legs flared. This was what she'd wanted the moment they'd kissed that night in Delhi.

Lost to her heady desires, Bea wrapped her arms around his neck, arching her back to bring him closer. Instead, Colin pulled away. His mouth rested near the side of her head, his harsh breath stirring the hairs near her temple. She was just about to demand he kiss her again when his tongue swept out, tracing the delicate shell of her ear. Bea quivered. He moved lower, his lips pressing to her neck, lower still to that valley between her breasts.

Above, just through the vines, stars twinkled like brilliant diamonds laid upon the goddess of night. Of promises to come. Over her own harsh breathing, Bea could hear insects chirping a symphony of seduction. She closed her eyes, reveling in the sensation of Colin's lips on her. She wanted this. She'd wanted Colin for so long. She had him now. Perhaps not exactly as she wanted him.

No, he wasn't on his knees confessing his love, but he was here, now, and that was all that mattered at the moment. And why not enjoy the moment? After all, if her family had taught her anything, it was that good moments never lasted and so she should enjoy them while they came.

Colin's warm hand rested low on her belly, shocking Bea from her thoughts. His thumb brushed across the soft curls at the junction of her thighs and her body caught fire. Slowly, he lifted his head, his eyes dark and fathomless in the night.

"Do you want this, Bea? Do you like it when I touch you here?" He slid his knuckle between her damp folds.

Bea bit her lower lip. He was taunting her. Trying to teach her a lesson as his finger teased. She didn't care. "Yes, please."

Two fingers replaced the one. Slowly, he slid them into her tight sheath. Bea sucked in a sharp breath, resisting the urge to arch her back and take him in farther.

"So polite. So English," he murmured, a wicked smile upon his lips, but there was no mirth in his eyes.

The flush of desire mixed with heated embarrassment. Bea turned her head, trying to hide her face in the cushions of the settee.

There was nowhere she could hide from Colin. He leaned closer, his chest pressing to her breasts. "Would you be so polite if my tongue replaced my fingers?"

His wicked words sent a thrilling chill through her body, but his fingers, oh dear Lord, his fingers were working a magic that made her want to beg for more.

Bea curled her fists, her nails biting into her palms as she resisted the urge to reply.

Colin leaned forward and licked the side of her neck. "Say please, Bea."

She whimpered, but kept her lips pressed tightly together. Somehow he'd gotten the upper hand in this seduction. She knew he wanted her as much as she wanted him and she wouldn't beg, not like this.

His mouth captured her right breast while his free hand

cupped her left. Bea gasped, her eyes opening as tendrils of pure delight swept through her body. The ache between her legs intensified, coiling tightly as her breasts grew heavy.

Colin moved lower, his lips pressing against her belly. "Say pretty, pretty please."

With a groan, she sat upright and pushed at his shoulders. He didn't budge. Suddenly, she was overwhelmed . . . by his strength so apparent in the sinewy muscles that refused to move, by her own emotions so consuming and utterly destroying. "Damn you, Colin!"

He lifted his head and crushed his mouth to hers. With his body and weight, he pressed her back into the settee, his heavy form holding her captive. His fingers, like manacles, latched on to her wrists. With a growl low in this throat, he lifted her arms and jerked them above her head, pinning them to the cushions. This wasn't the Colin she'd come to know.

"Tell me you still want me," he demanded against her mouth.

She turned her head, refusing to respond, but her body answered for her. Her breath came out in sharp, hot pants. She knew what this domination act was about. He was trying to frighten her. He wanted her to say no, to stop this madness. His knees nudged between her legs, spreading her thighs once more.

"Say it."

She lifted her chin and met his gaze, determined he wouldn't win. "I still want you." The words left her lips in a rush of air.

She couldn't deny the truth. She couldn't hold back her emotions any longer. She wanted him and she feared she always would.

She felt him shudder right before he lowered his mouth. "Damn you."

He crushed his lips to hers and his fingers found the soft curls at the junction of her thighs once more. As his tongue thrust into her mouth, his fingers thrust into her tight sheath.

White-hot need burst to life. Bea arched, arching her hips higher as her hands moved down his sleek back. She wanted more, more of him, all of him.

Frustration burned low in her belly, mixing with the deep ache and producing a desire that was uncontrollable. With a groan, Bea shifted, drawing his fingers deeper. She couldn't seem to get close enough, needed more . . . Desperate, Bea slid her arms around his neck, her fingers tugging on the strands of his hair until he lifted his head. Colin's hips shifted and she felt the tip of his arousal press to her folds. Breathless, wanting, she met his gaze and knew this time he wouldn't stop. This time he'd enter her fully.

Her heart sped up. With his eyes still locked to hers, Colin lowered his hips. His shaft slipped between her folds, sliding easily toward her entrance. Slowly, he stretched the walls of her sheath. It didn't hurt, but it wasn't exactly what she'd been expecting. Suddenly nervous, Bea's fingernails dug into his back, and she took her lower lip between her teeth. Perhaps she should explain that she wasn't quite ready after all. Perhaps . . .

With a low growl, Colin arched his back and thrust deep into her with swift determination. A slight sting interrupted the confusing reality of the moment. Shocked, Bea merely lay there, realizing it was done. She was no longer a virgin. She was completely and utterly ruined.

Colin paused then, his chin resting against her forehead, his breath harsh and loud, his body heavy. Tentatively, Bea shifted, testing the feel of him buried inside her. There, just below the shock, that ache resided, waiting . . . taunting.

"This is what you wanted." Colin said the words as if proving a point, as if she'd regret her decision.

She didn't. She wouldn't.

Angry, she slid her fingers into his hair and jerked his head down, taking his lips. At the same time, she arched her hips, sending his shaft deeper. This time, instead of pain, she felt only an aching pull deep within her womb . . . a heady need for fulfillment.

Colin groaned against her lips, his own hands slipping under her bottom, cupping her backside and pulling her up closer to him. Instinct made Bea slip her legs around his. Slowly, he moved, rocking against her. Bea's need flared, her nails digging into his shoulders.

"Please, Colin, please."

His thrusts became hard, faster, setting up a rhythm that sent her body tingling. Bea lifted, meeting him thrust for thrust. Again and again, he drove into her, sending a feverish spiral of need through her body. She would explode, the ache too deep, too tight. She wanted it to end, yet never wanted to stop. Finally, her body tightened. Bea arched, Colin's mouth found hers, trapping her shout. Her sheath tightened and Bea burst into that heady bliss of sexual release.

Every muscle in his body seemed to harden. Bea arched, for some reason needing to take him deeper. With a final cry, Colin thrust into her. She felt his seed, warm and wet, enter her body. For some reason, the sensation sent her muscles quivering with renewed pleasure.

He collapsed atop her, his weight heavy. He didn't move, didn't say a word. His breath fanned across her face, the only sound in the quiet night. Bea merely lay there reveling in the remaining pleasure, in her own seductive reality. She hadn't expected it to be so . . . so strong. So amazing. She'd felt this before, when he'd touched her, stroked her with his tongue down there. But never . . . never had she imagined it would be like this. She felt one with Colin. She felt . . .

Her eyes widened. She loved him. Dear God, she loved him and her heart would break.

Colin pulled back and slowly moved from her. She felt his loss as if he'd ripped out her soul. He didn't look her way as he picked up his clothes. He merely dressed as if she weren't even there, lying upon the bed like some virginal sacrifice.

He slipped his arms into the sleeves of his linen shirt and, not bothering to button it, turned so his back was to her. He paused then, for one incredibly long moment. "You got what you want, Bea. I hope you don't regret it." Without another word, without a backward glance, he walked away.

Shocked and numb, Bea sat up, watching him until he merged with the shadows. Gone, he left her, just like that. And she was in love with the bloody bastard.

Colin kept moving, kept going forward even as his soul screamed at him to turn around. His heart thundered in his ears, his pulse raced. He'd come inside her. She could get pregnant. Dear God, she could have his baby. And then what? She'd hate him? Despise him for trapping her in a marriage where they had no money, a marriage where she'd be forced to sit in some dingy shack and wait for him to return day after day as his mother had done with his father?

Ahead, a lantern burned in the window of his room, a beacon that called out safety. He focused on that light, even as he wanted to turn around and go back to Bea. How could he leave her like that? But how could he not? If he stayed . . . dear Lord, if he stayed, he'd want more . . . and if she even looked at him with a hint of desire in her eyes, he wouldn't be able to say no. His foot hit the marble patio with a thud that matched the beat of his heart.

His skin crawled. His body hummed. His mind raced yet nothing made sense. Like a drug, he needed her. Tasting her wouldn't be enough. He pushed the doors wide and stepped into his bedchamber, determined to leave her in peace, to let her gather her thoughts and realize the mistake of their intimacy. With a flip of his wrists, he shut the door. Shut Bea out.

At the fireplace, he paused, leaning his palms on the mantel. What had he done? He'd ruined her. An innocent woman who was intended to marry a titled gent, a rich titled gent. He'd ruined her. Leo's cousin. Ella's friend. And even worse, he'd abandoned her there, naked in the garden. He tore his shirt from his chest, the clothing suddenly too confining. The mirror that hung above the mantel showed a face full of confusion and anguish. He had to go back, he had to explain . . . But how did he explain? Hell, he didn't even understand any of it himself.

The door burst open, slamming against the wall with such force it made the flame in the lantern flicker. Colin spun around. Bea stood on the threshold, anger marring every inch of her beautiful body, from her clenched jaw to her curled, bare toes. The robe was in place, but hanging open without a belt to keep it closed and he could see every naked inch. She didn't seem to care.

"Bea, I—"

Her hands fisted at her sides. "How dare you." She stomped into the room, slamming the door behind her. "How dare you leave me like I'm nothing!"

Shocked, it took a moment for him to respond. "Bea, damn it, will you listen to me?"

Her eyes narrowed into mere slits, her breath harsh as she seethed. Fortunately, she paused and crossed her arms over her chest. Unfortunately, the movement only sent those soft mounds higher, taunting him. Colin blinked rapidly, trying to clear his lusty thoughts.

"Well? What do you have to say?" Bea threw her arms in the air. "That you took my virginity then left me like I was nothing? Please, explain."

He rubbed the back of his neck. "Well, when you say it like that . . ."

"You treat your mistresses even better, don't you?"

"Christ," he snapped, annoyed she'd bring up such a topic now, of all times.

She stomped closer, her eyes flashing in that way he so adored. "Oh, please. Yes, you see I'm not the innocent you think. I know what men do, I know they keep mistresses. And you, Colin, have just treated me worse than your mistress."

"Bea, I don't have . . ." She moved closer, only a breath away, and he lost his train of thought. Bea angry was a sight to behold. Her eyes sparkled. Her harsh breathing only raised her breasts, making her nipples brush against his chest.

She shoved her finger into his chest for emphasis. "I hope you get the pox, Colin Finch, and your thing falls off!"

Colin had to bite back a laugh.

"Don't you dare laugh at me!" She stomped her foot, and he thought for a moment she might slap him.

He held up his hands. "I'm not."

"You are! I can see it in your eyes. You're laughing at me. You just used me, discarded me, and now you're laughing."

Sudden tears shimmered in her eyes. Colin's mirth fled.

"You ruined everything, Colin, and I despise you!" Before he could guess her intentions, she raised her fist and swung at him. Her knuckles grazed his chin. Stunned, Colin merely stood there as Bea spun around and started back toward the door.

"You just hit me!" he yelled, irate yet oddly amused.

"And I'll do it again! Next time, harder!"

He reached her in two strides, reached her just as she was taking the doorknob in hand. Colin latched on to her arm and spun her around. The shock on her face was worth it all.

"No one hits me."

"What are you going to do about it?" she mocked, tilting her chin high, but her eyes, oh, her eyes bespoke not of arrogance, but insecurity.

A slow smile spread across his lips. "Are you afraid now, Bea?"

She backed up, her shoulder blades hitting the door. The bravado was gone from her eyes. "No."

"You should be." He grabbed her before she could get

away. With his hands on her hips, he threw her over his shoulder.

"Colin! Put me down!" Bea slammed her fists against his back with more force than he thought her capable of.

He tossed her onto the bed. Before she could move, he was on her, pinning her down with his body. "I'm going to teach you a lesson, darlin'."

His mouth pressed to her neck. Bea squirmed, struggling to move. He wouldn't let her.

"I mean it, Colin, get off!"

He pulled back, looking into her eyes. She was angry, yes, but there was also desire there. Damn, but she was amazing. "Why? When you enjoy my touch so much?" His lips trailed down her neck, to the tops of her breasts. Her fingers slipped into his hair and jerked back, pulling painfully at the strands.

With a growl, Colin took one of her breasts in his mouth. Bea sucked in a sharp breath, her hold loosening. The anger disappeared. She sighed, sinking into the bed as if her body had melted.

He pulled back just enough. "Do you still want me to stop?" He drew his tongue around her hard nipple and glanced up at her through his lashes, weighing her response.

Her brows snapped together. "Yes. No. I don't know."

He brushed aside her robe and moved lower, his mouth trailing over her flat belly. "Well?"

Her hands slid into his hair once more, this time in long, sweet strokes. "No. Please. Don't."

Her words sent his senses spinning. Any resistance was forgotten. She tasted good, so damn good. Her fingernails bit into his shoulders as her desire flared to life. "Please, Colin, come inside me."

He closed his eyes, resting his forehead on her stomach. He couldn't. Could he? Slowly, he lifted his head and met her gaze. "It's too soon."

"You'll be gentle," she whispered and there was a certainty in her eyes that flattered him. That amber gaze was hazy with passion, but something else . . . determination. She knew what she wanted. Bea always knew what she wanted. She wanted him. Dear God, how could he say no?

He moved up her and pressed his mouth to hers in a quick kiss. "Whatever you want, Bea."

He nudged his knee between her smooth thighs. She was ready for him, sleek, hot, and still wet from their last experience. He pressed the tip of his shaft into her tight sheath. Sweat broke out on his forehead. He tried to hold back, but Bea arched, taking him farther into her sweet body. It was torture. Beautiful, wonderful, torture and he never wanted it to end.

"Oh, Colin," she rasped, her voice as breathless as his.

It was as she called his name that he realized he never wanted her to stop. Damn, he had fallen too deep, too quick. It scared the hell out of him. He wanted to pull back. He couldn't. As he thrust, Bea lifted her hips, meeting him, drawing him closer. He watched her, his gaze pinned to her beautiful face as he buried himself inside her, giving over completely.

It was all he needed.

Again and again he moved against her. Time disappeared. Nothing mattered, until Bea moaned, her own body tightening in surrender. Fire pounded through his blood. With a roar, he threw his head back and emptied himself inside her. Bea trembled around him, her breathing harsh. He'd lost his mind once more and he couldn't seem to care.

Colin started to move, afraid he'd crush her, but Bea's arms tightened around his neck, holding him captive. She buried her face against his chest, hiding. Dear God, he'd never felt so wonderfully complete. His hold tightened around her.

"Please," she whispered so softly, he wasn't sure if she'd really said the word or he'd imagined it.

He waited.

"Please," she whispered again. "Please don't leave me this time."

Colin closed his eyes, his heart clenching. "I won't, Bea. I promise."

Chapter 25

"Colin Finch, you better have a very, very good reason for this!"

The low, feminine growl erupted into Bea's consciousness, dragging her from the dredges of slumber. She didn't open her eyes, she was too bloody tired, but lay still, wondering if perhaps she'd dreamt the familiar voice. After all, her body felt too languid and wonderful to be truly awake. Yes, most likely she was dreaming. With a sigh, she settled back into slumber and cuddled closer to the warm solidness that pressed against the length of her body.

"Privacy would be good," Colin grumbled, his voice a caress that stirred the hair at her temples. For one brief moment, Bea thought he was talking to her. He shifted, taking the warmth and pressure of his body away. Suddenly Bea was alone.

Confused, her lashes lifted. The ceiling glared down at her, refusing to give any answers, and so she lowered her gaze to Colin, who was sitting up for some odd reason, and even odder, he wasn't dressed. Why was he in her bed? And more importantly, why was he naked?

"Well?" someone demanded.

Bea jerked her gaze toward the voice. The dream became reality.

She wasn't in her bedchamber, after all. In fact, she was in Colin's, and Ella stood there wearing men's trousers and a white linen shirt. Her arms were folded across her chest, her face flushed red with . . . fury. Those blue eyes flickered between Bea and Colin as if searching for the answers to her question. Last night came rushing back on a torrent of emotions.

"Oh, dear God," Bea whispered, sinking into the bed and pulling the coverlet over her head. This was not happening. She hadn't been intimate with Colin, and Ella most certainly was not here . . . now of all times. Heat shot to her face, her stomach tightened into a knot that would surely never come undone.

"Dear God is right," Ella snapped, her voice muffled through the blanket. "What is going on here? There better be a very good explanation, Colin Finch!"

Bea pulled the covers down just enough to spy Colin and Ella.

Colin had grabbed his shirt and trousers and was holding them in front of his midsection, but his bottom was deliciously exposed to Bea. A gorgeous bottom, really, Bea thought, with a tilt of her head to get a better view. Last night she'd had no qualms about grabbing that backside. But now . . . blimey! The heat that had rushed to her face at Ella's appearance intensified.

"It's not what it seems," Colin said, jerking her from her thoughts.

Ella snorted at the same time that Bea rolled her eyes.

Apparently unconcerned, Colin smiled a wicked grin that produced both dimples. "All right, maybe it is."

Ella didn't relent, but continued to glare at her cousin. Apparently, she was immune to his dimples.

Colin sighed and raked back his hair. "Come on, Ella. Bea and I were together for days. You couldn't expect—"

"Oh, yes, *days*!" Ella flung her arms dramatically wide.

"How can a person go *days* without giving in to their basic human desires!"

"Good, so we're in agreement."

Ella stomped her foot and Bea flinched. "Ohhhh! You wretched man! I should have known better than to leave her with you! When Fran said Bea wasn't in her room, I was worried, but never did I expect . . ." She shook her head as if too disgusted to go on.

Bea resisted the urge to groan. She didn't think her life could get any more embarrassing. Did the entire household know?

Colin held up one hand, the other clutching the clothing to his private area. "Bea and I are two grown adults, lest you forget."

Ella was having none of his argument. She folded her arms across her chest once more and glared. "Yes, well, explain that to Leo." That glare turned into a tauntingly sweet smile. "Why, he should be here any moment."

"What?" Bea clutched the blanket to her chest and shot upright.

Ella quirked a brow, obviously enjoying the moment. "Yes, and I'm sure he'll be happy to explain what is appropriate and what isn't!"

"Oh, dear Lord." Going for the closest clothing, Bea reached over and snatched the shirt and trousers from Colin's fingers.

"Hey!" Suddenly naked, he had only his hands to hide his modesty.

Ella screamed and spun around, apparently horrified.

"Sorry!" Bea mumbled as she clutched the clothing to her chest and, naked, bolted toward the doors that led into the gardens. "Really." She pulled the doors open. "So sorry."

Colin merely stood there staring at her, his mouth agape. Seeing the shock on his face, Bea felt the insane desire to laugh. Instead, she shrugged, fighting her mirth, and pulled the doors shut.

Outside, with the early morning air fresh and crisp, she could finally breathe. From the bedchamber, she could hear Ella and Colin arguing, but the words were too muffled to understand.

She tilted her head back and looked to the pastel sky, the sun just beginning to rise. "Why? Have I not gone through enough? I mean really." She dropped the trousers and pulled Colin's shirt on, working the buttons up the front. "Ungrateful is what you are. I went to church every Sunday and this is how I'm repaid?" She shoved her legs through Colin's trousers and rolled the waistband until it hung low on her hips. She couldn't imagine what Leo would say. How could she ever look him in the face again?

Someone cleared his throat.

Bea froze, sending a silent prayer that the noise had been imagined. A low rumble of thunder shook the ground, a warning from the gods? Slowly, she turned. A gardener stood near the rosebushes, a shovel in hand. He bowed low, a small smile playing at the corners of his mouth.

Bea released a harsh laugh and crossed her arms over her chest, feigning a disinterest she sure as hell didn't feel. "Oh, good morning. Looks like rain." She took a step toward the stairs, her gaze pinned to him. Then another step. Finally she gave in to her urge and raced up the steps to her chamber. In her room, she slammed the door shut and leaned back.

With a peek at the ceiling, she glared. "Really? Do you hate me so much? Perhaps I should just prance naked through the streets of Bombay and get it over with!"

With a groan, she set off across the cold marble floor, raking her fingers through her disheveled hair. Heated embarrassment had settled into her body and didn't seem to have any plans of leaving at the moment. How would she ever face Leo or Ella again? How would she ever face the servants again? Colin's pants hung low on her hips, the cuffs tripping her steps. Her thoughts were in turmoil, spinning, colliding in her mind until she couldn't seem to catch hold of even one. She kicked the long legs out of the way and continued to pace. This was not how their morning after was supposed to unveil.

Ella. Ella had seen her naked in Colin's bed.

She sank onto a chair, moaning. How could Fran snitch on her? But no, that wasn't fair. Fran was probably worried and it was Bea's own bloody fault. What Ella must think of her! And she had no doubt Colin was blaming her at the moment, most likely playing the innocent and saying she attacked him when . . . when . . .

Bea lifted her eyes, staring unblinkingly at the cold hearth. When she had attacked him! Blimey, what had she become? Shiva was starting to look like a saint compared to her. Another rumble of thunder shook the room like a vocal agreement from God. She glanced mournfully toward the terrace doors. One stood ajar. Had she left it open? The rain would be here soon and the floor would take a soaking . . .

Oh, what did it matter? When Leo found out she'd been intimate with Colin, he'd ship her back to Scotland before she could bat an eyelash. She surged to her feet, crossing her arms over her chest. Well, she wouldn't. She wouldn't go back to Scotland. She'd . . . she'd stay with Fran. Yes. Fran had said she could stay and there was no doubt the woman owed her for blabbing. And if Leo and Ella didn't like it . . . well, they could . . .

The fine hairs on Bea's body stood on end. A whispered warning that sent a chill over her skin. Her lungs shrank. She couldn't seem to draw breath. Someone was in her room. Fear held her immobile as her heart thundered madly in her chest.

What to do? Scream? Run? But her legs had gone to weak and she couldn't seem to remember how to open her mouth. Through the tumbling thoughts in her mind, she managed to grab on to the one that urged her to turn. Bea spun around. There, in the shadows where the morning sun hadn't quite reached, stood a man.

Her brain kicked into action and Bea opened her mouth to scream. Without warning, a large hand clamped over her lips, trapping her cry for help. Bea tried to spin away, but an arm wrapped around her waist, jerking her back into a hard chest. Her body pinned to the large man holding her, she could do nothing more than squirm while trying not to gag on the man's unwashed scent.

The shadowed form in front of her shifted, moving casually closer, as if he had all the time in the world. Who was he? Too short to be Demyan. Bea stilled and narrowed her eyes. Yet . . . there was something familiar in that gait . . . The morning light that streamed through the part in the drapes hit his face.

Recognition swept through her, shock making her numb. Henry. The very man who had tried to kill Leo and Ella.

He smiled, a smile that spoke of false sincerity. "Hello, cousin."

Bea's stomach tightened. Too confused, too frightened, she didn't struggle with whichever of Henry's men held her in a tight grip. This was Henry, her cousin. She hadn't done anything to provoke him. He wouldn't hurt her, would he?

"Now," he said, moving slowly toward her. He was thinner than she remembered, but she hadn't seen him in over five years, and then only briefly. "If Sergio removes his hand, you'll keep quiet? I'd hate to have to hurt my own relative."

Her confidence wavered. Apparently, he *would* hurt her. With no other alternative, Bea nodded. Sergio's hand slipped away, but he kept his tight hold on her waist. Bea flinched, her ribs protesting the crushing embrace.

"What do you want?" she demanded, proud that her voice came out steady.

Henry's dark brows rose in mock surprise. "Want? Why, I want what everyone seems to want . . . money, power, knowledge. I want that statue, Bea. You're going to help me get it."

In a linen shirt and stained trousers, he barely resembled the man she knew. Time had worn him down. She met his gaze directly and shook her head. She would not cower to this man. "You don't need me and you know that. If it's true what they say about our bloodline, you don't need me. You can do it yourself."

His smirk fell but Bea didn't feel any satisfaction. Something wasn't right. A blush of red swept up his neck and into his cheeks. He looked away, a telling action. Was he embarrassed? "Yes, well, that would be true if my mother hadn't been a whore."

She shook her head. "I . . . I don't understand."

His gaze snapped toward her, ire flashing in his eyes. "Are you really so stupid?"

When she remained mute, he stepped closer, his breath warm and harsh. She could feel his anger like a blow, but managed not to flinch. "The blood flows through the male line. My mother slept with a local farmer. Understand? I'm another man's child."

The words sank heavy into Bea's gut. She and Henry weren't related? Nor were Leo and Henry? "All that anger toward Leo? That anger because he'd supposedly come back from the dead and taken your heritage, when you didn't even deserve the title?"

His eyes narrowed, his lips curled into a snarl, and Bea couldn't help flinching this time. "I deserve it more than that heathen!" For one breathless moment, she thought he would hit her. Finally, he cleared his throat and looked away, as if gathering himself. "So"—he was looking at her again—"as you see, I need you and your blood."

Blood. All sorts of horrible thoughts flashed through her mind. Bea trembled despite herself. "You really think you can escape without being seen?"

He laughed, the disinterest in his eyes making her nervous. "We got in, didn't we?"

A soft knock sounded on the door, a mere scratch of

hesitancy. A whispered warmth swept through her body and she knew who it was even before he called out. Bea cringed, her gaze jumping from the door to Henry, and her pulse gave a frantic leap. Henry didn't look concerned in the least.

"Don't answer it," Henry whispered.

"They know I'm here," she replied.

"Bea," Colin said from the hall. "We need to talk."

Bea didn't know whether to laugh or cry. Of course, now of all times the man wished to talk. Henry pressed his finger to his lips. "He dies if you say anything."

"He knows I'm in here!" she persisted, tears of frustration stinging her eyes.

"Bea, let me in. Please." There was a slight plea to his voice, so slight that anyone else wouldn't have noticed. But she did. How badly she wanted to call out to him. How badly she wanted to tell him she was sorry for being ridiculous when they first met. To tell him . . . to tell him she loved him.

"I'm not leaving, Bea, until you let me in."

"Colin, please, just leave me alone!" she cried before Henry or Sergio had time to stop her.

"I won't," he snapped, followed by a soft thud, as if he'd hit his fists against the door.

She looked helplessly at Henry. The man gritted his teeth, staring at her for one impossibly long moment. "Go then, open the door only slightly, understand? Get rid of him."

Bea nodded, eager to be released. Sergio loosened his hold. Wasting no time, fearing that Colin would break the door down, she stumbled forward. She didn't think about how hard it would be to see Colin. She didn't think about how her heart would ache, knowing this might be the last time they'd be face-to-face.

Her heart pounded with each unsure step. She'd only think about getting him to leave. She pressed her hands to the door as if she could feel him through the wooden panel.

Taking in a deep breath, she pulled it open only a crack. Hidden behind the door, Sergio was right behind her, his large body so close, she could feel his heat. She ignored the man and looked at Colin, prayed he'd leave, and at the same time prayed he'd understand the plea in her eyes.

How lovely he looked! Colin stood there disheveled, and delicious. He'd found more clothing, but his shirt hung untucked, his feet bare. He braced his hands on either side of the door jamb and looked at her with those pure blue eyes.

"Bea . . ."

She looked away, her heart clenching. "It's fine, Colin. It doesn't matter."

"To hell it doesn't. Bea, please, let me in."

"No!" she shot out, her gaze jumping to his. "You used me!"

Confusion worked across his handsome face. She could imagine what he was thinking. After all, wasn't she the one who had instigated their intimate night? But what she said seemed to be working and she knew she had to continue her rant for Colin's sake.

"You . . . you used me and now you'll toss me aside. Well, it was a lack in judgment, Colin, my lack. I'm going home. I'm sick of dirt, of bugs and heat. I'm going back to Scotland, where I can be with my grandmother in peace. Where I can marry a titled man with wealth."

The shocked look on his face told her she'd done her job well. "Bea, you don't mean—"

"I do! Damn you, Colin! Leave me alone." She slammed the door in his face. Her body trembled with emotion. The room fell silent, her harsh breathing the only sound. And she waited . . . waited to hear Colin's retreating footsteps.

"Very good," Henry whispered.

Sergio latched on to her arm and jerked across the room, toward the double doors that led to the terrace. Bea could merely trip beside him, too spent to argue. In her mind's eye she saw Colin, devastated.

"You're quite the actress, my cousin."

"I'm not your cousin," she seethed. "We're not even related!"

Before she could react, Henry slammed her against the wall, his fingers on her throat, holding her pinned to the plaster. "Keep your mouth shut. Understand?"

She couldn't nod, she couldn't breathe. She could only stare into the eyes of a man who had become a monster. Her lungs shriveled and panic flared. Her fingers found his wrist, her nails clawing at his skin, but he seemed immune to the pain. Giving up, she squeezed her eyes shut and prayed for her life to end quickly.

The sound of splintering wood broke through her consciousness. Bea's eyes opened as Henry's grip relaxed. Colin stood in the doorway like a guardian angel come to life.

"The infamous Colin, I presume?"

Colin's gaze flickered from her to her cousin. "Henry."

Henry smiled. There was no fear on his face. "But of course." His gaze moved from Colin to Sergio. "Kill him."

Sergio didn't hesitate. His burly arm lifted and Bea could only stare in horror at the small pistol that protruded from his fingertips. With a flick of his finger, a blast rent the room. It was over in a split second. Colin's eyes grew round in shock. For one brief, heavenly moment, Bea thought he was faking his death as he'd done in that temple. Then a brilliant red began to seep through the linen of his shirt.

Bea screamed. A terrifying sound that erupted from her very soul.

Henry slapped his hand over her mouth, trapping her cry. Someone latched on to her arms, tight manacles that refused to release. Bea jerked forward, desperate to get to Colin.

He sank to his knees, then slumped to the ground, his gaze locked on her. Bea couldn't move, couldn't help him. Someone pulled her back, but she was barely aware. Tears burned her eyes, streaming down her cheeks.

"Can you . . . can you get sick?" she'd asked him days ago.

"Yes," he'd said softly as he settled his bare feet on the marble floor at Shiva's home. *"I can. I was injured when my mother was murdered and I very nearly died with her."*

They were pulling her farther away . . . farther away from Colin. He fell back onto the floor, breaking eye contact. Her heart ripped in two.

Bea choked on a sob. Colin was dead. Lifeless and still on the floor.

They jerked her through the door, into the garden. Numb, she didn't struggle anymore. She didn't care.

Colin was dead.

A soft rain began to fall, misting her face. Suddenly the sunlight faded and blackness beckoned sweetly. Bea closed her eyes, allowing unconsciousness to overtake her as she slumped toward the ground.

"Is he dead?" a voice asked, a familiar voice . . . Where had he heard it before? Through the foggy haze of searing pain, Colin realized only one man would ask that question in such an even and unconcerned tone . . . Leo.

Colin curled his fingers, attempting to move, but the action only brought on an aching awareness that something wasn't right. He felt cold, yet each small tremor sent burning pain through his muscles. He parted his lips, intending to respond, but couldn't seem to find his voice. Liquid filled his throat, blocking air to his lungs. His eyes popped open, panic welling as he began to drown. Lifting his head, he coughed. Warm liquid splattered from his lips. Blood.

"Hurry, please," Ella replied. Soft hands rested atop his head like a mother's touch, gentle and comforting.

Colin breathed in shallow gasps and laid his head back, managing to keep his eyes open just enough to study those who hovered over him. Beside Leo and Ella, a stranger leaned forward, an older man with roughened skin and brilliant blue eyes that peered at him through scraggly gray facial hair. There was something in those eyes . . . something odd . . . something familiar.

The old man's lips moved, but a low buzz had entered Colin's ears, drowning out all sound. What had happened? Where was he? More importantly, why could he barely move? His chest felt wet, cold, almost sticky. And his body felt bizarre . . . as if he couldn't quite make out his legs or arms . . . just a head, floating in oblivion.

Confused, he met Ella's gaze, hoping for answers. Tears shimmered in her blue eyes, hovering at the tips of her spiky lashes. She was worried . . . about him?

She leaned closer, brushing the hair from his forehead. "He won't last much longer, please hurry."

And Colin knew in that moment that she spoke about him. *He* wouldn't last much longer. *He* was going to die. Shocked, he wasn't sure how to react.

Ella rested her hand on the old man's shoulder and peered up at him, as if the stranger were responsible for whether he lived or died.

Yet . . . someone was missing. Someone he needed to see.

The old man rubbed his chin, his eyes narrowing in contemplation as he studied Colin. "Then I suppose you must do whatever it is you do."

For one brief moment, Colin thought he was talking to him. Do what, exactly? Because frankly he felt like shit and wasn't about to do much of anything. Someone shifted, piercing his attention. Another stranger, Colin realized. An Indian man with a narrow face and brilliant blue turban atop his head. He felt suddenly surrounded and itchy irritation crawled up his skin. What the hell was going on?

"Can he hear us, do you suppose?" Ella asked, sniffling.

The old man nodded. "He can hear us. His mind's alert, if not his body. He's confused, all right."

For one blessed moment anger replaced his worry. Colin

wanted to demand answers. How the hell did he know what he was thinking? The Indian came closer, blocking the others from view and interrupting Colin's thoughts. His blue eyes focused on Colin. The man's young face grim, he settled his hands on Colin's chest. It was like someone had placed a branding iron on his bare skin. The pain was immediate, consuming. Colin sucked in a breath through gritted teeth, arching his back.

Just as suddenly as the pain arrived . . . it dissipated. A cool numbing sensation swept through his body.

"Go on then, we haven't all day," someone said.

Colin grappled with the words . . . trying to understand. But he couldn't make sense. Nothing made sense. Heat flared through his limbs. Colin gasped, his eyes opening but around him . . . all he could see was white light. Where had everyone gone? Was he dead? If so, he wouldn't complain. He felt better than he had in years.

Yet there was something not right, something pulling, tugging at his memory, something he seemed to have forgotten but needed to remember. The warmth spread slowly, bringing feeling to his limbs, his fingertips and toes. His entire form seemed to vibrate with energy as he floated through a peaceful bliss of reality.

And as the light enveloped him, taking away the pain and worry, a woman appeared. Her long dark hair fell in waves to her waist, her eyes glowing golden. An angel? Had he truly died? She smiled and realization dawned. Bea. Sweet, intoxicating Bea.

Memories flashed through his mind . . . Bea's eyes flaring with anger during that first meeting. Bea pushed against the wall as he cut her corset from her chest while they were escaping through the alleys of Delhi. Bea riding that damn elephant. Bea coming toward him . . . pressing her mouth to his . . . Bea.

The air suddenly changed from warm to bitterly cold. Bea disappeared and darkness enveloped him. Colin's lungs expanded. There was no warning. His eyes opened and he sucked in a bitterly cold breath as if he were drowning in ice water. Faces wavered before him, some concerned, some thrilled, others unreadable. He couldn't seem to catch his breath. Was he dying? Or had he just been saved? He started coughing, coughing on the dry air. The Indian man settled back, still silent, still watchful.

"That's it, well done," the old man said with a smile that produced dimples in his whiskered cheeks.

"Are you well?" Ella asked.

But Colin's gaze remained pinned to the old man, warily studying him. His face was barely readable through the full gray beard, but he knew there was something familiar about the man. Where had he seen him before? Colin moved his hands under his hips and attempted to push upright, but his body felt heavy and he barely managed to move. Ella was there, sliding her arm under him. She smelled like roses, he realized with a start, a strong, calming scent that he hadn't noticed before.

"What happened," he managed to croak past his dry throat. "Where am I?"

Curtains were thrown wide and light splashed into the room . . . too bright. Colin blinked, shading his eyes with his hand. Every tiny speck of dust floated on the beams . . . white, pure light. Beautiful, really, mesmerizing.

"You were shot," Leo explained.

"Shot?" Colin jerked his attention to him. It was then that he noticed the wetness of his shirt, clinging to his skin. Confused, he glanced down. Brilliant red soaked the linen, a hole in the center of the material.

A piercing, mind-numbing shock rushed through him. He pressed his hands to his chest and, with a swift movement, ripped the material wide. Buttons went pattering to the floor. His skin was pure, intact, if not stained slightly from the blood.

Wide-eyed, he looked up into their stoic faces. "How . . I . . . Am I dead?"

The old man chuckled. "This is a sorry afterlife if you are." He struggled to stand, the grunts and slowness showing his age. "No, you've been brought back to life. This is Sam, he carries the same powers as you." He nodded toward the Indian man, who bowed low but remained quiet. Colin doubted the man's name was truly something so American as Sam, but couldn't find the reason to argue.

He didn't understand. Nothing made sense. And Bea, he suddenly realized, was nowhere to be seen. "Powers?"

The old man shuffled closer. "We know. We know what you can do."

His gaze jumped to Ella and Leo. Had they told? But neither looked particularly guilty. "I don't understand."

The old man pulled at his beard, his face scrunched in contemplation. "We haven't time to explain. Not if you want to save that friend of yours."

"Friend?" Reality came rushing back, cold and gut-wrenching. "Bea."

"Yes, that's the one."

Fear pulsed through his veins, freezing him in place. Bea. They had Bea. His stomach tightened, his lungs tightened. His entire body tightened as frantic fear clawed at his insides.

"Bea," he whispered, so quietly no one could have heard, yet the old man narrowed his blue eyes.

"She's well. They won't hurt her. They need her."

He didn't feel any relief. Why didn't he feel any relief? Colin struggled to his feet, his breath coming out in harsh pants. "Bea. I have to find her. How long has she been gone?"

"Ten minutes, maybe fifteen," Leo replied, watchful, but Colin could read nothing else in the man's gaze, and for some reason that annoyed him.

"Don't seem too concerned," Colin gritted out. With a shove, he pushed Leo aside and stumbled toward the door.

"Colin, that's not fair," Ella said. "Please, wait, we're making a plan."

Colin threw the bedroom door wide and moved into the hall. "And as you're making plans, they're getting farther away!"

He could hear them following but didn't dare slow his pace. Panic pushed him forward. They'd keep her alive, he had to believe that. They needed her but he needed her more.

Akshay and Fran looked up as he swept down the steps toward the front door. At their feet were knapsacks.

"Colin?" Fran asked.

"Thank the gods, you're all right," Akshay said.

Colin gave him a quick jerk of his head, but didn't have time for sentimental reunions. "Weapons, I need weapons."

"Colin, you don't even know where she is!" Ella said, coming to rest beside him.

"The island."

Akshay handed him a pistol. "What island?"

Colin shoved the weapon in his waistband and took the knife Fran offered. "The map pointed to an island off the coast. A map Bea and I uncovered while at a forgotten temple."

Bea, just saying her name made his heart lurch. Was she well? Was she injured? If Demyan had done anything to her, he'd see the man tortured to death himself.

"The islands of Bombay," Akshay murmured, his dark brows drawn together in thought.

Colin strapped the knife to his thigh, annoyed and confused by his own lack of information. "No, it was between the Seven Islands. It . . . it pointed to nothing."

"Something underwater then?" Fran asked.

"Perhaps," Colin replied, taking a brief moment to mull over the possibilities. If it was underwater, they didn't have a chance in hell of finding the statue. At the moment, he didn't give a damn. The realization left him shocked. He finally understood Leo's lack of interest. When he had his wife, how could he care? If he had Bea by his side, the statue would be a minor irritation in his life instead of the consuming pain it had always represented.

Colin shook aside the feeling. "We have to go. Now."

"We have men trailing them," Leo explained, always so bloody rational.

Colin started toward the door. "I don't care. I'm leaving now."

"If he gets the statue, we're all as good as dead," the old man mumbled. "Who knows what could happen."

Colin spun around, his hands fisting. "Who the hell cares about the statue!"

They were stunned into a moment of silence.

"Oh, Colin, of course we're worried about Bea," Ella whispered. "But you more than anyone knows how important that statue is."

"Not as important as she is," he gritted out through clenched teeth.

Leo nodded, then looked toward the old man. "Did you get any information?"

"As I said before, they're headed to the coast, directly west," the old man said. "That was all I got out of them before they were out of hearing range."

Colin brushed off the man's odd comment, too impatient to care. It made sense. Due west would land them directly where the map pointed.

"We'll all go then." Ella started toward the knapsacks.

"No! You'll slow me down." Colin yanked open the front door.

"You can't go alone," Ella cried out. "It will take only a moment to finish packing."

Colin ignored them and started down the shallow steps to the front garden. Horses were saddled and waiting. They'd been preparing to leave. It gave him some hope, but they weren't fast enough for him. Already the sun was hot and rising; they were wasting valuable time.

"Then we'll follow," Akshay replied.

"I'll go with him," the old man said, hobbling toward another mount. "Sam will stay with you, in case you need him."

Colin latched on to the pommel and pulled himself onto his mount. "No offense, old man, but I'm in a hurry."

"You'll need his powers, Colin," Leo said, standing on the front stoop.

Colin froze for a brief moment as the words settled into his muddled mind. Powers? He slid the old man a glance.

In his own saddle the old man meet his gaze, a twinkle of defiance in his faded blue eyes. "That's right. You, Sam, and Ella here aren't the only ones. I've got my own special talent." Without another word, the man kicked his mount, urging the beast forward.

"And what would your powers be?" Colin demanded, nudging his mount into a cantor until he made it to the man's side.

The old man looked at him, something flickering in his eyes . . . amusement . . . but something else . . . determination. "I can read minds, my boy."

Confusion gave way to shock. The old man didn't wait for his response, but clicked his tongue and his mount burst forward, stirring up dust in his wake.

Stunned, Colin could merely watch him go. Only one man that he knew of had the power to read minds, and that man was supposed to be dead.

"You coming, boy?" the old man called out.

Colin nudged his heels into his mount's side and burst forward, his anger and ire directed at the man in front of him. "Yes, *Father*, I'm coming."

Chapter 26

"Wake up." A soft tap on the side of her face stirred Bea from the dredges of unconsciousness. She'd been dreaming . . . a lovely dream. She'd been with Colin, pressed next to him in his bed. She groaned, turning her face away from the persistent gnat. She didn't want to wake up. Darkness provided relief. Relief from what, she wasn't sure, but she didn't want to investigate.

Another tap, this time sharper. Her skin stung, yet she still didn't move, didn't open her eyes, for something warned her, hovering on the edges there, that she wouldn't like what she found when she awoke.

"Please, wake," a persistent feminine voice called out. Not Ella. No, even half-conscious, Bea recognized that the woman had an accent. French, perhaps? But that couldn't be possible. She was . . . where the hell *was* she?

Confused, Bea blinked her eyes wide. Dark clouds loomed above, rolling and tumbling across the sky as if in a hurry to get somewhere important. She wasn't sure what time it was. With the lack of light, it could have been morning, or evening. In the distance, birds cried and a soft rumble faded, then pulsed to life as if coming closer . . . closer.

"Where am I?" she managed to croak through parched lips.

A soft, cool breeze ruffled her clothing and hair. In the air hung the scent of brine and salt . . . the ocean. She curled her fingers, sand collecting under her nails and confirming her suspicions. She was at the ocean. Suddenly, the memories crashed down, suffocating.

Colin.

The woman muttered something, but over the rush of blood to her ears, Bea couldn't hear.

Colin shot.

Colin dead.

A deep ache ripped through her insides, tearing at her soul. She closed her eyes, fighting the sting of tears. Colin was dead. With a choked sob, she rolled to her side, curling into a tight ball, her face pressed into the warm, gritty sand.

"I've brought you water." The woman was speaking again.

Why wouldn't she leave her alone? A gentle hand settled atop Bea's head, but she didn't move, didn't bother to respond or open her eyes as the tears rolled across her nose and cheeks before pattering to the ground. Over and over in her mind she saw him . . . Colin with that stunned look upon his face as he tumbled to the ground. Colin as the brilliant red blood spread across the white linen of his shirt. She hadn't been able to say good-bye, to tell him she loved him, to kiss him once more. Just once more . . .

"You must drink something," the woman insisted.

"Allez en enfer," Bea whispered harshly.

The woman sighed. "If you want to live, you must drink, and telling me to go to hell won't help. I may be the only friend you have here."

Anger burned in the pit of Bea's belly, raw and consuming, replacing the deep ache. She opened her eyes just enough to glare at the woman.

"My name is Adelaide," the woman explained as she

cradled a clay jar to her chest. A brilliant blue scarf covered her head, the ends flapping on the breeze.

She was small, but curvy. If they fought, who would come out the victor? "Maybe I don't want to live and don't tell me you're a friend."

The woman settled back on her heels and gave her an exasperated look. She was dressed in men's clothing, as Bea was. But whereas the woman's clothing was just that, clothing, Bea's was so much more. Colin's shirt. Colin's trousers. She resisted the urge to bring the material close and breathe in his scent.

The woman lifted a black brow, the color striking against her pale skin. "Ah, your true love. Is that why you won't live?"

Bea didn't respond; she owed her no explanation. She owed no one anything. Instead, she found mindless, numbing escape in focusing on the ocean ahead, where gray waves crashed upon the shore and an odd fog hovered over the sea. It didn't matter what this French woman said. Nothing mattered. No one could hurt her more than they already had.

The woman inched forward, so close Bea was forced to look at her. She was attractive, she'd give her that much, with her long black hair and brilliant blue eyes. Blue eyes that reminded Bea of Colin. The thought tore at her gut with renewed pain so fierce, it was difficult to breathe. How would she possibly go on with such memories?

Adelaide darted a glance back over her shoulder. It was then that Bea noticed Henry and Sergio near a rowboat on the water's edge. Anger like she'd never felt roared through her body. She bolted upright, intent on rushing toward her cousin when the French woman turned back toward her.

Her intense gaze gave Bea pause. "And what if I told you your true love lives?"

Bea's heart skipped a beat, even as her mind denied the accusation. "I'd say you're crueler than I thought."

The woman frowned and settled the clay jar in the sand. "Nevertheless, it's true." She stood and brushed her long, dark braid over her shoulder. "So, if you want to be well for him when he arrives, perhaps you want to drink and keep your strength."

She turned then and walked away.

Bea couldn't move, too stunned to do anything more than repeat the woman's words over and over again in her head.

"And what if I told you your true love lives?"

Her heart leapt in her throat. Could it be true? How could that pixie woman possibly know if Colin lived? It was mad. So why, then, did hope flare to life, a tiny flicker that warmed her shattered heart?

Bea swallowed hard and reached toward the clay jar the woman had left behind. Tentatively, she brought the vessel to her lips. The water was warm and barely slipped down her dry throat but she kept drinking for Colin's sake. He would come for her. He still lived. She had to believe that. Tears had dried on her face, leaving her skin tight and itchy. But she didn't care about her appearance. In her mind remained the thought that Colin might be there at any moment.

With renewed energy, she took in her surroundings, intent on finding her escape. A long, white beach on either side. Behind her, thick vegetation. Just there, not far, two fishermen were pulling in a net next to their battered boat. The only sign of life on an otherwise desolate beach. Would they help her if she screamed?

"Finally," Henry said, strolling toward her and demanding her attention. He didn't pause until he was only feet from her, his hands on his hips. The sight of him made her nauseous. "You're awake. How do we get the statue?"

She was surprised by his question, although she refused to show it. If he didn't know how to get the statue, why had he taken her? She tilted her head back and looked directly at him. His clothing was tattered and worn, the white linen shirt stained, his hair mussed. The eyes of a man she thought she knew, now the eyes of a stranger. Fury flared through her body, churning bitterly in her gut. He'd ordered Colin shot as if he were nothing.

"You know, you always were a pathetic, greedy sod even as a child."

His jaw clenched, his throat working. She knew what would happen yet she didn't try to defend herself. It would be pointless. She didn't flinch as his arm came down and the back of his hand met her cheek. The force sent her tumbling to the side, her face hitting the beach. Bea lay there for a brief moment, staring at the tiny crystals of sand, resisting the urge to retaliate. Now was not the time. Her skin burned and tears pooled in her eyes, but she'd die before she'd let them fall. Slowly, she settled her hands underneath her chest and pushed upright.

"He's coming," Adelaide called.

Bea jumped to her feet, even as her weak legs threatened to give out. For one brief, wonderful moment, she thought the woman spoke of Colin. The smirk on Henry's face fell and Bea's hope flared.

Large palm fronds parted and an Indian man strolled into the clearing, machete in hand. Bea held her breath, waiting. Another man appeared, the green turban atop his head showing his ethnicity also as Indian. The leaves parted once more and a tall, gangly man stepped onto the sand. Bea's hope dissipated. Fear fought with fury. He surveyed his surroundings like a king would a newly conquered territory.

Demyan.

Finally, his gaze fell on Bea. She shuddered and looked away, focusing on the waves once more, barely aware of what Demyan and Henry spoke of as he came closer . . . closer to her.

It was only when he stopped directly in front of her that she managed to make eye contact. The silence stretched seemingly forever; still she wouldn't break but continued to stare at him determined to show no fear.

A small smirk lifted the corners of his mouth, as if he

thought her bravery amusing. "I see you found her, Henry. Well done."

"Thank you." Henry smiled, but Bea noticed it didn't quite reach his eyes. He was annoyed with Demyan.

She shouldn't have been surprised that Henry and Demyan were working together, but she was. Who else was involved?

"What will you do with me?" she demanded, annoyed her voice quivered.

Demyan's gaze flickered up and down her body. "That is not your concern." He turned toward the two Indian men and muttered something in a language that sounded like Hindi, but wasn't. They nodded and rushed to the small rowboat, not once glancing her way, and she knew, at that point, that no one would help her. Frantic, her gaze scanned the beach, hoping to see Colin come striding through the vegetation, rifles in tow.

"The necklace." Demyan held his hand out toward Henry. It was then that Bea noticed Leo's ring on his finger. She wasn't surprised that he'd found the piece when they'd left it behind.

Henry's cheeks flushed. "But—"

"Now, Henry."

Demyan quirked a brow, a man completely sure of himself. Henry paused for one brief moment, then reached under his shirt and pulled a pendant free. It was some sort of man, dangling from a silver chain. It had to be Ella's necklace, Bea realized with a start. The necklace Henry had stolen from Ella over a year ago. Stunned, Bea could merely watch as Henry jerked on the chain until it broke and, with annoyance working over his face, dropped the pendant into Demyan's pale hand. Demyan had both pieces. That couldn't be good.

"Now then, shall we?" Demyan turned back toward her. "You and I are going on a little trip."

He slipped the necklace into his trouser pocket and latched on to Bea's upper arm, his hand cold and painfully tight.

"I am coming as well, aren't I?" Henry whined like a child wanting to play with his older brother.

Demyan started toward the shore, pulling Bea along with him so her bare feet shuffled through the warm sand. "No room, Henry."

Henry snorted, his nostrils flared, and rushed after them like a bull about to charge. It was almost comical, and Bea might have laughed if she hadn't been so afraid.

"We are partners, Demyan," Henry said. "I demand to be allowed to go."

Demyan actually paused, as if thinking over the answer. Bea took the time to catch her breath and mull over her possibilities. Almost of their own free will, her eyes dropped to Demyan's pocket. The necklace was close . . . so close. She knew it was important, but why, she wasn't sure. Could she reach it? And then what . . . somehow escape a gaggle of men with pistols?

Finally, Demyan sighed and turned to face Henry like a father preparing to reprimand his son. "You tire me."

Before Bea could blink, he lifted his hand and pulled the trigger of a small pistol.

Bea gasped, jumping in surprise. Henry didn't even have time to beg for his life. Blood was already soaking his shirt. Her cousin's knees buckled and he slumped toward the ground. Bea merely stood there with her mouth gaping open, watching as he died. No one went to help him; not even the fishermen down the beach did more than glance their way. No one helped Henry, and no one would help her.

"I find I don't need you anymore." Demyan started forward toward the boat, dragging Bea along with him.

But her feet refused to work and she could barely stay upright. She wanted to be glad Henry was dead, how badly she wanted to be glad! She glanced back. His body lay upon the sand, unmoving. The sight sickened her. Her stomach churned, and she had to tear her gaze away for fear she'd get sick.

Too much death. Too much hate. Too much violence. Bea felt oddly numb as Demyan stood on the shore, but pushed her toward the small boat. She stumbled into a wave, the water splashing up her body, soaking her clothes and leaving the bitter taste of salt in her mouth. The two Indian men grabbed her arms and hauled her inside the vessel, dropping her to the floor as if she were a fish caught from the bowels of the ocean. Soft hands latched on to her upper arms, pulling her backward into a warm body. The feminine scent of flowers told her Adelaide was huddled beside her.

"Shh," the French woman whispered, wrapping an arm around Bea's waist and pulling her close. "Shhh, *du calme*. It will be over soon."

Bea hadn't realized she was whimpering until the woman spoke. Still, she couldn't stop the pathetic mewing sounds from slipping from her lips. Too much death. Too much blood. Demyan jumped into the vessel, his minions following. The boat shoved off and hit the first wave, sending them all bouncing into the air.

All except for Demyan, who sat upon the only bench, watching Bea through those eerie green eyes as if he knew so much more than she did.

Bea shifted her gaze and stared unblinking at the shore, hoping, praying to see Colin. If Colin was still alive, he would have come for her by now. If he was alive, she would have felt that warm pleasant sensation she felt when he was near. But all she saw was Henry's still body, becoming smaller and smaller until the fog wrapped them in its damp arms.

No, she couldn't rejoice in Henry's death because she knew without a doubt, the moment Demyan found the statue, she would follow Henry to the afterlife.

"Are you going to talk to me?"
Not if I can help it. Colin pressed his heels into the horse's

side, urging the animal forward, but the thick vegetation denied progress. He didn't bother to glance at the old man who rode beside him. Part of him was too disgusted to look at his father, the other half didn't give a damn. "There's nothing to discuss."

Besides, they didn't have time to talk. Talking would waste moments. Time they didn't have. What was done, was done. There was no use in reliving the past. He took in a deep breath. No, talking was ridiculous. He needed to focus on finding Bea.

"Slow down, lad. If they hear us coming, it will all be for nothing."

Colin ignored his father. Bea was close, he could feel it in his soul. But where was she exactly? He peered through the thick vegetation, listening with his body and instincts. Just over the cry of birds, the roar of the ocean could be heard. He leaned over the neck of his mount, searching the hazy green fog of plant life. Through the fronds, he spotted gray water.

"This way." He nudged his mount forward.

"Could be a trap."

"Is it?" Colin demanded, looking back at his father. The man didn't look tired, although he should have been after their frantic pace. Perhaps he wasn't as old as he appeared. Hell, he didn't even know the age of his own father.

The old man shrugged as he pulled gently at his scraggly gray beard. "No."

Annoyance warred with anger. "And were you going to share the information if it was a trap?"

His father's eyes twinkled as if he found the question amusing. "If you'd asked."

Anger won out. Colin's hands tightened on his reins. "Shit." He nudged his mount forward, trying to distance himself from the man supposedly related to him. How could his own father be so damn obnoxious? When he was a lad, all the neighboring women thought his father charming.

Colin blanched and slid the old man a look. Was this what he would become thirty years from now?

Overhead a brilliant red bird cried out, bursting through the brush and setting his nerves on edge. He watched the bird disappear into the dark shadows of the forest. Was this a trap? Was he walking toward death . . . once again? Did he have a choice?

"Where to then?" he finally asked his father.

The man smirked, as if he'd been waiting all along for Colin to ask for his assistance and was reveling in the moment. "The right."

Sweat gathered between Colin's shoulder blades. The heat hovering under the thick canopy of trees was almost overwhelming. Ahead, the light promised freedom and fresh air. But to go out onto the beach now could lead to disaster. There, anyone would see them. But here, in the trees, they were somewhat hidden.

He turned in his saddle, pinning his father with a glare. "What can you do, exactly? Can you help or not?" It wasn't as if the old man had been present during Colin's childhood for him to know his precise abilities. If he could tell him exactly where Bea was located, it would make things much easier.

The old man stopped next to Colin and shrugged. He looked rather unconcerned as he glanced about the forest. "Can sense people when they're near and can read minds. And I know for a fact you're angry at me."

Colin released a wry laugh. "We don't have time to talk about our feelings. I'm kind of in a hurry." He nudged his mount in the sides and the horse took off once again, stomping through the vegetation until the branches popped and snapped. How dare he want to discuss his life now, of all times. Bea was in danger, for God's sake. Besides, how the hell did he think he felt? Abandoned by his father, forced to fend for himself, thinking both parents were dead.

His father came up beside him. "A few minutes until we're there. That's enough time to talk."

Anger flared through him. Colin reached across and grabbed the man by his collar. Their horses shifted, uneasy being that close. "Damn you! What do you want from me?"

The old man didn't even flinch. "Enough, boy, I can still thump you."

"You want to try, old man?"

"You're worried about your woman and you're wanting a fight, and I'm not giving it to you."

Frustrated, Colin released his hold. How could the old man be so calm? His father smoothed down his shirt as if not the least bit offended. An image of his mother flashed to mind . . . dead. And it was his father's fault. The powers, the damn statue . . . all of it. And Bea could be next. No. He wouldn't think that way. He couldn't. He started forward again, this time heading directly toward that light. He didn't care about a sneak attack. All he knew was that he must get to Bea. He had to see her, to know she was well.

"I didn't want anything to do with the statue, boy." His father's voice was low, but steady.

Colin's anger wavered as he glanced at the man. There was an honesty in his father's face. Did he believe him? If he wanted nothing to do with the statue, why had he been absent so often? And why hadn't he come back?

"I had to pretend I was dead, Colin. You know that."

His ire flared. His father made it all sound so easy. He'd always wallowed in excuses and apparently time didn't change his ways. "No, I don't. And I sure as hell didn't when I was a child, scouring through garbage just to find a meal."

"They didn't know about you. At least, I didn't think they did." The old man looked away and shrugged. "I thought by dying, they'd end their search."

"And Ella? What about her? If you were so concerned, why did you keep visiting England, putting her in danger?"

"I tried to protect her as best I could."

"And who was protecting me and Mother?" The bitterness was apparent in his voice. He hated that, the obvious show of emotion. But it didn't make sense, what his father said. Why could he visit Ella, yet not them? Colin didn't trust the old man in the least. There was something he wasn't telling him.

"I told you, I didn't think they knew about you, but they did know about Ella."

Perhaps he was telling the truth, but it didn't help. "Even before all of this nonsense with the statue erupted . . ." Colin shook his head. "You were barely home, why?"

The old man gave his son a half smile. "You know how it is, my boy, the way a man likes to get out, see the world."

Colin's stomach churned. No, he didn't know what it was like. He wouldn't abandon his own child for the sake of adventure. Would he?

The old man sighed. "I visited Ella because she was . . . is . . ." He fell silent, a telling silence that said he hadn't told Colin everything. What were his secrets?

Confused, Colin studied him, trying to determine the truth. Something wasn't right. "Why, Father, why the fondness for Ella? She had her parents to . . ."

Suddenly it dawned on him. There was only one reason why a man would be so protective of another's child. "Damn."

Ella couldn't . . . she wasn't . . .

The old man shot him a wary look and it was there in his eyes. "Yes. Ella is your sister."

Frozen in shock, Colin could do no more than sit there, staring like an idiot. It couldn't be true. Not all this time . . .

"I didn't visit her any more than I did you," his father said.

He could have had a sister. He wouldn't have been alone. He would have found a way to protect Ella. "How," he whispered. "How can it be?"

The man looked away, the first sign of unease he'd shown

all day. Apparently his father did have a conscious. "Ella's mother was lonely after her husband died. We . . ."

"No need to go on." He wasn't sure if he should be angry or disgusted. Because his father couldn't control himself, he . . . he had a sister. Shit. What would Ella say? They barely knew each other. Had only met a little over a year ago.

"I kept you apart for your own good. But you're right, if it's anyone's fault your mother died, it's mine. I did what I thought was best. I guess perhaps it wasn't. But the truth is, you did a damn fine job of hiding yourself, boy. I probably wouldn't have done much better."

They fell silent as the trees thinned and the sand underfoot thickened. He'd spent enough time talking to his father. The past didn't matter; all that mattered was getting to Bea. Colin urged his horse forward onto the sandy beach. His mount dragged, exhausted by the fast pace. Would it be quicker on foot?

"No," his father said. "On foot would be harder and slower."

Colin gritted his teeth. His annoyance returning. "Stop reading my damn mind!"

He shrugged. "You're an emotional boy, you make it too easy."

Colin narrowed his eyes, pretty sure there was a verbal taunt in there. How badly he wanted to leave the man behind, but truth was, his father knew more about this mess with the statue than anyone. And the thought of finding out more about his powers overwhelmed his good sense. The trees faded, giving them no place to hide. They were completely exposed.

"This Sam. Where did you find him? How many others like us are out there?"

His father shrugged. "Can't say, and Sam found me."

Instantly suspicious, Colin demanded, "Why? How?" The beach was empty, save for a couple fishermen standing near a bank and pulling in their wares. An eerie fog hovered over the waves, limiting visibility. An odd fog, the likes of which he'd never seen before. Colin paused to look out upon the sand but saw nothing suspicious. Dear God, had he come this far, only to lose her?

His father was oddly quiet. He glanced back at him. A slight blush had moved into the man's weathered face. He scratched his head and looked everywhere but at Colin. "About Sam . . ."

"Oh dear God, don't tell me he's your son, too?" Colin said the words in half jest.

The old man shrugged, looking sheepish.

Shock gave way to pure annoyance. "Any others you want to tell me about?"

"Can't be sure."

"Christ, just tell me Bea's not related, for God's sake."

The old man smiled and shook his head. "Not that I know of."

Colin clenched his jaw. It was a joke, always a jest with his father. Bea's life was in danger and it was a damn joke to him. "Do you sense her or not?"

"This far away? Can't tell who is who." He scanned the beach, then the water. "But she's out there, still alive."

Colin clutched at that belief. He had to think she was still alive or nothing would matter anymore. He dug his heels into his mount, urging the exhausted horse forward. "Just a bit longer, darlin'," he murmured, patting the horse on her flank. He was getting close to finding her; he could feel it deep within his soul.

"You can't wrap your life around a woman, my son."

"What?" Stunned, Colin actually took the time to glance back at his father.

"I know what you're thinking. Truth is, my boy, humans are fragile. If you base your happiness on a human, you'll be disappointed because everyone dies in the end."

"You say that like we're not human."

"Maybe we're not."

"Ridiculous," Colin snorted and shook his head. His father had gone insane.

The old man sighed long and loud. "Love can be wonderful, for normal people. For us, love can be devastating."

Annoyed and confused, Colin could merely shake his head. "You're insane, you realize that? We're not gods. We can die just as well as any human." The moment the words left his lips, denial rang through his head. But not Demyan. He couldn't die. Colin's confidence wavered.

"My beliefs have kept me alive all these years."

Colin nudged his heels into his mount, urging the beast forward. "Really, and what do you consider alive, Father? Hiding out in foreign countries? Living alone because you think you're better than everyone else?"

Disappointment washed through him. His father was no better than Demyan. A sudden blast burst through the air. Colin stiffened, his heart leaping into his throat.

"Gunshot," his father muttered, confirming his worst fears.

"Bea," Colin whispered.

He nudged his horse in the sides and burst forward past the fishermen. He didn't slow as they raced around the bend, sand flying into the air. He didn't glance back to make sure his father followed. Nothing mattered but finding Bea.

There, near the shore, white cloth fluttered on the breeze. Colin's heart clenched. A body. He leaned lower over the horse's neck, urging the animal to move faster. The person turned his head, apparently hearing Colin's approach. A man, his shirt bloodied. Relief made his legs weak. Not Bea.

Colin slid from his mount before the animal had time to stop. His knees hit the sand with a thud that jarred his bones. Frantic, he scrambled upright and toward the body. Familiarity washed over him in a sickening wave.

"Henry." Colin didn't need his powers to know the man was almost gone.

"They've left," Henry whispered.

"Where?" Colin demanded.

Henry was losing blood fast. He'd die soon, but Colin couldn't let that happen before he uncovered Bea's location.

"A boat headed"—he paused, taking in a deep breath—"out to sea."

Colin glanced toward the waves. They couldn't have left long ago, yet with the fog thick and heavy, he could barely see two feet in front of him.

"Get the boat from the fishermen," Colin demanded over his shoulder, knowing his father stood there. He turned back toward Henry. "Demyan?"

Henry nodded, closing his eyes.

"Where are they going?" Colin demanded, gripping the dying man's shoulders.

"Statue," Henry whispered, his throat working as if saying that one word had been a trial.

Colin hesitated, knowing he must hurry to catch Bea, yet knowing at the same time if he didn't save Henry now, the man would die. Could he take precious minutes to save a man who had tried to kill them?

He shifted closer, his hands hovering over Henry's chest in indecision.

Suddenly, Henry latched on to his wrist. "Don't," he said, as if reading Colin's mind. "She knows." His breath came out in sharp pants. "The woman knows the future."

"What woman?" He didn't make sense. Was his mind merely gone?

"You . . . you will kill Bea." Henry's grip relaxed and his arm fell to the sand, his eyes wide and unblinking.

Chapter 27

"Stop here," Demyan demanded, standing so quickly the boat swayed.

Sergio pulled forward on the oars, his arms bulging with muscle as he attempted to calm the rocking vessel against the rough seas and Demyan's sudden movement.

Her destiny had arrived. Bea stiffened and slid her glance left, then right. She didn't want to stand for fear of drawing attention to herself. They were in the middle of the ocean. Nothing visible through the thick fog. Why had they stopped? It didn't make sense.

Demyan reached into his pocket and pulled Ella's necklace free. Bea's fingers curled, her breath caught. For one brief moment, as the pendant swung back and forth, gleaming in the dull light, she thought about grabbing that necklace, tossing it over the side of the boat where no one could abuse whatever powers it held.

"Don't," Adelaide whispered.

Bea glanced at the woman. How had she known? Instinct or something more? A shiver of unease whispered over her skin as she realized she didn't know any of these people and couldn't trust a single person. But no, that wasn't true. She trusted Colin. Just the thought of the man sent unwanted tears to her eyes. Colin hadn't come to save her. Perhaps he never would and Adelaide had lied.

Demyan brought the pendant higher, drawing Bea's attention back to him. She swiped her eyes with the back of her hand. Instantly her sadness was replaced with fury. How she loathed the man. How she wished she had a pistol, a sword, anything . . . something to take care of him once and for all.

Demyan brought Leo's ring and Ella's necklace together, and with a quick turn, the pendant popped open. Bea's breath hitched. What the hell was going on? She could see nothing from her position.

A slow smile spread across Demyan's face. "It's here. I knew it."

Bea glanced around but saw nothing out of the ordinary. Perhaps the fog had lifted slightly, but other than that, the sea looked as it had when they'd pushed off from shore.

"Hold it steady." Demyan stumbled toward her, his eyes gleaming with a light that instantly set Bea on edge. The two Indian men moved out of the way, while Sergio continued to keep the boat steady.

Bea shrank back, the edge of the boat biting into her shoulder blades. "What do you want with me?"

Demyan didn't respond, merely latched on to her wrist. Bea pulled back. The boat rocked dangerously to the left.

"Go," Adelaide whispered, pushing her forward. "It will only hurt a moment."

"Hurt? What will hurt?" Bea demanded.

Distracted, Bea allowed Demyan to pull her forward without a fight.

"Go with him. If you resist, we will all fall into the water and drown." No one glanced at Adelaide as she made that statement. It was as if a woman shouting out prophecies were an everyday occurrence.

Demyan jerked her upright. The boat tipped again and a wave washed over the side, soaking her trousers further. Bea tripped over the long legs of her pants and fell into the

Monster. Her hands flattened to Demyan's bony chest. His cold breath fanned across her face, creeping over her skin like a spider.

"Now, my dear, you'll behave, won't you?"

She gave a stiff jerk of her head but couldn't prevent the shivers that raced over her skin. She was terrified, and it was obvious.

"Come," Demyan demanded with a nod of his head.

Sergio stood, allowing the two Indian men to take the oars. The massive man latched on to her right arm. Bea gasped and tried to pull back, but Demyan slid a long arm around her waist, clutching her so tight, she could barely breathe.

"You promised you'd behave and I despise people who break their promises."

Bea met Adelaide's gaze. The woman gave her a curt nod. Bea understood her silent gesture. Stand still. Allow Demyan to do whatever he'd do. But how could Bea trust this Adelaide? Because she had a feeling the French woman wasn't here of her own accord and would just as likely want to see Demyan dead as Bea would.

With a soft swoosh, Demyan pulled a dagger from the sheath on his thigh.

Bea's heart slammed against her chest, her own harsh breathing drowning out any other noise. Her mind and body insisted she rebel, but she knew it was pointless. She jerked her attention forward, focusing between Demyan and Sergio, in the direction where the beach lay.

A sudden warmth swept through her body. Bea's entire soul stilled as she tried to grasp the meaning of the sense of peace she felt. There it was again . . . a whisper . . . a promise of hope. Colin. Her heart skipped a beat before racing. Colin was near. She could feel him . . . sense him. She didn't know how, or why, but she knew he was near.

Sergio's blunt fingernails dug into her wrist as he straightened her arm. But she didn't care. She didn't look as

Demyan brought the dagger down. She didn't even flinch when the blade sliced across her arm, slitting open her skin. She didn't cry out as wet, warm blood trailed down her forearm. Instead, she remained focused on that fog where the shore hid. Focused on Colin. She didn't care if she was imagining his presence. She didn't care if she'd gone insane.

Demyan shoved her arm over the boat, propelling Bea forward. Her attention broken, she latched on to the side of the vessel with her free arm, attempting to steady her balance. Waves crashed against the small boat, sending salty water onto her skin and burning the open wound.

"There, yes, now." A drop of blood hovered on the edge of her arm, before falling to the water. Two more drops followed in rapid succession. They splattered against the surface, diluting to pink before a wave tumbled forward, pulling the drops below into the vast sea. Demyan released his hold. Bea fell backward, landing on her bottom. She inched back, huddling into the bow and clutching her wounded arm to her chest.

"What the hell was that?" she whispered furiously, turning to face Adelaide.

"You'll see," the woman replied, her gaze pinned to Demyan.

Fog rolled over the edge of the boat, blanketing Bea in a misty veil so she could barely see Adelaide, who sat only inches from her. Shivering, Bea hunched lower, cradling her arm closer to her body, barely aware of the sting the cut produced. There, surrounded by the gray cloud, every harsh breath was magnified. Suspended in time, no one moved, no one said a word.

"I don't understand," Bea finally got the nerve to whisper. "What's . . ."

Ahead, the fog parted, drifting away like the train of a ghostly ball gown. A sudden golden ray pierced the gloom and fell upon their tiny vessel. Bea blinked rapidly, lifting her hand to shield her face from the light.

Demyan's smile grew, his excitement almost tangible. "There." He pointed ahead.

Bea turned, peering over the edge of the boat. An island stretched across the sea, an emerald against a sapphire ocean, the colors so brilliant and pure that Bea had to blink as she looked directly at the scene.

"Hurry." Demyan settled on his seat. Men rushed to their posts, Sergio at the helm, the two Indian men settling next to the oars as if they understood the direness of the situation. Bea could do no more than remain huddled on the floor, watching as the island came closer . . . closer.

"What is it?" Bea turned toward Adelaide. "What is that place?" She knew Demyan couldn't hear her over the grunt of the men rowing—not that it mattered. The bastard had set his sights on the land and didn't seem to notice anything else.

Still, Adelaide shifted closer as if afraid they'd be overhead. "The place where you'll find what you're looking for."

Bea snorted, more than annoyed with the woman's strange answers and the throbbing of her injured arm. "The statue? I'm not looking for the statue."

Adelaide pulled the blue scarf from her hair, and taking Bea's arm, she wrapped the material around the wound. "You should be. You have no idea what that statue is capable of, what could happen if it fell into the wrong hands."

"I've heard," Bea muttered and even as she wanted to dismiss the woman's words, a shiver of unease raised the fine hairs on her neck. "And I don't believe it."

"Do you believe this?" Adelaide nodded toward the island, so close now that Bea could make out the brilliant yellow and red birds perched in the trees that lined the shallow beach.

"Believe what?"

"Do you believe in this island?"

"It's an island, what's there to believe?" Bea hissed, growing more annoyed with each passing moment.

Her arm hurt, her head hurt, and she was desperately

attempting to reclaim that calming sensation she'd felt just before Demyan had gutted her like a fish. She pressed her fingers to her temples, unsure anymore if that sensation of Colin being close had just been in her imagination.

"You know it's not just an island. Deep down you know."

They hit a bank, the thud sending them all careening forward. Bea's palms slapped down hard on the bottom of the boat as she attempted to keep herself upright.

Having finally had enough, she managed to glare at Adelaide, who was also trying to steady herself. "They can't possibly think . . . they don't really believe this island appeared because of my blood?"

The woman shrugged as she stood. "Odder things have happened in this tale, surely."

Without waiting for help from the men, Adelaide jumped from the boat, her booted feet splashing in the shallow water. And Bea admitted, if only to herself, that she admired the woman's ease, the way she seemed to be in constant control of her surroundings. These men didn't worry her, nor the situation. What did she know, and how did she know it?

"Go," Demyan demanded, shoving Bea toward the boat's edge.

Bea bit her tongue, resisting the urge to curse him to hell. In a less than graceful manner, she stumbled out, splashing into the water. Here, the land was sunny, the gray clouds and fog gone. Slowly she turned. No other land was visible from where she stood. Surely, she should be able to see the mainland. They hadn't traveled that far.

"Go," Demyan demanded again.

Reluctantly, Bea moved toward the shore, her toes sinking into the silky fine sand. The place was a paradise, a heaven amid hell. Tiny yellow and blue fish darted around her ankles, stirred by the movement. In the thick green vegetation that ran along the perimeter of the shallow beach, brilliantly colored birds sung sweetly, their song mixing with the chirp of insects and coming together in a natural sound that vibrated in her very soul.

"What is this place?" she whispered, but the others were too far ahead, already upon the beach, to hear. Sergio and the two Indian men were cutting through the vines and vegetation with machetes. Obviously they hadn't come to the island to have a picnic and collect shells.

The moment she left the water, Demyan latched on to her arm, his long fingers biting into her skin. "Come along. We've a statue to find."

Bea glanced back at Adelaide, attempting to read her face, but for once the woman's expression was blank. Yet her footsteps remained sure, as if she knew what would happen and was eager to get it over with.

"This is ridiculous." Unable to keep silent no longer, Bea glared up at Demyan. "You're all ridiculous if you think an island can magically appear because of my blood."

He ignored her, following the path Sergio and the Indian men had cut. It couldn't be possible. It couldn't. Because if her blood could make islands magically appear, that meant the statue might be real. Which meant Demyan would be close . . . incredibly close to holding the sort of power no man should touch, especially a man like him.

"Really, when you see there is nothing here, how foolish will you feel?" No one responded. Even Demyan didn't seem to care about her taunts. Frustrated, and feeling slightly panicked, Bea blew a long breath through pursed lips. "Come, we're wasting time. You're completely and utterly mad if you . . ."

Bea's voice trailed off as the trees suddenly gave way. There, in the middle of a clearing, a stone temple loomed toward the sky.

"Nothing's written in stone, my boy."

Colin didn't bother to look at his father, merely put his ire to use by rowing through the thick surf. The crashing tide was intent on keeping them at bay, but he wouldn't relent. He would win this battle with the ocean, just as he would win back Bea.

You will kill Bea.

The words repeated over and over through his mind. What had Henry expected when he'd made that disgusting proclamation? Did he truly think Colin would stand aside and let Bea go? He wouldn't kill Bea. He *wouldn't*.

"What I'm saying is just because that insane lad seemed to think you'd, well . . . murder her, doesn't mean you will."

Colin's jaw clenched, his teeth grinding together. "I don't need your thoughts now of all times, old man. Just keep . . ." His voice trailed off as the fog shifted.

Something was out there. A shadow . . . a form interrupting the haziness. Colin stopped rowing, surging to his feet so the boat rocked, tipping precariously. "What the hell is that?"

"What?" his father asked, picking up the oars and steadying the boat as best as his wiry frame could.

Colin shrugged, unease making the hairs on the back of his neck stand on end. "I don't know. I thought I saw something. Trees."

"Can't be a tree, according to my calculations, we'd be between two of the Seven Islands, directly north of . . ."

The bottom of the boat scraped against something before settling to a stop. Colin wavered on his feet, attempting to regain his balance. "What the hell."

Clutching the edge of the boat, he peered over the side. Through the rolling waves he could see sand. Beautiful, clear water and at the bottom, pristine sand, almost white in color.

"A sand bar. We've hit sand." Just a bar . . . or something more? He looked up; there just barely visible through the fog was something green . . . something leafy . . . trees.

Colin glanced back at his father. "You were saying?"

The old man jumped over the side of the boat, landing with a splash that sent droplets into the air. "Doesn't make sense. It can't be land." He was silent for one long moment, his eyes narrowed in contemplation, the only sound the roar of the waves. With a sigh, Colin followed, jumping into the water. The liquid immediately filled his boots, annoying his already dark mood.

With a snarl, he latched on to the bow and dragged the boat up to the beach. He shouldn't have been surprised to see another boat there, yet hope flared all the same. Sunlight fell around them, glowing and warm, oddly keeping the fog away. "Then where the hell are we?"

He didn't expect an answer. They were lost.

"Lost is right." His father raced up to the shore. "A lost island." His father's eyes gleamed, his voice breathless with excitement. Instantly, Colin's suspicion flared. The old man might have claimed he didn't want to hunt the statue, but it was obvious he was still a treasure hunter at heart. He'd seen that same gleam in the old man's eyes when he'd told him stories years ago of lost fortunes to be found.

Colin trudged toward the trees, scanning the shadows. "Lost island?"

Father started after him. "Every culture has them. Tales of islands that appear and disappear at a whim."

Colin shook his head in disgust. He should have known better than to ask. "You're speaking about nonsense."

Father snorted. "You of all people should know how blurry the line between sense and nonsense is."

He had to admit, the man had a point. Colin mulled over the idea. Was this place really some magical island? It looked normal enough to him. Perhaps his father's senses were dull from the fog and age. They could, after all, actually be on one of the Seven Islands and that boat could merely be a fisherman's. Although he hadn't expected the Seven Islands to look like this, so rich in flora and fauna. So . . . perfect.

"I know what I'm talking about, *boy*, and my senses are not dull."

Colin threw the man a glare. "Damn it, would you stop reading my mind."

"There." His father pointed forward. "A trail."

Colin spun around. His heart jumped into his throat. His father was right. Newly cut leaves lay scattered about the area. Someone had just left them an obvious path. He didn't know if it was a trap and he didn't care. Patting his waist to make sure the pistol was still there, he started forward, the trees swallowing them into the dark, damp jungle.

"So you're saying this island magically appeared?" His heart thundered in his chest. He was eager to see Bea, to touch her, to make sure she was well. "How?" He needed as much information as he could gather in their short time before they found Bea.

The man shrugged, his gaze shifting away in a telling action.

"What is it?" Colin demanded, pausing in the middle of the trail.

The vegetation threw shadows over his father's face, making it difficult to read his expression. "Her blood, that's how."

Colin's stomach clenched. He couldn't seem to breathe. The trees above swirled in a dizzying whirl.

His father held up his hands, as if warding Colin off. "She's alive, she's well. But they used her blood in some way. How, I'm not sure. I'm only getting bits and pieces from their minds."

Colin started forward, faster this time, resisting the urge to run. He must stay calm, must be quiet. "Do they know we're coming?"

"No. Not that I'm aware of."

"This is insane. It's ridiculous to think that . . ."

Something didn't fit, just up ahead, there through the trees; something didn't fit in with the rest of the vegetation. Colin paused, inclining his head, peering through the branches. A different color, different shape. He bolted forward. His blood pounded through his veins, beating in time with each step he took. Faster, faster. The impatient need to see Bea overwhelmed his common sense.

The trail flared into an open area and Colin halted. There, in the middle of a clearing, stood a temple near the ocean. A beaten and battered place that showed its age. Vines clung to the gray stone, probably the only thing keeping some of the corners upright.

Swiftly, his gaze scanned the area. Were they walking into a trap?

"Inside," Father panted, coming to rest beside him.

Colin didn't wait for the old man but raced across the clearing and up the shallow steps to a dark, yawning opening that led into the temple. Inside, the air was musty and smelled of neglect. Darkness enveloped, suffocating. The only sound was his harsh breathing echoing through the building. Dirt and sticks lay upon the floor, footsteps interrupting the blanket of dust. Colin followed the tracks to another set of stairs, this one leading upward, toward a gaping hole in the roof.

"Slow down, my boy," his father whispered as he entered the building.

Colin didn't bother to turn. His mind was spinning, attempting to produce a sound plan to save Bea, but in the back of his thoughts remained Henry's taunting words.

You will kill Bea.

Impatient to find her, Colin's foot hit the first step.

"Stop," a feminine voice called out.

The woman's voice was soft, but it had the desired effect. Colin's heart jumped into his throat. Slowly, he turned. Two Indian men and a white woman stood not feet from them.

"Lift your arms." The woman demanded, her accent French. Colin ignored her and slowly lowered his arm toward the gun. Shit. This couldn't be happening. He slid his father a glare. How the hell hadn't the old man heard them

"Some people can block their thoughts," his father replied.

Obviously Colin wasn't one of those people.

"I should have known," his father went on, his hands held high. "It was too quiet."

Colin's fingers slid around the pistol. The woman was small, he could easily take her. The two Indians holding pistols, well, they wouldn't be so easy to take down.

"Don't," the woman said, taking a step back so she was behind the two men. "If you pull the trigger, the sound will alert Demyan to your presence."

Colin paused. How had she known what he was going to do? Did she read minds like his father? Hell, was she his sibling, too? His father's eyes had narrowed. Apparently, he was wondering the same thing.

Colin didn't release his hold on the weapon. He'd need a better reason than her weak excuse. "Why does that matter? Why do you care, sweetheart?"

Annoyance flickered behind her blue eyes. "Because if you die, then she dies and all is lost."

So she had a point, a sound point. She wasn't working with Demyan, but who was she working for? "What's the plan?"

"We tie them up." She glanced at the two Indian men, who obviously spoke not a word of English.

Colin released a wry laugh, rubbing the back of his neck. "And how do you propose we do that?"

She knelt and lifted the stick lying upon the floor at her feet. With a grunt, she swung the log forward. It struck the first man, bounced off his head, and hit the second man before he had time to understand. They didn't even see it coming. The whack was barely audible. They stumbled sideways, their eyes rolled back into their heads, and they slumped toward the ground. With a puff of air, she released the log, the limb clattering across the floor.

She swiped her hands on her trousers and lifted a dark

brow. "I'll tie them up. Now, go, time is wasting and your woman is waiting."

Colin hesitated. Who the hell was she?

She shooed him forward, waving her hands through the air. "Go!"

His father pushed him toward the steps. Colin needed no more encouragement. "How many above?"

She pulled a knapsack forward and knelt on the dusty floor. "Demyan and another man. One more thing. Demyan doesn't like water."

Colin paused, blinking down at her in surprise. "What does that mean?"

"Go! You must hurry. She'll die if you don't go now!"

Colin wasted no more time and bolted up the steps, not bothering to wait for his father. But as that light shone down, drawing him closer to the top, he couldn't help wondering . . . was he saving Bea by going to her rescue, or was he condemning her to the afterlife?

Chapter 28

Colin burst through the opening. Sunlight blinded him momentarily, making him blink and stumble backward.

"Whoa, lad." His father's hand rested against his shoulder, pressuring him to stop. "You need to settle down."

With a quick glance back, Colin saw the edge of the temple, the ocean a long, long way below. The water was peppered with rocks. His father had saved his life. Christ, he'd just made it up the stairs and almost gotten himself killed.

"Told you she was still alive," Father muttered.

Colin spun around. Demyan stood across from them near a rock pedestal, holding a golden statue in one hand, while his other arm was wrapped firmly around Bea's waist. Colin's legs went weak with relief. Consumed with need, he drank in the sight of her.

Her long dark hair hung loose, contrasting against her pale face. But other than the lack of color, she seemed well. She didn't move, but for the slight fisting of her hands, as if she was attempting to stay still. His clothing hung on her narrow frame, making her appear fragile. His heart lurched.

He stepped forward, unable to resist. "Bea."

"Colin, behind you!" she cried.

Colin turned. Too late. A huge, bulking fist slammed into

his face, propelling him backward. Colin hit the rock temple with a thud that pressed the air from his lungs. Above, the clouds spun in a dizzying whirl. People were shouting, but the ringing in his ears made it impossible to decipher the words. The bitter taste of blood seeped into his mouth.

Suddenly, the huge man loomed above him, a pistol pointed directly at Colin's chest. He'd almost died once; he wasn't about to do it again. Colin sucked in a breath and rolled to the side just as the gun went off. A bullet nicked the stone, sending a piece of rock twirling through the air. Wasting no time, Colin swept his leg forward, hitting the back of the man's knee. He went down like a great big oak, the gun flying over the edge of the rooftop, and when his body hit the stone, the temple actually vibrated.

Colin jumped to his feet, sparing Bea a quick glance. She still stood there in Demyan's evil embrace, her face even paler than it had been. Demyan, Colin realized, looked completely unconcerned. It was in that split second that Goliath regained his feet. Squared off, Colin stalked around the man, looking for prime opportunity.

The man's beefy fist lashed out again. This time Colin was expecting the attack. He spun away, out of reach. Thrown off balance, Goliath stumbled forward . . . too close to the edge. Colin sucked in a breath. The huge man's mouth gaped open in surprise as he teetered on the edge. He fell back, his cry echoing across the island. Then he was gone. For one impossibly long moment they all merely stood there. Finally a loud thud announced the man's demise. Colin cringed. Goliath hadn't hit water, unfortunately for him.

"Colin," Bea whispered.

He turned and met Bea's gaze. He could barely believe she was there, just across the rooftop . . . so close. His heart swelled, his body simmering to life. She was there, alive, well. He stepped forward.

Demyan stepped back, his lips lifting into a snarl. "Stop."

Behind him, his father shifted.

Stop! Do as he says, Colin cried out in his head. If his father read minds as well as he pretended, he should have gotten the message loud and clear.

The old man paused, but Colin could feel the tension radiating from his body. Colin slid him a warning glance. His faded blue eyes were hazy with desire; he was focused directly on that statue. Like a man needing a drink, his father's body trembled. He wasn't interested in the statue? Colin scoffed at his father's earlier comment.

Demyan tucked the statue under his arm. Made of pure gold, the object gleamed under the sunlight. Such a small object, odd how it could hold so much power. This was what he'd been searching for his entire life. And he'd been right all along—apparently the statues were separate. A smug smile lifted his mouth. His fingers curled, itching to touch the precious metal just once.

Demyan shifted his free hand, lifting a pistol to point it directly at Bea's head. "I'll give you the woman. You let me leave with the statue."

Colin sucked in a breath. Even as his soul rebelled, Henry's words whispered through his head. *You will kill Bea.* Colin's heart picked up speed, tripping in its haste to pump blood. The statue or Bea.

"It won't work, Colin," Bea said softly, her face stoic but her eyes . . . dear God, her eyes told the truth. She was terrified, yet accepting . . . accepting of death. "Just let him. *Let him.*"

Blood roared through his ears. Surely he misinterpreted her words.

"She wants you to let her go, my boy," his father whispered, confirming his worst fears.

"Shut your mouth." Demyan shook Bea hard.

Caught off balance by the sudden action, they both stumbled backward, close to the edge. Bea cried out in alarm. Colin's heart lurched and he started forward.

"Don't move!" Demyan swung the pistol toward Colin, then back at Bea's head.

Colin froze, his body trembling. "What's he thinking? What's Demyan thinking?"

His father shook his head. "I can't read him, my boy."

Shit. Just his luck. The man had somehow learned to block his thoughts. Colin's fingers curled, then straightened, his mind spinning. There had to be a way . . . *some* way to save the statue *and* Bea.

"The statue or the woman?" Demyan demanded.

Colin's gaze slid to Bea. She stood there stoically as if accepting her fate. Beautiful, wonderful Bea. Her personality so different from what he'd thought when they'd first met. But it had always been there . . . this unforgiving, uncompromising attraction. The moment he'd kissed her, he'd fallen.

His father sidled closer to him. "She wants you to let him shoot her and you can save her later."

Colin stiffened. Smart girl, she remembered what he'd said, that his father could read minds. She was sending his father messages, unless his father lied. Would his father lie about this? Colin swallowed hard, indecision holding him captive. "And if my powers don't work? If the shot is fatal?"

His father sighed. "There's another way. You shoot her. Shoot her in the leg, arm, somewhere that won't kill her. If she's injured, if Demyan thinks she's dying, she'll be of no use."

Demyan jerked Bea even closer. "Enough time. I am leaving with the statue."

"You can't let him do that, Colin," his father's voice whispered beside him. "We need that statue."

Colin glared at the old man. "You might need that statue, but I don't."

He grasped tightly on to Colin's arm. "Then think of the greater world, my boy. Shoot her. Do it. It's the only way. Make her worth nothing. You can save her after."

His frantic gaze met Bea's. So brave, she barely trembled. Could he shoot her? She trusted him, seemed to think he could save her, but what if he couldn't? And even if he could, would he be able to forgive himself for the pain he'd inflict? "You want me to risk her life?"

His father shook him impatiently. "It's for the better good! If Demyan unlocks the power of that statue, we're all dead."

Colin remained silent, his gaze pinned to Bea. She'd given up so much already. So much for her family, for him, and she was willing to give up more, even her life. He wouldn't let her die. His heart revolted. Henry was wrong. His father was wrong. He wouldn't let her die. Frantic, his mind flashed through the information it held.

Demyan doesn't like water, the Frenchwoman had said. It wasn't the only time someone had discussed water. Hadn't Shiva brought up the subject? His pulse skipped a beat. And at the abandoned temple Anish had sent them to . . . Demyan had made Bea go to the statue, made Bea swim through that water.

"You're not going to do it, are you?" his father asked, interrupting his musings.

"Wait," Colin implored, holding up his hand. "Just wait . . ." He needed a moment, just a moment.

"I've already waited too long." The old man pulled the pistol from his waistband, his gaze focused on Demyan. "Give me the statue now."

"What the hell do you think you're doing?" Colin resisted the urge to grab the weapon, knowing that if the gun went off, he might hit Bea.

His father threw him a glare. "What you don't have the guts to do. Saving the world, my son."

His words hit Colin like a punch to the gut. "You don't give a shit about the world. Admit it, you want that statue." Colin's anger flared beneath his skin. For one brief moment the man had made him feel guilty over wanting to save Bea.

Demyan laughed, a sound that came out shaky. "Try it, old man, see how well your bullets work."

His father pulled the trigger. At the same time Demyan swung his arm around and shot.

"No!" Bea screamed.

Colin's father crumpled to the ground with a cry, blood seeping from his leg. But the wound was the least of Colin's worries. Demyan had been shot. It wouldn't kill him, but the hit was enough to propel him backward . . . with Bea.

Colin's heart lurched and he dove for Bea as the man fell. He was too late. Demyan, with the statue and Bea, tumbled over the edge.

Demyan's hands fell away and for one brief moment Bea was floating . . . floating backward. Above, only the clouds were visible. A scream erupted from between her lips. She hit something hard, the impact knocking the breath from her lungs and cutting off her cry. Frantic, she clawed outward, praying for something . . . anything to latch on to. Her fingers swept across a vine. Instinctively they curled and she jerked to a halt.

Bea swung her other arm up, latching on to the thick vine, her feet shuffling against the rock until her bare toes managed to slip between the cracks in the wall. Safe for one blessed moment, she merely pressed her face to the rough stone and breathed. But her heart slammed against her rib cage, refusing to slow its mad pace no matter how many times she said, "I am safe. I am safe."

Her harsh breath fanned across the stone, sending dirt sailing through the air. Slowly, she managed to tuck her chin to her chest and look below. Sergio lay upon a rock, his body broken and twisted. Bea's stomach churned and bile tickled the back of her throat. If she would have fallen, she'd have hit one . . . would have died the same way as Sergio. And even as she thought the words, she realized that Demyan was not below.

Bea jerked her head to the right. The monster clung to the

wall with one hand, his other hand useless as it held on to that ridiculous statue. His gaze met hers, his eyes showing his anger and something else . . . fear. For the first time she saw real fear in the man's eerie eyes. How she hated him, how she hated that statue. Sweat had broken out across the man's pale forehead. He was, no doubt, in worse shape than she, and for a moment she felt a rush of glee.

"Bea!" Colin cried out and suddenly he was there, looming above them, his beautiful face pale. "Oh, thank God." She saw the relief in his eyes and didn't doubt it for a moment. She'd told the man to shoot her; he hadn't. Dare she think he truly cared?

"Take my hand! Help me!" Demyan cried out.

Colin's frantic gaze jumped from Bea to Demyan. Still, Colin paused.

"Damn you! Take my arm! Pull me up and I'll share it all with you! I swear!" Sweat trailed down Demyan's face, dripping to the ocean below.

Colin's gaze flickered from Demyan, to the statue.

Bea didn't say a word. Her fingers were shaking, her hands growing numb and damp with her own perspiration, but she didn't say a word. She wouldn't beg Colin to save her over the statue; she couldn't. Part of her knew the statue was more important than her measly life, and part of her didn't beg because she didn't want her last memories to be of Colin rejecting her. Her right hand slipped. She sucked in a sharp breath, before tightening her hold. As brave as she pretended, she couldn't prevent the whimper from escaping her lips. She was going to die.

"Think on it, Colin," Demyan whispered. "The girl or the power."

Sweat snaked between her shoulder blades. She knew how much that statue meant to Colin. He'd built his life around the treasure and protecting its powers. She'd seen what that statue could do to a person. The men in her family had fallen mad under its spell. Colin had, too. It was obvious. She was going to die. Should she let go so Colin wouldn't have to decide?

She tightened her hold. No, she wasn't one to give in. She'd hang on until she could no longer. Perhaps Colin could pull Demyan up and then save her. Even as she thought the words, she knew it was impossible. Perhaps she could climb up herself? She clenched her jaw. She didn't need a man to save her life. If she went slow enough, used the vine like a rope . . .

"The girl or the power," Demyan demanded once more, his voice coming out shrill with need and impatience.

And even as she swore she would ignore the two men, her entire body grew silent, waiting for Colin's response. She squeezed her eyes shut. The wind rushed around her, tugging at her hair and clothing. Not even a bird cried out.

A sudden shadow fell over her. That warming sensation lit her insides and she felt Colin before she heard him. "The girl."

Bea opened her eyes. Colin was leaning over the edge, his face set in determined lines, his arm outstretched, yet still impossibly far away. "Give me your hand, Bea. Just a little farther."

Her heart expanded and she choked on a sob. Realizing this was not the time to cry, she lifted her feet and inched up the vine. Her arms trembled, her muscles aching with the movement, but she wouldn't relent.

"Are you sure?" she whispered.

"Of course, now give me your arm."

"No!" Demyan cried out. "No, please! The statue, think of the statue!"

But Colin didn't bother to look at the man. "Just a little more," he urged, his gaze locked to hers, willing her to move closer.

She found strength in his gaze, in his very being. Gritting her teeth, Bea swung her right arm upward, rising on her tiptoes at the same time. Her fingers met his. Immediately

Colin's grasp tightened. As their palms came into contact, Bea's foot slipped. A strangled cry escaped her lips. She dangled, with only Colin's hand keeping her from death.

"It's all right," Colin breathed from above.

With a gentle tug, he pulled Bea upward, her forearms scraping painfully against the rock wall. She didn't dare look at Demyan. With one last pull, Bea crested the edge of the roof and fell into Colin's solid body. Bea cried out, wrapping her arms around his neck as the tears trailed down her cheeks.

He'd chosen her. Colin had picked her over the statue and its powers. She knew it was wrong, she knew she shouldn't be happy, but she was. His arms wrapped around her, holding her tight as he whispered calming words, words she couldn't understand over her sobs. She didn't care. She only cared that she was alive and in his arms.

Finally, she was able to pull back just enough to speak. "You have time. Time to save him, Colin."

He shook his head. "He's gone, Bea. He slipped the moment I pulled you to the top."

She pushed away from Colin's warm embrace. On her hands and knees, she scooted to the edge and peered below. Colin was right. Demyan was gone. The water had swallowed him whole, taking the statue with him. Only Sergio's body remained bent and broken across the rocks. The statue was gone. *Gone.* The realization sank heavy in her gut.

Slowly, she turned around to face Colin, attempting to read his mind. Was he upset? Angry? But his face was oddly blank. "Are you sure he's dead?"

"He's dead," an old man grunted from across the rooftop. He pushed himself upright, holding on to his bloodied leg. Vaguely she remembered Demyan's pistol going off as they'd tumbled backward.

"My father," Colin explained.

Stunned, Bea could merely stare open-mouthed at the old man. His wiry frame was the same height as Colin, although thinner. And yes . . . she supposed Colin did have the man's eyes, but that was where the resemblance ended.

"But . . . I thought . . ." She didn't need to finish her sentence. Obviously, Colin's father wasn't dead. But he would be soon if they didn't get his leg wound treated.

Colin slipped his arm around her waist and pulled her upright. She was thankful for his strength, unsure if she could stand on her own. Unconsciously, her gaze went to that rooftop ledge where Demyan had fallen to his death. She couldn't quite believe it was really over. "How do you know Demyan is truly dead?"

"Water." The old man managed to stand, his face pulled into a grimace. "His mind slipped right before he fell and I read his thoughts."

She wasn't sure what he meant but Colin nodded as if he understood completely.

"Water was his one weakness, the thing that could kill him. He drowned. He's dead." The old man didn't wait for them, but shuffled extremely slow toward the steps. He was angry, angry that Colin had picked her over the statue. She could see that in the hard set of his face. Would Leo be angry? Would Ella? Had she been selfish?

Alone with Colin, Bea was suddenly nervous. Why wasn't he talking to her? Why wasn't he laughing? Why wasn't he happy? "Will your father be all right?"

"Flesh wound," Colin replied, his voice still low and controlled, his face still stoic. Nothing. He was giving her bloody nothing to read. What was he thinking? Damn him! Was he angry at her? All she wanted to do was hold him close, to breathe in his scent, to kiss him . . . yet . . . yet he was being so cold.

"I'm so sorry, Colin," she blurted out as tears stung her eyes. "I'm sorry."

His jaw clenched, his throat working as if he wanted to say something, but held back. Suddenly, his large hands cupped her face and she thought he would kiss her . . . prayed he would kiss her. But he merely stared into her eyes for the longest moment. He didn't say a word. *Nothing*. Bea grew nervous. Finally, he jerked her forward. His arms wrapped around her, holding her tight, so tight she could barely breathe. Tears slipped unabashedly down her cheeks. Bea pressed her face into Colin's shirt, breathing in his scent.

"I'm so sorry," she whispered again.

He pulled away, his eyes hard, his face blank, as if he hadn't just hugged her as if his life depended upon the embrace. "Let's go."

She nodded, her tears of relief turning into tears of pain. He wanted that statue. It was obvious. He regretted picking her. And most likely Leo and Ella would be angry as well. She pushed away from his hold.

"I didn't tell you to save me, Colin Finch. You made the choice."

Without waiting for his response, she swept past him and started down the stairs, her legs trembling with each step.

"French girl's gone. Fled, is my bet," Colin's father said, glaring at her as she passed him, as if it was her fault. "What should we do with the two Indian men?"

She could hear Colin coming down the steps behind her but didn't wait for his response. She slipped outside, resting her back against the wall.

"Take them back with us, what choice do we have?" Colin murmured from inside.

He wasn't rushing after her. He didn't care. She stumbled down the steps. As her bare feet sank into the soft grass, she heard Colin's father. "What did you do, my boy? What the hell did you do?"

Bea froze. The anger and disappointment were obvious in the old man's voice. For a brief moment Colin might have thought her life was more important than the statue, but Colin's father never had.

Bea bit her lower lip, waiting.

"What you didn't have the guts to do," Colin replied.

Bea turned, confused by his answer. But Colin was helping the Indian men to their feet, his attention focused on them, Bea all but forgotten.

Chapter 29

"You're sure? Absolutely sure?" Ella's face was grim, the dark circles under her eyes showing her exhaustion. For two days they'd been ensconced in Akshay's home, but it was obvious Ella was still worried about them. Fortunately Ella hadn't been the least bit upset about losing the statue. In fact, she'd seemed rather relieved that the piece was somewhere on the bottom of the ocean.

Bea's guilt flared. It wasn't right that her friend should be so tired when she was with child. Part of it was Bea's fault, for the worry she'd produced. Yes, the faster Leo and Ella could be on their way home and be rid of her, the better.

"Very sure." Bea folded a dress and settled it carefully into the trunk she'd purchased for her trip. "Sam said he'd escort me. I can't be any safer than with him, right? He also said he'd hire a ladies' maid and two others as guards."

"Bea, I know Sam is Colin's half brother . . ." Ella took in a deep breath and settled on Bea's bed. "And mine, but we don't really know him. Please, let Leo and I come with you."

Bea sighed, moving across the room she'd been given. A different room from the room Colin had been shot in. No doubt they figured she couldn't take the memories. But the memories were still there, always would be.

"No, Ella." She'd be a burden no longer. With a resigned sigh, she picked up another dress that Ella had purchased for her in town that morning. "You need to rest. Especially in your condition. You need to go back home. Please." She clutched the gown to her chest. "Besides, I need to do this. For me. I have my own money, I want for nothing." But even as she said the words, she recognized them as a lie.

Ella nodded slowly, but it was obvious she wanted to argue. "And Colin?"

Bea bristled and shoved the dress into the trunk. "What about Colin?"

Ella didn't reply. Bea blew a breath between pursed lips and settled her hands on her hips. "I haven't seen him since. No doubt he blames me for losing the statue."

Ella tipped her head to the side in a sympathetic manner. "He doesn't."

"Then why, Ella? Why won't he open up to me? Why won't he tell me how he feels, *if* he feels the slightest bit of affection for me!" A blush immediately raced to her cheeks. She hadn't meant to sound like a shrew, and Colin was Ella's brother, after all. Shockingly enough, Colin had announced that little tidbit the moment they'd arrived at Akshay's home. "I'm sorry, I shouldn't burden you."

"You know he cares, Bea."

Bea snorted. "Yes, well, knowing isn't the same as hearing it."

Ella stood and took Bea's hands. "You already know so much more about him than most, isn't that enough?"

"Would it be enough for you?"

Ella looked away, her avoidance telling. "No, I suppose not."

"Well then," Bea whispered, giving Ella a strained smile.

She sniffled, trying to keep the tears at bay as she turned away from her friend. The entire journey back Colin had been silent, barely looking at her. It was obvious he regretted saving her life over the statue. He didn't care for her after all.

"Bea, I shouldn't tell you this but . . . well . . ."

Bea turned at Ella's words. Her friend was pacing the room, wringing her hands together in agitation. "Blast it all." She paused and looked directly at Bea. "There was a woman . . . before you. An Englishwoman. They were engaged."

Bea's heart hammered in her chest and the boots she'd just picked up thumped to the floor. Colin was engaged to another woman? How had she not known? Anger mixed with hurt. She hadn't known because he hadn't thought enough of Bea to tell her.

"I shouldn't be telling you this, but if it's my last resort, so be it. When he finally told her about his powers, she wanted to use him to make money." Ella sighed and went to the window, staring out on the rising sun. "I suppose part of me understands. She was an impoverished noblewoman whose family had lost everything. At first, I think Colin was a wonderful diversion. Then, after she found out about his powers, she realized she could use him to elevate her status to what it once was." Ella turned back toward her and shrugged. "Money and greed can make people do terrible things."

Bea sank onto the edge of her bed. Colin had been engaged. What else didn't she know about the man she supposedly loved? Did he still hold affection for his fiancée?

"Colin even wanted her to travel with him, but she scoffed at the idea. Better for both, I suppose. But it hardened him, I believe. He doesn't trust many with the knowledge of what he can do."

But he'd trusted Bea. The unspoken words hung between them. In fact, he'd practically begged her to believe and what had she done? Laughed and mocked his abilities. "And he still loves her?" Bea whispered, afraid of the answer.

"No. Not at all," Ella assured her. "But . . . well, it's hard for him."

Shock gave way to anger. "Well, it's hard for me, too, Ella."

"I know." Ella rushed to her side, taking her hands once more. "Just . . . try, one more time? Don't leave with any regrets, Bea. If you can travel to Morocco and be happy and never wonder what if . . . then great. But if you're going to always wonder what could have happened if you'd tried harder, then don't go."

Bea didn't respond. She didn't know what to say. She supposed Ella was right, but to try again would mean more coldness from Colin, more hurt, more heartbreak. Ella gave her a quick hug, the comforting scent of roses clinging to her body. "I'm going to have a hell of a time keeping Leo from demanding you return to England with us, you know."

Bea smiled.

Ella pulled back. "Just try, one last time, for me, but more importantly, for you." Without another word, the woman left, closing the door quietly behind her.

Bea released a long, shaky breath. Would she regret it if she didn't try one more time? Unwillingly her gaze went to the door. Colin was across the hall, his presence heated and pulsing beneath her skin. She didn't know how or why she could sense him, but she could.

Perhaps she would regret leaving without another try. But how could she possibly continue if he rejected her? Bea swallowed hard and stood. Only one way to find out. Slowly, she moved across the room on wooden legs.

The house was surprisingly empty. Quiet. Too quiet, as if in mourning. She didn't bother to knock on Colin's door, knowing he was in there and worried he would reject her calling. Like she belonged there, Bea opened the door, closing it immediately behind her. Colin stood near the windows, looking dour and confused. At the sound of the door closing, he turned. Bea's heart clenched. His hair mussed, his clothing wrinkled, he looked gorgeous.

It all made sense to Bea now. Why getting that statue and

its riches had been so important to Colin. He wanted to have money, to prove he was worth his fiancée's attention. Ella said he no longer loved her, but how well did Ella know the man?

"I'm so sorry," she whispered, the only thing she could think of saying.

He looked back out the window. "For what?"

He was speaking to her. At least it was something. "The statue, it's gone. Leo's ring. Ella's necklace. They're all gone. I know how important they were to you."

He turned then, and settled on the window ledge, watching her through wary eyes. "What do you mean? How is it your fault?"

She released a wry laugh and raked her trembling hands through her hair. "You know it's my fault. The money you could have had. The power." She started pacing, looking everywhere but at him. Her gaze landed on his bed and her heart jerked. That same bed where they'd made love. Where he'd held her, where he'd touched every inch of her body and where she'd thought, for a brief moment, that maybe he did love her.

"It wasn't about the money."

She jerked her gaze toward him and lifted a brow, not buying his answer for a second.

He shrugged and sighed. "Maybe a little. But mostly it was about keeping the statue safe and at the bottom of an ocean, near a mythical island . . . well, it can't be any safer."

He smiled briefly, then turned and strolled across the room in the opposite direction from where she stood, as if he couldn't stand to be near her. "Without *all* the statues, the riches will never be unveiled, according to legend. I suppose I'm free now."

The words gave Bea hope, a flaring joy that lit her soul. Truly, he didn't care about the money? Just as soon as the hope arrived, it dissipated. Why, then, did he still avoid her?

"The statues fit together." Bea took a hesitant step forward, willing to talk about anything just to have a few more minutes with him.

He shook his head. "What do you mean?"

Bea crossed her arms over her chest. "You were right along. The statues are separate, but they fit together, much like a puzzle."

He shrugged and looked toward the cold hearth of the marble fireplace, but not before she saw the flicker of interest in his eyes. "It doesn't matter now."

Frustrated, Bea took another step closer. She couldn't read his mind, didn't know how he felt. Was he still interested in her, or not? More importantly, could she bare her soul and risk everything?

"Come with me," she blurted out.

He glanced at her, the surprise evident on his face.

"I'm going to Morocco, then perhaps Italy. I don't know yet. It doesn't matter. I want you to come with me."

His smile was kind, the sort of smile a father gave a petulant child. "I'm not the husband type, darlin'."

Annoyance burned in her gut. Bea's hands fisted. "I didn't ask you to marry me."

He turned away from her once more. "We can't travel alone; it will ruin your reputation."

She laughed then, an almost hysterical bubble that welled within. "My reputation is already ruined."

"You deserve a husband, a titled husband," he went on, as if he hadn't even heard her.

Bea swept toward him, standing so close, he was forced to look at her. "I think I know what I want, and I want you."

His jaw clenched and he closed his eyes. The coward. "What do you want me to say, Bea? You come from a titled family. I come from the streets of New York. I had to beg for food at times, sleep in alleys. Is that the kind of life you want?"

"Do you think that matters to me?"

He looked at her, his gaze hard, unrelenting. "It matters to me."

Her heart sank into the pit of her stomach. "It doesn't matter what I say, does it?"

He didn't respond. And she knew there was nothing more she could do. She'd opened her heart, she'd told him what she felt. But she couldn't change his mind or how much, or little, he felt for her.

"I can't change who I am. And I don't want to."

He smiled fleetingly.

"I can't change who you are. And I don't want to. I love you, Colin Finch."

His nostrils flared slightly, his only reaction.

Bea took a step back. "I love you, but I can't change your mind. I can't change how you feel and I can't change who we are."

She swallowed hard and turned, walking steadily toward the door, knowing he watched her. With her hand resting on the doorknob, she paused. "I'm leaving. I'll be on that ship this evening headed to Morocco. If you feel enough . . . if you want me enough . . . be on that ship when it leaves."

She didn't pause, but forced herself to walk out the door knowing this could be the last time she saw him, yet knowing for her own sanity, she had to let him go.

"You'll write?" Ella asked, her lower lip quivering. She'd tied her beautiful blond hair into an upswept knot and worn traditional English clothing, a blue dress with a wide skirt that wavered in the wind and a jaunty little hat that perched atop her head. Standing on the deck of *The James*, they looked like any English family heading home. Leo was equally English in his black suit, although he looked far from comfortable.

Bea nodded, biting her bottom lip to keep from crying. She, too, had dressed for the occasion in a golden-colored gown that matched her eyes, according to Ella. But whereas her English clothing had felt normal when she'd first arrived in India, now it felt confining, too tight. What would Colin think, seeing her dressed so? She banished the thought as soon as it arrived.

"You don't have to go," Leo replied softly, so softly that he was barely audible over the flapping of canvas sails and the cry of birds hovering above, waiting for a fishy morsel.

She smiled and threw her arms around his neck in a sudden fit of emotion. He was stiff at first, then finally relented and returned her hug. Perhaps people could change after all.

"Yes, I do." She pulled back and looked directly at Leo, then Ella, willing them to understand. "Not only do I need to do this for myself, but when would I ever get the chance to see the world again?"

Leo frowned, but Ella smiled through her tears. "I suppose you're right. Once you're married and have children, you'll want to settle down."

Bea forced her smile to remain in place. Marriage? Children? The thought made her want to laugh. She couldn't imagine ever trusting another man, not after Colin had broken her heart.

Her amusement fled. She looked away, fighting her sorrow. All around them, sailors rushed past, shouting out orders, while travelers boarded their cabins. And in every face, she looked for Colin.

"You'll come back to us, in England, not Scotland, right?" Leo asked.

Bea nodded, her smile suddenly sincere. She had no desire to return to that moldy castle with her brooding grandmother.

"I'll count the days until we're all together again." Ella pulled her close. "The baby will have her wonderful aunt nearby!"

Bea rolled her eyes. Yes, the doddering old maiden aunt.

Ella pulled back, her eyes sparkling. "You'll tell her stories about all of your adventures!"

Bea laughed, forcing herself to feel better. She *was* going to have adventures and she didn't need a man for that. In fact, a man would only stifle her longing for independence. Yes, she was better off alone.

"We have to go," Leo broke in, leaning forward and pecking her on the cheek. His scent swirled around her, earthy and male, making her feel protected. For a brief moment she almost relented. Almost begged them to take her with them.

Bea bit her lower lip and gave Ella another quick hug. "You be careful on the way home. Take your time. Rest for the baby."

Her gloved hands took Bea's. "I will. And you be careful. Come back to us soon, all right?"

Bea nodded and stepped out of arm's reach, afraid if she didn't let go now, she never would. Leo slipped his arm through Ella's and they started down the plank, back toward dry land. Bea kept that ridiculous smile upon her face, kept waving even until her arm began to burn. Even after the ship shoved off from the dock, Bea kept waving. Even as her heart broke piece by piece, falling into the roiling pit of her stomach, she kept her smile in place.

The land grew smaller, the people indecipherable from the coastline. She had no idea how many minutes passed. Time no longer held merit.

All that mattered was that Colin hadn't come.

The soft fall of footsteps had Bea stiffening, and even though rationally she knew it was impossible, she couldn't keep the hope from flaring to life. Could it be? She spun around.

Sam stood there in his Indian garb, his face unreadable. "You are well?"

Bea hid her disappointment and nodded. His eyes were the same blue as Colin's, but then they were brothers. Still, the realization struck her hard. How would she look at him every day and not think of Colin?

He gave her a curt bow. "I shall see to the luggage."

Bea nodded and glanced back to the shore, where Leo and Ella had disappeared. Her heart leapt in her throat as her chance to escape faded. Above, the sails flapped in the wind, those birds still following them, but nothing else was the same.

She was stuck. What the hell was she thinking? Traipsing around the world with three people she'd hired and barely knew? Her stomach clenched. Oh God, she was going to be sick. Panic welled, threatening to close off her throat. She couldn't do this. She closed her eyes. She *must* do this.

She forced a breath of salty air into her lungs. She'd traveled through India, for God's sake. She could do this. She couldn't go back now. She would see Morocco, have a wonderful time, and then . . . and then . . .

A tear slipped down her cheek. He hadn't come. Colin hadn't come.

Another tear followed, dripping to the churning ocean below.

Colin hadn't come with her. She pressed her gloved hand to her stomach. She'd told herself, *forced* herself, to think about the possibility, yet deep down she supposed she'd assumed he wouldn't let her leave alone. Now, with no other choice, she allowed the reality to finally sink in. She was alone. Completely alone.

Another tear slipped down her cheek.

"Here," a man said with a thick English accent. A white handkerchief suddenly appeared in front of her face, wavering on the breeze.

Wanting to be alone and not wanting to court conversation, she didn't dare look at him. Bea focused on the scuffed deck boards and snatched the cloth from his tanned hand. "Thank you," she whispered.

He didn't move away and annoyance flared through Bea. Couldn't he tell she hadn't the desire to make conversation?

"You know . . ." He braced his elbows on the railing and

leaned forward. From the corner of her eye she could see that his suit was a fine black material that hugged his muscled arms well. "It's terrible to see a beautiful lady cry."

Bea almost sighed in exasperation. She turned her back to him, looking everywhere but at the man, wondering when Sam would return. Blast Colin. If he hadn't left her alone, she wouldn't feel so exposed. She inched away. She'd see Colin again, yes, most definitely. And when she did . . .

"In fact, it rips a man's heart quite open."

"Listen." She started to turn toward him when a warm tingling sensation broke through her ire. *No*. It couldn't be. Her body began to tremble and the handkerchief fell unheeded to the churning water below. Slowly, she turned.

Colin grinned down at her and winked. For one long moment she merely blinked up at him, wondering if perhaps the sun was playing tricks with her mind. She reached out, letting her fingers skim his warm arm. Realizing he was quite real, she jerked back, her fingertips tingling with the contact. He looked so wonderfully real, the suit fitting his broad shoulders perfectly, the wind playing with his curls. Even those dimples were on full display. Dear God, he was real!

"How'd you like my accent? I've been practicing."

The clouds above began to spin. Bea's mouth fell open, and just as quickly snapped shut. She would not faint!

Wariness settled in his blue gaze. "You don't look very thrilled to see me."

Bea's anger flared. "You . . . you led me to believe . . ." She stomped her foot and Colin's brow lifted in surprise. "You bastard! How could you make me go through this? How could you?" She hit his chest, and since it felt so bloody good, she hit him again.

Colin started laughing, a deep rumble that warmed her insides, much against her will. "Now, darlin,' you have to understand, I had things to do . . ."

She pulled back, trembling. "Don't you *darlin'* me, you . . . you arrogant arse!" She spun around and started across the deck, anger fueling her forward. She had to get away from him before she did something insane, like kiss him!

"Bea, I promise, I got here as soon as I could. But I had things to do, things to procure . . ."

Shocked and annoyed by his words, she stopped. Unbelievable. The man was unbelievable if he thought she'd accept his sorry excuse! "Really, Colin, what was so important? I'm most eager to hear what was so important that you didn't have the time to tell me you were coming?" Bea spun around to face him, but looking at that beautiful face was almost more than she could handle.

"Bea." The seriousness in his gaze gave her pause. "This." He held out a little jeweled box.

Confused, Bea couldn't stop herself and stepped closer. He'd bought her a present? Was he really trying to gain her forgiveness by giving her a measly present? "What is it?" She crossed her arms over her chest, feigning indifference.

A smile lifted the left corner of his mouth. "Open it."

She paused only a moment, then with trembling fingers she took the box and lifted the lid. Inside a beautiful gold ring with an odd gold and brown stone rested on a velvet pillow.

"It's called a tiger's-eye. I thought it matched your eyes, and your mood sometimes." He was smiling, but in his gaze there was something else . . . worry? Anxiousness? He was waiting for something . . . waiting for her response.

Confused, Bea shook her head. "I don't understand."

That pulse in his neck flared to life as he stepped closer. The seriousness in her gaze took her under and held her captive. "I love you, Beatrice. Will you marry me?"

Her heart plummeted to her toes and panic mixed with utter happiness. "No, you don't mean it." Tears pooled in her eyes and she shook her head once more. "You don't. You hate me for making you lose that statue."

Colin's brows snapped together. "No. Of course I don't." He reached for her but she stepped back.

Bea swiped angrily at the tears that slipped down her cheeks. "Then why were you so hateful? Why didn't you talk to me? Why'd you ignore me?"

Colin sighed and cupped her shoulders, bringing her up against his hard chest. "Bea, I had almost lost you. I'd just realized my father is the ass I worried he was. And the only person I cared about, *you*, had almost. . . . God, Bea, I had nothing to offer you. I *have* nothing to offer you. Nothing."

The anguish in his voice tore at her heart. She wanted to shake the man. She wanted to bring him close and kiss him until he'd never doubt her love. "I told you, Colin. I only want you."

His jaw clenched, he focused on the sailors, climbing masts and yelling out orders. "I know, but . . . Damn it all." His gaze met hers. "Bea, tell me you still love me."

She closed her eyes and waited, taking one long moment to savor the feel of his hands on her.

"Bea?" he whispered, his voice catching.

She could let him suffer no longer. Happiness flared through her very being. It no longer mattered. Not the statue. Not their past lives. Nothing but them. "Of course I love you!"

Relief washed visibly over his features. Yet his hands gripped her upper arms, his fingers tight. "Tell me you'll marry me."

She paused, letting the moment sink in. He wanted her as his wife. Her gaze took him in, that fine suit he wore, the way the wind touseled his curls, and his eyes, so serious, so loving, and so insecure, pleading with her to have him. But he was a cad, wasn't he? A woman in every country . . .

"Colin, are you sure? What if you get second thoughts? What if you decide . . ."

He growled low in his throat. "Will you stop talking and kiss me already?"

A smile quivered on Bea's lips. She held the jeweled box between them. "Only if you put that ring on my finger and make me a proper woman."

Colin grinned, a heart-stopping smile that spoke of success, but mostly of love. With hands that visibly trembled, he took the ring from the box and slid it upon her finger. "Well?" he insisted. "Say the words."

"Yes," she whispered. "Yes, Colin. I will marry you." She threw her arms around his neck and pressed her body up close to his, heedless of the stares from passengers and crew. His hold felt right, so incredibly right.

She tilted her head back and slid her fingers into his curls, warmed by the sun. "Tell me you love me again," she whispered.

He scooped her up into his arms. "I love you." He gave her a quick kiss and started toward the stairs that led to the cabin area, ignoring the hollers and cries of delight from crew members.

The sky was perfect and blue, the gulls overhead crying out their own cheers of delight. "Tell me again," she whispered, nuzzling his neck.

"I love you," he whispered.

"And again," she demanded as he ducked under the overhang and opened his cabin door.

Colin let her slide down his body as he closed the door behind them. "I love you, Bea, forever and always." With those words, he pressed his lips to her mouth, and showed her exactly how much he cared.

Books by Bestselling Author
Fern Michaels

Available Wherever Books Are Sold!
Check out our website at www.kensingtonbooks.com

Thrilling Suspense from
Beverly Barton

More by Bestselling Author
Hannah Howell

Available Wherever Books Are Sold!

Check out our website at
http://www.kensingtonbooks.com